# Dead Lift

## LUX BRUMALIS
### BOOK 2

## KRIS BUTLER

 Created with Vellum

# dead LIFT

## KRIS BUTLER

# Contents

I'd worked hard to escape the penalty box life had placed me in.

I started somewhere new, giving Reese and myself a clean slate. I found a job I loved and met three guys who made me feel alive.

I should've been prepared for life to smack me upside the head again, but in my defense, I'd been a little distracted by my hot roommates and trying to win games.

My life had become a mess, and I didn't know where to start. Everyone wanted something from me, and it was hard to know whom to trust.

The one thing I thought I could count on was hockey, but it no longer felt safe—not after the secrets and lies I'd uncovered.

The pressure was suffocating, and I knew I had to make a choice soon and pray it wasn't wrong... or someone might end up dead.

Hockey was meant to be only a game, but this time, it looked like we were playing for keeps.

*This is book 2 in the series. Penalty Box must be read first. This book does end on a cliffhanger.*

# Foreword

This is a contemporary why-choose hockey romance intended for 18+ due to language and content. This book deals with some themes that might be difficult to read. I always try to do my best to handle things with care for my characters and the reader. But please make sure to take care of yourself first.

## SOME THINGS TO CONSIDER ARE THE FOLLOWING:

- Family member dies from cancer
- Feelings of not being good enough/self doubt
- Past drug use
- Mild bullying of non-binary character by peers

- Violation of consent (shared videos)
- Mild mental/psychological abuse
- Keeping things from others
- Mild violence (outside of harem)
- Use of they/them pronouns for NB character

## THEMES AND/OR TROPES TO EXPECT

- Double penetration
- Anal Penetration
- Group Scene
- Praise
- Dirty Talk
- Voyeurism /Exhibitionism
- Explicit sex scenes
- Foul language
- Found Family

## HOCKEY

This book attempts to portray hockey in its truest form, but the author has taken some liberties to make things fit within the world of the book for the story. So for any hockey purest, be kind; it was done purpose-fully to tell a story. This book highlights women in sports and the inequality many face. I could go on all day about this, but since you probably want to read this book and not listen to my soapbox, turn the page to continue Henley's story.

# Introduction

Deadlift:

*noun*

a direct lifting without any mechanical assistance.

a situation that requires all one's strength or ingenuity.

*This book is dedicated to the power of female friendships.*
*Together we can rise up.*

# CHAPTER 1

## Fletcher

MY HANDS RUBBED up and down my legs as I watched Henley's game on TV. I hated that I couldn't be there, but at least I got to watch it before my game. The school they played against had its own broadcasting program and televised the sports teams as practice. It wasn't the most sophisticated setup, but it was better than nothing.

Henley looked so fierce from the box that it was hard to take my eyes off her and watch the game. The door to the garage opened, and I smiled as Dax entered the room.

"Hey, dude. How's the game going?" he asked, taking a drink from his Hydro Flask. His face was sweaty, and his shirt clung to him; I expected he'd rushed home to watch the game without showering.

"It's almost the end of the second period. Henley's looking great."

We both watched the last few seconds before the buzzer sounded, and the team headed off the ice. I peered at Dax out of the corner of my eye.

"It's great that you rushed over here, man, but if

you try to sit on this couch before you shower, I will tackle you to the ground and sic Lady Sterling on you."

Dax rolled his eyes, chuckling. "I'm going. No need to resort to violence." He practically ran to his room to shower. An excited Dax was new, but I'd welcome it any day.

Turning my attention back to the game, I watched as the kids returned with Henley and Reed, Kurt nowhere to be found. When Henley exited off the ice, I grabbed my phone and sent a message, not liking that she was about to be alone with Kurt. The clock counted down, my anxiety growing each second that she didn't reappear.

Kurt returned to the ice with a minute to spare, and I couldn't ignore the smug expression on his face. Reed approached him, shaking his head when Kurt didn't respond and exiting the ice himself.

A lump lodged in my throat as I watched the clock get closer to game time. I didn't know which option I preferred; Reed going after Henley or allowing Kurt to coach. When the buzzer sounded, the teams getting into formation on the ice, I knew it didn't matter. It was too late—the last period was starting.

I paced in front of the TV for the hundredth time, hoping the image would change when I looked back. But just as it had been every time before, Kurt still stood in the player's box with a smug smile as he watched the game play out. I couldn't be certain, but it also looked like Reese had been benched.

This wasn't good. Something had happened. *Something bad.*

Pulling out my phone, I sent another text to Henley and Reed. When nothing came back, I tossed it onto the couch, my hands pulling at the strands of my hair.

"Fuck!" I shouted into the room, my anxiety creeping up. I didn't know what to do at this point.

Sitting down, I picked up my phone and scrolled through the news sources, both dreading and hoping to find something. Maybe she slipped and fell and had to be rushed out? Perhaps a student had gotten injured, and she went with them? There were a million possibilities that weren't the worst-case scenario, so I tried to remind myself of that.

My thumb stopped scrolling on a news alert, the words sending a bucket of cold water over my head. The dread in my stomach bottomed out, forming a pile of rocks.

What. The. Fuck.

*News Alert! News Alert! News Alert!*

*Reports of Henley Henshaw and Dakota Hughes rekindling their relationship are coming through after a tweet went out this afternoon. Sources close to the pair state that they've been working through Henley's issues to get back to being the power couple America loves. Her coaching at Lux was a ploy to grab Dakota's attention, and it worked! We have it under good authority that Dakota rushed to the game to support her and proposed as well. What will this mean for the Blizzards? Will Henley be returning to the league? Stay tuned for our evening broadcast to find out more.*

I stared dumbstruck at the phone. This couldn't be true. She hadn't been leading us on this whole time, had she? And talking with Dakota behind our backs?

I shook my head. No. There was no way. I didn't believe it. I wouldn't believe it until I heard it from Henley. I owed her and our relationship that much.

Feeling settled, I took a deep breath, letting it out slowly. So was this why she wasn't on the ice? Dakota had shown up and thrown all of this crap at her? Yeah, that sounded more feasible. With the way Kurt was smirking, I had a feeling he was involved as well.

Dax raced back into the room, a towel rubbing at his long locks, an excited look on his face. The changes in Dax made me hope he could handle this news.

"Are they back? Who's winning?"

"Well, they're down two goals, but Henley's not on the ice."

"Where is she?" he asked, taking a seat.

"I don't know. She left before the third period started and didn't return. I can't get a hold of her or Reed. And... Kurt's coaching." I pointed to the TV, where the camera had zoomed over the box, showing Kurt standing there.

"He looks entirely too happy about something," Dax said, scrunching his eyes.

"Yeah, I think he and Dakota did something."

Dax turned to me then, lifting his eyebrows. "What?"

Handing him my phone, I had him read the news article, watching every minuscule move he made as I calculated his reaction. When he handed it back to me, rolling his eyes, I relaxed.

"You don't believe that, do you?" he asked, giving me a skeptical look this time.

"I'll be honest. For a second, I wondered. But no, I don't believe it's true. Do you?"

He scoffed, shaking his head. "I might not be as far along in my relationship with Henley, but I know she'd never get back with him. Plus, between practices and conditioning, she hasn't had enough time to lead a double life. It logistically doesn't work."

Dax took another swig of his water, not even bothered by what he read. I realized then how much he had come on board with this crazy plan, even if he wasn't fully aware. It made me believe we could make this work no matter what.

"You're right. I think my insecurity got the best of me for a moment." I sighed, rubbing my beard. "What do we think it means, then? Should we be concerned about Dakota? Do we tell Dmitry?"

"Oh, we for sure should be worried about Dakota. That dude sounds like a royal jackass. I'm not sure what his endgame here is, but he wants our girl for it, and that's not okay."

I smiled, nudging his shoulder.

"What?" he asked, turning and looking at me.

"You said 'our girl.' It's nice."

Dax's cheeks redden to a shade I'd never seen on him before. "Yeah, well, Henley's special. I realize that now."

"Good. I'm glad you got your head out of your ass." I clapped him on the back, my smile dropping as my brow furrowed in concentration. "We need a plan. I don't like not knowing what's happening. Maybe I should drive to their game," I mused, rubbing my beard a little more. At this rate, I was going to have a bald spot.

"No. You have a game. You can't let your team down; they need you. I'll go check on Henley. Maybe you could talk to Dmitry and get ahead of this for her?" Dax nodded and snapped his fingers, a plan forming behind his eyes. "Yeah, let's do that."

"Okay, but I need you to text me or call the second you find out how she is. I want visual proof she's okay. Promise me?"

Dax grabbed my arm, squeezing it. "I will. Let's go fight for our girl."

He smiled, and I noticed how genuine it was. One of the few I'd seen on the man in our years of knowing one another. A tightness in my chest lifted, and I nodded, slapping his back in response.

"Our girl."

Standing from the couch, I grabbed my stuff and headed toward the door. I needed to catch Dmitry before the game. Dax nodded as he headed to his room, presumably to change and grab whatever he needed for his trip.

I realized this was an important step in our relationship—trusting the other to handle something and ensuring she was safe. Knowing I didn't have to do it alone was also a relief. In the past, this would be when I'd burn out and let the relationship falter on its own, too tired to carry the load for both parties.

Not only was Henley fully a part of this relationship, but I had two other guys to balance me. As crazy as it sounded, it was the healthiest relationship I'd ever been in.

The drive to the school was quick, and I marched into the admin building within minutes. I didn't stop at the office, heading straight for Dmitry's door. Thankfully, it was open, and I barely paused to knock before I stepped in, shutting the door behind me.

Dmitry was on the phone, his eyes meeting mine as I entered. He lifted a finger when I took a seat, letting me know he saw me.

"I hear you, and I will look into it. Thank you for your advisement." He hung up without saying anything else, rubbing his temples before he glanced at me.

"I'm assuming you're here about Coach Henshaw?" he asked, surprising me.

"Yes." I swallowed, trying to remember the speech I'd repeatedly been saying since I'd walked out of the house. "Dakota's up to something. I don't believe this engagement is true, or that she was using the school. I think he's in league with Kurt to sabotage Henley, and I don't want you to penalize her until we have the full story."

I took a breath, realizing I'd practically shouted at the director of the school, my boss.

"Apologies. I'm just concerned about her and don't want false rumors to affect her any more than they have."

Dmitry watched me, giving me a moment to compose myself before he began. Despite feeling calmer after sharing my concerns, I was still on edge, waiting for him to disagree.

"I agree with you, Fletcher," he said, stealing all the fight from me.

I sat back, waiting for him to tell me the solution. If he agreed with me, that meant he had to have one.

"So, what does that mean, then?" I asked when he didn't say anything else.

He sighed, leaning back in his chair, steepling his fingers. "It means that I know something else is going on here. I'm not sure what it is, but I trust Coach Henshaw and know she hasn't used us to get back in the league. Once I get in touch with her, we'll release a statement and set up a press conference if needed."

"What about Kurt? If he's involved?"

"If we find out that one of our own went against another to further their own agenda, then they will no longer have a position here. Lux isn't about one person prospering; it's about an entire community. If we can't unite and fight as a school, then they don't belong here. I won't let what happened last year be the legacy we leave."

I sighed, feeling hopeful that things would be okay. "Thank you. I was worried..."

"I get it. It's hard to trust when that trust has been broken, but I promise that I'm striving to make a different environment here."

"Yeah, I'm starting to believe it. Have you heard anything?" I asked, wondering if maybe he had information I hadn't been able to gain yet.

"No. When Henley didn't return, I sent a message to one of my contacts. Shortly before the period started, Reed went searching for her, leaving Kurt in charge of the team. Neither one of them has returned to the game. I'm hoping they're just in the locker rooms, waiting it out since they can't return to the box."

"Yeah. Same." Thoughts circulated as I wondered what made Henley leave her team in the first place. "Dax is headed there since my game starts soon. I'll let you know if we find out anything. You'll do the same?" I asked.

"Of course, Fletcher. Good luck."

Nodding, I stood and headed out the door, waving at the receptionist as I walked past this time. My head was in the clouds as I returned to my car and drove to the hockey arena.

The parking lot was beginning to fill as parents and townsfolk filtered in. I spotted Ty and Cody as I entered the locker room, both of them seeming to relax at my arrival.

"Everything okay?" Ty asked, moving closer.

"I'm not sure. I can't get a hold of Henley."

"I saw she wasn't in the box. What do you think happened?"

"Kurt did something. I'm just not sure what yet. Dax is headed there to find out. In the meantime, I'm going to focus on the game and pray my girlfriend is okay."

Ty patted me on the back, understanding in his eyes. "We got you, Fletch. Take your time getting ready. We'll get the kids warmed up."

"Yeah," Cody nodded.

"Thanks, guys. I won't be long. It's easier to have something to focus on."

They headed out toward the team's locker room, and I sat on the bench, folding my arms on my knees. I sat for a few minutes, breathing, reminding myself I couldn't do anything at the moment. I had to trust and believe.

After about twenty times of saying it, I felt a little better. I checked my phone but knew that Dax wasn't there yet. It wouldn't be until midway through the game that he'd arrive. So, for now, I'd just have to focus on what I needed to and have confidence in the plan we had in place. No matter what happened, we'd get through this together.

Dakota Hughes had no clue the amount of wrath he was about to unleash from the three men he'd just pissed off by messing with their girl. With that thought, I finished changing and then charged out of the locker room onto the ice; a fire lit within me.

Henley Henshaw was our girl, and it was time the world knew it.

# CHAPTER 2

## Henley

THE WORLD CAME BACK into focus slowly, like I was moving underwater. Everything was fuzzy around the edges as I tried to latch onto something. A hand squeezed in mine and, like an anchor, it pulled me forward.

"Hen, can you hear me?" the husky voice asked. I instantly felt safe and warm, knowing it was okay to come to the surface.

Reed's face swam over mine, his blue eyes staring down at me. They swirled with concern as they traced over every inch of my face.

"What happened?" I asked.

I started to sit up, but the world spun around me.

"Whoa. Go slowly."

I obeyed his command, letting him guide me to an upright position. I blinked, taking in the room we were in. It looked like an ordinary office. The carpet was blue, the walls gray, and a desk with a filing cabinet sat to the left of us. I was on a leather couch, and Reed kneeled before me.

"Do you remember anything?" he asked, his eyes still on me.

"I..." Memories resurfaced as I recalled finding my belongings trashed, Kurt and Dakota conspiring, and then the media bombarding us. I glanced at Reed, his face letting me know none of it had been a dream. "Yeah, I remember. I'm just not sure what the media was saying."

His jaw flexed, his hand tightening in my grip before he let out a long breath.

"I'm not sure exactly what's going on, but it doesn't sound good. You fainted when they cornered you, and I could barely get you out of there. We're hiding out in this office until the media clears out."

"The game!" I shouted, moving to stand. The world tilted a little, but I pushed it away. I needed to see how my team was doing.

"It's over, Hen. You can't do anything about it now." Reed gritted his teeth, holding back what he really wanted to say.

"*Do* anything?" I asked, peering into his eyes.

"Kurt."

Before he could say anything more, a shout could be heard in the hallway. Reed stepped away, going to the door to see what it was about. I glanced down at what I was wearing, discovering I was still in my hockey padding and skates.

"Dax?" Reed asked before stepping out into the hall. At the name, I glanced up and moved closer to the door. What was Dax doing here? He should be back in Oak Crest.

I approached the door, but I didn't get far before they stepped back in. Dax's eyes met mine, and instantly he rushed to my side. His hands touched my face, looking for something.

"Are you hurt? What happened?" he asked, turning slightly to Reed when I didn't answer.

"What are you doing here?" I asked instead.

"She's not hurt," Reed answered, giving Dax a soft smile. "Not that I'm not glad to see you, man, but why are you here?"

"Fletch and I got worried when she didn't return to the ice. Then there was the news story…" he trailed off, searching my face.

"News… Yeah, I don't know what that's about."

He relaxed, giving himself a small nod. "Then neither of us could get a hold of you, and with Kurt on the bench coaching, it worried us. Fletch had a game, so I drove up here."

"It's an hour away," I said, realizing the gesture he'd just made.

"Yeah, I might have broken a few traffic laws on my way." He cringed, but it was one of the sweetest gestures ever from Dax.

"Sorry, my stuff is still in the locker room, and Henley's got trashed. We were on our way to find a janitor when we were ambushed by the craziness out there."

"What is all that? Are high school games usually that well covered by the press?" Dax asked.

"No." I shook my head, pieces of the puzzle beginning to slot into place. "Dakota did something, and I think my mom helped. I don't know why, though."

"The last news bulletin said you were engaged to Dakota." Dax swallowed, fear entering his eyes.

I laughed, shaking my head no. "Fuck that," I cursed. Dax relaxed, pulling me into a hug as much as he could with all my padding.

"It's a shitstorm, but we'll get through this together. I better let Fletch know you're okay. He was going out of his mind," he said into my ear.

Nodding, I let him pull back, immediately looking to Reed. I expected to find him angry, but instead, he watched us with a knowing look on his face. When I lifted my eyebrow at him, he smiled, showing his teeth. It was a whole new look for the man who usually wore a scowl.

"What?" I asked when he didn't stop. It was contagious, though, my own smile gracing my lips.

"Just this," he said, stepping closer to grab my hand. "I'm happy to be in this with you, Hen."

Pulling his jersey, I kissed him briefly on the lips, wanting to savor this moment. Drawing back, I caught Dax's hungry eyes. It surprised me since he'd been a bit standoffish about our relationship, but seeing him here changed something in me. I cleared my throat, needing to get the lovey-dovey thoughts out of my head.

"What do we do now? I don't want to face the

media, but I know I can't leave it either. Plus, the game should be over. The kids need someone to reassure them things are okay. Not to mention, I still need to deal with my room being trashed."

"Alright, I'll go back to the locker room and assist with the kids. Dax, can you go with Henley to find a janitor and get that cleaned up? Half of the students are going with their parents, and the other half staying overnight in the hotel to attend the Junior classic tomorrow. Once everyone is sorted, I'll meet you back at the hotel, and we can figure out what to do next. Avoid the media at all costs," Reed demanded, making parts of me wake up. I'd never heard him be so commanding before, and it was definitely working for me.

"Yes, sir," I said, giving him a shit-eating grin. The corner of his mouth tilted up, his eyes sparkling. Some of the darkness from earlier dissipated, making me feel better.

He didn't say anything as he headed out the door. The sounds of the arena could be heard as cheers and jeers rang out around it.

"Come on, let's get this over with." I pulled Dax with me, heading in the opposite direction of Reed. We didn't find a janitor, but we stumbled upon a staff person who said they would send someone to take a report. I took off some of my pads as we walked, wanting the extra weight off of me.

"You sure you're okay?" Dax asked, eying me out of the corner of his eyes.

"Right now I am because I have to be. I need to be strong for Reese and the others. I need to show them the bullies aren't getting to me."

"What about later, when you don't?"

"I'll face that when the time comes," I said.

"Let me be strong for you when it does. Let us."

I stopped walking, shocked by what Dax was saying. "I don't understand."

"I know we're still getting to know one another, but the thing I've learned about you, Petal, is that you take care of those around you. You strive extra hard to ensure everything is good for others, often neglecting yourself. I get you need to do that and feel a sense of obligation to protect these teens. So, I'm not going to tell you to stop. I admire your strength. It's sexy. But later, when we're alone, and the world isn't demanding anything from you, I want you to give in to me. Let me take all the worries and take care of you. Understand?"

With each word he spoke, he moved closer until his hand gripped my chin, forcing me to stare at him. Not that I protested. I'd stare at Dax any day of the week. His words were beautiful, and a part of me wept inside at the comfort he offered me.

Because he was right. I was responsible for everyone else. Making sure they were safe and taken care of. I didn't mind doing it; I enjoyed it most of the time. But I'd never had anyone looking out for me.

In my entire relationship with Dakota, or even my mother for that matter, they had never taken something off my shoulders or done anything to just help.

They were users, only wanting from me what they could take and never offering anything in return. Whatever I got from them was scraps, and they manipulated me to be happy to receive those.

It was twisted and morbid when I thought about it, and I hated that it had taken me until this point to fully see the reality of it.

I licked my lips, my breath catching in my throat. His eyes were molten lava as they stared at me, waiting for an answer.

"I understand," I whispered. It was the only amount of sound I could get out, but it seemed to work when Dax leaned forward and sealed my words with a kiss.

He stepped back before I could relish it, taking my hand as he pulled me forward. My heart dropped when we turned the corner, and I spotted Reese and Braden staring into the makeshift changing room.

One more thing I'd failed to protect them from.

"Hen!" Reese shouted, rushing toward me when they spotted me. Their arms went around me as best as they could. "I was so worried. What happened?"

"This." I pointed toward the room. "When I left to

find someone, I was locked in. It wasn't until Reed came that I could get out."

"You were locked in?" Dax asked, his face turning stormy. I guess I'd forgotten to mention that part earlier.

"Yeah. The janitor's cart had been pushed in front of it, the mop handle over the latch."

"Fuckers," Reese seethed, catching me off guard.

"Hey," I said, narrowing my eyes.

"You know this was planned, right? He trapped you and benched me the instant you didn't return." I'd never seen Reese so angry before. Their face was red with anger, their eyes barely slits, their hands bunched into fists.

"We can't prove it yet. But I'm working on it," I said, hoping to calm them. "It doesn't help that there's a media mob waiting out there. Mom and Dakota set something up," I warned.

"Mom?" they asked, peering around their shoulders.

"Yeah. We need to avoid the media if we can. I don't trust her."

Before I could say anything else, a janitor appeared around the corner with the worker I'd found earlier. I talked with them about the damage and made an official complaint with the league.

"Now, ma'am. I'm sure you're blowing this out of proportion. You don't need to get the league involved," the arena employee huffed, crossing their arms.

"First, yes, I do. Our belongings were trashed, and our space was violated, making it unsafe for anyone not part of the main team. Second, I'm Coach Henshaw. I'm not a simpering woman for you to cajole. This was a clear violation of our agreement to play here, and if I have to get the elective board on the phone for the Junior division, then I will. So, how about you tell me how you'll fix this instead of trying to brush it under the rug?"

I would've felt bad for the employee if he hadn't called me *ma'am*. But after the day I'd had, it was the last straw on the pile of disrespect I'd been served all day.

"Yes, *Coach*. I'll get the director here immediately."

They scurried away with their tail tucked between their legs as they rushed to find someone who could actually help. I prayed there was some footage to use in my complaint. I wanted to prove it was Kurt, but it would only be hearsay without evidence. It wouldn't be enough to get him out of the school.

At this point, though, I wasn't sure I could continue to coach or trust him in any capacity. Not after what I'd seen and heard.

Braden and Reese were helping the janitor go through what could be salvaged while Dax and I waited. He wrapped his arms around me, leaning down to whisper into my ear.

"That was sexy as hell, Petal."

I opened my mouth to respond but stopped when

Reese stepped out. "I think there's an outfit you can change into at least," they said, eyeing me and Dax, a coy smile playing on their lips.

"Thanks." I stepped away from Dax, stopping before I entered. "Let me know if someone shows up." He nodded, the simple act making my heart flip. It felt nice to lean on him.

I looked through the things Reese found and agreed it should work for the time being. We took them across the hall to another room since ours was being cleaned by the janitor.

Reese was quiet as we changed, and I wanted to ask them what they were feeling, but I didn't know how to broach it. Eventually, I left it, knowing if they wanted to talk, they would.

"You still going to stay with Braden and Briana this weekend?" I asked when we stepped out into the hallway.

"Yeah, unless you need me?"

It was the sweetest thing they could've offered. Tears brimmed my eyelids, but I shoved them back, not wanting to appear too feminine at the moment. It wasn't safe yet. I pulled Reese into a hug, placing a kiss on their forehead.

"Thanks, but I'll be okay. Be mindful of where you are and keep me updated. You should be good to be off campus for the weekend with everything."

They nodded, squeezing back, taking their hockey gear, and walking off with Braden. He gave me a nod as he took Reese's padding, throwing it over his shoulder.

I didn't get to ponder too much about them when the director showed up, and I went back over my grievances. He was a lot more apologetic, promising to send me any footage they had and replace anything that was beyond repair.

"Thank you; we appreciate that. Is there an exit out of here that will avoid the media?" I asked, tiredness weighing me down.

"Yes, absolutely. If you're ready, I can show you out." Grabbing the few things that had survived, I walked with Dax when he grabbed my pads, almost mirroring what Braden had done for Reese. It made me smile, the gesture not going unnoticed.

When we got to the back door, Dax hurried to his car to pull it back to us, avoiding any sightings. Thankfully, we seemed to avoid everyone; the hoodie he'd loaned me covered my hair. It all felt too similar to when I first ran into Reed for the first time, and my brain wanted to shut down and avoid remembering those things.

I looked at Dax and knew I wasn't alone this time, so I held my head up high and would face whatever the world wanted to throw at me.

I might've stumbled today, but I wasn't down for the count. I'd gotten up, and I would keep getting up until the world got the message that I wasn't going anywhere.

# CHAPTER 3

## *Henley*

DAX and I made it to the hotel unscathed, avoiding reporters as we checked in. I hated that I wasn't with the team, but I'd be more of a hindrance to them right now. I had to hope Reed could be my voice until we had everything taken care of.

Sighing, I sat on the bed as Dax set down his things. I didn't have much. Most of the stuff I'd brought had been ruined by the vandalism. My phone was still unaccounted for, as well. Though, I had a good guess where *that* had gone.

"Can I use your phone?" I asked, looking over at Dax.

Dax didn't say anything, pulling it out of his pocket and handing it to me. I smiled at him and kissed his cheek, letting him know I appreciated his help. Typing in one of the numbers I knew by heart, I sent a message to my sibling.

DAX

Hey, Reese. It's Hen. My phone's missing. You can reach me here for now.

REESE

Got it.

How much trouble would I get in if I
punched someone?

DAX

Probably a lot. Why?

REESE

Kurt. He's acting like he led us to
victory. We still lost by 1 point.

DAX

Ignore him for now. He'll get his due.
Let me know when you make it to the
twin's house.

REESE

You sure you're okay, Hen?

DAX

I will be. Love you lots, turd.

REESE

Back at ya, nerd.

Giggling, I closed out the chat and peered up, spotting Dax smiling at me.

"Reese?"

"Yeah, how did you know?" I asked, handing him his phone. "I told them to message you if they needed me. Hope that's okay?"

"Of course, Hen. I'm here for you. Even if that means you just need me for my phone." He paused, grinning. It was such a different look for the dour man

I'd come to know. He shifted, crossing his arms. "I knew it was Reese, because you're always happy when you're talking to them."

Warmth spread over me at that statement. Both from his acknowledgment and also the fact he respected Reese and their pronouns.

"Thank you," I whispered.

Dax's smile tilted crookedly, making him even more dashing, if that was possible.

"So," I cleared my throat, my body responding to his look. "What should we do until Reed's free?"

Dax's smile grew, his eyebrows going up into his hair. "Well, Petal," he purred, "I know a few things."

My face heated, the memory of his hands on my body replaying in my head. He smirked, crossing his feet as he leaned back against the dresser. Dax kept watching me like he was waiting for a signal.

Shifting my legs, I was about to give in when his phone vibrated on the dresser, surprising us both. Dax glanced down, rolling his eyes as he answered.

"Hey, man. Yeah, we just got to the room. Hold on," he groused, pulling the phone away and placing it on speaker. "You're on speaker now, Fletch."

"Henley?" he asked. His voice had tears fighting to return. It was gentle, warm, and full of concern.

"I'm here. I'm okay."

"What happened? Dax just said there was something with your room?"

"Yeah. I left to check on a player and found mine

and Reese's changing room destroyed. While looking through it, I overheard Dakota and Kurt talking. When I tried to leave the room to confront them, the door was locked. Reed said it had been done purposefully."

"Shit. I'm coming to you."

"No. You don't need to, Fletch. We'll be back in the morning. I didn't want to fight the media tonight, so we're staying in the hotel. Dax and Reed are here. No one will hurt me."

Fletcher sighed, and I could practically picture him rubbing his face and beard. Over the past week, I'd learned it was his nervous gesture when he was stressed.

"I don't like it, Hen. I won't feel good until you're back here."

My whole face warmed. I'd gotten so lucky to meet Fletcher Cromwell again.

"You're sweet, Fletch. I wish you were here too, but there's no reason for you to drive all this way. I promise we'll leave early tomorrow. I want to be back on campus as much as you want me to be. Then I'll need to talk with Dmitry and figure this all out."

"Actually, I did that. He's in full support of you. He knows something is amiss here. We just need evidence to prove who is behind it. Were you able to get anything?"

"We're waiting to see. The rink said they'd send it over once they'd gone through it. I'm not hopeful, though. Dakota is too smart to be caught on camera."

Dax's jaw clenched, a stern expression crossing his face.

"I won't let her out of my sight, Fletcher. I'll protect our girl."

I knew he was saying it for Fletcher's sake, but as usual, Dax's words lit a fire in me, scorching my body and liquifying my panties.

"Fine. I won't come. But I want updates every few hours. I don't like that they're spinning the narrative right now, and we don't know what they want," he grumbled.

I snorted, amused at the level of mastery Fletcher was giving Dakota. He wasn't an evil mastermind, just a narcissist covering his back.

"The only thing Dakota cares about is his appearance. Whatever his real purpose is for doing this, he'll try to get what he wants while making himself look like a saint in the process. It's not any more sinister than that. Guaranteed. He's a douche nozzle, but he's simple in the fact he's always looking out for number one. Himself."

Dax snickered, his grin returning to his face. I could hear Fletcher chuckling, too.

"When will Reed return?" he asked, changing the subject.

"Should be soon. I doubt the after-game pep talk was all that long. He was going to make sure Reese made it into Braden's parent's car unscathed before heading here. How's your game?" I asked.

Dax motioned he was going to step out of the room, giving me some privacy. I took the phone and sat it on the bed as I rolled over and lay on my stomach.

"Surprisingly, it's going well. I've been a little distracted… but the team has come through. We're up by one goal with the last period to go." I could hear the admonishment in his voice, and that wouldn't do.

"Fletcher, the players are good because you're an excellent coach." I smiled, wishing I could see his face. I heard rustling and knew he was scratching his beard again.

"Hmm, maybe."

"Don't be playing coy with me, Fletch," I teased. "We lost another one. Even though I wasn't there for the last period, I feel responsible."

"Because you have a kind soul and competitive spirit, Hen. But you can't let this get you down. Watch the film, learn from it, and make better calls. I trust your skills. You're going to know what to do to get your team to win."

"Thanks, Fletch. You always did give the best pep talks."

"I much prefer giving them when you're naked and in my bed," he purred, the conversation changing.

"Oh? You're going to have to demonstrate this technique when I return. I must have the full experience." My voice grew huskier the longer we talked, the arousal building in me with his words.

"Shit, time is up, and I have to return to the game. Pause this, Hen. I will make it up to you when you get home."

"I'm going to hold you to that. Bye, Fletch. Good luck!"

"Bye, baby. Keep me updated."

"I will."

The phone clicked off, and I laid my head on my arms, staring into space. My mind was filled with naughty visions of how I wanted to greet Fletcher tomorrow when I returned to the house.

It wasn't much longer until the door opened and two voices entered. I peered up, finding Reed was back. Dax carried a duffle, presumably Reed's, since his hands were full. He had one of my bags under his arm and a couple of shopping bags in the other. I sat up, curious about what he brought.

"Hey, how did it go? How's the team?" I asked, wanting to check in first.

He grinned, dropping the items onto the bed. "I love that your first question is about the team." He bent over, kissing me before moving back. He sighed, taking a seat beside me on the bed. Dax placed the bag on the dresser, resuming his position from earlier.

"The team's split. Most of them were concerned about you, asking what happened. The ones loyal to Kurt were practically gleeful that you weren't there. I don't know what he said before I entered, but I tried to calm the situation by saying that you were just handling something and would let everyone know what was going on when we returned to campus. I'm sure Kurt made some claims, instilling fear into the kids."

"Shit. Ugh, why is he so out to get me?"

"Because you're better at hockey than him, and he can't take it," Dax said matter-of-factly.

Reed snorted, nodding in agreement. "And he probably thought you'd be interested in him. He's not used to women saying no."

I scrunched up my face; the image of Kurt naked was not one I wanted to envision. "No offense, but ew. He's *so* not my type." My body shuddered, all remnants of desire leaving with it too.

"Good to know," Reed said, squeezing my leg. He rubbed his neck with his free one, turning toward me. "The media is loving the drama. I heard that Dakota is having a press conference in the morning to address your tweet."

"That can't be good." I bit my lip, worried about what his angle was. Why would he send something out to the world that wasn't true? How did he plan to spin this in his favor? Whatever it was, I needed to get ahead of it.

"It's a long shot, but I have an old buddy who might be able to find out what Dakota is up to if you're interested."

"Yes." I nodded fervently.

Reed stood and pulled out his phone, heading toward the hallway, leaving Dax and me alone again.

"How was your chat with Fletch?" he asked, raising his eyebrows.

"Great. It was great," I said, crossing my legs as I cleared my throat, remembering what we'd been talking about. "Man, is it warm in here? Maybe I should take a shower now."

"Hmm, is that what you really want to do?"

"No, but if I let myself give in to you now, I won't leave this room," I said, meaning it.

Dax stopped his forward progress, searching my eyes. "You make that sound like a bad thing, Petal." He arched an eyebrow at me, questioning my reasoning.

"In most cases, it wouldn't be. But you're right. My head's too cluttered with everything at the moment, and if I give in to you, I'm worried I'll lose myself. Give me a few hours to figure some things out. I'm not saying no, just not right now."

"Okay, I can give you that. Whatever you need, Petal." He raised my hand to his mouth, kissing my knuckles. "Go shower. I'll order some food and start making a game plan."

"You've been amazing today, Dax. Thank you."

I pulled him closer, wanting him to know how much I liked him. Kissing him, I forgot where I was for a second, Dax's lips consuming me. His hands dropped to my hips, pulling me flush with him.

The keycard beeped, so I pulled back, giving him one more brief kiss before moving away. Reed smiled, continuing to show me how okay he was with this arrangement.

"I'm going to shower. Dax is ordering food."

"Perfect. They'll call me back in a few minutes once they speak with Dakota."

Leaning forward, I kissed Reed, loving the feeling of being able to kiss them both. "I got you a few things on my way here. Reese told me what sizes and where to go. Let me know if you need anything else. We might have it or can get it for you until we get back home."

Grinning, I took the bag and stepped into the bathroom. Inside were a pair of underwear, a tank top, leggings, a hairbrush, a toothbrush, and some toiletries.

Dumping it on the counter, I turned on the water, ready for it to rinse off the feelings of inadequacy threatening to overtake me.

Not today, sucker. Not today. There was only room in this bathroom for badasses, so kindly get the fuck out.

Shaking off my negative emotions, I lifted my chin as I stepped into the shower, a surge of pride welling in my chest.

They'd have to try a lot harder to break me.

# CHAPTER 4

## *Reed*

MY BLOOD PUMPED FURIOUSLY through me as I paced up and down the hall. We'd driven back to school early this morning, beating the team bus. All night, Henley had been quiet, withdrawn into herself as she fought the demons in her head. Dax and I had tried to comfort her, but it wasn't something we could fix sitting in that hotel room.

None of us had slept, so when she rose at 5 am asking if we could leave, we agreed. Henley had called Dmitry on our way here, arranging a meeting with the PR team. The guys had wanted to come, but Henley felt she needed to do it on her own. I only made the cut because Dmitry wanted to hear my side of what had occurred.

Once I recalled it, they'd asked me to step out into the hallway to wait, but I couldn't sit still, so I paced and continued to ruminate over everything. The whirl-wind of emotions I'd gone through in the past day had me in a frenzy. I'd gone so long not feeling anything that now they consumed me as they rushed through my body.

Fear. Panic. Hate. Relief. Anger. *Love.*

They battled it out, and my thoughts jumbled as I tried to make sense of it all.

Especially the last one. I hadn't loved anyone in my life outside of my mother. To feel it for a woman I'd known for a month felt overwhelming.

But I couldn't deny it wasn't true. I just wasn't sure what to do with it.

So, I focused on the anger and hate for the men who'd done this to her. My old teammate hadn't been able to pull anything from Dakota, stating he'd closed up the second he asked him a question. It infuriated me to not know how to protect Henley in this. Pulling out my phone, I read the tweet and article for the millionth time.

*Dakota Fucking Hughes.*

I'd always despised the man. He was a lazy player who wanted to find the easiest way to his goal, no matter who he skated over in the process.

But this was a whole new level. Using Henley as a pawn in his sick game made me wish he was right in front of me so I could punch his face.

They'd have to pull me off because I wouldn't be able to stop.

The door opened down the hallway, and I pocketed my phone and hurried back. Henley was shaking hands with a few people as I approached.

"Thank you," she said. I was too far away to gauge her emotions in those few words.

Dmitry nodded as I neared, squeezing Henley's

shoulder before he stepped away. Her shoulders deflated, and I rushed the last few steps, needing to hold her.

Wrapping my arms around her, my hand held her head to my chest as she sank into me, her arms going around my waist. I squeezed her tight, breathing in her shampoo as I waited.

"What did they say?" I asked when I felt her body relax.

"It's not good. But they're going to help me fight it. So there's that."

Her voice was small, making me want to punch Dakota even more. Henley was fierce, and I hated that she doubted herself. She let out a breath, stepping back.

"Let's head back to the house. I know the guys are probably getting nervous," she said, her eyes not meeting mine.

Wrapping my arm around her shoulders, I drew her to me as we walked from the building, wanting to shield her from anything else. Since we'd left so early, we'd avoided the media, and none were allowed on campus since minors were present. Dmitry had sent out a campus-wide email reminding them of the code of conduct and warning all students of an immediate suspension if they talked to the press.

The threat to their careers was enough of a warning for the majority of them. I hoped the rest would follow suit as well. Henley didn't need any more trouble to contend with.

The drive back was quiet; Henley stared out the window the whole way. The need to make this right grew the longer she wasn't herself. The problem was I didn't know how to fix this outside of using violence, and that wasn't an option at the moment.

Feelings of helplessness wanted to overcome me, but I pushed them away, not wanting to make this about me. I just needed to be here for her. She wasn't a damsel in distress, needing me to show up and rescue her. Henley Henshaw was her own white knight.

Suddenly, I realized what I needed to do. I couldn't make it go away, but I could remind her who she was.

Pulling into the driveway, I didn't shut off the engine right away, wanting her to wait. She turned, blinking at me.

"Hen, I don't know what's going through your head, but you're not alone in this. Not that you need any of us. You're strong and a force to be reckoned with. As cliche as it sounds, that's why Kurt is intimidated. He knows you're a better player than he is and can't accept it. It doesn't make it right, but use that against him. We need to quit playing defense right now and score some points ourselves. The time to let it blow over is gone. The clock is ticking, and you have one play to make it happen. What do we do, Coach?"

Henley licked her lips, her eyes searching mine. I watched as she digested my words; the plan forming in her head. Her face hardened, the same look I'd seen on the ice as she prepared to go in for the kill.

"We take out their weakest link, distract them with a phony play, and shoot it right between their legs." She smiled, the one that set my heart on fire, and I knew she'd returned.

Pulling her face to mine, I locked my lips to hers, kissing her hard as I held her there. When I drew back, her lips were puffy, and both of our breathing was labored, but her eyes were shining with the light that Henley infused in others.

Dropping my forehead to hers, I brushed my thumb across her cheek as we caught our breath.

"Thank you for reminding me who I am, Reed."

"Anytime, Hen."

A knock on the window had us jumping. Henley turned, and I glared at the man who'd interrupted our moment.

"Sorry!" Fletcher said, holding his hands up. "Just curious if you're going to come in or if we should have the meeting in the car?"

Rolling my eyes, I turned the keys and pocketed them. Henley chuckled, opening her door once Fletcher had scooted back.

"I can barely fit in that car. I doubt four of us would," I grumbled, walking toward the house.

Henley and Fletcher laughed as they followed.

"I wondered why you had that car," Henley said as

we stepped into the house. "It doesn't seem like your style."

"It was what the rental company gave me. I have a truck back home. I'm tempted to lease something here so I can get rid of the tuna can. But I rarely have to drive anywhere, or I can tag along with you guys, so it hasn't been too much of an inconvenience."

"Hmm, yeah, I guess that's true. You can take my Jeep whenever you need, man," Fletcher said. I nodded, accepting his olive branch.

I wasn't actually irritated with him. The accumulation of little sleep, the stress of the game, and fear for Henley had drained me. Thankfully, he let my sour mood go, directing us into the living room.

Dax was already seated on the couch, standing, when he spotted us. "So?" he asked, apparently unable to wait for a second longer.

Henley kissed his cheek before taking her own seat.

"The video footage the arena sent had been tampered with. While it gives credence to the sabotage, it doesn't give us a culprit, meaning there's no evidence it was Kurt. The school will release a press update on my absence from the last period to stop any more rumors, though the damage is likely done. They want me to focus on the next game and show the league that the school is behind me and I'm committed to the team."

She took a breath, her shoulders dropping. Dax's jaw clenched, his hands flexing at the news.

"Dmitry is going to keep a close eye on Kurt. He's going to have him give a statement for documentation purposes and said he would ensure Kurt understands that if anything comes to light about his involvement or if there's another incident, his contract would be voided."

"That's not enough!" Dax shouted, surprising us all. Henley stood and walked over to him, taking his hands.

"I don't like it either, but there's not much I can do. It's he said, she said. Without proof, they'd have to suspend us both. This buys us time to get to the bottom of what's happening. There's something bigger at play here."

She turned back to Fletcher and me on the couch as Dax wrapped his arms around her, pulling her into his body. He seemed to calm at her touch, his head resting in her hair on her shoulder. He struggled with the verdict, and I wondered if it triggered something from his past. I'd have to check in with him later.

The part of me that hadn't had a friend in so long realized the momentous shift that had just taken place in me. It was jarring but gave me hope. I was building something more here than my resume. I was building a family.

"And Dakota's thing?" Fletcher asked.

"Dmitry said he could arrange a press conference if

I wanted to address it. The PR team encouraged me to let it go and ignore it, stating that giving it any more attention would only keep it in the news. My agent said she could release a statement if I wanted to avoid the cameras as well."

"What do you want to do?" Fletcher asked, leaning on his elbows.

"I'm not sure." She bit her lip, her eyes dropping to the floor in thought. "I don't like the idea of him spreading lies about me. But I agree that responding would be like pouring gasoline on the fire, and I don't want to give him what he wants—the attention. I guess if my agent sends out something, it's the lesser of two evils."

"But would it be enough? They could see it as a sign of admittance. I think this is a case of either striking hard or letting it go," Fletcher said.

"What was your plan you had in the car? The one about taking out the weakest link and distracting them while you scored?" I asked.

Henley's eyes lifted to me, her smile returning.

"There was one thing I didn't tell Dmitry and the PR team. When I overheard Dakota and Kurt, they mentioned a society. Have any of you ever heard of it?"

Fletcher shook his head, but I stayed quiet. I hadn't heard mention of the Society in years. I'd almost forgotten about it.

"What is it, Reed?" Dax asked. I met his eyes, realizing he'd been watching me. The other two turned, looking at me, too.

"Do you know, Reed?" Henley asked, her face hopeful.

Exhaling, I nodded, my fingers tapping on the couch's armrest. "It's a secret society for hockey players."

"Are you a member?" Fletcher asked, his eyes wide.

Scoffing, I shook my head. "Do I strike you as the type of guy to join organized clubs? Secret ones at that?" My eyebrows rose, the incredulousness thick in my voice. The others laughed, loosening some of the strain on my shoulders.

"Okay, what can you tell us then?" Henley asked.

Shrugging my shoulders, I ran my hand through my hair. "Not much. I told them to fuck off. A teammate approached me, stating there was an easy way to advance my career. I just needed to know the right people. I laughed him off, stating I wasn't interested in him like that. He cornered me in the locker room, spouting off how the Society was so old and secretive that only those they deemed worthy could utter their names, and I'd been tapped by a member to join. While he kept talking, I got this weird feeling in my gut, so I stayed away. I haven't thought about that since then."

"Did he ever try to approach you again?" Henley asked.

"No." My brows bunched up as I recalled that time.

"In fact, he was traded to a different team the next day. I haven't talked to him since. I never put the two together."

"They moved him to keep you from asking questions?" Fletcher asked.

"Maybe. Or it could've been the advancement he was talking about. He was traded to the Baltimore Barons, who won the Stanley Cup that year."

"And who Dakota plays for," Henley added, her eyes wide.

"So, you think the Society is the one pulling his strings?" I asked, curious.

"Maybe. It sounded like that was what Kurt was wanting."

"Then, what's your plan? I'm not sure we're up to taking down a secret society." I leaned forward, Fletcher and Dax looking between Henley and me.

"I'm not interested in taking down a secret society. As far as I know, they haven't done anything to me. That responsibility lies on Dakota's shoulders."

"Perhaps, or they could be using Dakota as a means to an end," Fletcher mused, rubbing his beard.

"It's too dangerous," Dax growled, tightening his grip on Henley.

"I agree. Until we know more, we can't make any decisions. I don't want to make myself an enemy to the Society if they've done nothing other than have the bad taste to accept Dakota." Henley shuddered at his name, making me want to punch him again. "For now,

I want to ensure Kurt can't do any more damage here. I'll go along with the school's plan unless something changes."

"I still think we should prepare. Offense, Henley."

Sighing, she nodded. "You're right. Do you think you could get in touch with that player and learn more about the Society then?"

I thought it over, and as much as it pained me to reach out to the man, I'd do it for Henley.

"Yeah, I can."

"As for the rest, no one leaves Henley alone with Kurt, *ever*," Dax said, glaring at Fletcher and me.

"Agreed," Fletcher and I said, much to Henley's annoyance.

"I can take care of myself," she huffed.

"We know. This is for us, Baby Shaw. Can you appease our frail male egos so we feel better?"

She rolled her eyes but nodded. "Fine. But no one is coming to pee with me. There are some boundaries I'm not ready to cross."

"Deal," the three of us said, laughing at the face she made.

We'd be alright. I had faith in the four of us to ride this storm. And if the opportunity came, I'd knock that smug grin right off Dakota's face.

# CHAPTER 5

## *Henley*

THE GUYS IGNORED their phones and the media for the rest of Saturday, and we just had fun. We played board games, baked, and put together a massive cat tower for Lady Sterling.

"I guess she approves," I said, standing back and watching the gray cat lick her paws from her perch. Reed chuckled, pulling me toward him, his hand resting on my hip.

"Yeah, it seems so. Have you heard anything from Reese?"

"Not yet. I told them to call yours if they needed something. I'll go into town tomorrow and get a new phone. Though, I might call them later to make sure they're behaving."

He kissed my temple, his breath warm. "You're a good sister."

"I try to be. It's hard to know the balance between sibling and guardian."

"To me, it seems you're doing what works for you two, and that's what matters."

I tilted my head to peer up at him. His crystal blue eyes still took my breath away. Reed was a handsome man with dark hair, a sharp jawline, and intense eyes, but his heart was what had attracted me the most.

"Thanks, Reed. You always make me feel better."

"Food time!" Fletcher yelled from the kitchen, breaking the stare-off between Reed and me. Smiling, I stepped out of his grip and followed my nose to the smells.

"Mmm, it smells wonderful."

In a spirit of rebellion, we made all the bad things the trainers were always telling us to avoid. Dax had grimaced the whole time and tried to convince us to add vegetables or get the whole-grain version. In the end, we added a salad, but I didn't think anyone outside of Dax planned to eat it. Who wanted leafy greens when there were cheese and carbs to eat?

Filling my plate with pizza rolls, pretzels, fried pickles, and mozzarella sticks, I took my food into the living room. I felt like a kid breaking curfew with the delicious fatty carbs on my plate.

"We need a bigger couch," Dax grumbled when he entered last, finding both Fletcher and Reed sitting next to me.

"Nah, it's the perfect size," Fletcher teased, his eyes heating and reminding me of our sexy encounter at the last movie night.

I stuffed a pretzel in my mouth, deciding to keep quiet. Reed snorted, covering his face as he tried not to choke on whatever he was eating.

"What?" Dax asked, looking between the three of us.

"Nothing!" I shouted, making him narrow his eyes. "Hit play, Fletch."

Reed and Fletcher snickered, the couch shaking with their laughter. I ignored them, reaching over to hit the button myself. Dax kept looking at them, knowing he was missing something as he took the chaise.

The movie began, and I slid off the couch onto the floor, deciding not to reward their teasing. Their laughter stopped abruptly as they tried to cajole me back, but I ignored them, enjoying my food as the movie played. When Dax and I finished, I climbed off the floor and walked over to him, curling up in his arms, settling the tug-of-war game they'd started.

Dax's body was warm, his hands smoothing over my back as I watched the movie. At some point, my eyes fluttered closed as the exhaustion from the last twenty-four hours caught up to me.

Strong arms carried me against a hard chest. I stirred, my eyes attempting to open.

"Ssh, Petal. Go back to sleep."

My body was laid on a soft surface, covers pulled over me. I quit fighting the sleep and let it pull me back under as arms wrapped around me.

*"You'll never beat me, Henny. I'll always win. Just like I have already."*

I bolted upright; the dream disappearing as I caught my breath. Dakota's voice played in my head, his threat still clear as day. I couldn't figure out if it was a memory or something twisted my mind had created.

A warm hand slid up my leg, stopping high on my thigh as it squeezed.

"You okay?" they muttered into the pillow.

Blinking, I nodded until I realized they couldn't see me.

"Bad dream," I whispered, laying back down.

Dax's hair cascaded around him, his blond waves splayed across his pillow. He looked otherworldly in the mid-morning light. His arms reached out to me, pulling me to his bare chest, his heart a steady beat against my ear.

"I didn't take you for a cuddler," I teased, needing to focus on something other than Dakota's threat.

"Mmm, only for the special ones, Petal."

My lips curved up at the statement, loving that I got to know Dax as more than the manwhore he'd pretended to be. My fingers trailed over his abs, loving the way his muscles dipped. He was hard and soft in all the right places. When I got to a small patch of hair, I couldn't stop my fingers from trailing through it.

"You're going to wake up another part of me, Petal."

"Maybe I want to," I teased.

Despite Dax being the first of the three I'd slept with, we hadn't since we'd entered into this new relationship. My body yearned for the pleasure it remembered, how he had wrung orgasms out of me like it was his job.

Traveling further down, I found the elastic of his boxers. Without hesitation, I snaked my fingers below the band, his breath hitching as I grasped him.

"Fuck, Petal," he hissed.

Smiling against his chest, I inched further down as I stroked him, his cock growing hard in my hand. Pushing his boxers lower, I wiggled around until my ass was closer to his head and my mouth could reach his tip.

Licking up the length of him, I felt his legs tense as he cursed behind me. Slowly, I swirled my tongue around his tip, pursing my lips as I sucked him down. Everything disappeared as I focused on Dax's cock and wanting to bring him pleasure.

My hand stroked him halfway as I sucked the rest. Humming, I felt his hands move but ignored it, continuing my mission. Moving down, I took him a little further, his thick cock stretching my lips as I wrapped them around him.

Stroking up and down, I watched the way his dick twitched with my touch. His hands caressed my butt, the only warning I got before his fingers dipped and plunged into me.

Squeaking, I tightened my grip as he chuckled. "Fair play, Petal," he purred, his voice a dark and husky tone that had my toes curling.

"You're lucky I didn't have you in my mouth then, or I might have bitten something off," I taunted.

"Why do you think I waited?" he hummed.

He arched his fingers, hitting my g-spot easily from his angle. His fingers moved quickly, making my legs shake from the pleasure.

In an attempt to regain control, I doubled down and sucked and squeezed him with everything I had. My tongue swirled around as I sucked in my cheeks, my free hand stroking his base. Drifting down with my other hand, I rolled his balls around in my palm. I was determined to make him come first. It felt like an important win.

"Shit, Petal. Your lips feel too good around me."

"Then give me what I want, Dax," I said, hoping I sounded more sensual than out of breath.

His hips lifted, his legs tensing as I continued. His breath hitched again as his fingers stalled inside of me. Feeling victorious, I sped up my actions, his hands grabbing my hips as they flexed. Dax moaned, giving me time to move away if I wanted. But I stayed, wanting my prize as he came, his cum filling my mouth. Swallowing him, I pulled back, licking my lips in satisfaction.

Turning my head, I gave him a big smile, finding

him spent against the bed. Giggling, I turned and crawled back up to him.

"I win," I cheered, not hiding my glee.

"You're a fucking minx, Petal." Dax pulled me into his arms, locking them around me. "Don't think I'm not repaying the favor. I'm going to finish what I started. I just need a second for the blood to return to my head."

Chuckling, I relaxed into his arms. Everything that'd happened on Friday felt so far away now. Sighing, I kissed Dax's cheek, his face turning toward me, a brow raised.

"Thank you for coming on Friday. It meant a lot to me."

"You mean a lot to me."

His green eyes traveled my face, his thumb lightly brushing my hair to the side. Staring into his eyes, I felt something shift in him. His shields dropped, letting me see into his soul.

Tilting my head up, he kissed me, not caring that I'd just had his cum in my mouth. His body pressed into mine, making me feel safe. When he pulled back, we stared at one another for a few seconds, emotions passing between us that words couldn't describe.

"Come on, let's take a shower," he said, pulling me with him as he climbed out of his bed.

"I thought you were going to finish," I pouted.

Dax chuckled as he led me into the bathroom he

shared with Fletcher, locking the doors and turning on the water.

"Oh, I plan to, Petal."

His eyes heated as he charged me, lifting me up and placing me on the counter as he stripped off my clothes, quickly tossing his too. After thoroughly reminding me about his tongue skills, Dax washed my hair, taking extra care with the action, showing me his gentle side.

After the shower, I walked to my room and grabbed some clean clothes, remembering everything I needed to do today. Running a brush through my hair, I walked further into the house, spotting Fletcher at the breakfast table.

"Good morning," I sang, snatching his attention.

"Good morning, Baby Shaw. I take it you slept okay?"

"Mm-hmm," I said, pouring myself a cup of coffee. "Any chance you want to go into town with me?"

He took a bite of toast, watching me. "You're ready?"

"Yep. I need to get a new phone, and I refuse to let the fear of the press saying something about me stop me from living."

"Okay. I'd love to go with you then. I need to drop off the food order for the week and pick up a few things."

"Thanks, Fletch." I smiled, enjoying my coffee.

A short while later, I pulled out of the driveway and headed into town. Fletcher directed me to a bookstore, where he picked up a book he'd ordered, and then to a specialty coffee store, where I got lost in the aisle of coffee beans. We also picked up a few bundt cakes for the house and grabbed a few cat toys for Lady Sterling.

"This has been fun," I said, walking with him toward the phone store. It felt like we were an everyday average couple out running Sunday errands.

"Everything is fun with you, baby." His voice dipped, making my toes curl.

Luckily, there weren't reporters or photographers during our outing, making me more relaxed. I had to trust the PR team that it would all blow over and focus on the team. That was who needed me.

"Can I help you?" the salesclerk asked when we entered the store.

"I need to get a new phone. My other one was stolen."

"Of course. Is it backed up to the cloud?"

I bit my lip, nodding. "Yeah, I believe so."

"Would you like me to wipe it then?"

"Yes! That would be perfect. Thank you."

"No problem."

Giving them all my info, I looked around at the displays, contemplating whether I wanted a different model or if it would be better to stick with the one I had. Fletcher trailed behind me, focusing on his phone while I searched.

"Henley," he said, his voice strained.

"What?" I asked, the nerves roaring back to the surface.

He looked around, grabbed one of the remotes, and switched the TV to a different channel. It was a talk show, and sitting in the guest chair was none other than my ex—Dakota Hughes.

"Turn it up," I said, fear clawing at me. My hands shook, so I shoved them into my pockets.

*"We all have to know about the tweet, Dakota. Is there a wedding in your future? Have you and Henley rekindled your romance?"*

*Dakota sighed, shaking his head, his face resigned. "I'm sorry to be the one to tell you that there will be no wedding, Laura."*

*"Oh?" the host leaned forward. "Is there news to share?"*

*"Just a desperate attempt by my ex to gain publicity, I'm afraid."*

A ringing sounded in my ears as I tried to process the lies Dakota spouted.

"What the actual fuck?" I hissed, my eyes wide as I turned to Fletcher.

"It seems Dakota has decided to play dirty. You can't let this go now, Henley."

My face heated, and I fought for my breath as I tried to come to terms with what was happening. Dakota Hughes had pissed me off for the last time. I wouldn't stop now until I'd taken him down.

# CHAPTER 6

## *Henley*

STORMING INTO DMITRY'S OFFICE, I barely contained my outrage as I waited for him to hang up the phone. He lifted his hand, motioning for me to take a seat. Huffing, I flopped down into the chair, crossing my arms over my chest. My leg bounced up and down as I waited.

Fletcher dropped me off after we'd raced out of the phone store with my new phone in hand. I'd been too keyed up to drive after I'd failed to start the car three times. Fletcher had taken the keys from me, coaxing me into the passenger seat with the promise to bring me straight to the administration building. He'd then gone to pick up the guys, stating I wasn't doing *this meeting* alone.

It felt nice to have the support, so I agreed. Mostly, I just wanted to get a game plan together and take Dakota down. I was so over his bullshit.

"Yes, she's here now. Uh-huh, bye," Dmitry said before hanging up the phone. He sighed, rubbing his face, and I instantly felt terrible for bringing all this drama to his school.

"I'm sorry," I started, but Dmitry's head jerked up, cutting me off.

"You have nothing to apologize for, Henley. I told you to wait, and now we've lost the upper hand. I'm sorry for not taking the opportunity when we had it." He sighed, sitting back in his chair.

"I won't let him get away with this," I hissed, sitting up.

"I didn't expect you would. I've already had a call with the PR team. They're setting up a press conference."

"Okay, good. That's what I wanted to talk to you about." I deflated, sinking back against the chair.

"That wasn't who I was on the phone with, though."

Scrunching my nose, I lifted my eyes to the director of the school. "Who else knows about me?" Fear sank into my belly. Shit. The parents.

"As you can imagine, I've been fielding calls from a few concerned parents all weekend, but that wasn't who I just hung up with."

"You're killing me, Dmitry. Just spit it out already!"

He laughed, and I rolled my eyes. I was glad he thought the demise of my career and life was humorous.

"Apologies, I'm not trying to be difficult. One of my old friends and alumni, Carly Conway, who you might know as—"

"Carly Makarov," I said with awe.

"Yes, so I see you're familiar with her." He grinned as I nodded. Carly had been the best women's hockey player in the world when she played, setting records and breaking glass ceilings her whole career. She was the reason women's hockey was where it was today.

"Carly wants to meet you. She thinks what you're doing here is phenomenal and understands the media backlash women in hockey face. She could be the ally you need to set things right with the media."

"She wants to help me?" I asked, still star-struck.

"Yes, Henley. She'd like to invite you up to her place this weekend to strategize, if you're willing to wait until then to deal with Dakota. Carly thinks attacking too soon will only stir the pot. She has some ideas but said she'd only share them with you. So, what do you say?"

I nodded without even thinking it through. If Carly Conway wanted to help, then I'd let her. My head spun at the news, the earlier anger dissipating with each second. Clearing my throat, I glanced back at Dmitry.

"What about the PR team?"

"That's still up to you. You can hold off, give a general statement, or go full force and take his balls."

My jaw dropped, a laugh escaping me as I stared at my boss.

"What?" Dmitry asked, his brow lifted. "I'm not allowed to want that man's blood? He disrespected my school, our team, and my employee, whom I respect greatly. I hope you rain down on him everything he deserves. I have no doubt you'll force him to his knees and make him beg for mercy."

"Um, what did we miss?" Fletcher asked as he, Dax, and Reed stepped into the office. All three men looked at me; their eyes caressed my body as they looked for any signs of pain. Their concern warmed my heart.

"Oh, just Dmitry telling me to take Dakota's balls," I snorted.

The guys looked from me to the director, clearly as confused as I'd been when he'd first said it.

"What?" he asked, a slow smile spreading across his face. "I'm not just a pretty face, guys."

My three guys broke out in laughter, buckling over as they hooted at Dmitry. Shaking my head, I felt lighter and more assured in myself. This school continued to show me this was where I needed to be.

When they'd calmed down, Fletcher turned to me, a question in his eyes. "What's the game plan?"

Glancing at Dmitry, I debated what the best decision was. The need to respond in kind didn't feel as vital; vengeance and retaliation no longer overpowered me. I needed to be smart here. If there was one thing I knew about Dakota, it was that everything he did had a purpose. If I wasn't careful, I'd fall into his trap as a willing piece of leverage.

I was neither of those things—willing or leverage.

"I'm going to stick with the original plan," I said, exhaling. The guys immediately protested, their voices growing loud in the office. "And this weekend, I'm going to meet with Carly Conway and see what she has to say."

Reed and Fletcher immediately shut up, their faces reflecting the same awe I'd shown. Dax looked between everyone, knowing he was missing something.

"Who's Carly Conway?"

"Only one of the most prolific hockey players in the world," Reed said. It didn't slip past me that he'd said hockey, not women's hockey. I knew there was a reason I was falling in love with him.

Whoa. Where had that come from? Love? Was I ready for that?

Shaking it off, I focused on the men in front of me.

"What? How?" Fletcher asked, still a bit dazed.

"She's an old friend of mine. Though, don't tell her I said old. She'd murder me," Dmitry said with a chuckle. "Carly wants to meet Henley and help her. She's invited her up this weekend."

"Just her?" Dax asked, his eyes zeroed in on me.

"Oh, I don't know." I bit my lip, realizing I didn't want to be alone. I would if I needed to, but the guys had become part of my life, and to be without at least one of them felt empty.

"I'm sure Carly would love to have Henley and her guests," Dmitry assured, calming my heart rate. "I'll let the PR team know you'll stick with the original plan and only release the statement about the game. I agree this is the right course, Henley."

"Thanks, Dmitry. Sorry for barging into your office. I seem to be doing that a lot lately." I cringed, realizing how often I'd been in here over the last week.

"It's always open, Coach."

With that, I stood, giving him a nod of appreciation as I walked out with the guys. The trek to the car was quiet, whether from surprise or not wanting to say anything in public; I didn't know, but no one spoke until we reached my SUV.

"Are we really going to meet Carly Conway?" Reed asked, looking at me.

"Yeah, I think so." The dread I'd been feeling lifted as excitement took over. "First, we just have to get through the week."

Which turned out to be easier said than done.

"You going in?" Reed asked. I'd been standing outside the door to the locker room for five minutes. I knew I had to face Kurt, but it took everything in me to do it.

"Just trying to get my game face on." Pushing my shoulders back, I shook out my hands and lifted my head.

"I'll be right by your side, Hen."

Reed's words pushed me to open the door and step

into the locker room. My heart raced, but I kept my face blank, showing no emotion.

Kurt was lacing his skates as I turned the corner. Ignoring him, I walked to my locker and pulled out my gear. Reed fumed next to me, his body vibrating with anger at whatever Kurt was doing behind my back.

Turning slowly, I sat on the bench with my skates in hand. Kurt glared at me with a smug smile, and I'd never wanted to smack his face more than I did at that moment.

"Something you want to say, Kurt?" I asked, going about my business and putting on my skates.

"It's too bad you missed the last period of the game, Henley. What happened?" he asked, with about as much fake concern as a grizzly bear.

"Yeah, about that. I know you trashed my room and took my phone. It's only a matter of time before I prove it. I'd watch your back if I were you."

His face turned red as I finished tying my skates. Grabbing my stick and helmet, I walked away, Reed hot on my tail. Stopping at the door, I didn't turn around as I raised my voice.

"And it's Coach Henshaw to you. Don't fucking forget that again."

My skin was littered with goosebumps as I walked out the door, the sound of something banging against the wall following us. We took two steps before Reed stopped, bending at the waist as he laughed. Rolling my eyes, I pulled his arm, dragging him down the corridor. I couldn't make a grand exit and get caught standing outside the door a second later. It would lose the whole effect.

A few kids were already on the ice as we approached the rink, Reese one of them. I nodded, glad to see them after everything that had occurred this weekend. We'd talked briefly the night before when they'd returned to campus, but it was nothing like seeing them in person.

Falling into my warmup, I skated up and down the ice, running plays through my head. If I could focus on the game, maybe I could ignore the whispers and questions.

My breath misted out in front of me as I stopped to lean against the boards and catch my breath. I'd need to do some more conditioning with Dax this week, and not the naked kind.

I blew my whistle, headed to the middle, and gathered the kids to the center. I tried not to notice that a few kids were missing—Anders and his posse included.

"Today is the start of a new week. The mistakes of last week's game are in the past, and we'll use them to make us stronger. This Friday is our first home game. It will be our chance to show our families, friends, and peers that we're not giving up. Break out into your groups. Group one, you're with me; group two with Reed."

The kids looked at one another, questions in their

eyes, but I didn't have time for them. Blowing my whistle again, I moved off toward the right side of the ice, gesturing for the kids to move. Eventually, everyone got into place as I ignored Kurt and left him stewing on the side.

The following two hours were the most challenging practice I'd ever run, and it wasn't from the intensity. Any respect and leadership I'd gained over the summer and term were lost over the weekend. Outside of a few, the team was sluggish and unresponsive to my calls, only going through the movements.

I pushed them hard, running them through drills and forcing them to skate harder than they ever had, but it didn't matter. No one smiled. No one laughed. No one played the game like it was the air they breathed. They just skated, and it broke my heart.

"Alright, that's it for today."

I skated off, not looking back, wondering if I'd just ruined the best opportunity for Reese. Maybe I should quit? What was the point in coaching if no one listened?

# CHAPTER 7

## *Dax*

PRESSING the leg of my last client into position, I glanced at the clock, checking the time. Usually, I didn't care how long sessions went, focusing on the work and not the minutes passing by. Today, though, I wanted to catch Henley after her first practice back with the team.

"And release," I said, stepping back. "How did that feel?"

"Good," my client, Ryker, said. He sat up and turned from side to side. "I feel better than new. You're a miracle worker, Dax."

"Yeah, well, don't go and get reshot. I can only do so much," I joked.

Ryker laughed, grabbing a towel off the bench to wipe his brow. "My girlfriend feels the same way, man. I'm retired now. Nothing but golf and house projects in my future."

Wiping down the equipment, I chuckled, not believing a word he said. "I don't think golfing's your sport. I'm not sure you could pull off the outfit."

Ryker slapped me with his towel, laughing at my comment. "Yeah, you might be right about that. It feels like I've worked every day for the past ten years. I'm unsure what to do with myself now that I'm out of the game."

I wasn't given much information about Ryker, but I knew he'd been a leader of a covert organization that took down bad people. He'd gotten injured over the summer and had come here for rehab since his girl-friend, Finley, and one of her other boyfriends, Milo, worked at the school.

"Whatever you do, you're free of me. You just grad-uated from physical therapy, man."

"And I know the perfect way to celebrate." He smiled wide as thoughts clearly ran through his mind.

Shaking my head, I gathered my things. "I'd say be careful, but what's the fun in that? Just don't break anything. I don't want to see your ugly mug back in this gym."

"Ah, you're going to miss me, Dax, aren't you?"

"Nah. I'll miss Milo's blueberry muffins he sends with you."

Ryker threw his head back, letting out a loud laugh as we walked out of the room.

"I'll be sure to let him know. You headed to see Henley?"

I turned to him, lifting my eyebrow. How did he know about her?

"I noticed you watching the clock, and the gossip on the street is that you're dating her, along with your other two roommates."

"Fucking gossip," I cursed, running my hands through my hair. It was one more thing for Henley to deal with.

"Hey, I didn't mean to upset you. Believe me, Finley's dealt with more than her fair share. It was easier since none of us had been here before, though. The other female instructors had laid claim to you and Fletcher, at least. From what I hear, Henley taking you both off the market put a target on her back. If you guys need anything, we're there for you all. Not everyone gets the unconventional dating relationship."

"I'm still trying to get my head around it, if I'm honest. Did it come naturally for you?"

"Hell no. I planned to steal her away from those three knuckleheads." He grinned, no shame in his statement.

Snorting, I felt better knowing not everyone jumped into a foursome with a smile. Reed and Fletcher had accepted it so readily that I sometimes felt like the third wheel to them.

"I sorta thought the same thing," I admitted.

"I could see that. But then you caved when you saw her with the others, didn't you?"

Nodding, I sighed, not even upset about giving in. I got to have Henley in my life. That was what mattered.

"It was the same for me. It helped that I also wanted to be with Cohen, but I saw the family and team they'd become, and I desperately wanted to belong. What we've built is unlike anything I've ever been part of before."

Ryker's words echoed the feeling I experienced when I was with Henley and the other guys. It was acceptance and a connection that transcended societal norms.

"Yeah. I get that now." My smile grew with ease, and I wanted to get to my girl even more. "Take care, Ryker."

He waved, heading off toward the parking lot while I headed to the ice. When I got there, she was already heading off in the direction of the locker room, a determined stride in her step. I caught Reed's eyes as he gathered some kids, nodding for me to go after her.

Without hesitation, I quickened my pace and bolted down the hallway to the locker room. I didn't know what had happened, but I could guess it wasn't good. I just hoped Kurt wasn't involved, or my fist might slip and hit his ugly face.

Pushing open the door, I yelled out her name. "Henley?"

"Dax?" a quiet voice said from the stalls. I could've sworn I heard a sniffle, my body hardening with the need to punch something even more.

"Petal?" I asked softer when I neared the bathroom area.

A door opened, revealing Henley sitting down as tears ran down her face. My feet moved before I could think, swooping in and gathering her in my arms.

"Hey, it's okay. What happened?"

"They all hate me. Only Reese and Braden were even trying out there. Everything I've worked for is over. He's ruined me in a weekend."

Her tears fell harder as she clung to me, the grief heavy in her voice. Smoothing my palm up and down her back, I held her to me as I tried to find the right words to say, but everything left my head. None of the usual positive motivation I spewed seemed good enough for her, for my petal.

"It's just one day, Petal. I know it's hard and sucks, but it's just one day. If you keep showing up, then they will too. They just need to know they can trust you."

"Why does that sound like 'if you build it, they will come' logic?" she asked, her tears slowing.

"Because one, *Field of Dreams* is one of the greatest movies ever filmed, and two, it always works."

She giggled, the sound making me feel like I'd won the lottery. She sighed, pulling back to wipe her eyes. I pulled off some toilet paper, softly dabbing her cheeks.

"I know you're right, but logic isn't in the building at the moment. I'm solely in my emotions. Reason number five hundred why having a female coach is a disastrous move."

"Bullshit. You're a great coach. You're just having a bad day. I guarantee there have been men in here crying just as much as the women. Don't discredit yourself because of one bad practice. Shake this off and find that Henley spirit that no one can ignore. If they're going to act like little shits, then treat them that way. Be smarter than your prey, Petal."

She blinked, her head nodding slowly. "Yeah. You're right."

"I love when you say that," I teased. Henley slapped me, but it brought a smile to her face, making it worth it.

Opening my mouth, I was about to give her my best advice on how to spend our time when the door opened. Figuring it was Reed, I debated on a way to scare him, stopping when I heard Kurt talking instead.

"It's all clear," he said, moving through the locker room. "I guess the bitch already tucked her tail and left for the day."

Henley flinched, her muscles tensing as she prepared to walk out there and give Kurt the beating he deserved. Thinking quickly, I pulled the door shut, grateful the stall walls went all the way to the ground. He wouldn't be able to see us unless he opened it.

Motioning to move closer, I held Henley as we leaned against the wood, eavesdropping on Kurt. I could hear him pacing back and forth, and I figured he had to be on the phone since we'd only heard one person enter. Pulling out my phone, I hit record; Henley's eyes lit up, a smile spreading.

"Our plans are already in motion. Half of the team didn't show up for practice, getting the message to meet me after hours. The other kids barely listened to her outside that weirdo of a sister and our top right winger. He'll fold when he realizes he's on the losing side."

Henley's face hardened, her fists clenching as her jaw ticked. Shaking my head, I told her to stay here with my eyes, reminding her I had my phone out.

"When do I get my official invitation to the Society? I heard their parties are legendary." Kurt chuckled, the sound lecherous even to my ears. "Yeah, okay. I have the parents on board. The bitch will be gone by this Friday, mark my words."

Silence fell around the locker room as he ended his call and changed. I stopped the recording and shoved my phone back into my pocket. It just became the most important object here. Footsteps grew louder as he neared, presumably headed for the stall. Henley sucked in a breath, the movement stopping.

"Hello?" he said, coming further into the room. Henley shook as nerves rushed through her. Thinking quickly, I pulled my phone back out and sent a text to Reed and Fletcher.

DAX

Locker room NOW!

I didn't have time to see if they got it, putting it back in my pocket for safekeeping. I suddenly feared dropping it in the toilet and our evidence drowning with it. Holding Henley's hand, I squeezed it, trying to calm her. I'd take the chance to beat his ass if I needed to, jail be damned.

The door to the first stall slammed open, making us both jump. Henley squared her feet, the movement making me smile. She was sorely mistaken if she thought I'd let him get his hands on her.

The door next to us slammed open a second later, but neither of us jumped that time, tensing as we prepared for him to open ours. His steps neared, stopping right in front of the stall. Preparing to throw open the door first and take him by surprise, I dropped my shoulder just as the main door slammed open.

"What's going on?" Reed shouted, and I exhaled in relief.

"What do you want, asshole?" Kurt spewed as he moved away.

Our bodies relaxed as his voice grew smaller with each step he took. Until I realized Reed would probably end up in a fight with Kurt.

"What did you do?" Reed asked, his voice hard.

"Nothing." I could almost hear the glee in his voice.

"Bullshit. Those kids acted like they'd never played before today; not to mention, half of the team was missing. So, I'll repeat it one more time. What. Did. You. Do?"

"I'm just making things right. Hockey is meant to be played a certain way."

"You're a sexist pig. Open your eyes and see how much you suck as a player and then ask yourself why you didn't get the job."

Something slammed into a locker, and I cursed, debating about opening the door and joining him.

"Break it up!" Fletcher yelled, stopping whatever had occurred. "Kurt, take your gear and leave."

"Fucking, fine. I won't have to deal with you all much longer."

A rustling could be heard before feet stomped out of the room, the door slamming behind him. Henley and I waited a few seconds, making sure the coast was clear. Opening the door, I peeked out, finding Fletcher peering around the wall.

"Over here," he said as Reed joined him.

Pushing the door all the way open, I grabbed Henley's hand and stepped out. Fletcher and Reed moved toward Henley, touching her and looking her over. Neither of them missed her red eyes or puffy cheeks. Almost in unison, they turned to me for an explanation.

"Thanks for the assist. We recorded his conversation and didn't want him to discover us."

"Wait, does that mean?" Fletcher asked, his eyes wide.

"That we have some evidence," Henley said, some of her spark returning. "I want to stake out the arena tonight. He's apparently holding a practice after hours. I want to know who attends and if there are any other supporters we need to be aware of."

"Should we tell Dmitry? He's been on your side. If

he hears what you have, he might be able to do something about it," Reed said.

"Yeah. We can stop by on the way home," Henley said, moving toward her locker. "Dang it! I really wanted to stay out of his office for one day."

We all chuckled, watching her tie her hair back before picking up her belongings. She made the simplest things captivating. I looked over at the guys, Ryker's words about belonging and connection ringing in my ears, knowing he was spot on.

It might not be everyone's cup of tea, but this quad-ship worked for us, and that was all that mattered.

"I'll catch you guys at the house. I have practice soon," Fletcher said, kissing Henley goodbye before he started putting on his own pads.

Reed grabbed her hand as I placed my arm around her shoulders, and the three of us walked out, a sense of purpose in our steps.

# CHAPTER 8

## *Henley*

WE SNUCK INTO THE BOX, keeping the lights off as we set up the video equipment. Dmitry had given us a key so that we could stay hidden. He'd been furious when we played the recording and immediately agreed to help us stage this coup. Whatever went down tonight would set the future path for the school. It was quite terrifying to think about.

The guys were silent soldiers beside me, none of them willing to stay back. Reed sat stoically, his eyes searching the ice and looking for anything to move. Fletcher paced behind us, his head down and arms crossed as he thought. Dax fidgeted, changing position every two seconds, his fingers tapping against his leg.

Reaching over, I linked our fingers together, stopping his movement. "I never thanked you for coming for me today," I whispered. Despite being miles away from the ice where no one could hear us, staying as quiet as possible felt appropriate.

Dax relaxed, his face open as he looked at me. "Anytime, Petal."

Even at a whisper, his voice was smooth and husky, sending shivers through my body. Squeezing his hand, I stared back out at the ice, afraid of what I might do if I didn't focus. Anxiety always made me want to take my clothes off, and now was not the time for any recreational activities.

Dax leaned closer as I crossed my legs in a different direction. "I can read everything going through your mind right now, Petal. We can follow up with it later," he promised, kissing my cheek.

My body shuddered; the action and promise were too much to hide.

"Did you know an ice rink is often referred to as a barn?" I blurted, my voice like a shot in the dark. The guys looked at me, their eyes making my skin heat even more.

"That's interesting," Dax said, his voice low. "Why?"

I could hear the teasing in his words, but I didn't care. It gave me something else to focus on.

"Because ice hockey was first played in barns, and the design of the first hockey rinks often resembled barns," I said, my voice low and husky—a combination I should not have when talking about barns. But nonetheless, there it was.

Fletcher bent down, whispering over my shoulder, his beard tickling my ear as his spicy cologne enveloped me. It was really unfair how easily he could flip my switch.

"As interesting as your knowledge of *barns* is, Baby Shaw, I'd rather hear you moan my name, the sound echoing for hours." My fingers gripped the chair as I sucked in a breath. "But first, let's catch this asshole."

He stepped back, my breath barely returning to me as my pussy throbbed. I could see his smirk reflecting in the glass as he watched me. But I couldn't turn my head for fear of attacking one of them with my lips, but I could imagine the other two wore similar expressions. I had a feeling they were trying to take my mind off things, but it didn't help the soaked situation I had going on downstairs.

Fueling my rage at the rev-up with no reward, I pushed the lust away. "Don't think I won't forget this. Turnabout is fair play, guys."

They chuckled, but I meant every word, a plan to repay the favor already developing in my mind.

A door sounded below, and we all quieted as we leaned forward as far as we could to watch. Sure enough, Kurt walked out with another man as they spoke, laughing between themselves. He wore a long overcoat that covered most of his clothes. It looked fancy, complimenting his shiny dress shoes and slacks.

"Do you know who that is?" I asked, zooming in on the camera. Up close, his impeccable style was more noticeable, his hair coiffed to perfection, and his face clean-shaven even at this late hour.

Reed and Dax shook their heads, but Fletcher squinted in thought. "It might be a parent. I think I've seen him at a game before."

"Has to be Mr. Michelson then, Anders' father."

Fletcher nodded, his eyes still watching the pair. We couldn't make out what they were saying, making me wish we'd set up surveillance or something below.

"Shit. We can't hear anything," Dax grumbled, shifting in his seat. "Should I go down there? I'll stay hidden, but if they see me, I'll pretend to have come from a workout or something. I won't be as suspicious as you three."

I chewed on my lip as I wrung my hands, debating. It would be nice to hear what they were saying, but at what cost? Was it worth splitting up?

"I dunno. I don't want anything to happen to you," I said, turning to face him. Dax's face softened, and he reached out to cup my face.

"As sweet as that is, I'll be fine. I promise. I don't plan on needing to, but if it comes down to it, I can handle myself. Besides, you have it recorded. So if they try to say anything, we have evidence."

Taking a deep breath, I nodded, realizing he was right. It would be nice to hear what they were saying as well.

"Okay. Just be careful. I kind of like your grumpy butt."

Dax smirked, his eyes practically twinkling in the dark room. He kissed my lips quickly before vaulting over the seat and sauntering toward the door. Sighing, I turned back to the front, hoping to put the potential danger out of my head. Fletcher took Dax's seat, his hand squeezing my leg. It helped to ground me, knowing they were still here.

The two men below were still talking against the boards, looking like they were waiting for someone else. Fletcher's phone vibrated, so he pulled it out, putting it on speaker when he saw the caller.

"Figured this would be easier. I'm going to put you in my pocket. Mute your side unless there's an emergency," Dax said.

Fletcher did as he asked, setting it on the ledge in front of us. I could hear movement as Dax walked, then a door, his breathing coming through the phone. As he moved closer, we could start to pick up voices, but it was still faint. The three of us collectively held our breaths, anxious as Dax neared. When we could pick up words, I almost wished we hadn't.

"I don't care what the Arbitrator says; women's hockey is not the future," the well-dressed man said.

"You got that right. They don't belong on the ice. It's meant to be a brutal game of grit and physicality. Women offer nothing to the game. It's time they got the message and stayed in the kitchen, or better yet, on their backs," Kurt spewed, laughing at his own joke.

"Once we get rid of the whore, you'll be able to take this team all the way. It's going to do great things for your career. As long as my boy stays front and center. He's the real future of this team."

I looked at the others, anger stemming from my eyes. Any doubt this wasn't Anders' father evaporated.

The boards by the locker rooms opened, and kids spilled out. I tried to identify them, but from this viewpoint, it was difficult. They all looked the same in their practice jerseys, with the numbers faded and their helmets covering their faces. When I could make out a number, I wrote it down to keep track. Within twenty minutes, the ice was filled with players.

"Son of a bitch," Fletcher cursed, catching my attention. "There's some of my players here too. He's poaching from both teams."

He'd zoomed in on his phone camera, snapping pictures of players when he knew them. It would explain why there were different color jerseys with so many players out there. Gulping, my leg shook again, worried about what this would mean.

Kurt skated out onto the ice, his voice easier to pick up from there as he shouted. I glanced at where Dax was but couldn't see him. Wherever he was hidden, he was out of sight. The well-dressed man took a phone call, some of his words carrying through Dax's phone. I tried to listen to both of them but couldn't.

"You focus on Kurt; I'll listen to Daddy-o," Reed said, placing his hand on my knee. The shaking stopped, and I nodded, peering down at the rat bastard trying to take my team from me. It hurt to see so many students against me being their coach.

Maybe I should take that as a sign and give up. I was so tired of fighting for my place among these men. To prove my worth in a game I loved.

"Thank you all for coming. We won't have to practice like this for much longer. But until we can get rid of some trash, this is when we'll practice. On Friday, her team will be so demoralized they won't take the ice, and we'll swoop in, saving the school."

"So your plan is to get rid of Coach Henshaw? Not challenge her for it?" someone asked.

"What's the point in challenging her for something that's already mine? She has no right to be here. So I'm proving it. If anyone has a problem with that, you're welcome to go back to her trash of a team. But speak of this, and you'll regret it. We have eyes and ears everywhere."

The kid that had spoken up slapped a few of his teammates, and they skated off, shaking their heads. I couldn't hear them, but the phone picked it up.

"That's bogus. I thought this was an extra practice, not a takeover."

"Coach Henshaw doesn't deserve this. It was weird at first, but she knows her stuff."

"If he can't follow the school's challenge system, then what's the guarantee he'll follow it when we're playing? He won't. I'm not throwing my future away on a guy who can't take on a girl. Makes me think he's scared of her. I'd rather be with the girl he's scared of challenging than him."

While they weren't wholly team Henshaw, they respected me as a player and the school enough to not give Kurt credence. It pushed the dark thoughts away, vanishing them from my mind. As long as there was one player that believed, then it was worth it.

"Do you think that's enough evidence for the board?" I asked, glancing at the guys. Both wore dark expressions, their jaws clenched tight. It made me wonder what I'd missed on the phone.

"Yeah. It's enough."

Sending Dmitry a message that we had enough, I sat back with a smile, excited about the next part.

"Is it bad that I'm not going to stop recording?" Fletcher asked.

"Nope. I plan to watch this next part on repeat every night." I smiled, rubbing my hands together as the guys laughed.

Kurt started some lame drills, proving to me that he didn't even have what it took to be a coach when all the lights in the arena came on.

Grinning, the three of us stood as we watched the clusterfuck below. The kids stopped their plays, looked around, and asked each other what was happening. Kurt's face turned bright red as he searched the arena. The well-dressed man conveniently slipped into the shadows, but it didn't matter. He was done for.

A slow clap sounded, echoing around until Dmitry eventually revealed himself. Kurt's shoulders drew back, a smug smile on his face, and I couldn't wait to see how he spun this.

"Wow, I had no idea we had practices this late at night," Dmitry said. "Where's Coach Henshaw?"

The kids shuffled back to the boards, separating themselves from Kurt. They'd already sealed their fate, though. Fletcher stood and went to the back of the box, fiddling with some cords. I didn't know what he was doing, so I focused back on the showdown on the ice.

"She couldn't be here," Kurt said, crossing his arms. "It proves how much more committed I am to this team."

Dmitry frowned, looking around at all the kids. "Is that so?"

"You saw what happened at the last game. I'm the coach our school needs."

"Yes, I wanted to talk to you about that. This evening, I received an interesting phone call from someone who said they had some footage I needed to see from Friday. Shall we all watch it together?"

"Um, footage? What footage?" Kurt asked, his arms dropping as some of his confidence waned.

Dmitry snapped his fingers, pointing a finger in the air. "Oh, and I just remembered. Coach Henshaw is here. I think it's only fair if she gets to watch it with us too, since it involves her. Don't you, Coach?"

Dmitry looked up at the box, and I swallowed, unsure of what he was doing. This hadn't been part of the plan! Everyone looked around, searching the stands.

"Go to the window, Hen. I promise it'll be worth it."

Standing, I stepped up to the glass, looked below, and waved. Dmitry winked, making Reed growl, the entire act making me relax.

"Ah, yes, there she is. Go ahead and hit play, Fletcher."

I watched Kurt, his face turning bright red as his eyes bored into me. If he could've killed me with his thoughts, I'd be dead.

On the Jumbotron, a video started to play. It was shaky at first; the video coming from a phone as the person moved it to show what they were aiming for. Through a small crack, they captured Kurt tossing mine and Reese's stuff. When he didn't find what he wanted, he spray-painted it. When he found my phone, he sighed in relief and placed it in his pocket before finishing destroying the room. The video stopped then, but it was enough to prove that Kurt had vandalized our things and stolen my phone.

I glanced back at the ice and realized a few other coaches had come out to hold Kurt. Apparently, during our viewing, he'd tried to escape. Coward. He kept looking to where Mr. Michelson had been, but no one was there. Sorry bud, you weren't getting rescued.

"Kurt, this is your notice that you've breached your contract and will no longer be a member of our staff. I've also notified our legal team and will speak with the police on Coach Henshaw's behalf. Your days in hockey are over. I hope whatever this was about was worth it because you just lost everything. The boys will follow you to your locker and help you clean out your stuff. You have two hours to vacate the premises, or the police will escort you out."

Kurt struggled against his escorts, his face molten red as he cursed at everyone around him. It wasn't a good look, and I wanted to feel sorry for him. But he'd made his bed; time to lie in it.

Dmitry turned back to the kids remaining on the ice. "As for you, we'll discuss your future at Lux in the morning. Don't try to deny your presence here. Your cards were scanned in, and we have video proof. Now, get some sleep."

With that, Dmitry turned and walked out, leaving the kids to skate off the ice, their heads hanging. Reed pulled me to him, and I sagged in relief.

We'd won a huge battle tonight, but I had a feeling the war was only beginning.

# CHAPTER 9

## *Henley*

FLETCHER SAID goodbye on his phone, motioning for us to follow him out of the box. He locked it and took my hand when we exited, leading us toward the stairs.

"Dax's going to meet us outside. He followed Mr. Michelson and needs to tell us something."

My mind raced as we descended the stairs. When we'd approached Dmitry, I'd hoped something like this would happen, but what would it mean in reality? What would happen to the kids?

As much as I wanted them to suffer, I couldn't hold them ultimately accountable. They'd trusted an adult who'd led them astray. Though, I didn't necessarily want them to be on *my* team either. Hopefully, Dmitry would have a viable solution in the morning.

Stepping out into the night air, I rubbed my arms. The temperature dropped rapidly at night here, and I hadn't gotten used to it. Reed pulled off his zipped hoodie, placing it on my arms.

"You might not get this back," I teased, pushing my arms in it.

"Worth it." He smiled, his blue eyes dancing.

Walking across the parking lot, we spotted Dax leaning against the side of my SUV. He straightened when we neared, his eyes searching me.

"What did you hear?" Fletcher asked, unlocking the SUV.

"Inside," he said, looking around us. It was pitch dark, and no one else was around. I wasn't sure who he thought would overhear us.

Climbing in the back, I chuckled at how the guys seemed to be driving my car more than me lately. Once we were seated, Dax turned, looking at us all.

"Spit it out. You're making me nervous," I blurted.

"Sorry. I'm just trying to get my head around it. What did you hear over the phone?"

"We heard most of their conversation together. When Kurt went to the ice, it was harder to hear what Mr. Michelson was saying. I only made out a few words," Reed answered.

Dax nodded, wiping his hands on his legs. "Michelson was talking to someone. He was happy at first, saying that everything was on track. He wasn't on the phone with them for long. When the lights turned on, he moved, staying in the shadows. He called someone next, maybe the same person, maybe a different one. I don't know. I followed him, but hearing him on the move was harder while keeping him from spotting me. He stopped at one point, cursing as he yelled into the phone. I caught, '*Do what-*

*ever it takes,'* and *'It can't come back on me.'* It sounded like he was calling in a favor."

Dax shook his head, fear evident on his face. I noticed his hands were shaking, so I reached out and grabbed them, holding them in mine.

"A car pulled up to the back door, and he climbed in. I spotted a woman in the backseat, but I didn't know who she was. The whole thing gave me a bad vibe."

"Do you think he was suggesting someone hurt Henley?" Fletcher asked, shocking me.

"What?" I gasped, my hand coming up to cover my mouth.

"Maybe. I don't know. It's just... it sounded bad. You need to be careful, Hen. I don't think the threat is gone just because Kurt is out. It might be worse because now we don't know who's coming for you."

The earlier glee I'd been feeling evaporated. Whenever I thought I'd got ahead in this sport, I was yanked back and reminded of my place. The guys were quiet as they digested what Dax said.

"Nothing's going to happen to you, Hen. I promise," Reed said, searing his words into me with his eyes. "You've got us."

The guys made sounds of agreement, making me feel marginally better. But the fact remained someone out there didn't want me here, and they were willing to go to extreme measures. At some point, I had to put my pride aside and ensure I was doing what was safe for Reese and myself.

Fletcher started the car and drove back to the house, no one speaking. We'd had a victory, but like I'd assumed, we were far from winning the war.

My eyes were barely open as I stepped into the conference room. It had taken me forever to fall asleep. When I finally stopped tossing and turning, the sun was already beginning to rise. I was currently on my second cup of coffee, and I was going to need a third.

When Tyler walked in with a tray of cups, I practically jumped up and kissed him.

"Marry me?" I asked, taking the beverage.

"She asking him or the coffee?" Cody asked, placing a box of donuts down.

"The coffee," Reed and Fletcher said together, making the room laugh.

Flipping them off, I didn't care as I inhaled the aroma, taking a big drink. Sitting back in my chair, I sighed as the coffee slowly woke me up.

The guys talked about things going on around campus as I sat with my eyes closed, occasionally opening them when I took a sip.

Dmitry walked in with two people I didn't know, just as I finished my cup. Sitting up, I observed the strangers, trying to gauge their importance.

"Thank you all for coming in this early. This is Callum Blake and Patricia Sanchez, two of our board members. They're here to hear our case against Kurt Kuga and our plans moving forward."

Fletcher stood and hit some buttons, allowing the video feed and recording we made to play for the room. Tyler and Cody's faces grew angry as they listened, making me like them even more. They'd always been kind to me, and it felt nice to know it had been real.

Everyone turned to Dmitry and the board members when it was finished. He turned in his chair to address them.

"Do you need any other evidence?" he asked. His tone brokered no nonsense. I could finally understand how he managed to create such an elite school. Dmitry was a force to be reckoned with when he fought for what he believed in.

The two members put their heads together for a few seconds as they spoke with one another. When they faced back to Dmitry, I held my breath, knowing this would factor everything.

"We agree that Kurt's contract has been voided. We'll sign off on your recommendation to fire him," Callum said, Patricia nodding.

"Good. Based on the number of students present last night, what do we propose we do? Fletcher, can you list off who was present?"

I glanced back as he read the names and which

team they were from. I hadn't known he'd done that. It made me wonder how late he'd been up as well. Guilt that I should've done it as the head coach rose up.

"That's half of the senior team and a large portion of the juniors," Tyler said, cursing as he leaned against the table.

Dmitry nodded, sighing, resting his elbows on the table. "It leaves us in a difficult situation. It's also hard to tell which were pressured by their peers or Kurt himself, and which were there of their own volition."

"What do you have in mind, Dmitry? I know you well enough to know you have something up your sleeve," Callum said with a smile on his face.

Dmitry smirked, a soft chuckle escaping. "That you do. Here's what I'm thinking." He leaned forward, grabbing everyone's attention. The more I saw him in his element, the more the natural showman appeared. "We need to restructure the teams, and we can do that in two different ways."

He stood and walked over to the whiteboard along the wall.

"The first way, we put all the players that weren't at the practice onto one team, and all those that were onto another."

I raised my hand, making Dmitry smile.

"Yes, Henley."

"In theory, that sounds like a solution. But we can't forget that even those that showed up for practice weren't participating at their full capacity. Nor does it take into consideration the ones who might've been bullied into attending."

"Which is why I think option number two will be our best bet. We hold another tryout. The rest of the week will determine who gets to play the game on Friday. And those who weren't at the practice will get extra one-on-one time this week, so they have an advantage. It rewards them for loyalty."

I debated it in my mind, rolling around the pros and cons, realizing while it wasn't perfect, it at least made it fair. I glanced at the other coaches to observe what they thought of it. Everyone seemed to be considering it.

"There's going to be some backlash that we need to prepare for, too. There will be some kids pulled. Their parents had already threatened to do it after last week. This might send them over the edge. Which is why we have the board here to sign off on our plan since it could affect school enrollment."

The thought of kids leaving because of me made me queasy, but I wouldn't apologize for being a woman. I'd done it enough my whole life, and I was sick of it.

"I'm for the second plan," Fletcher said, bringing my attention back to the room. "I'd also like to be considered for Kurt's role."

"But you're a head coach now. If you did that, you'd be an assistant," I said, my heart jumping into my throat. I didn't want him to throw away his career for me.

Dmitry assessed Fletcher, both of them ignoring my protest. Huffing, I crossed my arms, not liking that they were contemplating this without my input.

"I'll consider it, but let's get through this week first," Dmitry said. It wasn't a yes, but it wasn't a no. I decided I'd do all I could this week to make Fletcher want to stay where he was.

"I agree with the second plan," Tyler said, followed by Cody.

"Me too," Reed added, leaving only me.

I looked around the room as all eyes landed on me. "I agree as well. Hopefully, it will make those on the senior team realize their spot isn't guaranteed."

Dmitry looked at the two board members, waiting for their approval. They spoke to one another again, and this time Patricia answered.

"We'll approve it, with the suggestion that you open up mid-term transfers to help replenish any dip in enrollment."

"I'll add it to my list of things," Dmitry said, nodding at the two. They stood, shaking his hand before nodding at us when they left the room.

Dmitry turned back to us, leaning against the table. "Do you have any friends or teammates that could help out for a week? If so, give me their names, and I'll make the calls. I don't want you guys to wear yourself out with extra training hours. If we can get some other help, it might encourage the other kids, too."

A few of my teammates that had retired came to mind. Seeing some friendly faces, especially of the female variety, would be nice.

The rest of the meeting focused on dividing the time and reorganizing the schedule to accommodate everyone being on the ice at the same time.

We walked out together to meet the students in the rink when everything was sorted. I tried not to count, but I could tell kids were missing.

The five coaches made a line against the boards, with Dmitry next to us. Everyone had agreed I needed to be the one to address them and update them on how things were going to be.

"If you haven't heard, Coach Kuga is no longer part of our staff. Because of his actions, several of you were at an unsanctioned practice last night. Kurt's direction was wrong, and he put your careers in jeopardy. Because of this, we're changing things up. There is no longer a junior or senior team. Everyone will start at zero, and you must re-earn your spot. This week, we'll all train together and run through drills to prepare for the games on Friday."

"Why are we getting punished if we didn't attend their stupid meeting?" someone shouted.

"Can you honestly say you showed up ready to play yesterday?" I answered back. "I'll go ahead and respond for you. *No.* Outside of a handful of players, the rest of you were a disgrace to hockey yesterday and Lux. But, because you didn't attend an unsanctioned practice, you'll receive extra training this week from some outside pros we'll be bringing in."

Excited chatter filled the ice as the kids speculated who might be here.

"Yes, I can see that makes you excited. So, here's the deal. If you were on the junior team, this is your chance to show us what you've got and move up early in the season. If you were on the senior team, you'd need to bring it to prove you deserve to be where you were. We'll post the extra workouts on the app and how many people can sign up for them tonight. Final rosters will be made Friday morning. Any questions? No?" I ignored the hands, lifting my whistle to my lips.

"Suicides, begin!"

I turned, heading back to the boards with the others; the sound of sticks hitting the ice as they skated off was music to my ears. I didn't have to turn to know that this time, no one had hesitated. Coach Henshaw was back, bitches.

# CHAPTER 10

## Fletcher

WATCHING Henley transform into the coach she was always meant to be, brought goosebumps to my skin. I had to keep reminding myself to focus on the players I had in my own rotation and not get sucked into watching her.

"Alright, let's rerun those shots. I want you to make the goalie work for it," I shouted.

"Ah, man," Gregory cried. He was already sweating, but he hunkered down and got into position.

The majority of the players had responded well to the restructuring, especially the ones who'd been part of the secret practice, knowing it was their only shot. There were a few disgruntled players, though, still grumbling. I suspected they were the same ones who'd lagged the day before. This process might be more productive than intended if it cleared out some of the lazy kids.

"Line up," Henley shouted, blowing her whistle. Was it weird I now had an obsession with the object? Yeah, it probably was. But the thought of her in her jersey, blowing that whistle, made me hard all over.

The kids panted as they leaned on their sticks,

waiting for everyone to gather around. It had been an intense practice, separating those who really wanted it from those who didn't.

"Grab some lunch, and then you have conditioning this afternoon. You've been divided into three groups among the trainers and coaches. All the information is on the app. Tomorrow we'll have our first scrimmage game in the afternoon. The teams will be assigned in the morning. Don't be late."

Henley skated away and started her after-practice routine of doing laps. Cody and Tyler waved as they headed off, and the kids were subdued as they went to lunch. Reed skated over to where I'd taken up a position against the boards, watching.

"She was incredible today," he said in lieu of a greeting.

"Yeah. The love of the game shone through. It was epic. I hope these kids realize the magnitude of what occurred today."

"You staying to watch?" Reed asked.

I nodded, meeting his eyes. "I got her."

He smacked my shoulder. "I've got a call to make. I'll see you two in the locker room."

My eyes went back to Henley, enjoying watching her in her element. After about twenty laps, she slowed, her hands on her hips as she coasted to me.

"Feel better?"

"Yeah." She nodded, catching her breath. "I had this energy building up and needed to get it out." She shook out her hands like some residual tingling was still there.

Reaching out for her, I pulled her to me. "I know some ways to help with that," I said, my voice low and husky.

Henley's breath hitched, jolting my cock to attention.

"We couldn't. Not here." She looked around like she could see people.

"Oh, Baby Shaw. I've worked here for three years. Do you not think I know all the secret hidey-holes?"

She reared back, a scowl on her face. "Ew. I don't want to go to your booty call room."

My face reddened when I realized how that had sounded. Huffing, I cradled her chin, tilting her head back to stare at me.

"That's not what I mean, baby, and I think you know that."

She squirmed, her skates moving back and forth as she kept her balance. Her pulse picked up under my fingers, exciting me more.

"Is that a yes or no, Henley?"

Her eyes searched mine, her fingers gripping my jersey. Her breaths came out as a puff of fog, the cold temperature beginning to settle into our bones the longer we were still. Time seemed to stop as I waited.

"Yes," she breathed, the word skating over my skin like a hot poker.

Turning, I pulled her toward the opening, barely

stopping to put on our skate guards. If it wouldn't fuck up my blades, I'd have tossed her over my shoulder and already had her naked by now.

Neither of us talked as we ran through the halls, turning and twisting through the building. When I came to the empty medical room, I hurried in and shut the door behind us as I pressed her up against it.

"I want you so bad, Baby Shaw. Watching you command the players was such a turn-on. Every time you blew your whistle, my cock jumped. I'm so hard, I was worried I wouldn't be able to skate off the ice."

Her eyes widened at my confession. My hands cupped her face, my fingers sinking into her hair.

"It's going to be quick and dirty. I'll make it up to you later when I can devour every inch of you."

Henley gasped, her mouth opening as her head tilted back. Her hands gripped my hips as she angled her leg between mine. Taking the opportunity, I pressed my lips to hers, my tongue sweeping in with no apology. It had been too long since I'd kissed Henley, and my body responded in kind. My dick throbbed, reminding me I had a purpose for coming here.

Henley's moans were music to my ears as her hands ran up my back and pulled my jersey over my head. Breaking the kiss, I smiled at her, pulling her over to the exam table.

"It's not the sexiest, but I'm hoping it works," I said, realizing how it might look.

Henley smirked, pulling off her jersey and standing in front of me in her sports bra. Thankfully, neither of us was in pads, or it would've been a chore to get undressed. I dropped mine to the floor as her eyes scanned over my abs.

"I always forget what you're hiding under that," she whispered.

"Just ask, and you can look anytime, Baby Shaw."

"I'll remember that."

Giggling, she pushed her pants down and turned, propping her arms on the table, looking over her shoulder like the vixen she was.

"I'm ready for my exam, Doctor," she cooed, shaking her butt at me.

"Fuck, if you only knew how hot that was," I groaned, palming my erection through my pants. Pushing down my pants, my cock sprang up now that it was free.

Caressing her ass, I said a prayer of thanks for all the workouts that made her butt look like that. "You've got such a great ass, Hen. One day, I want to take you there. But for today..." I reached down, my fingers finding her folds already wet and plump for me. Stroking them, I coated my fingers in her wetness and rubbed her clit.

Henley gasped, a moan escaping as I leaned over her, my fingers working between her legs. I placed kisses on her back, loving her exposed skin.

"If your sports bra didn't scare me, I'd demand it

be taken off," I muttered, continuing to kiss down her spine.

"Yeah, it's not going back on after it's off," she hissed, followed by a moan.

Chuckling against her back, I plunged my fingers into her welcoming pussy, her legs spreading a little to give me more access.

"More, Fletch. You said quick and dirty; where's the quick?"

"Sorry, when I get you in my hands, I can't help but adore every inch of what I can."

"That's sweet and all, but if you don't give me your dick in the next ten seconds, I'll go find Reed or Dax. I'm sure they'd be happy to accommodate."

Growling, I rose up, gripping her thighs as I spread them wider. Her wet pussy tempted me to bend down and lick it, but I knew she'd meant every word of her threat, and I wasn't losing this chance with her.

"Mine."

"Then show me," she challenged, her eyes daring.

Staring at her, I held my fingers to my lips, licking them as I lined up. Keeping her focus on me, I plunged in one move, her eyes closing at the force. Dropping both hands down, I held her tightly and gave her a second to adjust.

"More," she demanded, tossing the word over her shoulder, her teeth biting her lip.

Not needing to be told twice, I pulled out and

thrust back in, the table rocking with the force. Her fingers gripped the edge, her eyes searing into mine.

Keeping my balance on skates proved difficult with each thrust, my legs burning from the movements. Ignoring the burn, I fell into the rhythm, driven by the need to feel her tremble around me. Her pussy wrapped around my cock like a glove, each slide in and out more luxurious than the next.

"Shit, shit," I cursed, the tingles at the base of my spine beginning.

"Yes, yes, give it to me," Henley demanded, her voice needy. Her walls tightened as she pulsed around me, her moan a siren song.

My balls took that as the go signal, drawing up as my orgasm took over, my cum spilling out in thick ropes. Groaning, I held her tight as she came, her muscles tense beneath my fingers. When I had nothing left, I pulled out, falling next to her on the table.

Smiling, she rubbed her hand over my beard. "That was exactly what I needed. Thank you."

Chuckling, I pushed her hair out of her face, staring into her eyes. They twinkled, the shadows of the past few days gone.

"I'm pretty sure this was my idea. Don't be taking credit for it now," I teased.

Henley stuck out her tongue, slapping me playfully on the shoulder. It wasn't the most ideal place to have a moment, but I was glad we were.

Sighing, I pushed up, looking around the room for something to clean up our mess. Wobbling on my skates with my pants at my ankles wasn't the easiest thing. I probably looked like a penguin. When Henley laughed at me, I had a feeling she agreed.

"We didn't think through the mess part," I grimaced, opening a few cabinets. "Aha!" Finding an old box of tissues pushed back into the corner. Grabbing it, I waddled back to the table and handed her some as I wiped off my dick.

"I really need a shower," Henley moaned.

"Yeah. Let's head there before we go to lunch. Just need to be clean enough to put clothes back on."

Henley nodded, pulling up her pants and grabbing her jersey. I found mine on the floor where it'd landed and did the same. We double-checked one another before heading out, checking both ways before we exited. Snickering as we walked down the hallway, I felt like a kid sneaking around behind his parents.

The locker room was empty when we entered, and we both grabbed our stuff, heading into separate showers. As tempting as it was, I didn't want anyone to walk in and create problems for Henley.

Dressing into regular clothes, I was surprised when I found Henley already dressed and on the phone at her locker station.

"Seriously? Oh, that would be amazing. I'll give your number to Dmitry and see you soon. Alright, bye!"

She hung up, turning to me with a grin. "Two old teammates are coming to help this week."

"One of them isn't my sister, right?" I asked, cringing.

"No. But you should ask her. It would be fun," she teased.

Rolling my eyes, I grabbed our bags, tossing them over one shoulder and wrapping my arm around her other as we headed out of the locker room.

"As much as I love my sister, I don't want to share you with her anymore. Besides, she hasn't been on the ice in years. I doubt she's any good."

"I'm so going to tell her you said that," Henley said, giggling.

"Don't you dare," I warned, tickling her as we walked down the hallway. She avoided my hand, skipping ahead, giving me a carefree grin. It hit me right then as I watched her, my heart full and overflowing in this simple moment with her, that I was head over heels in love with this girl.

I stopped, my heart racing, and I tried to catch my breath. It felt like I'd just been hit by a defenseman on the ice.

"You okay?" she asked, stepping back to me.

Blinking, I nodded, taking her hand. "Absolutely. Just hungry."

"Let's get you some food then so you don't turn into an angry bear," she teased, linking our hands together.

I couldn't help but commit this moment to my memory as we walked, knowing that to her, it was just a random walk to the cafeteria. But I knew one day I'd be telling our grandkids this was the moment she became my whole world, all from a simple smile.

# CHAPTER 11

## Henley

BOUNCING ON MY FEET, I ignored the others in the room as they chatted, my gaze fixed on the door in front of me. When it opened, I smiled, preparing to bound over when Dax walked in. Dropping my shoulders, I pouted, much to his amusement.

"I'd almost be offended if I didn't know you were waiting on your friends," he teased, dropping a kiss to my forehead as he moved toward the others.

I waved him off, ignoring the slight embarrassment. Checking my phone, I glanced at the clock for the fifth time in a minute. Arms wrapped around me, the smell of mint tickling my nose as Reed pulled me to him.

"They'll be here, Hen," he whispered, his head resting on my shoulder.

"Easy for you to say. Your friend's already here," I groused.

Reed chuckled, the sound vibrating through my body. "You're cute when you pout. Speaking of friends, I'd like to introduce you to him if you can tear yourself away from watching the door."

My leg bounced, and I debated telling him no when I realized how ridiculous that sounded.

"Yeah, okay," I sighed.

He snorted, pulling me back toward the new group in the room. The group of imposing men stopped talking as Reed approached. My body tensed as I prepared to face a bunch of hockey guys, unsure how it would go.

Most thought it was 'cute' that I played hockey, dismissing women as real players and instead tried to hit on me, offering to show me how big their sticks were. That had been the majority of my experience; Dakota's teammates were the worst of the bunch.

Only a small percentage of male hockey players saw me as an equal, acknowledging my skill. Considering four of the coaches here fell into the group, I wasn't holding my breath that more would.

I wanted to believe that there were more good men out there, but history hadn't been kind to me, making me doubt the odds were in my favor.

"Maks and Monty, this is my girlfriend, Henley. Though you can call her Coach."

"Henley Henshaw, it's a pleasure to meet you. I've followed your career for quite a while. You're a damn good player," Monty said, stretching out his hand. He was a tall man in his mid-thirties with dark brown hair. He had kind chocolate eyes and a friendly smile, so I shook his hand. It was a warm grip, making me release a breath.

"I could say the same about you, Montgomery Boyer. I saw you when you got your 10th hat trick with the Ice Breakers." My body relaxed. One down. I could do this.

"Monty, please." He smiled, dropping my hand, and looked between me and the others, his brows drawn down. "Girlfriend? I thought I saw the blond guy kiss her a second ago."

My shoulders tightened again, worried I would have to deck Reed's friend and one of the greatest left wings.

"You did. He's her other boyfriend, along with Fletcher." Reed said it so matter-of-factly that even I didn't question it. Monty paused for a second before nodding.

"How does that work exactly?" he asked curiously, with no hint of disgust.

"We're still trying to figure that out, but for now, openness and communication."

"I'm glad to see you happy, friend." Monty slapped Reed on the back, accepting his choice. It was such an easy exchange; I wondered if I was sleeping. My face must've shown my confusion because Fletcher laughed, catching the other two's attention.

"Did you expect something else?" he asked.

Nodding, I widened my eyes. "Uh, yeah. I expected some bashing or insults at the very least."

"We're guys." Monty shrugged. "I can tell how happy Reed is. If it's working for him, I won't judge."

"I've been around my fair share of male hockey players, and most do not act like you guys," I said, looking around the circle.

None of them liked that; even Cody and Tyler frowned.

"You show me who, and I'll take care of them," Maks said, surprising me. He'd been quiet while we'd talked, watching.

He had a reputation for being a brute of an enforcer. His stature alone was intimidating at six-foot-six and as wide as a refrigerator with muscles to spare. He earned the nickname MakTruck because most guys felt like they'd been hit by one after encountering him on the ice.

"You're assuming she'll need it," Fletcher boasted, making my cheeks flush red.

Maks lifted an eyebrow, turning to me. He raised his fist, knuckles out, and presented them to me for a fist bump. Touching mine to his, I smiled.

"Respect. Pleasure to meet you, Coach."

"You too, Maks."

The third guy I didn't know stepped forward, looking between all the other guys as he offered his hand. "Hey, Henley. I'm Keaton Snow."

"Nice to meet you, Keaton. I'm sorry, I'm not familiar with who you play for."

"That's because I'm not on a team," he said, shuffling his feet, his cheeks turning a light pink. He was shorter than the other guys and didn't have the body mass hockey players tended to, but I didn't know why else he'd be here.

"Keaton's not a hockey player," Dax said, drawing my attention. "He's my nerdy college roommate that has created some of the most groundbreaking hockey equipment on the market."

My brain flicked through the information I knew, the last name sounding familiar. When it came to me, my eyes grew big.

"You're SnowPoke Unlimited?" I blurted. He nodded, his blush deepening.

"Yes, that's my *nerdy* company."

I slapped Dax, my mouth still hanging open as I stared. "Be nice to the smart man!"

Everyone laughed, apparently amused with my shock and reprimand of Dax. I shrugged it off. Instead, focusing on the possibilities running through my head at this new knowledge. I was so stuck on the information I didn't even hear the door open.

"Henshaw! Get your cute butt over here right now and give me a hug, woman!"

Dropping Reed's arm, I spun around and screamed, bolting toward my two friends and grabbing them into a group hug. The three of us laughed as we all tried to talk, hugging one another as we bounced on our feet.

"Holy shit," someone said behind us.

"I've never seen her be so girlie before," said another.

I ignored them, just happy to see two of my former teammates.

"Suze, your hair is so cute like this. Oh my god, Scar, I love your shoes! I'm so glad you're here." Tears pricked my eyes, the emotion overwhelming at having some female companionship.

"I'm so glad you called. We've missed you, Hen," Susie said, squeezing me tight.

"Girl, who are all these yummy men staring at you?" Scarlet asked, her eyes going over my head. Giggling, I wasn't surprised it was Scarlet who'd noticed the guys first.

When Scarlet Stephens wasn't stopping goals on the ice like no one's business, she was flirting and sleeping with anyone who caught her fancy—men and women alike. She was a free spirit who loved with all her heart and was a good friend. Standing six feet tall, she was an imposing force with red hair, blue eyes, and a smile that broke hearts worldwide.

Susie and I laughed, rolling our eyes. We were used to Scar finding her next bed partner in every new place we went. Scarlet was sex on skates, simple as that.

While Scarlet was in your face with her sex appeal, Susie was at the other end of the spectrum. She always kept men guessing, wondering where they stood with her. She was more timid, preferring a good old fashion setup over a dating app. With her chin-length brown hair, hazel eyes, and freckles across her nose, she fit most guys' girl-next-door fantasy. She also gave the best hugs, making you feel instantly better afterward.

The two of them were complete opposites off the ice but forces to be reckoned with when they held a stick in their hands. They'd become two of my closest friends over the years, supporting me through taking in Reese and dealing with the league.

Turning, I took in the group of guys watching us like hawks. I wasn't surprised to find a few of them checking out Scarlet; it was a rite of passage to fall for her. It was Maks' focus on Susie that had me smiling.

"Girls, come meet the guys you'll be working with this week. But first, meet my three guys—Reed, Fletcher, and Dax."

I pointed them out, watching their expressions. A tiny part of me worried they wouldn't support my choice. But like the amazing women they were, they accepted it with ease.

"Ooh, a harem. I've thought about getting myself one of those. You'll have to tell me more later," Scarlet said, winking. The guys laughed, but I caught the assessing gazes in a few. Scar might have her wish before she left Utah.

"I always knew you were Wonder Woman," Susie teased. "I can barely deal with one man's socks on the floor."

"You know, they're surprisingly tidy outside of Fletcher's room. You need to wear your full hockey pads to not break anything in the middle of the night."

Fletcher laughed, nodding in agreement. "It's true. I can keep everything clean but my room." He shrugged, not caring that I'd outed him. He moved closer to me, wrapping his arm around me.

"It's nice to meet you, ladies. I look forward to watching you on the ice this week." He shook their hands, warming my heart at his heartfelt welcome.

Dax and Reed also introduced themselves, making Scar give me an approving look afterward.

"Tyler and Cody are coaches here at Lux," I said, pointing them out. They exchanged greetings, looking at the other three. "Maks and Monty have joined us this week, like you two, to help with specific skills."

"It's nice to meet you both," Monty said, shaking their hands, his eyes lingering on Scarlet. Maks gave a fist bump to Scar before turning Susie's hand and kissing the top, making her cheeks scorch red.

"And who is this yummy specimen?" Scar asked, turning to Keaton and stepping closer to him. She eyed him like a gazelle she was about to pounce on. His ears turned beet red along with his cheeks as he shuffled his feet. When he didn't appear to have any words, I jumped in to save him.

"This is Keaton Snow, the brain behind SnowPoke."

"A cutie and brain," she purred, her fingers running up his chest. He gulped, nodding, letting out a breath when she stepped back. When she winked, I worried he might pass out.

"Alright, now that we're all here, let me explain what to expect this week."

Everyone took a seat as I stood at the front, reviewing the past few days' events and our plan. When everyone was clear on their roles, I stood back, amazed at the talent in the room.

"Any questions?"

Scarlet raised her hand, and I knew I was about to be embarrassed.

"Yes, Scar?" I asked, hoping my tone told her not to test me.

"Is it me, or did Henley get a million times hotter when she used her coach voice? Where do I sign up to join your harem? Are you still taking applications?" she asked, leaning forward and fluttering her eyes at me.

Face flaming, I threw the marker I'd been using at her as the room broke into laughter.

"I so regret inviting you," I huffed, placing my hands on my hips.

"No, you don't. You love me and know I'm the best goalie around," she bragged, leaning back in her chair.

Some days, I wished I had the confidence that Scarlet Stephens seemed to embody so naturally. I knew firsthand it hadn't always been easy for her, especially since she was bisexual. A lot of the girls in the league had shunned or bullied her, afraid she'd sneak a peek at them while undressing.

"Any *pertinent* questions?" I asked, ignoring Scarlet's hand. "Alright, practice starts in thirty minutes. You're welcome to observe and get a feel for the players, or Dax can show you to the fitness rooms or cafeteria. Be ready to be spoiled. Lux has better amenities than most professional stadiums." I chuckled, remembering how stunned I'd been at everything during my first week here.

"See you on the ice."

Heading out with the other coaches to get ready, I had a renewed sense of purpose. We were making a difference, and this week I'd get to show these kids everything I had to offer.

# CHAPTER 12

## Henley

BY THE END OF PRACTICE, I was pleased with the progress the players were making. There were still a few stragglers, but it just made placing them easier. I could tell the moment the kids noticed the new faces in the stands. Deciding it was enough for today, I called everyone to attention.

"I've noticed an improvement in a lot of you. You're playing at the level you should. Some of you are still sleeping through the movements. So don't be surprised Friday when you're not on the team you want. You only have yourself to blame." There were a few grumbles, but I saw some other kids gulp, nodding to themselves.

"Now, you might've noticed some folks behind me. The students who didn't attend the unsanctioned practice, this is your upper hand. Let me introduce you to some of my friends, new and old."

Turning, I took in the four opposing players, each holding their own in their skates and pads. The biggest difference was always Susie and Scarlet. Off the ice, they were fun and carefree, but the second they stepped into their gear, the hard-ass player emerged.

Maks and Monty stood on the outside, bracketing the girls. I wondered if that had been intentional. Either way, it was cute and presented them as a joint force.

"Montgomery Boyer, former all-star for the Ice Breakers, will be working with the offense this week and stick-handling clinics." Gone were his kind eyes and smile as he assessed the kids. He nodded, keeping his arms crossed. While the kids were awed at his presence, I could tell most of them were scared.

"Scarlet Stephens, a former Cardinal and the best damn goalie I know. She'll be working on goaltending, and if you're lucky, she might teach you her trademark shot."

Scar nodded her head but kept her face stern, her game mask on and ready.

"Next to her is Susie McNeil, the current record holder for most points as a center in women's hockey. If you can outscore her this week, I'll be shocked." I laughed, making Susie blush. She gave a small wave, her manners overriding her beast mode.

"And the giant on the end is Maks Petrov, an enforcer from the Tigers and known to give more concussions than any other player in the league. He'll be working with defense and proper blocking this week." He growled, the sound menacing, and I wondered if any of the kids had pissed themselves based on how the ones in the front jumped.

I turned back, taking in all their faces, seeing the awe in most of them, the envy in others.

"That's it for today. If you're signed up for extra sessions, you have an hour to take a break and grab some food. All the instructors will report to me at the end of each day, so just because none of the coaches are here, don't think you're not being assessed. Everything counts this week. If you have questions, I'll be around later to answer them. Dismissed."

I blew my whistle, watching them skate off in different directions, their eyes glued to the four newcomers. I skated over, meeting them at the boards.

"Thoughts?" I asked, wanting to know if they saw anything in practice.

"There's a lot of talent out there. How many females do you have?" Susie asked.

"There were two on the senior, four on the junior, and one non-binary on senior."

"That Reese?" Scarlet asked, and I nodded.

"Yep. It hasn't been an easy transition, but they've enjoyed playing here more than any other school. So there's that."

"It's easy to identify the kids who sided with that asshat," Monty said.

"Yeah?" I asked, curious about what he'd noticed.

"They have a chip on their shoulders like they think their positions are owed to them without the work. I've played with their kind before. It's easy to spot if you know what to look for. "

"Hmm, I think I know what you mean. Sadly,

you're not even seeing the overt ones. About fifteen kids were pulled by their parents."

"Good riddance," Maks said, his voice hoarse.

Despite his outward appearance, the big brute had a heart of gold, something I was learning about him. It made sense how he was friends with Fletcher. He had the biggest heart of anyone I knew.

"Well, I'm going to get some food and work on some plays. I'll pop in during your time to see how things are going."

"We got this, Hen," Scar assured, winking.

"They're in our hands now, Coach," Monty added.

Thanking them again, I met Reed and Fletcher where they'd waited for me. They waved to their friends as we moved out of the rink and into the hallway.

Both men squeezed me into them before we headed to get some food.

"How are you feeling, Baby Shaw?" Fletcher asked me once we sat down at a table.

"Better than I was on Monday. I'm hopeful things will work out, and we can turn this program around. I'd like the kids to respect me, but I mostly want them to become the best players they can while loving the game."

"Spoken like a true coach," Reed said, his eyes warming as he looked at me. I'd been noticing it more and more, but I was too afraid to ask what it meant.

"I hope so. It's become important to me. Don't get

me wrong, I want to win and prove I'm just as talented of a player without an extra appendage between my legs. But at the end of the day, it's the smiles after a well-played game, knowing you did your best; that's what I'm realizing is most important."

"God, you're sexy when you get all inspirational," Fletcher teased, turning my cheeks pink. I tossed my napkin at him, but he ducked, catching it in his hand.

"Let's go see how these sessions are going," I said once I'd gathered my stuff, the guys following.

When I got to the bleachers, I was surprised to find some of the students not permitted to attend were watching from the stands. It made me wonder if I should make this a closed practice. Most of the kids watching were good players, and I hoped it meant they'd been bullied or pressured into joining Kurt. If they were taking the initiative to learn something by watching, then I wouldn't punish them for that. As long as they didn't become disruptive, they could stay. It was a smart move on their end.

I spotted Keaton off to the side, so I moved over to join him. I didn't understand his purpose here yet and wanted to learn more.

"Hey, Keaton," I said, startling him.

He waved, gesturing to the spot next to him.

"How did practice go?" he asked, keeping his eyes on the players. He wrote down numbers on a notepad that looked like some complex mathematical equation.

"Better. I'm hoping tomorrow will be the turning point for the rest of them."

"Teenagers are impetuous and impulsive creatures, but in my experience, they know when something is the real deal. And I think that's you, Henley."

He glanced over, stopping his note-taking.

"Oh, well, thank you. Is that why you're here? You're a fan?"

His cheeks tinted pink again, his eyes sparkling. "Um, no. I mean, I am, but that's not why I'm here." He turned back toward the ice, his face relaxing as he peered out at the players. "I've loved hockey for as long as I can remember. Unfortunately, I didn't have an athletic bone in my body. I tried for several years to play, but after my second broken arm, my mom put her foot down. It didn't quell my love of the sport. I watched every hockey game I could on TV or in person. It didn't matter if it was professional, junior, or peewee. I just wanted to be a part of it."

Keaton turned back to me, a wistful look on his face. It was a look that spoke of heartbreak and hopes, all wrapped in one. A game he loved had betrayed him, but he kept persevering because he loved it too much to stop. It was a look I was personally familiar with.

"I wasn't coordinated enough to skate, but I had the brains, as Dax said. I saw patterns and numbers in everything. Through a lot of experimentation, I designed my first aerodynamic hockey stick when I was fifteen. My best friend was willing to use it, and it improved his game by almost 200%. Suddenly, all these kids who'd made fun of me wanted to be my friend too. I had to learn who I could trust and who just wanted to use me."

He paused, taking a deep breath.

"By the time I was in college, I'd designed my first helmet to help reduce concussions with padding that was lighter and more durable. I'd become a millionaire overnight, making it even harder to know who my real friends were. Dax never treated me differently. He gave me a hard time, but it was out of respect and not malice. He was a true friend. So, when he told me about you and the struggles you'd faced in the league and at Lux, I knew I needed to meet you."

"Me? You're here for me?" I asked, confused.

He chuckled, his ears getting in on the red action now. "I mean, yes, but also no. Let me explain." He took a deep breath, his pen tapping a rhythm on his notepad.

"Hockey has always been my first love; numbers are the tools I use to get to enjoy it. SnowPoke has allowed me to do more of the things I love. This year, I started an initiative to help young players reach their goals while highlighting diversity in the sport. So, I'm here for two things. First, I'd like to help the players with custom sticks, pads, and helmets."

"Seriously? That's beyond gracious," I gushed, making him go pink again.

"And the second, I'm doing a campaign, and I'd like for you and Reese to be in it."

"As in marketing?" I asked, needing all the details.

"Yes, and sponsorship, if you're interested. I have two other players that have agreed as well. The four of you would be the new faces of SnowPoke to show that hockey is for everyone."

My jaw dropped; the magnitude of what he was offering would be monumental. Keaton continued to blink at me, enjoying my shock for once. SnowPoke was the second biggest hockey company in the world, only outmatched by Hat Trick Co. This was a game-changing offer. Collecting myself, I looked out at the ice, watching Reese.

"I'd love to be part of it, but I'll need to check with Reese. They've faced a lot of backlashes already in their short career, and this would put a magnifying glass over them. They'd be the one dealing with it, so I want them to be sure before I say yes."

"I understand. Just let me know by the end of the week. As for the other, if I could spend ten minutes with each player to measure them and have them run through my program, I can get the demographics for their gear."

"Yes, of course. I'll set it up."

"I'm glad Dax met you, Henley. He seems more grounded and accepting of himself. His ex-girlfriend damaged him. I was worried he wouldn't be able to get past it. It's nice seeing him laugh and joke again."

"Dax's a special guy. I'm glad to have met him, too," I said, my body warming.

"Can I ask a personal question?" he asked, tapping his fingers against his thigh.

"Shoot. I'll let you know if it's *too* personal."

"Your friend... she's going to eat me alive, isn't she?" he asked, the blush back full force.

"Oh, honey." I giggled, nodding my head. "She's seriously the best, though."

"Well, at least I'll go out with a smile on my face."

Chuckling, I bid him good luck as I moved down toward the boards to watch the rest of the practice. Keaton's offer kept running through my head, and I couldn't wait to talk to Reese about it.

# CHAPTER 13

## Henley

THE GIRLS FINISHED FIRST, skating off the ice together and talking animatedly. When they spotted me, their eyes brightened, and I knew they were up to something.

"What?" I asked, lifting my eyebrows.

"We should all go out tonight. A little get-together for the adults," Scarlet said.

"Hmm, that sounds a lot like 'let's get tipsy and do questionable things.'" I laughed, already knowing I would say yes. It did sound fun, and I hadn't been out much since I'd been here.

"Pish, posh," Scarlet replied, waving her hand. "Is that a yes?"

Rolling my eyes, I smiled and nodded. "Yeah. That could be fun. I'll talk to the guys. I just need to speak with Reese first. Are you staying in the guest suites?"

"Yep. Message when you're ready."

They both hugged me before heading toward the locker rooms. I sent a quick text to the guys as Reese's group made their way off the ice.

HENLEY

The girls want to go out. All of us together. You game?

FLETCHER

You had me at go out.

DAX

Who is all of us?

REED

If you're going, I'm going.

HENLEY

Message the guys. Everyone. I think the girls are eyeing some of the guys, and it seemed mutual.

FLETCHER

On it.

HENLEY

Talking with Reese, and then I'll be home.

REED

I'm still here. Let me know when you're leaving, and I'll head out with you.

DAX

Why is the word home so sexy suddenly?

FLETCHER

I'll explain it to you later.

Laughing, I put my phone away as Reese neared. They eyed me, knowing I had to be here for a reason.

"Hey, sis, what's up?"

"I just wanted to touch base with you about something."

They nodded, waving to Braden as they walked off with me. I decided to head to the office for privacy. Stepping in, I sat on the edge of the desk and waited for Reese to shut the door.

"How are things going? Are you getting any backlash?" I asked, realizing I hadn't checked in since everything had gone down.

"There's been some grumbling, but for the most part, people have left me alone. A lot of the team is excited about the chance to prove themselves, especially now that so many of the assholes are gone."

"How was it with Monty today?"

Reese's face lit up as they told me all about what they'd learned. "He's so cool. I can't believe I'm getting to train with him."

"I'm glad you're enjoying it. You're playing well."

They bit their lip, looking at the wall for a second before turning back to me. "Mom's been calling some more, but I've sent her to voicemail."

I raised an eyebrow, surprised by that. "I didn't know she was still hounding you. It might be best to keep her out of this for now. She had to be behind the media at the last game."

Reese nodded, shifting as they waited. "Is that all you wanted to talk about?"

"One of the people here today is from SnowPoke."

"Wow! So cool!" Their eyes sparkled as they smiled, and I knew it was the happiest I'd seen my sibling in a while.

"Yeah, it is cool. They're going to meet with everyone and outfit the team with customized helmets, sticks, and padding."

"What? That's crazy! I can't wait to tell Braden! Their stuff is the best. I know most people think Hat Trick is, but I've always preferred SnowPoke. HTC hasn't been the same since the ownership change," Reese rambled as they paced back and forth.

"Well, Keaton, the owner and brain behind Snow-Poke, wants to highlight diversity in hockey and has asked me to be part of a campaign with potential sponsorship if I decided to play again."

They jumped up, giving me a big hug. "I'm so happy for you, Hen." I smiled into their shoulder, pulling back to watch their face.

"He also asked if you wanted to be part of the campaign."

"Me?" Reese asked; their eyes were wide as they stared at me in shock.

"I told him you would get to decide. It would be a great opportunity, but it would put you directly in the limelight. I didn't know if you wanted to be the poster child for non-binary players."

"Whoa, um, I don't know what to say." They sat down, blinking as they thought about it.

"How about you think about it tonight and let me

know? I want to make sure you consider all your options. It could be a cool thing, but it does come with risks."

"Yeah, okay, I will. Thanks, Hen."

"No problem. You know I'll always look out for you first."

"Yeah, I know." They stood up again and hugged me, holding me for a little longer than usual.

"Alright, you're free to go. Eat something and relax for the rest of the night. Tomorrow is going to be tough."

"Ugh. My hockey coach is such a drag," they teased, waving as they walked out.

Chuckling, I shook my head, feeling lighter. Some days the doubt I hadn't made the right call to be Reese's guardian would surface, all my insecurities flaring to life. It was nice in moments like this where I could see firsthand that I absolutely had—Reese was blooming here.

Checking my phone, I found two messages. One from Reed telling me where he was, and another from Fletcher letting me know the guys would meet us at the pub in an hour. I quickly sent a message to the girls, asking if they needed a ride as I made my way to where Reed was.

SCAR

Are you finally offering, hot stuff?

SUZE

She means no, we're good.

Snorting, I couldn't help but have some fun with Scar.

HENLEY

It's always been you, Scar.

SCAR

I knew it. Let's run away together.

SUZE

Sometimes I wonder how I became friends with you two.

HENLEY

Because we're awesome. Duh.

SUZE

Debatable.

SCAR

I'll see you soon, lover. Now go take a shower and get pretty for me!

HENLEY

Already telling me how to dress. This relationship is doomed.

Finding Reed a few minutes later, he gave me a funny look when he spotted me.

"What?" I asked, wondering if I had something on my face.

"You seem lighter. That's all. It's nothing bad. I like it."

"Oh." My face warmed. "I forgot how good friends can cheer you up. I'm glad the girls are here."

"And here I thought my dick had healing properties."

A choked cough left me before I sputtered, my eyes wide at Reed. "Oh my god, you just made a sex joke. The guys have corrupted you!"

Reed laughed with me as we made our way home, happiness filling my veins.

"Then Henley got in the girl's face and says, 'I'd give you a nasty look, but you're already wearing one,'" Scar shared with the table. Her arms were wide, in full storytelling mode, as she regaled the others with stories about me. The table laughed, only encouraging Scar more. I groaned, resting my forehead in my hands as I smiled.

We'd been here for at least an hour, sitting around a large round table. There had already been a few beers drunk, along with several appetizers devoured. Despite being in the hot seat as Scar shared embarrassing stories about me, it had been a fun evening with everyone.

Maks and Susie had been talking while Scar entertained her entourage of Cody, Keaton, and Monty. She flitted back and forth between all the guys, making me wonder if she really would have a harem before she left. Cody and Keaton hung on her every word with doe eyes whenever she flirted with them. Monty was harder to read, but the sexual tension between them was palpable. He might be the first guy to give her a run for her money.

"I want to hear a story about Reed, Dax, or Fletcher. Henley torture hour is over!" I declared, slapping my hand on the table.

The guys looked at one another, debating if they'd share any tales. Monty got a gleam in his eyes, and I knew I had a winner.

"Oh, you have something, Monty. Spill!"

Reed stiffened next to me, eyeing his friend, which spurred on Monty more.

"During our rookie year, we went out celebrating after our first win. Well, when Reed has a certain amount of drinks, he turns into happy-go-lucky and touchy-feely Reed," Monty said, turning Reed bright red.

"Oh, god. Not this story, I beg you," Reed pleaded.

Monty chuckled and continued. "We stopped at a gas station on the way home, and everyone got out. While we were inside, Reed went around and slapped everyone on the butt, laughing as he ran off. He went up to the guy at the register and slapped him square on the ass, making the poor guy turn around, his face red. Reed froze, realizing it wasn't his teammate like he thought. The guy looked at him and goes," he stopped, a laugh breaking free. "He goes, 'Sorry, you're handsome and all, but I'm more into the bearded ones.' Reed stuttered, running out the door as we all laughed our asses off. The guy shrugged and left. I followed him, wanting to check on Reed."

Monty broke out into more laughter, stopping himself from being able to continue as he wiped tears from his eyes. The table joined in as Reed hid his face, shaking his head. I'd never seen his face get so red before.

"What happened next?" I asked, giggling as Reed narrowed his eyes at me. Monty wiped his face, finding his voice again.

"So Reed ran out of the store and got into the car, wanting to hide from his blunder. When the guy stepped out of the store, he stopped dead in his tracks, and I almost bumped into him. Looking at him, I didn't know why he'd paused suddenly until he spoke again. He goes, 'I guess I'll try anything once.' I followed his gaze and found him staring at Reed. That's when I realized Reed hadn't gotten into our car, but this guy's."

The table roared with laughter as Reed turned crimson. Taking pity on him, I kissed him, whispering in his ear. "He didn't know what he was missing, babe."

Reed scoffed but kissed me back; some of the redness dissipating. The others shared more stories, each person being put in the hot seat at least once.

"We need more beer!" Scar announced.

"I'll grab it. But I'm on water from here on out. I have an earlier call time than you."

"Praise be to that! I *so* don't do mornings anymore," she said, making everyone laugh.

Taking the empty pitcher, I walked to the bar and handed it to the bartender. They motioned that it would be a second, so I turned to take in the rest of the pub.

For a Wednesday night, it had a decent turnout, though it was far from being full. Most people were in groups of four, with a few pairs scattered throughout. Our group was by far the largest and loudest in the place. We should probably call it after this pitcher before we got kicked out. Turning back, I noticed a woman dressed in a designer suit, slicked back dark hair, and bright red lipstick sitting by herself. She stood out from the rest of the crowd. When she noticed my staring, she waved.

"Sorry, didn't mean to stare."

"It's no trouble. You having a good time with your friends?"

"Uh, yeah. I am."

"That's good. Having a group of friends is important."

"For sure." I nodded, not sure what else to say to this woman. It felt strange she was talking to me, but I guess alcohol made people chatty.

The bartender sat the pitcher down in front of me,

drawing my attention. I picked it up and glanced at the woman, nodding toward my hand.

"I guess I'll be seeing you. Have a good night."

"You too, Henley. See you around."

The use of my name had me stalling, but the woman placed down some bills and stood to walk out, her heels clacking on the floor with each step. Telling myself it wasn't too strange someone in this town knew me, I returned to the table, forgetting about the strange woman the rest of the night.

"Okay, I think it's time to call it," I said with a yawn. Fletcher agreed, standing to go pay the tab.

"Ah, no. Do you have to go? It's just getting fun," Scar said, grabbing my arms to dance.

"Yeah. I'm beat. Will you guys be okay making it back?" I asked, looking between the two girls and the group of guys hanging off their words.

"We'll take care of them," Monty promised, and I wondered if that was meant in more ways than one.

When Fletcher returned, Dax and Reed said their goodbyes, and the four of us left, feeling high on life.

# CHAPTER 14

## Henley

THURSDAY HAD FLOWN by with practice and conditioning. It was the last chance the players had to show their skills. The afternoon sessions with the auxiliary instructors had gone well, and more kids had shown up to watch from the stands. They'd kept quiet, so I hadn't made them leave. It made me wonder if we should hold more clinics throughout the year. It was something to bring up with Dmitry after this week.

It was now Friday morning and time for my breakfast check-in with Reese. The cafeteria wasn't as busy today, and it astonished me how much of the enrollment the hockey kids had been. I understood the board's position about opening it up mid-season now. Even with the kids still here, it would be difficult to make up two full teams. If there were any injuries throughout the season, we'd all be screwed.

Sipping my coffee, I waved as Reese entered. Their hair was still damp, the ends getting longer. Their wire-frame glasses sat on their nose, the large lenses making their eyes stand out. Wearing a long sleeve shirt and sweatpants, they blended in with the rest of the athletes.

"Good morning," I said when they neared.

"Morning." Reese yawned, placing their tray on the table and running their hands through their hair.

"Rough night?" I teased.

"Oh, you know, just a drill sergeant of a coach. Everything hurts. I think they take delight in seeing us suffer."

"Ah, is that the word on the street?" I stuck out my tongue as they laughed, picking up their fork.

"Have you thought any more about the campaign?" I asked, leaning forward.

Reese nodded around a bite, finishing before their eyes met mine. "I want to do it. I know it might open up more bullying, but it's a great opportunity for my future, and I can't help but think about the other people out there that might see it and feel represented."

I nodded, feeling proud of my sibling. "It's not easy being the poster child. People believe they have the right to tell you whatever they want, regardless of how it might make you feel. You'll need to be careful of social media and set up good boundaries, so other people's comments don't penetrate you."

They sighed, nodding as they continued to eat. I sipped my coffee, watching them closely.

"If it was Mom proposing this, then I'd run away.

She wouldn't protect me in this. But because it's you, I know you'll help me navigate it."

My cheeks warmed, my heart feeling full from their compliment. "And I will, Reese. Especially if I can help you avoid some of the mistakes I made early in my career."

"You're my role model, Hen. I admire everything you've done. I just wanted you to hear me say that."

"Thanks, Reese." Tears brimmed my eyes, so I took a big gulp of my coffee, needing to focus on something else so I didn't start crying in the cafeteria.

"Okay, enough mushy gushy stuff. How's it going with your roommate?"

"Briana's great. I don't get to see her too much since our schedules are a little different. Especially this week. I feel like I've basically lived on the ice."

"True story. What about tutoring? How is it?"

"Not bad. It's nice to get it out of the way and have the rest of the day for hockey. My tutor has helped me learn things in new ways, and it's really sped up the process," they said as they finished their food.

"Oh!" My eyes grew big as I remembered something I hadn't told Reese yet. "Guess where I get to go this weekend?"

"Where?" they asked, their brows rising above the wire-frames.

"Carly Conway's house."

Reese's mouth dropped open as I smiled, sipping my coffee smugly.

"No way. She's like your idol! Ten bucks you pass out when you meet her."

Chuckling, I shook my head. "I'll take that bet."

"Video proof, or I won't believe you," Reese teased.

Rolling my eyes, I agreed. "You'll be okay alone here this weekend?"

"Yeah. I won't really be alone. The twins are staying this weekend too. Plus, it's a boarding school. Most of the kids here are without their guardians year round."

"Okay, okay. I just worry." I lifted my hands, sitting back.

"I know. But you don't have to so much. I know taking me in wasn't part of your five-year plan. You're still trying to figure out your life and career." Reese dropped their eyes, playing with things on their tray.

"True, but I've never regretted taking you in. It might not have been part of my plan, but I think it's turned out okay. We make a good team. Don't we?" I asked, wanting Reese to know I meant what I said.

"Yeah. We do. I'm glad that you've met the guys here. They're bringing out something new in you. I like it. And after this year, I'll be heading to college. You're almost free of me." They smiled, meeting my eyes.

"Thank god," I groaned dramatically, making them relax. "You'll never be free of me, squirt. Siblings are for life." I hooked my finger out in the middle of the table, waiting for them to respond.

"Forever." They hooked theirs with mine, smiling

at our gesture. When Reese had been small, I'd taught it to them, stating it was our secret handshake.

"You headed to tutoring?" I asked, noticing the time. Reese nodded, picking up their tray.

"Yeah. I'll see you at the meeting."

Standing, I gave them a brief hug before we headed out of the cafeteria together, happy our breakfast hadn't been interrupted by bullies this week. They waved as they walked off toward the library, and I headed toward the rink. It was time to make the final roster.

I twirled in the chair, tossing the smart pen into the air, catching it before it hit my face. We'd been in this room for almost two hours and were stuck on the last few players. Everyone had a different opinion, making it difficult to gauge. I'd zoned out a few minutes ago, trying to find a solution. Somewhere in the middle of everything, I'd become paralyzed in my ability to make a decision, too worried it would be the wrong one.

"What's your gut saying, Henley?" Reed asked, the room going quiet at his question.

I sat up, facing the table, looking at everyone, and swallowed. Reed's crystal blue eyes bore into me, ever steady.

Taking a deep breath, I looked down at the list on the smart tablet. What did my gut say? Checking the names we'd already divided, I looked at it from a coach's perspective.

Daniels was good, but we already had a player like him. O'Malley wasn't the best at reading plays, but he was excellent under pressure, making almost all of his penalty shots. For the next twenty minutes, I reviewed the list and looked for what the team needed. When I was done, I glanced up to see everyone smiling. They'd been able to watch the moves I made on the smart wall behind me.

"There's our Coach," Scar said, winking.

Exhaling, I sank back into my chair, feeling tired and excited in the same second. Before I could change my mind, I hit submit, updating the lineup on the app.

"Thanks so much for all of your support this week. It's been nice having y'all here. I'm going to miss you."

The girls stood, coming over to hug me. "Don't think you're getting rid of us that easily. We have a suggestion."

"Oh?" I asked, leaning against the table. The guys had moved closer, peering at one another.

"Let's do an exhibition game as a fun surprise for the kids. We just need one more player to make it even," Susie said, practically bouncing on her toes.

"Oliver's home," Tyler suggested as I thought about it.

"It could be fun, but when? We have practice soon and a game tonight. And then I'm leaving tomorrow to go to Carly's."

"You've had a million practices all week. At most, you just need to run through some plays with the final players. You won't wear everyone out before the game, and you know it. That leaves plenty of time to have a little fun. Plus, it will help you blow off some steam."

I looked around at the guys, taking in their faces. "You're all in on this?"

"Yeah, it's been a while since some of us have played together, and Dmitry already approved it," Fletcher said before his eyes heated. "Unless you're not up to the task, worried you might lose."

Narrowing my eyes, I met his, knowing precisely what he was doing—pushing my competitive button.

"Fine. You're on. Just don't cry when my team beats yours."

"Yes!" Scar said, pumping her fists. "Wait, how are we dividing teams? I call Henley!"

"You can't call teams," Susie said, rolling her eyes before glancing between Fletcher and me. "Wait, can you? I call Henley too."

Chuckling, I shook my head, loving my girls. Maybe I had needed this more than I'd realized.

"Henley and Fletcher can be the team captains. Oliver said he's in as well. He needs to burn off some calories from eating desserts all week," Ty interjected, making everyone chuckle.

"Should we draw them out of a hat or just pick?" Monty asked, looking between mine and Fletcher's stare down.

"Henley can pick her team. I'm confident in everyone here," Fletcher said, crossing his arms as he gave me a smug smile.

"Fine, I'll also take Cody and Tyler," I said after thinking it through. If my hunch was correct, then I'd just put someone who wanted to sleep with the other on opposing teams. Things would be interesting, at least.

"May the best team win," Fletcher said, reaching out to shake my hand. Gripping his, I smiled, knowing exactly how to beat them.

"Oh, we will."

We spent the next ten minutes reviewing the rules before heading to change. If anything, the game gave me something to focus on instead of the roster and game tonight. I wasn't sure if it had been deliberate, but I was thankful nonetheless.

It was quiet when I entered the player's locker room, Reed and Fletcher behind me. For a second, I worried no one was there, but as I turned the corner, I found everyone who'd made the senior team waiting. Tyler and Cody were meeting the junior players in their locker room.

"Thank you all for bringing your A-game this week. I know it has been stressful with all the changes, and I applaud you for sticking with it. This wasn't an easy decision. In fact, we all argued over who should go where all morning. So, if you're here, it's because we believe in you. We're going to have a short practice to run through some drills, and then after, the coaches and guest instructors are playing in an exhibition game."

The players talked excitedly, shifting in their spots. Looking around the room, I took in the faces of the players, excited to see two girls had made the roster, along with Reese.

"Get changed, and I'll see you on the ice."

The noise in the room grew as I headed out, needing to put on my gear. The guys were quiet behind me, and I worried I'd said something wrong. When we stepped into our locker room, I stopped and turned, surprising them.

"Everything okay? You've been quiet."

Reed and Fletcher looked at one another before turning back to me with predatory smiles. They stepped forward together, backing me against the wall. Sucking in a breath, I tried to focus on one of them, but they both kept pulling my focus.

Their heads dropped, one on each side of my neck, as they kissed and nipped me. My legs turned to goo as I stood against the wall, my hands gripped in their jerseys.

Just as things heated up, my clit quivering with need, they stepped back, taking their heat with them.

"We know what you're doing, Hen. So how about we make it fair?"

"What do you mean?" I gasped, trying to find my balance as my legs shook.

"You plan to use sex as a motivator to win," Fletcher said, calling me out.

Giggling, I couldn't deny it. "What are *you* suggesting, then?"

"If we win, you have to fulfill one of our fantasies, and if you win, we'll do the same. No matter what it is."

"No matter what?" I breathed, licking my lips as ideas ran through my head, like making Fletcher clean his room.

"You in?" Reed asked, his voice practically smoldering.

"Oh, I'm so in. Let's do this, boys. Game. On."

# CHAPTER 15

## Reed

THE RUN through had gone well, and the newly established team made progress in gelling as a unit. Though, the best part for me was watching Henley coach. I enjoyed the time away from the pressure of playing. It helped me remember why I loved hockey in the first place, and I knew coaching was temporary for me.

But for Henley, it seemed like it was in her blood. When the kids got over the fact she was a woman, they followed her every word, waiting for any nugget she offered. Watching her across the ice now with her friends made me happier than I'd thought possible.

"If you keep looking at her like that, they're going to win before we even start," Fletcher teased, nudging me.

Grunting, I pulled my focus back to the other four players. Maks and Monty were also staring across the ice, each focusing on a different girl. Snorting, I couldn't help but adore her genius. She knew what she was doing when she picked teams. Even with the bet Fletcher and I had with her, I had a feeling she'd still come out the victor.

"You guys are toast," Oliver said, chuckling.

"Like you're not worried about losing to Tyler," I taunted, narrowing my eyes at his bluff.

"Nah. It's different with guys. We thrive off competitiveness. Now, if it was Sawyer, I'd have a harder time. Mostly because she's decent at hockey and can skate circles around me and do jumps."

The guys chuckled, nodding.

"Just how many people here are in multiple dating relationships?" Monty asked curiously.

Oliver leaned on his stick as he thought. "Hmm, I guess there are three groups now. Though mine's the biggest." Oliver chuckled at his dirty joke, making the rest of us roll our eyes.

"Size doesn't matter if you know how to use it," I countered, ducking his slap. "You thinking of joining your own foursome, Monty?" I asked, turning back to my friend.

"Before this week, I would've thought you were crazy. I don't judge anyone who makes that decision," he said, instantly backpedaling. "I just didn't think I'd ever make it. But now..." He shook his head, his eyes focused on the redhead across the ice. "Something tells me I might be willing for her."

Oliver slapped him on the back with a proud sigh. "Welcome to the club, man."

The rest of us chuckled, focusing on the plays Fletcher wanted us to try. I was glad Oliver had joined us. He kept things light, reminding us to have fun. It was completely contrary to the player he'd been back in his pro days, but I happened to like this version better.

"You boys ready?" Henley shouted, skating to the center of the ice where Rhett waited. He'd agreed to play referee for us. I looked out into the stands, finding them fuller than I expected. There were several kids, along with other instructors and parents.

Oliver skated toward the middle to face off with Susie while the rest of us got into position. Anticipation built in me as I bent my knees, my stick resting in my hand as I waited for the moment it became me and the game.

The whistle blew, the puck dropped, and everything faded as the sound of sticks hit against the ice, and everyone moved into action. My favorite part of a game was the feeling of a team coming together for one purpose—to win.

Susie got the puck and passed it to Tyler before spinning out to block Maks. Pushing off on my skates, I headed toward Henley, wanting to guard her. The puck passed between a few people, heading toward Henley just as I reached her.

In a surprise move, I stole the puck and pivoted toward the other goal, Henley hot on my heels. Monty moved to my left, and I checked my peripheral, passing it to him as Tyler checked me. Smiling, I spun out as he cursed, Monty already moving down the ice with the puck. When he got to the goal, he hesitated before he struck, Scar easily catching his shot.

She dropped it in front of him, smirking behind her mask. Monty chuckled, shaking his head as he skated back toward the center.

And so the game went on, with us all trading pucks back and forth, but neither team could score. Fletcher had stepped in as the goalie for our team, stopping all the attempts the girls made. After the first period, we were all panting as we took a moment to regroup. Shit, I needed to up my conditioning.

The crowd had grown some, cheering for us all equally, filling the stadium with their chants and cheers. It turned out to be one of the most fun games I'd ever played, and the score was zero to zero.

"Ready to give up?" Henley asked as she skated toward me.

"Never. You?"

"Nope." She smiled, winking before skating backward, keeping her eyes on me.

A few minutes later, the second period started, and I grabbed the puck from the center and made a breakaway. I could feel someone hot on my heels, but I pushed off with my skates, biting into the ice to move faster than I'd ever moved.

When I neared the goal, I didn't hesitate, lifting my stick high before coming down on the side of the puck as it soared through the air, heading for the left corner. Scar reached out for it, but it was a second too late, and the puck dropped into the net, the red light going off with the point.

Henley stopped next to me, her eyes sparkling as she looked at me.

"Felt good, didn't it?"

"Yeah. Might be my favorite goal ever," I teased, not breaking eye contact. She smiled, shaking her head before skating back toward the center. The guys patted me on the back as the game resumed.

Henley and Susie retrieved the puck, passing it between them, and scored next, bringing it to a tie at 1-1 before the buzzer sounded, ending the second period.

Our team huddled together, going over some plays.

"They're using the girls to distract you, so I think Cody and Tyler should be easier to go after. They're blocking, allowing them to get through."

"Ah, man," Oliver cursed, making us all turn to him. "I lied, okay. I don't want to block him. He'll definitely hold it against me and get Sawyer in on it too. Give me someone else to block."

The guys chuckled at his expense, understanding how he felt.

"I'll take the little guy," Maks said, cracking his knuckles. Oliver's face went pale, and he swirled from Ty to Maks.

"You know, on second thought..." he backtracked but shut up when Maks stared at him. "Just be gentle."

He grimaced, hanging his head. I had a feeling this wasn't any better for his love life.

Maks growled, giving off a toothy grin, making the gesture hilarious and frightening. Fletcher reworked the plays with the new players, putting me on Henley. I raised my eyebrow, wondering if he was trying to sabotage me.

"You've been the only one to get close," he clarified.

The whistle blew, and we broke our huddle, falling into our positions. Henley was in the center, so I met her there, her eyes sparkling as I neared.

"Oh, this is going to be fun," she purred, making me grit my teeth as my body responded to her voice.

Getting into position, I tried to focus on the puck and not the beautiful woman in front of me. The whistle blew, the puck tossed into the air, and I watched as it flipped over and over, time slowing down as I waited for the perfect second to snag it.

When I felt it, I reached in with my stick, feeling the weight of the black disk as it landed on the edge, and I turned, flipping it to Maks. Henley pushed into me, making me chuckle as she grumbled, skating off. I watched them fighting it out as Susie came up to my left.

"You love her, don't you?"

I didn't even hesitate, nodding. "Yeah, I do."

"Good. She's the best."

She skated off, and I followed this time, not

wanting to get distracted with hearts in my eyes. Everyone was skating hard but also laughing and having a good time together as we played. It was fun, and I wish we could do games like this more often— where the only thing at stake was your pride. The girls scored again, taking the lead and bringing the score to 2-1.

We all gathered in the middle when the buzzer ended, shaking hands and hugging one another. The crowd cheered, starting a chant for more. Henley skated over to the microphone so she could address the onlookers. Her face was red, her hair plastered to her head from the helmet, but she looked as sexy as ever. Maybe more. I guess the woman I loved in hockey pads really did it for me.

"Thank you all for coming to our little game. It's been an honor to have all our guest instructors this week, and I hope to have more of them and others throughout the year. It's a great way to learn new skills from the pros and get that extra advantage that Lux provides. Can we give Monty, Maks, Susie, and Scarlet a round of applause for their help this week?"

The crowd stood, clapping for the four as they stood in the middle, waving. I watched my friend, seeing him happy as he acknowledged the crowd. It could be the girl next to him, or maybe like me, he'd found the love of the game again. Either way, I was happy for him.

"They might be willing to stick around after the

game to sign autographs if anyone is interested?" Henley asked, placing her hand to her ear to get the crowd to respond loudly.

"Yeah? I'll see what I can do." She laughed, blowing a kiss to her friends who were acting put out on the sidelines.

"Now, the serious stuff. This week, the hockey team has undergone a lot of restructuring, and we've replaced players who weren't here to make our team and school the best they can be. I know everyone is still getting used to me as the head coach, and that's fine. I can take it. But don't take it out on these kids. They've worked harder than ever this week to show everyone what Lux and the Blizzards are made of. So, I hope to see everyone back here in a few hours to support them! Thanks again for coming out. Senior team, get some food and meet in the locker room in an hour for your last surprise. Go, Blizzards!"

The crowd talked, people getting up and leaving as Henley put the microphone down and skated back over. I pulled her into my arms, glad we were back on the same side.

"You have fun?" she asked as we waved to the others.

"I did. We should do that more often. Though next time, I want you on my team," I said, pulling her closer.

"Oh? Was it too hard playing against me?"

"The only time I want you against me is when I'm

naked," I purred into her ear, watching as she shivered. Henley licked her lips, her eyes dilating at the thought.

"Hmm, that could be arranged."

As much as I wanted her, I wasn't sure if there was enough time to fulfill the plans in my head. When we stepped into the locker room, my hope was dashed as we encountered Keaton and Dax.

"Great game, Petal," Dax said, snagging her from me to give her a kiss. With her skates on, she was almost the same height as him. "Oh, this is different."

Chuckling, I changed out of my pads and skates, needing a few hours without them. Henley did the same while she chatted with Keaton, letting him know that she and Reese would be part of the campaign.

"Thank you, Henley. It's going to be great. I'll let the marketing team know and be in touch on dates and times. I'll ensure it's the weekend so it won't interfere with school. Then I'll send over the scholarship information for Reese."

As I watched Henley, I dreamed about the future and what it would look like. Before, I hadn't thought much past the next day, especially after Mom died. Now, it felt like a new world of possibilities was opening up to me. I just wasn't sure which direction I wanted to go yet. The only thing I knew for sure was I wanted Henley by my side.

# CHAPTER 16

## *Henley*

PACING UP and down the locker room, nerves overtook my body. I'd been so focused on finalizing the team that I'd conveniently forgotten about the game and the fact that outside people like the media could be here. I'd been in my safe bubble all week, and now it had burst.

"It's going to be okay, Hen," Reed said, stepping in my path. "You're ready for this. What happened last week won't happen again. We got you."

Taking a deep breath, I glanced from him to Fletcher and nodded, knowing he was right. I didn't have to address the media if they showed up. I'd figure that out this weekend. For now, I just needed to focus on the game.

"Okay, I'm ready."

"That's my girl," Fletcher said, stepping closer to kiss me. It was soft but full of heat, making me chase his lips when he pulled away. "You get more after we win." He slapped my butt, making me squeal.

Reed chuckled, bending down to give me a kiss as well. If they were trying to work me up before the game. It was working.

Fanning myself, I focused on the plays and players as we made our way to the team locker room. The guys both smirked next to me, pleased with themselves, and I decided to think of a way to return the favor. Not to mention, I had a fantasy to cash in.

Stepping inside, my bad bitch mask slid into place as I embraced the coach I wanted to be. The players quieted as we neared, their faces solemn and alert. It was a drastic change from last week and this past Monday that made me believe in our chances to win.

"I've given my fair share of speeches this week, so I'll save you from having to hear one more." The kids chuckled, making me smile. We might not have the numbers we did before, but the players left were the ones I wanted to be here—the true athletes. "There's one more thing you all get before the game."

The door opened, and I turned, spotting Keaton as he walked in. He gave a shy wave, taking in the kid's faces.

"You all met with Keaton this week so he could study your swing and how you play. What you don't know is that he's the founder and owner of Snow-Poke." The team's eyes grew wide as they glanced around at one another, a few of them grabbing the arms of the player next to them as they waited in suspense. "Do you want to tell them, Keaton? I don't want to steal your moment."

Keaton nodded as he stepped forward, clearing his

throat. He pulled his hands from his pocket, clapping them together.

"Ever since I was little, I've loved hockey. It's been an honor to watch you all play this week and give your all in order to play tonight. So I wanted to give you all something to help you perform your best. When you did my tests, I collected data so I would know which equipment you'd need."

Fletcher and Reed pulled back the two dry-erase boards that had been in front of the new gear. Sticks, helmets, and pads were separated and marked with each player's name. The kids screamed excitedly as they took in the shiny new things. Standing to peer around one another to get the best view.

"Okay, let's do this in an orderly fashion and not maul one another before the game," I yelled, grabbing their attention.

Thankfully, the kids contained their excitement long enough to maintain a semblance of order as Keaton and the guys made their way around the room, handing out things. Once everyone had their new stuff switched out, I clapped to grab their attention once more.

"Alright, it's game time. You've all shown you love hockey this week, so go out there and play with your heart. Your body knows what else to do. Blizzards on three."

I tossed my hand into the center as they piled theirs on. "One, two, three, Blizzards!"

The players gathered their gear, and I checked in with Reese, taking their nod to let me know they were good. Fletcher slapped all the players on the back as they walked through the door, telling each one of them something too quiet for me to hear.

As much as I hated that it felt like he'd stepped down to support me, I couldn't deny how nice it felt to have him on the same team.

Once the kids were clear, I headed toward the ice, reminding myself to stay focused. The head referee met me as I stepped into the box, and I handed him our final roster. Reed gave me one last look before he headed up to the box to oversee the plays.

I observed the other team as they began their warm-ups, taking in the players and coaches. I ignored the crowd in the stands, not wanting to lose sight of the game. There was too much at stake to crumble under the pressure. These kids counted on me, and I'd do whatever it took to be here for them.

The buzzer sounded, and I blinked, not realizing how quickly the time had gone. Everyone skated off the ice except the starters, joining me in the box. The whistle blew, the puck dropped, and the game was afoot.

After the second goal, I released a huge sigh, feeling my body relax as the game continued. I almost couldn't believe it was the same team, but I suppose, in a lot of ways, it wasn't. There were new players, and every single one had undergone a transformation this week. That process changed them, making them different players from a week ago. It was exciting to watch it in action.

"Go, Henshaw. Score!" the player next to me yelled, making me happy to hear Reese had some support. The crowd roared in cheers when they scored, making my body relax the rest of the way.

When the first period ended, we were up 3-1, and the team was riding a high as they chatted in the locker room.

"How is everyone feeling on the ice?" I asked, wanting to check-in.

"Good. It feels like we've finally come together," Daniels said. A couple of players next to him nodded in agreement.

"It's been nice to play and feel confident in my teammates," Braden added.

"Everyone is doing great. So keep it up. Trust in each other. Let's get back out there and keep scoring."

The team cheered and filed out of the locker room, their spirits brighter as they returned to the ice. By the end of the second period, we were up by four, and it looked like we would have our first win of the season. My heart was full, and my spirit was overjoyed.

Of course, it all had to go to Hell in the third.

"Where's the penalty, ref? Do you need to have your eyes checked?" I screamed as I leaned over the railing.

Daniels limped back toward the box as Reese took

their spot, my anxiety ramping up even more. The ref gave me a warning look, and only knowing Reese was out there had me sitting down and shutting up for the moment.

Turning to Daniels, I checked him over as the play started. "What happened? What hurts?"

"It's the enforcer, #78. He's checking when no one is looking. He pushed me into the boards and tripped me. And he's saying things to all the players, trying to get us to cross the line and fight so they get penalty shots."

"Son of a... biscuit eater," I cursed, remembering where I was. "Ice your shoulder and knee, but you should be fine. We'll have the doc check you out, just in case." Daniels nodded, heading toward the medic to get some ice.

I turned and tried to focus back on the game, fear and rage fighting it out for which emotion would dominate. My fingers dug into the wood as the game went on, nerves traveling up my throat and choking me. Time slowed as I zoomed in on the player Daniels had warned me about. And just like he said, as soon as the ref turned his back, he checked someone, sending them into the boards.

This was when I wished high school was managed like the professionals, with a panel viewing the game from up top and instant replay. Logically, I knew there was only so much they could see, and they tried to catch everything. But when my sibling was on the ice with a dirty player, the refs' imperfections were a glowing nuclear bomb about to explode.

Braden passed the puck to Quinn, who spun out and avoided their player. Two more closed in on them, and he managed to hit the puck back to Reese. I held my breath as the clock counted down, and they skated toward the goal. My eyes searched for the enforcer, realizing I'd lost him in my observation of the game.

My eyes landed on him, and I sucked in a breath as he barreled down the ice toward Reese. He was coming from behind, in their blind spot, and it would be too late for them to move as they pulled their stick back to strike the puck.

The crowd held their breath; the clock running down as Reese slapped the puck and it flew through the air. They stood still, waiting to see if it would be good, the enforcer still skating toward them. The referee blew his whistle, but the player kept going, too focused on hitting Reese.

Screaming at the top of my lungs, I watched as Reese turned, realizing what would happen as the player neared. They braced their arms to protect their head as they scrunched down to cover themselves. At the moment of impact, Braden intercepted, pushing the player away as the three of them crashed into the ice and boards.

The buzzer sounded, but everyone was focused on the players lying still on the ice. Jumping over the side,

I didn't care if the game was still technically in play, needing to see how my players were, how Reese was.

The ice filled with both teams, and chaos erupted as players came to their teammates' defense. I ignored them, despite knowing I should tell the team not to fight. I was too focused on the three players lying in a heap.

Someone else got to them at the same time I did, my knees sliding on the ice as I stopped my forward movement. My hands hovered over the prone body, trembling as I pushed them over to inspect them. My heart ran rampant, bile grew in my throat, and sound ceased to exist outside of the pounding in my ears.

It felt like a lifetime as I waited, pushing the helmet visor up and checking their eyes. Reese blinked up at me, my heart crashing back into place at the simple gesture. The medic hovered over my shoulder, shining a light in Reese's eyes.

"Does it hurt anywhere?" I asked.

"No, I just got the air knocked out of me. I'm sure I'll feel the hit tomorrow, but I'm okay."

I glanced at the medic, who nodded, moving over to the next player. Helping Reese sit up, I gently pulled them into my arms as I held back tears. I couldn't break down on the ice. I took a deep breath as relief swept through me. They were okay. They were okay.

"You scared the shit out of me," I whispered, drawing back to look at their face again.

"I didn't do it on purpose," they said, looking around and remembering what happened. "Braden!"

Reese turned and looked over their teammate, who was holding his shoulder as the medic checked him out. My rage surfaced when I saw the player responsible for it all holding his knee and gesturing toward Braden to his coach. A hand squeezed my shoulder, stopping me from getting up and slugging the bastard as he continued to make false claims.

"Take Reese to the medical room, Hen. I'll get Braden and meet you there. Reed will handle the rest," Fletcher said, grounding me in the moment to focus on what mattered.

Nodding, I stood, taking in the rest of the ice for the first time. Both sides had been pulled apart and were held back by the other coaches. I spotted Tyler and Cody on the ice while Reed was arguing with the ref. Trusting they had it, I did as Fletcher said and helped Reese up as we skated toward the break in the boards.

The crowd clapped for Reese, so I waved, thanking them for their concern while stewing inside and wondering how I could get payback on a teenage boy.

# CHAPTER 17

## Henley

CLOSING the medical room's door, I took a deep breath as I tried to reassure myself that Reese was okay. The moment only lasted a second before Sera and her fiancé Sean, Braden's dad, rushed over, Briana hot on their trails.

"How is he? How is Reese?" they rushed out, overwhelming me.

"They're both fine. You can go in and see Braden. His shoulder is a little swollen, but they don't think he's damaged it. Otherwise, they just have a few bruises from the fall."

"I swear to God, if I ever see that kid off the ice, I'll pummel him into next week," Sera said, practically spitting.

Sean had relaxed at my update, smiling down at his fiancée, my old teammate, like she was the cutest thing he'd ever seen. Sera might appear cute and fluffy, but she was feisty. She'd started her fair share of fights on the ice, which for women's hockey was rare.

Sean wrapped his arm around her as they headed in. Briana stopped in front of me, twisting her hands. "Could I see Reese?"

"Yeah. Go on in. They're next to Braden."

Briana smiled as they stepped inside, leaving me alone once again. Tilting my head back against the wall, I let my body relax, trusting that everything was okay for now.

"Hey." Dax's voice was soft as he stepped near me, taking my hand in his. I dropped my head onto his shoulder, letting him support me for a moment.

"Reese okay?" he asked after a few minutes.

Lifting my head, I looked up at him. "Yeah. Bruised, but okay. It could've been so much worse."

"But it wasn't. And it looks like that kid will get suspended from a few games. The ref tried adding Braden to it when Reed showed him footage of how #78 had been charging Reese, and Braden stepped in to shield them."

My blood boiled at that, my hands clenched into fists. "That kid better stay the hell away from me, or I'll be going to jail," I seethed.

Dax chuckled, making me angrier.

"I would!"

"Oh, I believe you. I'm just laughing at how cute you are, even when you're angry. It's really unfair, Petal."

My mouth gaped open, unsure if I was offended or turned on that he found me cute. The door opened, saving me from having to decide.

"Really, I'm fine," Braden said, rolling his eyes as he stepped out with his shoulder wrapped in a giant ice pack. "I'm not coming home just because I got hurt. I'll be okay here."

Sera went to argue when Sean placed his hand on her arm. "Fine. But I want you to check in with me twice a day just to make sure."

"He'll be fine, Dad," Briana added, stepping out with Reese.

"Yeah. We'll hole up in our room and watch movies and do homework all week. It will be relaxing," Reese added.

"I dunno. Maybe I should stay here this weekend," I said, the need to take care of them overpowering.

"Not needed, Sis. It's just a bruise, and I have a paper to write. I'd be the most boring person to watch. Besides, it's not every day you get to meet Carly Conway."

"Carly Conway!" Sera screeched, making me grimace from the high pitch.

"Just announce it to everyone, Sera," I teased. Her cheeks reddened as she leaned closer, whispering this time.

"Carly Conway? You've been holding out. I didn't even know Susie and Scar were here until lunch today."

"Oops." I cringed, realizing I'd unintentionally ignored Sera for the past month.

"You're forgiven. I know you have a lot on your plate. How about you go meet your idol, and the kids stay here, but they promise to come over for Sunday dinner? How does that sound? Fair compromise?" she asked, looking between the three teens and me.

The teens smiled, nodding that it would work, and I relaxed, happy to have good friends to help me manage this parenting thing. Satisfied with everyone's answer, Sera wrapped her arm in mine as we walked down the hall.

"Don't think I didn't notice the blond hottie from the pool. We need a girl's night when you get back."

"I will gladly take you up on that offer. I have lots to tell you." I wiggled my eyebrows, making her giggle.

"Oh boy, they're up to something," Sean said from behind us. I glanced over my shoulder, finding Dax walking with him, talking to him about the game.

When we got to the end of the corridor, Fletcher and Reed were waiting for us. They handed Reese and Braden their bags, having collected their gear and stored it for them while they were with the doctor.

"One of these days, I'll get to be there for the after-game speech," I mumbled, making Dax shake his head as he hid a smile. The guys looked me over, despite only being out of their sight for an hour.

"Thanks, Fletch," Reese said, taking their bag. They turned, looking at me. Taking a step forward, I pulled them into my arms, holding them gently.

"Call me if you need anything. Promise me you will."

"I promise."

"I'll see you on Monday then. Rest and recover.

That's an order." I pulled back, cupping their cheeks, before kissing their forehead.

"Bye, Coach," Braden said as they moved to step through the doors. When applause broke out, I was shocked, stopping to find what it was all about.

The rest of the team had waited in the lobby, along with some instructors and parents. When Reese and Braden exited, they stood, clapping for them. I'd figured everyone had left by this point, so seeing the team waiting for their injured teammates moved me.

Following them out into the lobby, I was shocked even more when the crowd started chanting, "Coach! Coach! Coach!"

Stunned, I stopped a few feet in, looking around at the faces gathered in disbelief. Fletcher stooped down, his beard tickling my cheek as he whispered into my ear.

"They're all here for you, Baby Shaw."

Tears wanted to fall, but I held them back, lifting my chin and nodded as I gathered myself. Once I didn't feel on the verge of breaking down, I cleared my throat as the crowd quieted.

"Thank you all for your support. Tonight's game ended roughly, but I hope you can see the effort the kids are putting into this sport. Now go and rest up; practice resumes on Monday."

The students groaned good-naturedly as they picked up their gear and headed out the doors. A few parents stopped by to tell me how well their child was playing, reminding me I wasn't failing at this. By the time they were all gone, it was just my guys and me.

"Did you know?" I asked, looking at them suspiciously. Dax smirked; Reed looked elsewhere while Fletcher met my eyes with a heated look.

"It was their idea, and I didn't discourage it because I knew you'd be beating yourself up. I wanted you to see what I heard all game and what the three of us know. You're an amazing coach, Hen. I hope you're starting to believe that."

Nodding, I went to them, letting the three of them hold me between their arms, the tears finding a safe place to fall.

I always thought hockey would be my only true love, but these three men were showing me I just might be wrong.

SHOVING MORE CLOTHES INTO THE DRYER, I SERIOUSLY reconsidered the three-boyfriend thing. Cursing at the clothes, I managed to shut the door and remember to hit start this time.

"Why do I always wait until the last minute to do laundry? And why did I agree to do more? I'm going insane. Three dicks are too greedy, so the balance is insanity," I mumbled, folding the clothes on top of the dryer.

After finishing with the fifth black tee, I regretted

ever thinking how hot Reed looked in them. The stupid shirts were no longer desirable when I had to fold them.

"Stupid shirts," I grumbled, taking my aggression out on the socks next.

A chuckle behind me had me freezing, spinning with the socks as I spotted my eavesdropper. Planting my hands on my hips, I glared at the intruder.

"How long have you been there?"

Reed grinned, sauntering forward in a sexy stroll before trapping me against the dryer. "Long enough to hear you're going crazy from too much dick. And apparently, my shirts are stupid?" He lifted a brow, the words leaving my brain as I breathed in his minty fresh scent.

"They are stupid," I said, though I couldn't remember why now that he was standing before me.

Reed threaded his fingers through my hair, his nose brushing against mine as he held my jaw. His crystal blue eyes shimmered as he searched my face before his lashes fluttered against his cheeks as his lips brushed against mine. It was a soft kiss, full of passion and want. Our lips moved against one another, treasuring the feel.

"You don't have to do this all on your own," he whispered, pulling back to plant kisses on my cheek and forehead. "We're all capable of managing it." He moved to the other side, his lips warm as he traveled over me.

"I know. I just thought it would be nice," I said, knowing how ridiculous I sounded. Reed dropped to my neck, sucking a little before kissing lower over my shoulder, pushing down the strap of my camisole.

His big hands trailed to my hips, sliding up my torso under my shirt. His thumb brushed against my nipple as he continued to kiss my hot flesh. Words no longer formed in my head, and I suddenly enjoyed doing laundry a lot.

In fact, I wanted to do laundry every day if this was how it would end, forgetting that being dick greedy had gotten me into this mess to begin with.

But when a hot guy kissed you senseless, to the point you forgot your name and how to breathe, it didn't seem like such a big deal anymore.

Reed lifted me, sitting my butt on the washer and stepping between my legs. He lifted my shirt over my head, dropping his lips down to my breast, sucking it into his mouth with his devil tongue.

I rocked my front against him; my hand clutched in his silky hair as I tried to find more friction. Reed's hands dropped to my thighs, spreading them wider and stopping my motion.

"More," I whined, not caring if I sounded like a whiny bitch.

"Patience, Hen. I only reward good girls. Now, let's see if you're wet for me."

His dirty words had me squirming against his

hold, my need for him becoming more and more apparent.

Reed's nose traveled down my torso, his tongue leaving a trail as he went. When he got to the elastic of my shorts, he didn't stop, trailing over my center with his nose. Gasping, I leaned back on the washer, bracing my arms on the machine as it spun below us. The gentle vibration sent tingles through my body, setting off every nerve ending.

At this point, I could feel myself dripping wet, my clit throbbing in tandem with my heartbeat. I had to have a damp patch on the front of my shorts, but I was too aroused to be embarrassed by it. Reed breathed me in, pressing the material of my shorts in as he exhaled. My legs shuddered, the slightest bit of pressure practically sending me over the edge.

Reed's palms moved up my thighs, his thumbs sneaking under the fabric of my shorts. I wished I had magic so I could make them disappear; the desire to have him reward me was too much to bear.

"Please," I begged, no longer able to stop myself.

Reed's eyes looked up, giving me only a second to catch his smile before he suctioned his lips on my clit, making me spasm like I'd been electrocuted. My back arched, my hair falling down my bare back, sending goosebumps down my spine.

"Fuck," I moaned, my legs shaking. My shorts were ripped off me, Reed's mouth replacing them as he thrust his tongue through my folds. He pulled my legs higher, resting my thighs on his shoulders as I convulsed on top of the washer. Everything together sent me flying over the edge, soaking Reed's face with my cum in the process.

He growled, licking his lips as he stared down at me with hunger. Barely able to catch my breath, Reed lowered my legs back on the washer before replacing his tongue with his dick. Gripping onto his shoulders, I clung to him as he held me to his chest, my nipples rubbing against him. My knees hung over his arms as he lifted me, fucking me into oblivion.

"Ah, yes. Oh my god, yes," I moaned, no other words forming.

"You're so wet for me, Hen. Your tight little pussy takes my cock so well. All I can think about is when I can be inside you next. You've made me addicted, Hen. I can never get enough of you. So, if you're greedy, then I'm a willing participant. So, take what is yours and squeeze my cock until I'm coming so hard I blackout."

"Fuck, Reed!" I screamed, pulling at his hair with one hand, digging my nails in his back with the other as I came hard, my pussy twitching and clenching around him.

Hearing me roar his name as I did exactly what he commanded, Reed cursed, pumping deep one last time before he shouted, his orgasm taking over as he unloaded into me. I clung to him, my whole body tingling from a million pinpoints. His head fell to my neck, and I wondered if he did pass out.

The washer buzzed, sending vibrations through us both as we groaned and then laughed. Reed moved back as I caught my breath. I smoothed the hair off his face, staring up at his handsome face so lovingly. It was on the tip of my tongue to tell him how he made me feel.

"I—"

"I want to volunteer to help with laundry next time," Fletcher interrupted. "I still owe you for winning the game."

Reed and I glanced over, spotting him leaning against the doorframe as he ate a bowl of cereal, a cheeky grin on his face. His pants were tented, and I wondered how long he'd been there.

"Fuck off, Fletch," Reed cursed, pulling me closer.

Giggling, I untangled us and grabbed a towel out of the basket that I'd just folded. I guess that was handy.

Once we were both redressed, Reed helped me finish folding the clothes, putting the last load in the dryer as we headed to bed. And I knew I'd volunteer to do laundry again too.

# CHAPTER 18

## *Henley*

MY LEG BOUNCED as the plane descended, the reality of today sinking in. The morning had been a whirlwind of packing, copious amounts of coffee, and double-checking on Reese. Now that I thought about it, the bouncing could be from the pot of coffee I'd drank. Yeah, that was it. I wasn't nervous. I'd met celebrities before.

Despite my reassurances, I knew deep down I was scared shitless. It wasn't every day you met your role model. Carly had paved the way for so many women. She never apologized for her stats and demanded that men pay attention to her. She never let her gender get in the way of her dreams, and I admired that.

I wanted to be like that. Too often, I started strong, to only bow to the pressures the world placed on me when the weight got too heavy. I hoped Carly would have some advice on how to stop doing that.

"You excited, Petal?" Dax asked, nuzzling my neck. He'd been sleeping most of the flight. His shoulder-length blond hair was pulled back, his emerald green eyes still sleepy as he watched me.

The plane touched down, and my throat jumped

into my throat. We were almost there. Squeezing his hand, I nodded, too worried I'd get sick if I opened my mouth right that second.

"I thought you liked flying," Fletcher said from across me. Reed was sitting next to him in almost the same state as me. Focusing on him, I relaxed and smiled at him, hoping to distract him from the plane. We landed a second later, the plane slowing as it pulled around.

Even though Carly had sent us her private jet, I hadn't been able to appreciate it; too busy freaking out all morning. Reed took a deep breath, removing his fingers from the armrests. The plane stopped, and the overhead lights came on.

"I don't mind it. I'm more nervous about meeting Carly. What if I say something dumb? Or she tells me I'm the worst thing to happen to women's hockey?"

The guys and I unbuckled our lap belts, stretching as the flight attendant came out. She eyed my guys again, making me mad. Thankfully it didn't seem like any of them had noticed, but it had set my possessive radar off.

Fletcher wrapped his arms around me, pulling me to his chest. "She's going to love you, Baby Shaw. Now, why do you look like someone kicked your puppy?" His eyes sparkled with mirth, and I had a feeling he knew but wanted me to say it.

"Nothing," I uttered, stepping out of his arms to

grab my bag. He snorted behind me but let me get away with it for now.

Reed was the first one off the plane, the tension in his body leaving him as he touched the pavement. He tilted his face to the sun as he took a deep breath. Smiling, I descended the stairs, still amazed this was my life.

Private jets and limousines weren't my normal.

Fletcher and Dax joined me as we took in the view. I'd never been to Oregon before. The view was picturesque, with tall pine trees that had thick trunks. The mountains were off in the distance, giving a surreal feeling of nature all around us.

"Miss, your ride is here," a soft-spoken man said, gesturing toward the limo I'd seen earlier but ignored.

"That's for us?" I asked, confused.

"Yes, miss. Do you need anything else?" he asked, glancing between the guys and me.

"We're good. Thank you," Fletcher said.

I smiled to myself as we all walked to the limo. The driver took our bags and placed them in the trunk. Fletcher had been stepping up as the leader of our little group. I didn't know if it was because he was the oldest, already in his 30s, or if it was just his nature. Either way, I was waiting for the perfect opportunity to tease him with a 'yes, Daddy or Sir' and see what his face did.

"Something to share?" Fletcher asked after we were all seated.

"Nope." I giggled, the action helping to release some nerves.

"How long do you think the drive is?" Dax asked, rubbing his hands together.

"Not sure. Why?" I arched an eyebrow, wondering what he was up to.

"Limo sex," he purred. I shifted in my seat at his words, the thought making me hot all over.

"I will not do that in someone else's limo! Same for the plane, so get those thoughts out of your head." I sat back, crossing my legs and arms to keep myself from giving in to the idea.

"What I hear her saying is she isn't opposed to the ideas, just not in Carly's. Well, boys, we know what we must do when we get back," Dax teased.

Snorting, my face flamed because he wasn't wrong. "When did you get funny? I thought you were the broody one?" I asked, trying to change the subject.

"Broody one? Do we have roles, Petal?" he asked, moving closer to fan his hot breath across my neck.

"Yep. If you don't know what it is, I'm not telling. It's more fun that way," I teased, moving away, but it was too late as goosebumps spread across my skin.

"Am I the sweet one?" Reed asked, his brow scrunched. He looked really confused by the word.

Chuckling, I shook my head. "You're sweet, but it's not your natural inclination."

"I think you need to share with the class, Baby

Shaw," Fletcher commanded, and I almost caved as a fire lit within, but I shook my head, holding firm.

"Nope. This is more fun."

Reed continued to think; his brow furrowed as he stared at the ground. It made me want to tell him so he didn't look so confused.

"I know," Dax said, grabbing everyone's attention. "I'm the dashing one, not broody," he corrected, giving me a wink. "Fletch is the bossy one, and Reed is the punchy one." He sat back with a smug smile, proud of himself.

Fletcher coughed back a laugh while Reed appeared offended, scoffing at Dax, no words coming to him.

"Still wrong," I teased.

"Oh, come on, Petal. We both know I'm the most dashing."

"Nah. More like most annoying."

The other two chuckled. Reed, having recovered from Dax's proclamation, kicked Dax, narrowing his eyes at him.

"I'm not punchy."

Dax glanced down at his leg where Reed's foot had just been. "Sure, tough guy. You were ready to throw down for me the first day we met."

"That was different, and you know it," he hissed, arms crossed and eyes narrowed.

"And who was it that punched Kurt first?" Dax continued.

Reed's mouth opened then shut, his lips forming a line as he stared at Dax.

"And you want to punch me right now. Don't you?" Dax teased, leaning back, proud of himself.

Reed's face became more agitated, and I worried he was taking Dax's assessment to heart. Sighing, I reached across and pulled Reed's hands from his arms.

"Reed, you're my strength and reassurance. You ground me and remind me who I am when I forget it. You bring me balance and faith." He blinked, his face softening as I spoke.

"You mean that?" he whispered. This was why I didn't want to say it in front of the others. It felt like a moment just for us.

"Yeah, I do." I leaned over and pressed my lips against his before sitting back in my spot. Since Dax had been the instigator, I turned to Fletcher next. He stared at me with hungry eyes, making me have to swallow before I could speak.

"Fletcher, you're my light and confidant. You remind me to have fun and help me not to focus on the problems but see the solutions. You listen to me, offer your shoulder to cry on, and make me feel like I can do anything. You're the backbone of our little group, leading us toward our future."

"But like a sexy compass, right?" he asked, making me laugh and proving my point.

"Yes, dork." I kissed him, his hands gripping my waist and not letting me get away with a peck.

When I sat back, I was flustered, my heart racing from his kiss. His heated eyes told me he'd done that on purpose. Once I had myself centered, I turned and looked at the last man who held my heart. His eyes were half-lidded, his teeth biting into his lip. Dax looked worried, his confidence having disappeared.

"Dax, you're my passion and spirit. You show me how to push boundaries and break free of the things that have limited me all my life. I love how you challenge me to live free and not be ashamed of what I want. You showed me I could want so much more than I'd ever allowed myself to dream."

"No one has ever said anything like that to me," he whispered, placing his forehead against mine. His hand trembled as he cupped my cheek to lift my chin. His green eyes were glossy as he stared into my soul. "I was so dumb to think I could resist you, Petal. You've rewritten my heart, so it only knows your name."

His lips crashed down on mine, and I accepted them, knowing he needed this belief in himself, in us. I knew the other two were in the limo, but for a second, it felt like it was just Dax and me, and maybe that was what I needed to do more. Make sure they each knew their value and place in my heart.

The car turned as it slowed, breaking the moment between Dax and me. I peeked over at Fletcher and Reed, and they nodded, letting me know they understood.

Glancing out the window, I took in the trees lining

the driveway; up close, they seemed like they were 20ft tall. We drove up that windy road forever before stopping in front of a sprawling wooden mansion. The front had massive floor-to-ceiling windows with large wooden beams forming a triangle.

"Whoa," I whispered in awe. "This place is bananas."

The door opened, and I jumped, a squeal escaping me before I covered my mouth and laughed. The driver looked down at me in concern.

"Sorry, you surprised me."

"Apologies, Miss Henshaw." He bowed his head, offering me his hand to step out of the car. Glancing back at the guys, they nodded to accept it. Climbing out of the limo, I dropped the man's hand as soon as I cleared the door. I took a few steps forward to peer at the landscape around me.

Trees surrounded us, the house and buildings were the only things I could see. There was a garage and another large complex off to the right of the house. It made me wonder if she wanted this much privacy or needed it. Fame had a cost.

The guys stepped beside me, shielding their eyes as they looked around. A gentleman in a black suit descended the stairs, clearing his throat when we didn't acknowledge him, too busy taking in our whereabouts.

"Oh, hello." I waved awkwardly, feeling out of my league here. I hadn't grown up with a lot of money, and women's hockey didn't pay as much as men's. So while I'd always done well, I wasn't loaded. This was a whole new level. I didn't know everything about the guys' backgrounds, but I doubted they were on this level, either.

"Greetings, madam. I'm to escort you and your guests to your rooms so that you may freshen up. Mrs. Conway will meet you for lunch in the formal dining room."

"Oh, okay." I turned to the others, finding it a little strange she wasn't greeting us now, but I couldn't assume she was free all weekend just for me. She probably had a lot of other things to do as well.

We followed the butler into the house, having to focus so we didn't get left behind as we peered at everything. We climbed two flights of stairs before he led us down a hallway. He stopped a few doors down and pointed.

"Here are your rooms. There's an itinerary on your bed and the rules of the house. If you do not have suitable attire, clothing can be found in your closet. If you find you may need something not provided, please ring the box by the door, and staff will see to it."

He bowed his head and walked off, all the information he'd told us filling my head. "Thanks," I remembered to say, but he was already gone, turning around the corner and out of view.

The four of us looked at one another, shock and

curiosity mirroring what I felt. "I guess we try a room?"

The guys nodded, stepping into the first one. A note was laid on the bed with Reed's name. He picked it up, reading it out loud.

"Welcome to Chateau Conway. We hope you enjoy your stay. While on these premises, please be mindful of the other guests and respect the off-limit areas on the map. Meals are served at 8 am, 12 pm, and 6 pm, with no exceptions. If you're not present, you will lose the opportunity to eat until the next meal. Please refer to the dress code for each mealtime. No exceptions are allowed. If you do not have anything that meets the requirements, accommodations have been made for you. Please see Gerald for anything you may require. Thank you for joining us at Chateau Conway. We hope you enjoy your stay."

Reed flipped it over, finding a map and dress code listed on the back. I glanced around the meticulously styled room, wondering what the hell I'd gotten myself into.

"Anyone else find it weird as fuck?" Dax asked, walking over to the closet.

"Yeah, but rich people are known for their eccentricities. Don't make any judgments yet," Fletcher offered, staring down at his phone, a perplexed look on his face.

He looked up, his smile returning as he put his phone in his pocket. I shook off the look, exploring the other rooms and discovering the same note on each bed. All the rooms were lovely, but I had an odd feeling in the pit of my stomach. I just hoped it was gas or something.

But I couldn't shake that saying... Never meet your idols.

Had I just walked us all into a bigger clusterfuck?

# CHAPTER 19

## *Henley*

AFTER OUR EXPLORATION, we'd all retreated to our separate rooms to get ready for lunch. The shower did wonders for my nerves, the anxiousness, and doubt dissipating to a reasonable level. Some of that could also be attributed to the clothes I'd discovered in the closet.

The appropriate attire for this meal consisted of slacks, a nice shirt with no tie for the guys, and an above-the-knee length dress or skirt for me. The guys might have something that worked for them, but I hadn't packed any dress clothes outside of slacks. I wasn't crazy about wearing a dress, but the ones she'd picked were lovely.

I'd chosen a green dress with wide straps covering my shoulders with a deep v in the middle. If I had bigger boobs, it would show a lot of cleavage, but since I didn't, it was tastefully seductive. Slipping on the shoes, I twirled in the mirror, taking in my appearance.

Everything fit perfectly, and I found it odd that some stranger knew our sizes so well. I was hoping there was a reasonable explanation for it. Snapping a picture for Reese, I sent it to them as I checked how they were recovering.

REESE

Look at you, sis! Where'd you get that dress?

HENLEY

She had it for me. That's weird, right? There's a dress code to eat!

REESE

Maybe, maybe not. At least they provided you with something since you didn't know. It would be worse to find out there was a dress code and then walk down there in your cut-off shorts.

HENLEY

Fair. But I'd so rock those shorts, and you know it. I think I'm just nervous. How are you doing?

REESE

Fine. Just like I was the other hundred times you asked. We've been working on homework, and now we're watching movies. Braden is asleep, and Briana wants to draw on his face.

HENLEY

As his coach, I say be nice. As your sister, I say send a pic!

REESE

Duly noted. Now go and have fun. Let me know what she's like.

HENLEY

Ok, ok, ok, ok. Bye, dweeb.

REESE

Bye, older dweeb.

HENLEY

You're just cruel.

REESE

*tongue sticking out emoji*

Chuckling, I slipped my phone into the pocket of the dress. Because besides this dress fitting perfectly and feeling like butter on my skin, it had pockets! It was seriously the unicorn of dresses.

A knock on my door had me jumping until I realized it was probably the guys. Opening it, I stopped, my mouth dropping open as I took in their appearance.

Reed was in a black button-down and black pants, his dark features making his eyes stand out even more. He looked deadly and sexy, a dangerous combination.

Fletcher wore a hunter-green shirt that brought out the green in his eyes. The first button was open to show his chest. He wore dark gray pants that cupped his thick thighs, which made me drool. He looked like a tree I wanted to climb and never leave.

Dax wore a dark blue shirt with dark pants, and his hair was pulled back. His complexion seemed to shine, his muscles evident through the shirt. He looked more delicious than a bowl of macaroni, if that was even possible.

"Wow, okay, I'm digging this dress code thing. Though I wonder if you're on the menu because you all look good enough to eat."

They smirked, their eyes caressing me as I stepped out my door.

"You look divine, Hen," Reed said, his eyes heating.

"You're never allowed to wear this in public," Fletcher growled.

"Spoilsport, you just have to know how to keep the others away. We'll go dancing again, Petal." Dax winked, sending butterflies everywhere. Their attention heated my skin, and I suddenly wanted to return to the room and forget about this lunch.

"Please follow me," the butler said, pulling me from my lust daze.

The four of us trailed him down the stairs and to a room. I'd hoped we would get a tour of the place. It was gorgeous and massive. There was no telling what kind of rooms they had here at Chateau Conway.

When we approached a set of wooden double doors, another man opened them, bowing his head in our direction. The butler stopped, not stepping foot into the room.

"There are cards on your plates to let you know where to sit," he said before spinning and walking off in a different direction.

The staff here were odd. They were polite, but they

never showed any emotion. Maybe that was what the Conways wanted, but it seemed strange to me.

The table before us was huge, but only a portion had been set with place settings. There were three on the side, two on another, with one at the head. Walking forward, I glanced at the cards, finding all three guys sitting together with my name next to Carly's.

"Oh my God, I'm going to be sitting next to her," I panted, fanning my face. The guys chuckled, watching me.

"It's going to be hard to keep our eyes off you in that dress, Hen," Fletcher said, stopping my freak-out. I was starting to rethink the whole dress thing. If they responded this way, it could be worth the pain. It just needed to have pockets. Those were a must.

A door opened to the right stopping my rambling thoughts, and Carly Conway floated through, her scarves floating behind her like wings. She appeared even more majestic in person. I knew she had to be in her fifties since I'd watched her play when I was a little girl, but I wouldn't have known it by looking at her. She smiled at me as she approached, and I almost fainted.

"Henley, I'm so happy you were able to accept my invitation. It's lovely to see you, dear." She stepped toward me, enveloping me in a hug, her scarves and perfume embracing me.

I was at a loss for words, so I just hugged her back,

hoping I wasn't drooling on her. She pulled back, smiling at me as she looked me over.

"Did you find everything okay? This dress looks darling on you. I'm so glad you picked this one."

I nodded, too many words wanting to exit at the same time.

"What Henley is trying to say is that it's been wonderful. Thank you for your hospitality," Fletcher said, jumping in to save me like a well-bred pro.

I turned to him, finding him smiling at me, giving me time to compose myself.

"Yes, thank you. Your home is so beautiful."

"Ah, bless you. We do love our home," Carly said, turning to the man I hadn't seen enter. He was tall with dark hair and eyes. His frame was slim, and he wore a black sweater and pants. Everything about him was dark, from his features to his outerwear. He smiled down at Carly, the action changing his whole face.

"It's been a labor of love. Please, have a seat. Lunch will be served shortly." He gestured toward the table, pushing us all into motion.

"This is my husband, Geoffrey," Carly said as she turned to me. "I have to say. I was surprised when Dmitry said you'd have three suitors traveling with you."

"Oh, um, yes. Our relationship isn't conventional, but it's what works for us," I said, placing the napkin in my lap. I didn't want to be rude, but I wasn't ashamed of our relationship and wouldn't let anyone else make me feel that way.

"Well, I think it's lovely. More women should feel empowered to do what they want. My family disapproved of Geoffrey, but I said 'screw it' and married him, anyway."

The door opposite the one Carly entered through opened as waiters appeared with food bowls. They set them down in front of us before leaving as quietly as they'd come.

"This is my favorite," Carly said, picking up her spoon. I glanced at the guys who'd already picked up theirs and tried the soup. I followed suit, surprised by the flavor as it rolled over my tongue.

"Oh, that's delicious," I said, licking my lips. Carly chuckled, nodding as she continued to eat. She never offered to tell me what it was, and her husband ate silently. It was a bit odd, but I wasn't one to judge. If they were happy, then it was none of my business.

"How did you two meet?" Fletcher asked after a few minutes.

"It's not that interesting," Carly said, dabbing the corners of her mouth.

"What she means is that it was a scandal," Geoffrey offered, speaking up. His voice was deep, surprising me.

"None of that, Geoffrey. They don't want to hear old tales."

"But I love a good love story," I said, trying.

"Hmph," she said, tapping her fingers on the table. I realized we were prying into this woman's life. It wasn't what we were here for.

"Sorry, you don't have to tell us. We're strangers," I said, fiddling with the cloth napkin.

"It's alright, dear. I just haven't had anyone ask in so long." She glanced at her husband, admiration and love passing between them. She reached across and took his hand, setting their joined palms on the table. "I met Geoffrey my first year playing at UNC. He drove the Zamboni at the hockey rink."

"I used to wait until her games to clear it so it would be fresh for her, and I'd get to see her," he said.

"My family didn't think he was good enough for me and wanted me to focus on my career. I listened to them at first, but by the time I was twenty-two, I knew he was the one for me."

"At that point, I'd started my own Zamboni company and had employees that worked for me. But it didn't matter. I was still the kid who worked a blue-collar job to them. I hadn't gone to college, but I'd made something of myself."

"So I told my parents they could either get behind our marriage or not, but I was going to marry him. They eventually came around, but it took a while. And now Geoffrey owns an empire. He's worth more than my family and my hockey career."

It was a cute story, making you want to cheer for their love. They told it together, finishing each other's sentences, showing their undeniable bond. But that pit in my stomach reappeared, making my smile tight. Something felt off about it, but I didn't know what.

More food appeared so the conversation changed, and I pushed the anxiety aside, wanting to focus on the people in the room. So far, Carly had stayed on safe topics, asking the guys what they did and how they liked Lux. Fletcher did most of the talking with Dax, interjecting occasionally. Reed was silent, only answering questions that were directed at him with minimal words. It was a surreal experience to be sitting in the home of Carly Conway and eating a meal with her.

I couldn't forget why we were here, though, so once dessert was delivered, I broached the subject.

"Dmitry said you might have some ideas on how I can fight the media and Dakota's claims?"

She waved me off, picking her napkin up and placing it over her plate.

"No discussion of those matters at the table, dear. We'll focus on that later. We need to hurry so we don't miss the party." She stood, pushing her chair back. My mind spun, not understanding what she was saying.

"Party? What party?" I asked.

"Just a little get-together I'm throwing in your honor. Some close friends of ours wanted to meet you. It was on the itinerary. Didn't you get one?" she asked, looking at our faces when none of us stood.

I cleared my throat and shook my head, trying to

remember what it said. "I believe it said drinks by the pool. I didn't realize that was with other people."

"Hmph, well, I understand if you don't want to join us, but it might appear rude to the guests that have arrived."

I glanced at the guys, feeling like I'd just experienced whiplash. "I could go for a swim. We didn't bring any swimwear," I hedged.

She waved her hand, walking into her husband's arms. "There are plenty of suits in the pool house. Come on. We can't have the party without the guest of honor."

Carly motioned for me to follow her, taking my choice away after giving me one a second ago. I was trapped in a loop. What I wanted was only an illusion. I had to go; otherwise, I'd appear rude and be labeled a bitch. But if I cooperated, I told them they could break my boundaries, and my choice didn't matter.

The polite thing would be to go along with her demands since she'd invited us here, and ninety-eight percent of my body was already agreeing and accepting the choice that had been made for me. But that two percent wanted me to fight for myself.

The guys stood, watching and waiting, as I stalled in my chair with indecision. Why did this feel like such a pivotal moment?

But as the loop commanded, I succumbed to the pressure of politeness, forgoing my consent. I prayed that the two percent screaming to hold my boundaries was the trauma part of me that never trusted anything —that or indigestion.

Yep, my inner voice had been whittled down to trauma and indigestion. What did that say about me?

Ignoring everything, I stood and took the hand outstretched for me with a forced smile on my face.

# CHAPTER 20

## *Dax*

SOMETHING about this situation felt off, but I couldn't put my finger on why. I was the only non-hockey player in our group, so maybe I was overreacting. But the look on Petal's face had me following close behind, just in case.

I'd worked with a lot of rich people, so I knew they could be odd at times, and this lady was no exception. The dynamic between her and her husband was strange, along with the dress code and itinerary. I didn't understand the purpose, but I brushed it off as my past clouding my view. If this lady could help Henley, then I'd do whatever crazy things they suggested as long as she was okay. And so far, no request had been too far out in left field.

"Here's the pool house. Please exit the other side into the pool area when you're dressed. Everyone is already there."

Carly and Geoffrey turned and went down a different hall, leaving the four of us standing in the hallway before a door.

"Was that weird? That was weird, right?" Petal

whispered, making my anxiety spike. Shit. If she felt something, then maybe I wasn't overreacting.

"A little, but I think it's harmless," Fletcher said, shrugging. "Let's go inside before we're caught by someone whispering out here."

He pushed open the door and led the way through the pool house in his calm and collected way. We entered into an oversized bathroom with four shower heads along the wall with partitions dividing them. On the lower part of a wall were two rows of cubby storage with towels and sandals stuffed in the bottom ones and baskets with guests' names in the top. Above it, a rack hung filled with swim shorts and suits in various sizes and colors.

Picking up a pair of trunks, I turned them around to inspect them. They looked like basic black board shorts, but the price tag sticking off them listed them at a hundred and fifty dollars. Was the material made of mermaid's tears or something crazy like that? Fuck.

"I still find it creepy that they have our sizes," Henley muttered as she pushed a few swimsuits aside to find one she liked.

"A pool house with extra suits isn't all that strange. That's more common than you'd think," Fletcher said, folding his clothes to put into the basket. He was so unaffected by this whole thing, it made me question myself more.

"Really? I keep waiting for them to have life-size mannequins of us stashed somewhere to try them on,"

Reed grunted, looking over his shoulder like he expected it to jump out.

Henley pointed, nodding. "Yes. See!" She turned to Fletcher with her hands on her hips, her eyes so wide, I didn't think she could blink. Okay, maybe it was just Fletcher who'd drank the Kool-Aid.

Fletcher stopped folding, looking up at the three of us, and realized he was the only one who'd changed. His brows dipped as his lips turned down, making his beard move as he glanced at us back and forth.

"Did I miss something?"

"Something's nagging at me. I don't know what it is. Just a feeling," Henley said, releasing a breath.

Fletcher relaxed, walking over to place his hands on her shoulders. "I'm sure today has been a lot. You met someone you admire, plus the anxiety of dealing with all the stuff back at Lux. Take a deep breath and remember that we've got you. You're not alone in this, Baby Shaw."

Henley took a deep breath, her eyes closing as she let the tension out of her body. She took one more, her shoulders dropping back before she opened her eyes.

"You good?" Fletcher asked, and Henley nodded. "Now, I think you should wear this one." He picked up a yellow and black two-piece and handed it to her. The top looked similar to a sports bra, the bottom more like shorts.

"And here I thought you'd pick the string bikini,"

she teased. Seeing her more relaxed, in turn, released the tension in me.

"If it was just us. Fuck yes. But I don't know who these guests are. I don't want anyone else to be getting a look at our woman," Fletcher growled, tilting her chin up in his hands.

I watched as Henley sucked in a breath, her eyes dilating at his words. My fingers itched to reach out and make her scream my name in their presence. The desire to stake my claim was strong as I figured out my place in this relationship.

I knew our individual one was growing, and I was secure in where it was, but the one between the four of us was still new to me. I didn't know where I stood when we were all together. It didn't help that I knew they'd both been with her before, making me feel like I was still on the sidelines watching.

Henley gulped and nodded. "I'll wear this one."

Fletcher smiled, kissing her before he stepped back. I glanced over at Reed, finding him watching as well. He didn't appear jealous, but it was hard to gauge Reed's emotions most of the time. He was either stoic or pissed. I was still learning the other sides of him.

Reed turned, catching me staring at him. He lifted a brow when I didn't say anything. Shaking my head at his unspoken question, I pulled the shorts off the hanger and walked to a bench to change. I kept my hair pulled back, not wanting to deal with it when it got wet. Snagging a towel and sandals, I glanced at the others.

When I spotted Henley, I sucked in a breath. The swimsuit didn't show much skin, but it hugged her in all the right ways, displaying her curves and ass.

"Fuck. If you look that hot in this one, I'm afraid I would've died of a heart attack in the other," I whispered.

Henley blushed, putting on a black see-through robe. It fluttered around her, covering up her body. It was a shame but necessary in this crowd of strangers.

"Thank God for that," Reed hissed, swiping his hand through his hair. "I'm with Dax. You look amazing, Hen."

"Me? Look at you three with your stupid abs on display! I'm going to push a lot of women into the pool today," she sighed, wrapping her arms under her chest. It pushed up her boobs, making them even more delicious looking.

"We can wear shirts if you want?" I asked, grabbing one. "I don't enjoy being mauled by older women who think it's okay to touch me."

"Good point," Fletcher said, with Reed hot on his tail to grab a shirt.

It was just a cotton shirt, but it was soft and covered my upper body. If I were going to get in the pool, I'd take it off, but just standing around and talking to people, I'd rather have more layers. Henley nodded in approval, her arms dropping to her sides as she smiled.

"Should we do this then?" I asked, motioning to the door.

"Yeah, let's get it over with." She walked toward the other side of the pool house, taking a second to take a deep breath before she pulled the door. The instant it was open, loud music poured in, making me question the insulation of this place. We hadn't heard a peep until the door opened.

The three of us caught up to her, stepping out onto the pool deck as she did. The place was packed with people drinking and dancing with a few in the pool. It was a mix of young and old guests, some looking familiar.

"Holy shit, is that Taylor Serrano?" Henley gasped. Her head swung to the other side, her hand pointing out more people. "And Abbie Vaughns and Lucas Harrell!"

"And that's Matt Gibson," Fletcher said, his voice just as shocked.

"You've lost me," I said, stopping when I spotted one of my old clients from LA. "Shit. Um, guys..." I turned, but they'd moved to the other side, talking to some people I didn't know.

Ducking my head, I hoped I'd kept myself hidden as I rushed to catch up. I'd never felt at a disadvantage on campus by not playing the same sport as all of them, but here, among what I assumed was hockey royalty, I did.

Eyes trailed us, but people stayed in their spots as they talked to their companions. Everyone was dressed similarly, with the women wearing a wrap or cover-up, their tops on display. Most men wore open shirts, giving glimpses of their chests, while others had shirts on, like the three of us. There was a handful that strutted around, preening for attention.

I kept gathering information as I cataloged the crowd, wanting to know who we were up against. It made me feel like I was back in LA among the social elite, never measuring up to their standards. Shaking off the unwanted feelings, I focused on our group.

Henley chatted animatedly with a woman a few years older than her. Reed and Fletcher were likewise engaged in a conversation with one of the biggest guys I'd ever seen. He was at eye level with them sitting down. His arms were crossed over his chest and were as big as a tree trunk. This guy either worked out for hours a day to build those muscles or used something to help him. Something told me it was the latter.

I didn't see Carly or her husband anywhere in the crowd. Nor could I figure out how we'd missed all these people coming into the house. A caterer walked by with a tray of drinks, so I grabbed one, hoping it helped ease some of the crazy feelings I had rushing through me. Lifting the glass, I placed it against my lips as I surveyed the crowd.

"Dax? It is you!"

My eyes bulged as I took in the person across from me. The sip I'd just taken left me in surprise, spraying everywhere as I stared. She jumped back, avoiding my sprinkler impression, her face tight with worry.

"Jenny? What are you doing here?" I whispered, my voice vacating the premises, along with my confidence, as my eyes stayed locked on the woman who'd broken my heart.

"Oh, we're here—"

Before he even interrupted, I knew in that instant my brother was also there.

"*Brother*. Interesting bumping into you here. I didn't realize you knew anyone in this tax bracket." He laughed, wrapping his arm around Jenny and pulling her to him. My eyes shuttered, and I wished I was literally anywhere else but here. I'd take Gareth punching my face in again to avoid this agony.

"Funny, Derek. You really missed your calling as a comedian." I tossed back the last of the glass, swallowing it this time before anyone else could jump out and surprise me.

"It's good to see you, Dax," Jenny said, her voice sad. I didn't know what she had to be sad about. She was the one who'd cheated on me with my brother and was now getting married to him.

"Can't say the same," I grumbled, shifting on my feet. Derek watched me, searching for something.

"So, really, what are you doing here?" he asked. It

was stated as a question, but there was no missing the command in his voice to answer it this time.

"Oh, you know. I ran out of important clients to scam in LA, so I thought I'd try Oregon. Got any friends you want to introduce me to?"

Derek's eyes narrowed, his mouth tightening in a line. When I'd been arrested, it had brought shame to our family, so my joking about it was not appreciated by my brother. I snorted, finding the whole thing funny. He pretended to care, but he was really only interested in his career and the fallout he'd face.

"Did you follow us here? This is a private event for a very important—"

"Dax, there's someone I'd like you to meet," Henley's voice said, her arm wrapping around my waist. I'd almost forgotten they were here. I didn't know if any of them had heard the conversation or not. At least I'd already shared this garbage with them, so it wouldn't be a dumpster fire waiting to happen.

Tilting my head to peer at her, I spotted concern and a touch of possessiveness in her eyes. Henley had heard enough to be pissed on my behalf. I sank into her touch, wrapping my arm around her shoulders and drawing her closer.

"Who's that, Petal?" I purred, not even having to try when I looked at her. My body automatically turned toward her, the crowd fading until it was just the two of us.

"Hi, I'm Jenny, Derek's fiancee." A hand appeared

between us, breaking the spell we'd fallen under. We turned back to face them, Henley's smile in place as she took the hand.

"It's nice to meet you. I'm Henley, Dax's girl-friend." She said it with such ease I melted on the spot. "And I'm assuming you're Derek? His brother who slept with his girlfriend?"

If I'd taken another drink, I would've spewed it all over them at her words. Henley had just stood up for me and taken my brother down a peg in the same breath, sealing herself permanently on my heart. I could no longer claim that I wasn't in love with the girl. This right here cemented it. I just didn't know what to do with that.

Derek sputtered, his face turning red at being called out. Jenny withdrew into herself as shame covered her features. I watched as my brother did nothing to comfort her, more enraged his character had been attacked. For the first time since she broke my heart, I felt sad for Jenny.

Derek wasn't a better man than me. If anything, he was worse. He was consumed by his goal to become the governor. He didn't care about Jenny's feelings, just that she was a hot piece of ass he could easily control. The fact he got to stick it to me as well had been a bonus. I could see it all now, and it made me feel pity for her.

But that was all I felt when I looked at her. *Pity.* Gone was the love and lust I thought I'd never lose.

She glanced up, catching me staring, and her eyes sparked, a smile growing as she looked at me. I quickly turned back to Henley, not wanting to give Jenny the wrong impression.

"That's ancient history. The question I'd like to know is why you're here? I'm not going to let you take advantage of these people." Derek puffed up his chest like he was single-handedly saving the upper echelon from my swindling ways.

"Speaking of ancient history," I muttered, rolling my eyes. Derek professed he wanted us to reunite, but the second I stepped anywhere near his world, he made it his goal to put me in my place—beneath his foot.

"Henley! There you are, my dear. It's time for me to announce you as my special guest. Come, come." Carly gestured for us to follow her.

I wasn't sure if she'd overheard my brother, but the timing had been impeccable. Not able to stop myself, I took one more look at my brother, his face stuck between a look of shock and torment. It made me wish I had my phone so I could capture it and use it for my screensaver.

# CHAPTER 21

## Henley

DAX'S HAND clutched mine like a lifeline, and I berated myself for not noticing sooner that he needed me. I'd gotten so caught up in meeting people that I'd left him behind. Then he'd been ambushed by the two people who made him question his worth.

Jenny wasn't how I'd pictured her in my head. She had a heart-shaped face, soft brown eyes, and perfect hair. There wasn't a strand of her brunette strands out of place. She didn't even have any frizz, a miracle in itself and something I envied. The most surprising observation was how sweet she seemed. There hadn't been any jealousy in her eyes; if anything, I caught sadness and perhaps some regret. She didn't seem like the type to cheat on her boyfriend, making me wonder how much had been Dax's brother's influence.

There was no doubt Derek was a shark pretending to be a goldfish.

He had that same cold yet perfect smile that my ex-boyfriend wore. He was an opportunist, waiting for any moment to exploit for his gain. His eyes were the same color as Dax's but completely different in their depths. They'd raked over my body, making me feel dirty as they filled with rage when I'd claimed Dax. It was unsettling.

We'd need to watch him. I didn't trust he'd let Dax thrive. He needed Dax to suffer to feel superior for whatever reason.

"You okay?" I asked as Carly led us through the crowd of people.

"Yeah. Because of you, I am." Dax squeezed my hand, the corners of his mouth tilting up the slightest.

"You've got me and the others, Dax. We're here for you. Don't forget that."

His emerald eyes scanned my face, searching for something. I let him, knowing he needed to find his landing ground after his encounter with his brother. Not for one second had I thought he wanted Jenny. I hadn't felt threatened or insecure by her presence, and I knew that was because of Dax. He showed me how he felt about me in a million ways, and I trusted him.

I wondered if he even realized it had been his brother's presence that had made him stiffen? Not hers.

Cupping my cheek in his hand, he kissed me, his mouth pressed hard as his tongue demanded entrance. My mind went woozy, the taste of his lips on mine the only thing I noticed. He pulled back a fraction, his eyes no longer searching as he stared straight into my soul.

"You're it for me, Petal. I'm all in. No more straddling the line. No more standing back. I'm here for the long haul."

"I know, Dax. It's been written all over your face for at least a week."

Shocked, he blinked before a grin spread across his face, changing him into a new person as some of the shadows he carried fell away.

A throat cleared, reminding us we'd stopped in the middle of the crowd. I peered over Dax's shoulder, spotting Reed and Fletcher a few feet away. They hadn't gone far but gave us enough space to have the moment while keeping Carly contained.

"Come on, Petal, let's go see what shenanigans this lady has in store for us now." He winked, linking our hands, and we continued on our path. Reed and Fletcher started back when we neared, giving Dax a nod of support.

Carly gave me a tight smile, and I felt terrible for making her wait, but I wouldn't deny my men if they needed something. She might be my role model, but they were my heart. There was no hesitation when it came to them.

That proclamation surprised me, but I knew I meant it with every fiber of my being.

"Henley," Carly beckoned, reaching her hand out for mine. Keeping my polite smile in place, I took it, squeezing Dax's one last time before I let go. He stood beside Reed and Fletcher, forming a sexy and formidable trio behind me.

Standing next to one of the most decorated women's hockey players, I tried to remember why I was here and not focus on how hot my boyfriends were and the activities she was keeping us from.

"Good afternoon, everyone. I'm beyond honored you've all graced me with your presence today. I'd like you to meet my guest, Henley Henshaw. You might know her from her days of playing for Cambridge Cardinals or her achievements at the past two winter Olympics." She turned and smiled like a proud parent.

The whole thing made me feel weird. Maybe because I'd never had any parent be proud of me, so it was a foreign concept, or perhaps it was the beauty contest/cattle auction vibes I was getting.

Whatever it was, I wasn't fond of it. I suddenly wondered if I'd stepped into something bigger than I'd intended. I'd been so excited when I heard her name and the fact that she wanted to help me that I hadn't stopped to question the why or how.

The crowd's hungry gaze fell over my body, the desire to cover myself growing stronger by the minute. Why would Carly choose a pool party to introduce me to people? At least everyone was dressed similarly, but I felt more naked than I wanted to be around a crowd of strangers, famous ones or not.

The way everyone kept staring at me, I wondered if they were waiting for me to break out in song or perform an interpretive dance. Perhaps I should moo? How did cattle exert their status?

A giggle escaped before I could choke it down, my nerves beginning to show as my mind jumped from one ridiculous solution to the next. Deciding on a wave, I lifted my hand and wiggled my fingers. I was about to bow when Carly grabbed my hand and pulled it down, stopping all movement.

With a strained face, Carly turned back to the crowd. "Henley and her companions will be around this afternoon and this evening. Please take a moment to introduce yourself and meet this upcoming star. Dinner is at 6 pm for those staying. Now, have some drinks and enjoy the afternoon."

The crowd cheered, returning to their conversations and drinks as the music played restarted. Carly squeezed the hand she held, grabbing my attention.

"This would be an excellent opportunity to meet some allies. Don't forget that all eyes are on you here. Everything you do will be remembered. I'd advised not to make enemies of anyone."

Too late for that. Her words were cryptic, delivered with a smile, and had my insides squirming.

"The pool party will end at 4 pm, so there's enough time to change and be presentable for dinner. Don't be late; that's where the real fun begins."

She continued to grip my hand, and I realized she was waiting for a response.

"Yes, of course. Thank you for having us here." It was all I could muster, still unsure how I felt about everything now that I was seeing beyond the glitz and glamor. There was something else at play behind the wealth and prestige; I just wasn't sure what it was yet.

Dropping my hand, she made a small noise of acceptance before she turned and disappeared into the crowd. Now that I wasn't forced to pretend, I dropped my smile and noticed her husband hadn't been with her. Nor had she changed into a bathing suit. Maybe more telling was that she hadn't mentioned that I was coaching at Lux. I didn't know her agenda, but I was beginning to believe it had nothing to do with me.

Scanning the crowd, I looked around the enclosed space, noticing the heating lamps and tinted glass. The area resembled a pool deck you'd find in southern Florida, tricking your mind into thinking you were there instead of Oregon.

Hands snaked around my belly, pulling me back into a hard body. I kept searching the room as they dropped their head onto my shoulder.

"What do you think?" Fletcher whispered as Reed and Dax came to my sides.

"I'm not sure. Something is going on. I don't know what."

"Agreed. We need to stay vigilant until we do," Fletcher responded.

"I have a feeling if my brother is involved, then it's not good. Plus, I saw an old client. I don't think we can trust anyone," Dax whispered.

"No one let Henley out of their sight," Reed commanded.

"I can take care of myself." The guys started to protest. "That being said, I'll stay with someone. I'm not taking any chances." They all collectively exhaled at my statement, making me chuckle.

"So, what do we do now?" Fletcher asked.

I shrugged, his beard brushing against my shoulder in the process. "There's Dax's brother to avoid, but otherwise, I guess we mingle?" I cringed, not knowing how I felt about that. I'd noticed people kept tossing our four-some glances over their shoulders every few minutes.

"There's Anya Kerr. I know her from college. She might be safe," I said, waving when she spotted me.

"Except, remember that friend I had that was connected to the Society?" Reed asked, whispering. "Riggs is with her."

"Shit. Do you think this is them?" I asked, my eyes bulging out at the thought.

"Don't know. But he hadn't returned my call, so I guess we can go see why."

"We need to stay even more alert then, if this is potentially 'you know who,'" Fletcher added.

Agreeing, I stepped out of his embrace and walked to Anya. She waved when I neared, smiling at me. The guys stayed back, talking amongst themselves.

"Henley. It's so nice to see you again. What has it been, six years?" she asked, hugging me and kissing my cheeks.

"Something like that. How are things with you?"

"Oh, you know, playing for Toronto still. I'm just getting back after maternity leave."

"Wow, congrats! That's so awesome."

She eyed the guys, then me, a question on her face. "You sure keep interesting friends. That's Reed Cole, right?"

I nodded, curious about where she was going with this. "Yep, and Fletcher Cromwell. Frankie's brother. We all work together at Lux Brumalis."

Her eyes widened as she took a sip. "You're not playing?"

"Um, no. Not this year. There was a whole thing with the league. I'm coaching my sibling at Lux for now."

"Coaching? What an interesting career choice."

"It's been amazing. I hadn't ever considered it, but I'm glad I did. It's revealing the parts of myself I'd buried long ago."

She gave a tight smile at my answer, and I tried to remember if it had always been this way between us and I hadn't noticed, or if it was new.

"I was sorry to hear about you and Dakota," she finally said, placing her hand on my arm. It was cold and clammy, and I didn't like it at all. I shuffled my feet, stepping back a smidge so her hand fell away.

"I'm not. We weren't right together, and he's shown his true colors and intentions by leaking the video. Dakota is all about himself, and no one else matters. I'm much happier now that I'm out of his clutches."

"Mmm, well, good for you then."

It grew quiet again, and I knew I needed to ask one last question before I couldn't take the awkwardness anymore.

"How do you know Carly?" I asked.

"You know how it is. So and so knows someone, who knows someone, and then before long, you know them. She was helpful to me a few years ago in my career and this past season while I was pregnant. You're so lucky that she's taken notice of you. Your whole life is about to change, Henley."

I tried to recall Anya's career and what she would've needed help with a few years ago. Her words felt empty outside of some jealousy that I didn't quite understand.

"I'll keep that in mind. It was great catching up with you, Anya."

"You too, Henley. Don't be a stranger now that you're part of the club."

"Club?" I asked.

"Carly's, you know..." She waved her hands around like she was looking for a word. When she didn't find one, she smiled and turned around to talk to someone else.

I glanced back, finding Reed had been watching.

"That was strange, right?"

"Very. I'm starting to wonder if we should leave."

I bit my lip, debating what he was suggesting. While things were secretive and odd, nothing had been over the line yet. It could be our only chance to find some answers and get ahead of Dakota.

"Not yet. There's still too much to discover."

Reed nodded, accepting my answer, and I prayed I hadn't led us into a bad situation.

# CHAPTER 22

## *Henley*

WHEN THE BUTLER came out to announce the end of the pool party, I instantly sighed in relief. It had been a lot of work to mingle and pretend to be the old Henley—the one who cared about social necessities and others' opinions. It felt like a wet suit I'd put on. Too tight and chafing a little to the left.

"We'll have to continue this conversation at dinner, Henley," the couple I was talking to said as we headed to different pool houses. I guess that explained why we hadn't seen anyone.

The butler waited for us, directing our group to the pool house we'd entered earlier. He didn't stop when we got inside, continuing through the door to the house and ignoring the few people inside already changing.

"A warning would've been nice," Reed muttered as we exited. I snorted but agreed. I hadn't been prepared to see an older man's bare ass as he got into the shower. At least it hadn't been the front. The butler ignored us, pretending not to have heard or perhaps not caring.

"Your belongings have been transferred to your

rooms. You have two hours before dinner is served. Use them wisely as late guests are not permitted entry."

With that, he turned on his heels and marched down the hall, the tails on his tuxedo jacket flying out behind him.

"If anyone asks, the butler did it," Dax said as the man in question turned the corner.

The three of us laughed at his assessment. This place screamed murder mystery. I hoped we weren't the victims.

On our way to our rooms, I was surprised we'd been left unattended for the first time since we'd arrived. It was still odd that there didn't seem to be another soul in the house. All those people and it was as quiet as a church mouse in here. I didn't even spot any other staff as we climbed the stairs.

When we made it to the hallway our rooms were in, we all filed into mine without question. Once the door shut, I wanted to relax, but Fletcher held up his hand and pulled out his phone.

FLETCHER:

Be careful what you say. There could be listening devices.

REED

Why aren't we leaving again?

DAX

I'm with the quiet one.

HENLEY

I think there's info we can learn. It hasn't been dangerous.

REED

Yet.

Riggs was evasive. Anyone else have luck?

HENLEY

Nothing concrete. Anya was strange.

DAX

My brother's here. Whatever this is, it's got enough clout he either wants in or already is.

He's only focused on one thing. Power.

FLETCHER

I agree but also feel Henley is right. While it might feel weird, it's not dangerous. We should stay to see what info we can obtain.

I bit my lip as I paced. My mind raced, possibilities running through. To distract myself, I checked in on Reese.

HENLEY

Hey, kiddo. How are you doing?

I flipped back over to the guys' messages while I waited for them to respond. They'd continued to talk while I'd spaced out.

FLETCHER

Do you think the girl knows?

DAX

Jenny? Probably, but I'm not talking to her.

REED

He's in politics? That makes it harder to gauge since most everyone else was hockey.

FLETCHER

There were a few Fortune 500 people and CEOs, politicians included. They all kept to themselves.

DAX

How do you know all these people? I wouldn't know a politician if they were right in front of me. And that's saying something.

FLETCHER

I just do. Maybe watch a different channel other than bodybuilder ones.

REED

I didn't notice them either.

DAX

Is that what happens when you get older? You watch the news?

FLETCHER

What? Become more aware of the world around you?

REED

Boring is the word I think he was referring to.

HENLEY

Focus. We're not interrogating Fletcher for being more woke than the rest of us.

The guys chuckled as I rolled my eyes. I switched back over to Reese's text conversation when I felt it vibrate in my hand.

REESE

Sore, but nothing I can't manage. What's Carly like?

HENLEY

She's… interesting. Not like I expected at all.

REESE

Oh? What have you done so far? Is she going to help?

HENLEY

We haven't discussed that yet. We had lunch and then attended a pool party. Now, we're getting ready for dinner. There's a bunch of guests staying.

REESE

Your life is so cool.

HENLEY

It's something.

> If I don't check in again tonight, send me an update later so I know you're okay.

REESE

> Yes, big sis. *Eye roll emoji*

HENLEY

> Love you lots, tiny terror.

REESE

> Ha. Love ya too.

The guys were quiet, so I looked up, finding them watching me. I placed the phone down beside me on the bed.

"Checking in with Reese," I said.

"We know. You had your big sister smile on," Fletcher said.

Blushing, I leaned back on my elbows. "So, what's the plan? Get dressed and go from there?"

"Yeah, I guess that's a good start," Dax said, rubbing his hand over his head.

"What do you want us to do if your brother is there?"

He shrugged his shoulders, peering around the room like he was hoping the right choice would jump out and hit him over the head.

"Okay, we'll try to avoid him as much as possible, then. Should we have a code word or something in case... you know?" I asked, lifting my shoulders.

The guys looked at one another before moving

closer. Fletcher pulled me up, and they enclosed me in the middle of them. My body started to get ideas with them so near, focusing on the lust instead of the anxiety.

Leaning close, Fletcher whispered in my ear. "You're not very good at being a spy, Baby Shaw."

Giggling, my face flushed. He was right. I'd make a terrible spy. The only time I didn't broadcast my feelings was when I had blades strapped to my feet.

"Sorry."

"Don't be. It makes you who you are. How about tacos?"

I nodded, looking at the other two. They smiled, letting me know they'd heard Fletcher as well.

"Okay, good work, team. I'll see you in a bit?" My voice cracked as I tried to swallow down the desire.

"Can't wait," Reed said, stepping away first. The space gave me a second to breathe, my heart slowing from the gallop it had sped off at.

Dax winked, following Reed out the door and leaving Fletcher and me. Looking up at him, I sucked in a breath when I caught the look in his eyes. His lips fell to mine, stealing my breath more, his tongue dominating as he ravished my mouth.

"I've wanted to kiss you for hours. That should hold me over until later." He placed one more kiss on my nose before he let go and walked to the door, leaving me panting in his wake.

It took a few more minutes for me to collect

myself. When I saw the time, I raced to the closet, searching through the choices for the evening. The card from earlier said a long dress was required for dinner. There was a black one with sequins that was pretty but not my style. A coral one with a weird cut about it, and a pink one with a few too many ruffles. Pass and pass.

When my hands landed on the royal blue one, I was instantly in love. It was simple but elegant, with a high slit up the front. The skirt flared out at the waist, the top had a small v with skinny straps. There was no way I could wear a bra with it, though. I hadn't brought a strapless with me, so I'd have to try to go without. The mechanics of being a woman sucked.

Pulling off the swimsuit, I tossed it into the laundry basket in the bathroom. I didn't know if I should take it or not, so I'd err on the side of caution and not. Plus, I wasn't sure I ever wanted to wear it again and remember that bizarro pool party.

As I slipped on some underwear from my bag, I thought about the range of emotions I'd experienced since being here—nerves, excitement, anxiety, happiness, awe, anger, fear, and, lastly, disappointment.

I'd placed a lot of value on coming here, hoping that Carly would be the key to fighting my battles. Instead, it seemed I'd walked into something I wasn't prepared for. If this was the Society, how could it be bad if all these other people were involved? I knew a handful of them and had always thought they were nice, hardworking, and focused. I didn't think they'd be part of a sinister organization.

Remembering I'd wanted to look up what Anya was talking about, I walked to the bed and picked up my phone. Typing her name into the search bar, I grew frustrated when nothing outside her stats, social media posts, and news of her baby appeared. Tapping my finger against the case, I tried to think of who I knew who might know. An idea popped into my head, but I debated if it was wise or not to invite that attention in.

Taking a chance, I sent a text to an acquaintance in the media, hoping they'd remember what I was referring to and not sell me out.

I dropped the phone back on the bed and returned to the closet to pull on the dress. I had it up over my body when the door opened. I froze, peeking around to see who it was. At the sight of Reed, I relaxed.

"Can you zip me up?"

"Absolutely." He stepped further in, and my mouth watered as I took in his delicious suit.

"Damn, Reed. You look hot."

His cheeks turned red as he approached me, making me smile. I loved when I could surprise him.

"I could say the same about you." His fingers skimmed over my back before reaching the zipper. He lifted it so slowly, the pads of his thumbs caressing my skin in the process. "I don't know what I enjoy more. Zipping you in or out."

My body heated at his words, and I fanned myself, unable to control the lust. If they hadn't harped on the time for dinner so much, I'd have ripped off our clothes and had my way with him right that second.

"Thank you," I said, clearing my throat. "I'll be right back."

I grabbed my bag and took it into the bathroom, shutting the door to provide much-needed distance. I touched up my makeup, applying more mascara and lipstick this time. Brushing my hair back, I secured it into a low ponytail at the base of my neck. Adding on more deodorant, I spritzed my perfume and gargled some mouthwash, careful not to drip.

Stepping back from the mirror, I gave my skirt a little twirl as I took in my appearance. The dress brought out the blue in my eyes and went well with my complexion. It fit perfectly, again making me wonder how that was possible.

"I always thought my stalker would be a dude, but I guess there are perks to it being a woman," I mumbled as I exited the bathroom. I stopped a few feet from it as I took in the three men standing in my bedroom.

"Wow, you guys look incredible!" Their suits were a similar charcoal gray, but they each wore different color shirts and ties.

Reed wore a crisp white shirt with a black tie and fit him to perfection. I got lost looking at him again. Remembering I had two more boyfriends to drool over,

I turned to Dax. He'd pulled his hair down, his blond locks curly around his face. His shirt was the same color as the suit, with a green tie that almost matched his eyes. It was stunning, and I swallowed as I took him in. Turning to Fletcher, I didn't know if I'd survive, but oh, what a way to go out.

His shirt was black, his tie a deep red, and I wondered for half a second if he was related to the king of the underworld because he looked sinful standing there.

"How much time do we have?" I asked, my voice husky.

"Not enough," Dax growled, his eyes on me. "You look divine, Petal."

"He's not wrong, Baby Shaw. You're breathtaking."

I grinned, liking how their compliments made me feel. It never hurt for a sexy guy to tell you that you were divine and breathtaking. Sign me up for that all day long.

"Shall we?" I asked, glancing at the time.

The guys nodded, motioning for me to walk ahead of them. I stepped through the door and glanced back, watching as they did a quick round of paper, rock, scissors. When Reed and Dax won, they smiled and walked forward, taking my arms. Fletcher cursed, but good-naturedly followed behind.

We still didn't see anyone as we descended the stairs, where a staff member was waiting for us.

"Follow me. We'll be dining in the grand ballroom."

Lifting my eyebrows, I mouthed "grand ballroom" to Dax as we followed. In all my years living on this planet, I had never been to any function that required a distinction before the word ballroom. Stepping into the room, I was momentarily speechless as I took it in.

A massive chandelier hung in the center under a long table that looked to seat about twenty. Gold and ivory intertwined, with thick drapes and columns breaking up the space. Guests from earlier mingled around the room, having changed into attire similar to what we wore. It surprised me, but I guess some people were accustomed to this type of lifestyle.

The door shut a few seconds later as a clock somewhere chimed. Carly and Geoffrey appeared through another door, and I was starting to believe she had a thing for grand entrances.

"Good evening. Thank you all for being here. I look forward to the night ahead, but first, let's eat."

Caterers filled the ballroom with trays and stood behind chairs. The guests moved to the table, taking a seat. I glanced at the guys, and Fletcher took the lead, directing us where to sit.

Same as lunch, there were cards before the chairs, dictating where people sat. I relaxed when I spotted Reed's name next to mine. Dax and Fletcher went across the table and nodded when they found theirs. I didn't particularly appreciate that they weren't on the same side, but at least they were across from us.

Taking a seat, I glanced around at the other guests near us, spotting Dax's brother further down the table. Sighing, I practically jumped as the caterer placed the dish over my head and lifted the lid before strolling back toward the door they'd come through.

Everyone ate, apparently accustomed to these dinner parties and the etiquette required. I was too overwhelmed to talk, so I focused on the food and listening to the people talk around me.

# CHAPTER 23

## *Fletcher*

ON THE OUTSIDE, I portrayed a calm and collected exterior, exuding the perfect gentleman entertained by the ongoings of his surroundings. I was trying to hold it together and be the leader of our group, assuring them everything was okay.

But inside... inside, I was a fucking mess.

This all felt too familiar, too much like a life I'd left behind. One I hadn't told Henley or the guys about. I felt myself slipping back into that man with each second we were here. The one I promised myself I'd never be again. The edges were blurring, and it was becoming harder to remember where I began, and the other version ended.

I had to hold on tighter for them. They needed me to do this. To protect them.

I wouldn't fail *this time*.

So, with my weapon of choice loaded, I smiled at the other guests, pretending to be interested in their stories. If there was one thing I could do well, it was to be charming.

Dax was too self-conscious in this setting to trust

himself, especially with his brother and ex-girlfriend present.

Reed didn't give a shit about any of this, and it was obvious by the glares he sent to anyone trying to talk to him.

It left it up to me to swim among the sharks. I just had to ensure I didn't become chum, or we'd all be screwed.

"How's your family, Peter?" I asked, taking a bite of my food. We were on the second course, but it all tasted the same to me. I never acquired a taste for fine dining. I focused on my surroundings, mindlessly shoving food into my mouth.

"They're good. Gabe made the honor roll and was named captain of his hockey team, and Ariel landed the lead in the school musical. She's taking almost all AP classes as well. She's excited about college next year," Peter replied in his smarmy voice. I fucking hated this guy.

"Wow, they sure have grown so fast. I remember when Gabe had just gotten his first set of skates." My smile was tense, but he didn't seem to notice. If there was one thing you could count on for the upper echelon was their own narcissism, making them oblivious to anyone else.

"Time sure does fly. It feels like forever since Emi... Well, you know," Peter said, stopping himself, cringing slightly. My hand clutched the knife I held as anger rolled through me at his audacity to have her name in his mouth. My nostrils flared, and I had to remind myself to count to ten before answering.

These people didn't care. It didn't mean anything. They were nothing.

"Yes, well, make sure to tell the kids I said congrats," I choked out, shoving a bite of food into my mouth to chew. Peter nodded, turning to someone else, realizing his blunder.

I ate more on my plate, not wanting to see if Henley had overheard him. I didn't know if I was ready to open that door yet. I knew I'd have to sooner or later, but I'd been cashing in on the latter, hoping it never came. Emi was a part of my life that was best forgotten—even if no one else would let me.

My appetite evaporated, the taste of sawdust in my mouth. I glanced at our group, searching their faces for any clue they'd overheard. Reed and Henley were whispering together, and I hoped they had been for a while. Dax was nodding next to me; his face strained as he listened to whoever was next to him. He gripped the fork so hard his knuckles were white. I peered around him and wondered who it was.

"Hey man, I'm Fletcher Cromwell," I said, reaching to shake their hand. The man stopped whatever he was saying, his eyes brightening.

"Fletcher Cromwell. Vancouver lost a good man when you retired. It's a pleasure to meet you."

"Ah, thanks. It was hard to step back, but I'm glad I did. I'm sorry I didn't catch your name." My eyes narrowed, but my smile stayed on. Hurt one of my friends, and I'd ruin you.

"Brendan Gibbons. I own a few gyms in LA, along with the Ice Foxes," he said smugly. Inwardly, I rolled my eyes. Big. Fucking. Deal. But at least I knew how to handle this type of guy.

"How are they looking for the season?" I asked, pulling him into a conversation where he talked about himself so much he forgot about battering Dax.

I felt Dax relax next to me as the asshat rambled about the team and what players he thought would succeed. It might not be a huge thing, but it felt good knowing I'd helped Dax.

Brendan was interrupted a few minutes later when Carly announced it was time for the main event to begin. The caterers took all the plates, pointing us to the other side of the ballroom. Dax and I stood, buttoning our suit jackets as we did. Dax made a mad dash away from Brendan, so I followed, moving around the end of the table to meet up with Henley and Reed.

She might've been across the table from me, but it had felt like a million miles. Reaching out for her, my body sang as my hand wrapped around hers and pulled her to me.

"Hey, baby," I whispered into her ear, needing a moment to hold her. "You doing okay?"

She tilted back, nodding as she peered into my

eyes. "Yeah. So far, it hasn't been anything too crazy. Do you think this next part will be?"

"I'm sure it will be over the top, but not dangerous. Whoever this is, they're wooing you. This whole day has been a seduction to show you what they can do and why you should be part of them."

"How do you know?" she asked, licking her lips, my eyes dropping to them.

"I just do. It's my superpower."

She giggled, the noise so light and carefree I wanted to wrap it around me. I'd support her in whatever she decided, but these people didn't deserve someone like Henley. Just like they hadn't Emila.

But now wasn't the time for ghosts.

Stepping back, I walked with her to the side of the ballroom everyone had gathered. Reed and Dax stood to the side, watching us. It amazed me how we all seemed to sense when to give each other a moment with our girl. It was instinctual between us and what I believed would make us work in the long run.

As the tables were cleared away, I watched the servers, wanting to find any sign of what went on behind the scenes. They all seemed focused on their task, diligently working. I tucked it away, hoping it was from a good work environment, not a tyrant boss.

Sparks flew ahead of us, drawing my attention back to the front. Doors I hadn't noticed before opened as women and men dressed seductively entered. Some of them carried sparklers; others balanced multiple trays of champagne on their palms. When they were inside, they moved between all the guests as they oohed and awed.

Material fell from the ceiling before a man and woman climbed up them, twisting the fabric around their legs to suspend themselves in the air.

"It's like Cirque Du Soleil," Henley gasped in awe. "I always wanted to catch a show."

I had a suspicion Carly had somehow known that. From the food, the clothes, and the guests, it wasn't hard to tell that this was mainly to entice her and reward others. This party was exclusive, and the invitation was meant to be revered. I just wondered where the strings were because they had to be close. It was how these groups worked. What had these people sacrificed or done to be included?

Peering around at the other entertainers and guests, I watched as they enjoyed and imbibed the refreshments offered. They wanted everyone to let go, giving them something to use for control or something to crave more of.

"Don't drink or take anything," I whispered to our crew.

"You think it's spiked?"

I shrugged. "It could be, or it very well might just be regular alcohol. But this is a crowd you don't want to lose your inhibitions around."

"Got it." Henley grimaced, understanding dawning on her. The group gathered might be acting friendly to her now, but it didn't mean they wouldn't flip the second Carly or someone else told them to.

"How long do we have to stay?" Reed asked, already looking ready to bolt.

"We need to show our faces for a little bit. They want Henley for something. If we brush it off, they'll retaliate, and I don't want to add anything else to our plate. We have enough as it is."

"Yeah. Most of it mine," Henley said, cringing.

"Not all of it," Dax said, turning his head so he wouldn't have to look at his brother.

"Let's do a round. Every twenty minutes, we'll switch out Henley. After that hour, we should be able to escape without too much fuss. I'll take her first. I'd suggest the other two stick together as well."

"Aye, aye, captain," Dax said, saluting me. Reed snorted.

"Don't forget it," I said, not taking offense. Whatever worked to keep them safe was fine by me.

Soft music played as the guests danced, watched the performers, or mingled with one another as they drank refreshments. Pulling Henley into my arms, I rocked with her on the outskirts of the dance floor, wanting a moment to have her all to myself.

"This is nice." She laid her head on my chest, my hands wrapped around her waist, touching her bare back.

"You look fucking incredible in this dress. I'm half

tempted to squirrel you away to a dark corner and show you how hard you make me."

Henley's breath hitched, her head tilting to look up at me. Her eyes were hungry as she stared at me. Her fingers ran through the hair at the base of my neck, sending tiny shivers through me.

"I could say the same about you in this suit. I've had to stop myself several times from undressing you three."

"That can be arranged later," I purred, nipping her ear. "You still have a fantasy to cash in." Henley's body shuddered beneath my fingers, her breath gasping.

I glanced around to find if anyone other than Carly was interested in Henley. There were a few eyes on us, but none seemed to be more than a passing curiosity. When I landed on Dax and saw his stance, I cursed.

"Shit. It looks like our twenty minutes are up, Baby Shaw."

"What?" she asked, glancing around.

"Dax needs us. Come on. I think this one might need your magic."

"I really hope I don't punch someone tonight," she grumbled, making me love her even more. That was Henley in a sexy nutshell—fierce, protective, and loyal.

"Doesn't seem like your girl feels the same way about you, Bro. Lost another one," Derek taunted. He had a drink in his hand, and it didn't appear to be his first one with how glazed his eyes were.

"Stay out of my relationship, Derek. It's none of your business."

"That sounds like advice he should've taken the first time, too," Henley said, wrapping her arm in Dax's.

"You can drop the act. I know you're not with him," Derek slurred.

"Oh, I'm with him, Fletcher, and Reed. But that's none of your concern."

"Should've figured Dax couldn't hold on to anyone. He's too much of a pussy."

Henley's fist clenched, her arm raising up, but Dax beat her to it. Dax's fist connected with Derek's face, knocking him cold to the ground. His drink fell with him, spilling on him, making it look like he'd pissed himself. I peered around to see if anyone had noticed.

A staff member walked over, and I sucked in a breath, hoping they weren't about to kick us out. We all waited, shocked, when they handed Dax a towel with some ice.

"For your hand. That guy's a dick."

Dax took it, nodding his thanks as he laid it over his knuckles. Henley immediately inspected his knuckles, holding the ice to them once she was satisfied nothing was broken.

Reed bent down and lifted Derek to a sitting position against the wall, making it look like he'd just passed out. The rest of the crowd ignored us, and I suspected they felt the same about him as the server had.

"And you call *me* punchy," he teased as he stood. Dax chuckled, rolling his eyes.

"Maybe I just learned it from you." He shook his head, peering at us. "Fuck, I've wanted to do that forever."

"You beat me to it," Henley said, shrugging.

Dax smiled, his eyes crinkling at the sides. "Thanks, Petal. I'm glad you didn't, though. I wouldn't want you to mess up your pretty hands. Plus, it was long past due."

"Speaking of past due, can we leave now?" Reed asked.

I glanced at the clock. It hadn't been an hour, but based on the crowd, they were all getting drunk quickly. It was likely they wouldn't even notice our absence.

"Yeah. Why not? I think we've seen enough entertainment for the night."

Henley linked one arm with Dax, holding out her hand to me. Reed followed behind us as the four of us left the ballroom. I couldn't help but sigh a breath of relief the moment we were out the doors. We'd survived the night with the sharks.

# CHAPTER 24

## Henley

THE NIGHT HAD GONE BETTER than I'd predicted, with only one dick to contend with. It felt foolish now to be so suspicious of a woman I admired. She'd gone through a lot of effort as a host to ensure we had a good time. I still didn't understand her intentions, but maybe I didn't need to.

People could be good, and it seemed Carly was one of them.

The four of us stepped through the ballroom doors, the sounds of the party disappearing as we exited. The sudden absence of sound was eerie.

Fletcher took the lead as usual, directing us back toward the staircase. I wasn't sure how he remembered which way to go. This house was too massive, and I'd be lost without him.

"Henley! Leaving so soon?" Carly exclaimed as we came around the bend.

She was talking with another couple, her husband nowhere to be found. The three of them observed us, waiting for a response. Something about the woman caught my eye, a familiarity of some sort, but the day had been long, and I'd met so many people it was hard to determine what my brain was trying to tell me. I shook it off, remembering she'd asked me a question.

"It's been such a lovely day, Carly, but it's all catching up to me, the game yesterday, traveling, and all the wonderful things you've had planned for us. I can't thank you enough for being such a wonderful host," I gushed.

She walked forward, clasping my hands between her warm palms as she smiled.

"I'm glad you've enjoyed yourself, dear. We'll discuss everything in the morning before you leave. Get some rest, and don't forget, breakfast is at 8 am."

She patted my hands twice before she stepped back, her eyes quickly passing over the guys. With a nod, she dismissed us, walking back to her conversation. The woman had watched us the whole time, her eyes still assessing as they kept their voices low, talking amongst themselves. Peering at the guys, I shrugged a shoulder before continuing on our way. Lifting my dress, I climbed the stairs, cursing my heels with each one.

"How is it I can spend all day in skates, balancing on a blade, on ice, mind you, but heels feel like torture death traps sent to take me out?"

The guys chuckled as I continued to curse until one second, I was climbing, and the next, I was flying. A hard chest pressed against my side as the world righted itself. Peering up into hazel eyes, I smiled.

"Hi."

"I should've thought of that," Dax grumbled next to us.

"You snooze, you lose," Fletcher teased, taking the stairs two at a time, curses following him as they rushed to catch up.

Peering over his shoulder, I waved at Reed and Dax as they trailed behind. "This is how I always want to travel," I said gleefully.

"That can be arranged." Fletcher gave me a heated look. I didn't know who was enjoying it more—me or him.

The tingles from our dance earlier returned as I stared into his eyes. The flecks of brown almost looked gold in the light. I scraped my fingernails against the base of his neck, moving my other hand to cup his jaw and do the same to his beard. His eyes fluttered closed for a second as his steps faltered.

"Careful with her, or you won't get to carry her anymore," Reed hissed.

Fletcher regained his footing as he marched with determination toward my door. He glanced over his shoulder before he entered.

"I think it would be wise to stay in the same room tonight. That said, I plan to ravage and do filthy things to our girl. We haven't talked about what everyone is comfortable with, so I wanted to let you know now so you can make your decision."

Reed didn't hesitate, opening the door and

strolling through as he shucked off his tie. Dax paused for a second, his eyes dropping to mine.

"I understand," I said, not wanting him to feel pressured.

Dax's jaw ticked, and his eyes locked on mine. Swallowing, he met Fletcher's unwavering gaze.

"I'm not touching anyone's dick."

"No one is asking you to, bro," Fletcher said, smiling.

"It would be hot—" I started, stopping when they both stared at me and rephrased what I was going to say. "I'd love to be with all of you at the same time. But I want you to be comfortable with it. So, if you just want to watch, I'm good with that, too."

Dax stepped forward, his hand cupping my cheek. "As sexy as that sounds, Petal, I know watching would never be enough with you. If you want to be with all of us, then I'm here. All in, remember? I'll figure out how to deal with my stuff."

"Are you sure? I—"

His lips landed on mine, stealing the words from me. His tongue swept in, taking control as we kissed. Fletcher growled, shifting me in his arms and breaking the kiss.

"I'm not holding her for you to make out with her. If you're in, then walk through the door so we can all be part of this."

Dax stepped back, saluted Fletcher with a smile, and turned to walk in. I sighed in relief. I'd been worried he'd be out for this part, and I really needed them all tonight. I wanted to physically feel the bond I'd been experiencing all day between us.

Fletcher huffed, but I caught his smirk, knowing he'd done that on purpose.

"Sometimes Dax needs to get out of his head with a little push. I've lived with him long enough to know how to motivate him to do something," he said, winking.

"You're truly a remarkable man, Fletcher Cromwell."

His face softened as he stared at me, his lips moving closer to mine.

"I thought you wanted us all to be part of this?" Dax shouted from the open door. Fletcher sighed, dropping his head down to my forehead for a second.

"Fucking shit-stirrer," he muttered before lifting his head. "I'm so getting him back for that."

Giggling, I couldn't help but get giddy over their friendship. I loved watching them tease one another one second and be there to throw a punch the next. It was what connected us and made us a family—a real one.

Fletcher stalked through the door, slamming it behind him, and locked it. I slid down his body, my legs wobbly after that display in the hallway. His hands gripped my arms, steadying me. Kissing his cheek, I stepped back and lifted my heels one at a time so that I could take off the torture devices.

Dangling the pumps from my fingers, I walked backward, keeping Fletcher's eyes on me. Reaching my arm out, I dropped the shoes to the floor and continued to step back as my hand reached up to push off my strap.

I ran into a hard surface before I could lift my arm. Looking up, I found Reed smirking down at me.

"Need any help, Hen?" His hands trailed up my arms, his lips kissing my neck as he waited for an answer.

"Bring her to the front of the bed so we can watch the show," Fletcher commanded.

He pulled off his tie, a devilish smile crossing his face as he placed it on the bed. Reed turned me and directed me to the massive king bed in the center of the room. Dax was already shirtless, lounging on his side as he watched.

My eyes danced between the sexy men in front of me, wondering what new adventure they would take me on tonight. Each time I was with any of them, I discovered something new about myself and what I enjoyed in the bedroom.

From the praise to the dirty talk, I trusted them implicitly to take care of me, something I'd never felt with a bed partner before. I wasn't just physically naked with these men, but emotionally and mentally. I never knew vulnerability could be so sexy.

Reed's hands dropped to the zipper he'd helped me with earlier. His mouth landed near my ear, his hot breath fanning across my skin. "I've been thinking about this tiny little zipper all night. It's only fair that I get to lower it."

"Yes," I breathed, unable to say anything else. I watched as Fletcher unbuttoned his shirt, tossing it to the side when it was free.

"And that's why you have clothes all over your floor," I teased, a laugh wanting to bubble out of me. It was cut off as Reed's teeth sank into the space between my neck and collarbone. I gasped, a moan following it as the sting gave way to pleasure as he licked and sucked, sending goosebumps all over me.

His hands were warm on my back as the zipper fell, the air a welcomed relief against my hot flesh. I moved my other strap down, desperate for them to fall away so I could be free of this dress. The instant Reed was done, my dress slid off me like butter, leaving me in nothing but my barely there lace panties.

"Fuck," Dax moaned, his hand dropping to his erection in his pants. It was a struggle to keep my eyes open to watch the show before me as Reed kissed down my shoulder, his hands coming up to cup my breasts.

His thumb rolled over one, his palm gripping and caressing the other. My legs shook as I stood there, pleasure overriding me. I could feel his hard length behind me, nestled between my cheeks. My hands gripped his thighs as he lavished me with touches, my brain no longer able to think.

Reed's fingers traveled lower, my breath catching as he neared my center. His hand slid beneath the only fabric left between him and my pussy, his fingers knowing precisely what to do as he dragged it up through my wetness, my lips plump with arousal. My clit throbbed like a beacon, needing his touch to survive. The moment he made contact, my legs gave way as I shuddered in his arm that had banded around my torso.

"Holy fuck," someone from the bed cursed. I was too far gone to open my eyes to look. When Reed's finger pushed in, I couldn't take it any longer as an orgasm crashed into me, my walls clamping around him. But it wasn't enough. I needed more.

"More," I whimpered, hoping they understood.

"Bring her to me," Dax said, his voice like liquid heat to my ears. It was husky and low, and I knew somehow he would understand what I needed. His knowledge of the body gave him an advantage in reading my cues.

My knees were placed on the edge of the bed, and my underwear pulled off me as I fell to my elbows. I blinked, finding Fletcher in front of me. He was now naked, one hand wrapped around his cock as he slowly stroked it. He reached up with his free hand to cup my jaw.

"If it gets to be too much, just tell us, baby," Fletcher whispered. He leaned forward to kiss my lips, pulling back before I wanted him to. His eyes heated, his pupils overtaking the hazel of them.

Hands gripped my thighs from below as I was pulled down, my pussy landing on Dax's face. His tongue licked up my cum, his moan vibrating my insides as he ate me out like a man starved.

My thighs gripped his head, and I realized he had to be sitting on the floor with his head thrown back onto the bed for an all-you-can-eat buffet. The image was pornographic, making me wetter just thinking about it. My hips rocked with his efforts, and I leaned forward more to take Fletcher into my mouth.

He cursed, his hand stalling as I covered it with mine, wanting to stroke him as I licked. My tongue darted out to the tip, my lips wrapping around his thick shaft as I sucked him down. His hand moved with mine, following my mouth as we worked together.

I peered up at him, wanting to watch him unravel as I took him deeper. His head was thrown back, his lips slightly parted, and his eyes clenched tight. It was sexy as hell and something I wanted to burn into my memory.

Dax ramped up his efforts, plunging two fingers into my pussy as he sucked my clit. I trembled, another orgasm near as he continued. I was almost as full as I wanted, but it still wasn't enough; I needed more.

His tongue worked like magic, moving in time

with his fingers, and I was unable to hold back my orgasm as it ran up my spine, taking me like a tidal wave.

A sensation I'd never experienced overcame me as I came, my legs shaking as I moaned around Fletcher, my body exploding in a whole new way.

"Did she just?"

"Squirt all over my face? Yeah," Dax answered.

Even from my orgasmed-induced haze, I could hear the smugness.

"Lucky fucker," Reed hissed, making me laugh.

It was only for a second before Fletcher hauled me into his arms, spreading my cheeks as he speared me on his dick. I wanted to be angry for being tossed around like I weighed nothing. I was a professional athlete with a lot of muscle I worked hard for. But here they were, acting like I was light as a feather. It was a bit insulting.

But the girlie part of me liked being manhandled and possessed by these men.

I shouted as Fletcher filled me, finally giving me what I wanted. His hand gripped my chin as he tilted it to look at him. It wasn't hard, just enough pressure to take control.

"My turn," he grunted, his lips crashing to mine as he reared up, his dick hitting me so deep it was a wonder it wasn't coming out of my throat.

As Fletcher had his way with me, fucking me into

oblivion, I lost track of the other two, focusing entirely on the bearded man in front of me.

"You're such a good girl, baby, taking my cock like you did. You had me ready to explode down your throat. But I want to hear you scream my name when I make you cum again."

I whimpered, his fingers flexing on my throat as he continued his pace. My legs were locked around his waist, my thighs burning from the intense workout they'd already been through.

It wasn't long before Fletcher's hand on my hip moved to my clit, the sensitive bud too eager for his touch. With a few flicks, I was back to trembling around him, my walls clenching his cock this time.

"God, yes, Fletch," I screamed, my voice already hoarse.

His hips stilled, his head falling to my neck as he sucked on my collarbone, his cock jerking inside me. When he pulled back, his face was smug as he stared at his handy work.

"I'm not sure I want you guys to start a hickey competition."

"Too bad," the three of them said simultaneously.

Rolling my eyes, I panted as I caught my breath. I guess if I wanted them to all be okay dating me at the same time, I had to give into their little ways of one-upping each other.

"How do you feel about two dicks at once, Hen?"

Reed asked, holding a bottle of lube. "That is if Dax isn't scared of my dick."

Dax scoffed, crossing his arms over his defined chest. His cock hung hard between his legs, making me wet my lips. His chin shined with the evidence of my orgasm earlier as he stared at me.

"I'm not scared. Think you can handle two of us, Petal?"

I nodded, not needing to question it. Reed tossed the lube to Dax, stepping forward to take me from Fletcher. His arms tightened around me for a second before he kissed me and let me go, climbing off the bed toward the bathroom.

Reed laid me back on the bed, turning me on my side as he faced me. He took a moment to brush a few strands of hair that had slipped free back. His touch was gentle, and my eyes closed at the gesture. He kissed my eyelids, then my nose, before landing on my lips.

Lifting a leg over his hip, I felt his cock as it rubbed between my slick folds. His eyes fluttered closed as he took deep breaths. I didn't know what it was, but Reed loved being in me after someone else.

My hand trailed up his chest, running through the spattering of chest hair. His knee shifted, pulling me closer as his tip pushed in. His hands fell to my ass as he moved me forward, cursing when he slipped all the way in.

I sucked in a breath as I stretched around him. He

rocked slowly, making short thrusts as Dax climbed onto the bed. His hands ran up my back, tilting my head to look at him.

"I didn't know if I'd like this, but watching you come apart, no matter by whose hands, is sexy as hell, Petal."

He bent down to kiss me, Reed continuing to roll his hips forward, rocking his pelvis onto my clit. Reed moved one hand up to my breasts as he took them into his mouth. I could've stayed like that, kissing Dax while Reed fucked me softly. It was a gentle and intimate moment between the three of us.

Dax pulled back, leaving my lips puffy as he opened the bottle and squirted some lube on his fingers. Reed lifted one of my butt cheeks, inching forward a little more as I gasped. Dax spread the lube around, using some of my wetness to loosen me up. It felt so tight already with just his finger, I wasn't sure I'd be able to handle both of them, but I wanted to try.

When Dax felt I was ready, I heard the bottle again as he used it on himself. Reed stopped, letting Dax get in position behind me. His arm snaked under me, holding me to him as he put my other leg between his. Sucking in a breath, I let it out slowly as he pushed in.

Reed held my face, kissing me all over to keep my focus off the stretch. Dax's hand reached between Reed and me, strumming my clit as he continued. My body vibrated by the time he was in; the fullness was unlike anything I'd ever felt.

"Shit. That feels incredible," Dax hissed, kissing my nape. "Slowly, together."

I closed my eyes, unable to focus on anything as they moved. When Reed would pull back, Dax would push forward, ensuring I was never empty.

Whimpering, I held onto them both, needing their presence to ground me so I didn't float away. My body was spent; three orgasms were the most I'd ever had at one time, so I wasn't sure if I'd be able to have another.

But the guys seemed determined, hands roaming over my body, their thrusts becoming deeper and faster as they got used to it. My body responded in kind, the overwhelming feeling of completeness settling into me.

"Reed! Dax!" I shouted as my body gave way to an orgasm so big, my eyes rolled back as everything convulsed and trembled, tiny stars dancing everywhere.

"I love you guys," I slurred as sleep took me under.

# CHAPTER 25

## *Henley*

THE WORLD CAME BACK to me in waves. My muscles ached in a new and delicious way, evidence of a hard workout. The night was blurry in my mind as I tried to put the pieces together. Stretching, my arms connected with a body, a grunt alerting me to who.

I blinked my eyes, taking in the man in front of me. Dax's hair was a crazy mess around his head; his eyes closed tight. The hand that had struck him was now grasped between his palm and his chest.

"Go back to sleep, Petal."

"I think it's time to get up. We can't be late."

"Screw breakfast. It's not that important."

Giggling, I moved closer, my hand trailing over his face, touching him softly. He was too beautiful for words.

"I vaguely remember getting into bed," I whispered.

"That's because you were a zombie. Fletcher cleaned you up and put his shirt on you. I think he did it so we'd have to smell his cologne all night."

A smile grew as I thought of them taking care of

me. "Um, not to be ungrateful, but did I happen to go to the bathroom, too?" I winced as I imagined the potential UTI in my future.

"Reed handled it."

"Did he watch me?" I shrieked, realizing the implication. I wasn't ready for those kinds of peep shows.

"No, Hen." Reed chuckled from behind me. "I sat you down and then shut the door. You sang 'Tinkle, Tinkle, little pee.' And yes, you said tinkle."

I hid my face in embarrassment. "Shut up. No, I didn't."

"'Fraid so, Petal. I believe there's even evidence," Dax muttered, his eyes still closed.

"I hate you all," I groaned, my face heating.

"It was cute, Baby Shaw," Fletcher added.

"Ugh. At least you didn't watch me pee. There are some boundaries I refuse to cross. How did you know I was done?" I was curious and slightly mortified at what I might've done in my cum-oma.

"You were washing your hands. So I felt it was safe," Reed answered. The mattress dipped, and he kissed my cheek.

"He even made us all brush our teeth," Dax said around a yawn, his eyes slowly opening.

"You did?" I giggled, looking at Reed upside down.

His cheek turned pink, and he shrugged his shoulders. "Dental hygiene is important."

"I bet your momma taught you that, didn't she?" I asked, smiling.

"Yeah, she did." His voice was soft as he peered into my eyes. His hand traced over my face, waking up the rest of my body.

"Did I do anything else?" I asked, sitting up. I glanced down at the shirt and smiled as I lifted it to my nose. Sure enough, it smelled like Fletcher. When no one said anything, I looked at them, finding them all avoiding looking at me.

Reed and Fletcher were both dressed, their hair slightly damp from a shower. Both of them blushed, making me curious. Dax had his boxers on, still giving me a nice view of his back as he climbed out of bed. I still caught his pink cheeks as he stood, focusing on everything in the room but me.

"Um, okay? What is it? You're all avoiding me and blushing. Did I say something embarrassing? Make an awful sound? Oh my god, I didn't queef, did I?" My hands flew to my face as humiliation took hold.

Dax snorted, finally turning back to me. "Say what now?"

"I did, didn't I? Or was it worse? Did I fart, and it made that wet sound? That's it. I'm never having sex again. I can't deal with this embarrassment."

Fletcher gave a choked laugh before he walked to the bed and bent down. "You didn't do either of those things. But even if you did, I wouldn't care. I'm sure these two feel the same."

"Oh." My heart slowed as I calmed. "Then what aren't you telling me?"

Fletcher glanced at the other two, clearing his throat. "You said... you loved us before you passed out."

"Okay..." I shrugged, trying to figure out if I had missed something. "I mean, I do. Why would you avoid me? I don't care if you're not there yet."

Three collective sighs of relief sounded next to me. "That's not it, Hen. We didn't want you to say something you might've only felt in the moment. I guess we were all worried you'd take it back. I don't know about them, but I love you too, Henley Henshaw," Fletcher said earnestly.

Smiling bigger than I thought possible, I leaped forward and wrapped my arms around Fletcher's neck. He grunted but caught me, holding me close to him. His hand smoothed up and down my back.

"Me too. I love you, Hen. I didn't think it was possible, but you made me *believe* it was possible," Reed said, his eyes full of emotion. Leaning forward, I kissed Fletcher's cheek then moved to hug Reed.

Sitting back, I glanced at Dax, my heart full of warmth. He looked at the other two and then at me. "Can I have a moment with Henley?"

"Sure. We'll get our bags ready to go," Fletcher said, getting up from the bed. When he and Reed were gone, Dax moved closer, holding my hand. He stared at our fingers for a long time before he met my eyes. They were sad, scared, and a bit lost.

Scooting forward, I sat in his lap, wrapping my

arms and legs around him, needing to hold him to me. He took a deep breath, letting it out as he relaxed.

"The last time I said that, it was used against me."

I pulled back, cupping his face with both of my hands. Swiping my thumbs over his cheeks, I stared into his beautiful eyes.

"I know, and I'd never want you to feel pressure to say it when you're not ready. I know how you feel about me, Dax, even without words."

His eyes shuttered, and he nodded, the last of his tension fading away.

"I wish I'd met you before all that... before I was damaged. You deserve the best, Petal."

"So do you, Dax. I'm going to show you every day until you believe it, too. You're not any more damaged than I am. Besides, we met each other when we needed to. You showed me I could feel so much more than I thought possible the first night we met. Opening my eyes to how sex could be."

"I did?" he asked, shocked.

"Yeah. Now come on. We need to get dressed so we're not late for breakfast. I have a feeling it's going to be insightful."

"Even more reason to skip it." He nipped at my neck, his cock growing harder beneath me.

"As nice as that sounds, I need a little rest in that area after the marathon last night. Plus, the sooner we eat, the quicker we can head home."

"You're so sexy when you get all logical," he

growled, pulling himself away from kissing me. "Fine. Only because I'm ready to be home."

Chuckling, I climbed off him and went to my bag to get dressed, hoping that what I had brought would be sufficient this time. The new clothes were nice, but they weren't my style. It felt more like I was playing dress-up as someone else and not myself. It was another role I had to play, and I was tired of it.

Within twenty minutes, I was dressed in a cute shirt and shorts combo, packed, and ready to tackle the day. The guys and I walked down to the kitchen, and this time I felt nothing but happiness. No matter what Carly said, I had people in my life I could count on, and that was worth more than this entire estate.

Breakfast was subdued as we ate around a smaller table on the patio. It was a pretty view surrounded by trees and mountains, but I never knew someone who had so many different places to eat a meal. Was that what made someone rich? Multiple dining areas?

"The party was a lot of fun, Carly. Thank you for everything yesterday," I said after the quietness got to me.

"Of course, dear. I'm glad you enjoyed it." She smiled, taking a sip of her coffee.

"I didn't see you around much, Geoffrey."

"Yes, well, I'm not a big fan of crowds. I tend to let Carly do her thing, and I stay in the library."

"A library? Wow. I never got a tour. Your house is truly amazing."

"Thank you, dear." Carly drank her coffee, her eyes distant.

I took another bite, widening my eyes at the guys. The conversation felt stilted this morning, and I didn't know the cause.

When the meal was finished, I sighed in relief. Even if she couldn't help with the press conference, I didn't know if I cared anymore. I just wanted to get out of here.

"Before you leave, I'd like to discuss my proposition with you in my study."

"Sure," I said, standing. The guys stood as well, following me. Carly stopped at the door, glancing at them.

"I'm sorry, fellas. But this part is for the ladies only. You can wait in the foyer. I promise to return her to you in one piece."

I halted, glancing at the three men behind me. A million thoughts crossed between us all.

*What should I do?*

Is it safe?

*It's Carly, so I'd think so.*

We'll be close.

Fletcher grimaced but nodded for me to go. I acquiesced, knowing they'd be close.

Turning to Carly, I followed her inside the house to her study. The walk was quiet, with not another person in sight again. Was this house the *Haunted Mansion* and everyone a ghost?

Carly gestured toward a seat as she opened the door for me. The room was full of books and photos, with two leather wingback chairs, a matching leather couch, and a massive desk in front of a window.

Taking the couch, I sat down and crossed one leg over the other, placing my hands on my lap. There was a wooden table between the couch and chairs, the surface gleaming with wood shine. It made me nervous to touch it, worried I'd leave a fingerprint behind. Carly sat across from me, her posture perfect as she assessed me before she finally spoke.

"I remember the first time I saw you play, Henley. You reminded me so much of myself. You had fire and confidence most women lack on the ice. I watched your career and saw how the league used you to advance their agenda, not caring whether or not you were hurt in the process. I've wanted to reach out to you for years, but certain rules kept me from doing so."

"Rules?" I asked, clearing my throat. She looked off into the distance, ignoring me.

"I almost quit hockey. Did you know that?" she asked, her voice wistful.

"No, I didn't. Why?" I recrossed my ankles, my palms sweaty. She turned back, her eyes meeting mine.

"Much like you, the league used me to present a certain agenda. I was young and naïve, so I went along with it. I thought if I did what they wanted, they'd support me too. But when I needed them, they weren't there. They washed their hands of me and left me to deal with it myself."

"What happened?" I asked curiously. I'd never heard this part of her history before. Carly smiled, but it was sad.

"One night after a game, I was raped by a male hockey player. I went to the league, thinking they'd protect me. Instead, they made me out to be a problematic player, and I was traded from a well-funded and winning team to one that could barely keep the lights on. I ended up getting pregnant, and I contemplated suicide. Life felt meaningless without hockey, so why stick around?"

She sniffled, taking a tissue from her pocket to dab at her eyes. Her story was horrifying. In some ways, I could relate to how she felt about the league and the betrayal. I was grateful that I had Reese, who'd kept me from falling that low to where suicide felt like my only option.

"Thankfully, someone saw my distress and stepped in, helping me fight against the league and get my career back where I wanted it. They even held my hand through an abortion. I became a powerhouse and role model, stepping up for women's rights in hockey and making the men who ran it pay attention. I met Geoffrey again shortly after and got married, building this life I have now with him."

"That's a great story of triumph. You persevered and survived something horrible, and became a role model to girls like me growing up," I paused. "Is that why you're helping me?" I asked.

"Partially." She shifted, her eyes falling over me. "Like I said, I've been watching you for years. I believe you have what it takes to become the next me. To be that driving force to make big changes in women's hockey. You just need someone bigger behind you to help push."

"And that's you?" Nerves stirred in me; not sure where this was going. "What about Dakota? Isn't he part of this?" I asked, cringing when I realized she hadn't specifically mentioned the Society yet. Her eyes flew up to mine, calculating her next words.

"Dakota will be dealt with accordingly. He stepped over the line in his quest for greatness and needs to be reminded he doesn't *speak* for everyone."

I let that settle in, comforted that the Society didn't appear to condone his behavior. Though, I didn't know how much weight Carly had. She could be blowing smoke up my ass for all I knew.

"This could be your comeback moment where you stick it to the league and him. No one will dare question you again after that. You'd be free to do what you wanted and make significant changes for women for years to come," she said.

"I still don't understand how or why you'd do this for me."

"Because I believe you can be greater than yourself, and I'm willing to help you get there."

"That sounds great and all, but what's the cost? You wouldn't sacrifice so much for nothing." I crossed my ankles again, the urge to fidget and blurt out inappropriate things riding me hard. Carly gave me a soft smile that teetered on the edge of condescending.

"The only cost is membership into the world's most elite secret hockey club. The rest I can't tell you until you've sworn loyalty." And there it was. We were no longer pussyfooting around the subject.

"And my job, my relationships, my sibling, they'd all be left alone?"

"There will be many who balk at your relationship, but you can use it to push the agenda for women. You wouldn't need to work at Lux anymore. You'd be welcomed back into the league with whatever team you wished to play for. And your sibling, we'd help out with whatever we can." She pulled her shoulders back, pride radiating from her.

"I feel like there's a catch." It sounded too good to be true. I could hear the strings even if she weren't explicitly saying them out loud.

"When you're in, we all work together to be better, stronger. Your admittance into the club pays itself forward by helping others when needed. As you can tell by this weekend, we treat our members well, providing you with whatever you need."

Yeah, that told me nothing. And working together? I'd die before I did anything with Dakota. Either they had condoned what he did and now regretted it. Or they didn't control his leash as well as they thought they did.

"It's a lot to process. When do I have to decide?" I shifted again, my body itching.

Carly observed me; her brows creased, and her mouth turned down in confusion why I hadn't jumped at her offer. I could practically see the thoughts running through her head as she debated.

"You have a week." She halted, taking a breath, and I worried she wouldn't let me leave here with what I knew. "But you mustn't tell anyone else about us. It's what keeps us secret."

"A week. Okay, I can let you know by then. Thank you once again for the kindness you've shown me this weekend."

She smiled, though it was more strained than before as she stood. I followed suit, walking to the door, her words stopping me before I opened it.

"I look forward to hearing from you. Just one more thing, dear."

"Yes?" My hand wrapped around the doorknob.

"The Society will only ask once. I wouldn't linger if I were you."

# CHAPTER 26

## *Henley*

THE ENTIRE PLANE RIDE HOME, I tried to make sense of everything Carly had said, but the truth was I couldn't. When I met them in the foyer, the guys had given me a nervous look, but I shook my head, letting them know now was not the time.

I didn't feel safe talking about any of it while in that home.

Fletcher tried to engage me on the plane, but I still couldn't formulate words. After a few attempts, he stopped and pulled out a crossword puzzle. Dax watched a movie while Reed listened to a podcast through his earbuds. It was an uneventful flight, and we returned to Utah in the middle of the afternoon.

Powering on my phone, it flooded with messages, and I instantly cursed. I hadn't even looked at it between last night and this morning. It was dead when we'd gotten on the plane, so I powered it off to charge it.

REESE

Going to bed. Nothing new to report.
See you tomorrow.

REESE

Fire alarm pulled. Everyone is outside
while they investigate.

REESE

Two hours later, headed back in. So
much for getting some sleep.

REESE

When are you heading back?

REESE

Hen, is everything okay? Getting
worried since I haven't heard from
you. Text me back, or I'm sending out
a search party.

REESE

I hope you're alive because we have a
problem.

REESE

Mom showed up today. Made a scene
in front of everyone. She threatened to
call the cops if I didn't go to lunch
with her.

REESE

She got a new lawyer. She says she
will fight for custody, that I don't
belong here, and you're not a good
guardian.

REESE

Hen, I'm scared. Please call me soon.

I didn't finish reading the other messages when I
hit the call button. My anxiety had risen with each
one, and I needed to talk to Reese now. The guys were

placing our luggage into Fletcher's Jeep, so I walked a little farther away, nodding I was making a call. Their eyes followed me; concern etched all over their faces. Reese picked up on the first ring, and I sighed in relief.

"Hen? Is it you?" they asked with a slight sniffle.

"Reese, I'm so sorry. Last night and this morning were chaotic, and then my phone died, so I charged it on the plane. We just landed, and I got all your messages. Where are you?"

"I'm back in the dorms. I told her I'd make a scene if she tried anything. But I wouldn't put it past her to get a judge to agree with her. That new guy she's with apparently has money. Lots of it. He's some bigshot developer or something and knows a lot of important people."

"Reese, don't worry about her. She won't take you from me. You want to be here, right?"

"Yes," they answered quickly.

"And you want me to be your guardian?" I asked.

"Absolutely." My heart rate slowed, needing to hear that.

"Then I'll take care of it. She wants something and is using you as leverage, as usual. She has no leg to stand on, though. You'll be 18 in less than a year, attend an elite school for a sport you excel at, and I'm a responsible adult. There's nothing she can do, and no judge is going to grant her custody."

Reese started to protest, but I cut them off.

"But, if she does, then I will go above whoever I

need to, hire whoever I need to, to make sure you never have to see that woman again if you don't want to. Understood?"

"Yes, Hen. And I believe you. I know you'll fight for me. It's just... Mom mentioned your relationships. I think she'll try to say you're not a good role model."

I closed my eyes, pressing my palm against them as I held in a raging scream.

"It's not the first time someone has come at me for my choices; she won't be the last. I'm not going to be blackmailed or bullied. I'm sick of people judging my life choices like they have the right. If she wants to come at me, fine. I can handle it. Besides, I'm not alone anymore, and neither are you. Got it?"

"Yeah, I got it. I feel sorry for Mom now."

"Why?" I asked with a restrained laugh.

"You're going to clean the floor with her. You're scary when you want to be, Hen. I'm glad you're on my side."

"Always. We're leaving the airfield now. I'll swing by on our way home."

"I'm okay, but you don't need to," Reese said.

"Bullshit. I need a hug, so we're stopping. Do you need anything?"

"No, I'm good." I could hear the smile in their voice, settling some more nerves.

"Okay, kiddo. I'll see you soon."

"See you soon. Love you, Hen."

"Love you, too."

I ended the call and dropped my head, needing a few seconds to gather myself. It felt like I'd run a marathon in the last few minutes with the way my heart raced. An arm wrapped around my waist, a neck falling to the dip of my shoulder. The body was warm and comforting as clean cotton greeted me.

"Everything okay?" Dax asked.

"No," I answered honestly. My shoulders relaxed the longer he held me, and I turned in his arms, laying my head against his chest. His hands fell to my ass as he pulled me closer, wrapping me up completely. We stood together as I listened to his heart, my breathing beginning to even by the time he spoke.

"Whatever it is, we'll get through it together, Petal."

I nodded, agreeing. "I know. It helped to have you hold me for a second. We need to stop by the dorms before we head home."

Dax kissed my temple, taking my hand to lead me to the car. I loved how he didn't question my request, accepting that Reese was in my life and, therefore, his. It was everything I needed after that phone call.

Sliding into the back, I let out a loud exhale as I tried to calm my nerves. This was the last thing I needed on top of everything else going on, but something told me Carol chose this time on purpose. She had someone on the inside.

"What's going on?" Fletcher asked as he drove.

"First, we need to go see Reese. Our mother

dropped by today and made a scene, demanding she have lunch with her. It was only under duress that Reese went. Then Carol threatened and scared Reese that they would be taken away from me. So, I need to check on them. I know I owe you guys an explanation from earlier, but I just don't have the bandwidth to deal with it right now. Can it wait?" I asked, rubbing my temple.

Fletcher's hands tightened on the steering wheel, his nostrils flaring slightly, and I worried for the first time he wouldn't have my back.

"That fucking bitch. Of course, Hen, we'll do whatever it takes to help you with this. Reese won't be leaving with that woman."

Sighing in relief, I sat back, my body feeling exhausted from everything that had occurred in the past forty-eight hours. I needed a day off, but it didn't look like that existed anymore.

Sending a few messages to my lawyer and the family specialist assigned to Reese's case, I updated them on Carol's threats. By the time I'd finished, we had pulled up to Grayson Hall, and I ignored the rest of the messages as the need to confirm for myself Reese was okay surged forward.

The Jeep had barely stopped when I threw open my door, jogging through the parking lot up to the door. I wasn't sure if the guys would follow or wait, not caring either way. The desk manager looked up as I neared, waving me up. It didn't take me long to climb the stairs, knocking on Reese's door a moment later.

The second it opened, I pulled my sibling into my arms, needing to feel them. Reese made an 'oof' sound but wrapped their arms around just as quickly.

"Hey," I whispered, pulling back to check them over. I scanned their face and eyes, wanting to make sure they were as okay as they said.

"I'm glad you're back." Reese smiled, their dimple popping out. They stepped back, adjusting their glasses and letting me into the room.

I blinked when Reed stepped in behind me, not realizing he'd been there. He gave me a smug smile but turned to Reese.

"You okay, killer?" Reed asked.

"Killer?" I asked, confused.

"It's an inside thing." Reed shrugged like it was no big deal, but inside, my parts were liquifying into goo from how sweet it was that he had a nickname for my sibling.

I noticed Briana sitting at her desk, so I walked over, realizing we'd just barged in. "Hey, Briana. You survive caring for your brother and this one?" I asked.

Briana laughed. "Yeah. Reese wasn't bad. Braden was the biggest baby, though."

I glanced back at the other two, finding them talking in hushed tones. Curious, I nodded in their direction, letting her return to her studies.

"There weren't any problems with the others,"

Reese said as I neared.

"Good. I threatened to bench them all if anyone caused a scene. You feeling up to skating tomorrow?"

"Yeah. The bruises are healing. I'll be fine as long as I avoid any more trips into the boards."

Reese and Reed laughed as I huffed. "Yeah, let's not joke about that. You scared the shit of me."

Reese rolled their eyes but agreed.

"Anything else from Mom?"

"Just that she'll be in touch." Reese crossed their arms, pressing their lips together as they shuffled on their feet.

"I've already contacted the lawyer and the Guardian Ad Litem. We'll get ahead of this. Knowing Carol, she's angling for something and knows she won't be able to use you very much longer. She's desperate."

"I hope you're right because I don't want to go with her. I like being here with you."

"You have us in your corner now too, killer. We'll throw so many things at her; she'll have to give up," Reed said, surprising me.

"If she calls or texts, don't answer her. Just screen-shot and forward any texts to Rita. I'll leave you be, but call me if you need anything. I'm sorry I missed yours this morning. It won't happen again."

I pulled them into my arms one more time, kissing their head. Reese's arms squeezed me tight, soothing the fear that had appeared since I'd gotten their calls.

"See you on the ice," Reed said, squeezing their shoulders. I waved bye to Briana as we headed out the door, wiping a tear as I climbed down the stairs.

"I mean it, Hen. The three of us will help you in any way we can. I can get my lawyer on it too."

"Thank you, Reed, but I'm good for now. We had a really good one back in Massachusetts. I'll let you know if they don't think they can help. I'm not too proud to accept help when it comes to Reese."

Reed threw his arm over my shoulder, pulling my body to his. It made walking down the stairs a little awkward since he was taller than me, but the gesture felt too nice to step away from. When we got into the car, I gave the other two a brief update as we headed to the house. Now that the crisis was over, I checked the other messages I'd ignored.

SCAR

Breakfast in the morning? I have something I want to run by you.

HENLEY

Yeah, that works. There's a cute coffee place in town. Want to meet there, or I can pick you up?

I wasn't surprised when she responded instantly.

SCAR

Pick me up, lover. I'm too pretty to hitchhike.

HENLEY

I'll be there at 8 am. I have a meeting at 10, so you better be ready, Miss Priss.

SCAR

Oh, is that your pet name for me? I like it. Yes, coach, sir, yes.

SCAR

I'm leaning into the domme thing for you, sweets. If you get tired of hockey, you might have a career as a dominatrix.

HENLEY

I'll keep that in mind. See you in the morning.

SCAR

Bye, lover! XOXO

I already felt better as I went through a few more messages. There was one from Sera giving me an update on the kids, making me grateful she'd been here to check on them. Susie had left this morning and would be back in a few days but didn't say why, leaving me curious.

When I got to the last message I had, I dropped my phone just as Fletcher pulled into the driveway.

"Son of a bitch." My hands shook as my vision blurred. Biting my cheek, I used the pain to ground me. This wasn't the time to pass out.

"What's wrong? What happened?" three voices shouted.

Digging my nails into my legs, I counted as I tried to calm down. Reed picked up my phone, the message from the reporter still displayed. He glanced down at it, then back to me, asking permission. I gave a curt nod as I continued to breathe through the panic of wondering what the hell I was going to do.

RACHEL (HTC MEDIA)

Hey, girl. I think I remember what you're talking about. I'll see if I can find it in the archives.

RACHEL (HTC MEDIA)

JFC. I can't believe I forgot this. Some people are despicable. All online stories have been removed. I didn't find a trace of them, but we have a backup on our server. Whatever you do, don't let it get out. While I don't condone what happened, I know a cover-up when I see one, and I don't want on anyone's shit list.

RACHEL (HTC MEDIA)

You owe me a big favor after this, Henley.

RACHEL (HTC MEDIA)

*Link-Hockey Star Anya Kerr involved in a hit-and-run*

If the Society could cover up something as serious as a hit-and-run, just who the fuck were they and could I really say no?

# CHAPTER 27

## *Reed*

IT TOOK me a minute to comprehend what I'd read and why it had shaken Henley. Pressing my lips together, I knew we needed to get out of here and into the house. It was time we had that discussion.

"Let's get her inside."

"What's on the phone?" Dax demanded.

I ignored him as I climbed out of the Jeep and unlocked the door. Lady Sterling met me as soon as I stepped into the house; her purrs were loud as she wound herself around my legs. I paused and bent down, patting her soft fur for a moment. My panic ebbed as I scratched behind her ears and exhaled, letting more out.

The others entered shortly after, and I stood, feeling more centered. Lady Sterling greeted the others before meandering back to the cat tower, licking her paws like she didn't have a care in the world.

Taking a seat on the couch, I handed the phone to Fletcher, who looked like he was about to blow a gasket. Henley still had a startled look on her face, so I pulled her onto my lap, wrapping my arms around her as she nestled into me.

"What the fuck?" Fletcher hissed, his eyes widening when he looked up, his jaw clenching. His eyes flashed with fear for a second before they settled on rage, and I dismissed it, focusing on Henley.

"What's going on?" Dax asked, taking the phone. He read it but shook his head, his mouth turned downward. "I don't understand."

Henley kissed my cheek before turning. "When I was talking to Anya at the pool party, she mentioned something about Carly helping her a few years ago. I remembered there had been something in the news, but then it had died down, and I forgot. So I messaged someone I know in the media, asking if they remembered. That's what they found."

"So... you're saying that Anya Kerr hit someone with her car, and Carly made it go away?" Dax asked.

"Yes. Or well, the Society did." Henley bit her lip as she thought.

"It's confirmed, then? That *was* the Society?" Fletcher asked.

Henley nodded. "Yes. I'm not supposed to tell you, but they want me to join. Part of their pitch was to make all the problems I'm facing go away, including Dakota."

"Isn't he a member?" I asked.

Henley shrugged. "Carly said he stepped over the line and has been too focused on his own agenda or something. She said he'd be dealt with. Whatever the fuck that means."

"Are you going to join?" Fletcher asked. His tone was even, but his hands gripped the phone with so much force I was surprised it hadn't cracked in half.

Henley blinked, looking up at him. She licked her lips and swallowed. "I... I... Do I have a choice? If they're this powerful, how can I fight against that?"

Fletcher's face relaxed, and he bent his legs, squatting in front of her to take her hands into his. Dax stood at the end of the couch, his hands in his hair as he paced. Something had shaken him.

"What are they asking from you, Baby Shaw?" Fletcher asked softly.

"She didn't come out and say. Just that members help other members. But I don't want to help with things like this." She shook her head, her lip trembling. "It makes me sick to think about someone getting away with it."

"What are they promising you?" I asked, wanting all the information.

"Everything."

"Everything?" I asked. She nodded, tilting her head slightly to look me in the eyes.

"Back in the league for any team I want. Protection for Reese. All the negative publicity goes away. She wants me to take up her mantle to push for equality in women's sports."

"You can't do it," Dax said, finally stopping his pacing. His hands were still in his hair as he pulled.

"You can't, Hen. They'll corrupt you. I won't let them do that to you."

Henley stood and walked over to Dax, wrapping her arms around his waist. His freak-out stopped as his arms dropped to wrap around her. I knew the feeling. It was hard not to hold or touch her if she was near. After a few seconds, Henley returned to the couch and sat down next to me with Dax on her right. I picked up her hand, needing to have some contact back.

"When do you have to tell them? I'm assuming there's a deadline?" Fletcher asked, pulling the topic back around.

"A week. I'd planned to say no, but now it doesn't feel as clear."

Dax grumbled, not liking she was considering it. If I was honest, I wasn't either. It felt like they'd try to keep us apart. If she had this part of her life separate from us, it would only be a matter of time before they convinced her we weren't good enough for her.

"No matter what, we'll make this decision together. I promise," Henley said, squeezing the two hands she had, looking at Fletcher.

"Should we tell Dmitry? Do you think he knew? He's friends with Carly, after all," Fletcher questioned.

Henley blew out a breath, throwing her head back against the couch with a groan. She withdrew her hands and rubbed them against her face. I missed her touch but knew she needed to process things.

"Why does everything have to be so complicated? Just as I progress in one area, I'm attacked by another. It's impossible to know what to focus on first. The team, Reese, Dakota, and now the Society. This weekend was supposed to help make one of those easier, not add more to my plate."

"You're right, Baby Shaw. We need to take a moment and assess everything, but then I think we should take the night off."

"I don't know if I can," she admitted, dropping her hands.

Fletcher sat on the coffee table, rubbing his palms up and down his legs. He pulled out his phone and made a list.

"Okay, the team. What are you worried about with them?" he asked, looking up when she didn't answer.

"We still need to find another coach. And though we won, it was only one game. We have to win a lot more to make it to the championship."

"Those are far-off worries, though, yes?" I asked, realizing what Fletcher was doing.

"Yeah. I guess." She bit her lip, tugging it between her teeth. I reached up, pulling it free. She blinked, not having realized she'd done it.

"We still need to work and improve the team, but it's coming together. It's no longer an immediate need. Dmitry will take care of the coach for the junior team. Let's rate it as low and ongoing." He made a note, looking up at the next item.

"Next was Reese. You messaged the lawyer and the caseworker. Anyone else we should notify?" Fletcher asked in complete boss mode. I wondered if he knew how much big daddy energy he was exuding right now. Even I wanted to sit down and listen to what he said as if it would solve everything.

Henley sighed, shaking her head. "No. Not until I hear from them. I'm not calling Carol."

"Okay, so while it's a higher priority, everything has been handled for now. Correct?"

"Yes," she grumbled, crossing her arms.

The corner of Fletcher's mouth ticked up, but he kept his focus on the phone as he typed. He was enjoying this.

"That brings us to Dakota. Do you want to ignore it like you've been doing? Or use the things you've collected against him?" Fletcher asked, looking up.

Henley's head flopped back and forth on the back of the coach. "I don't know. I'm at the point where I don't care, but the thought of him getting away with it infuriates me."

"Can I ask a favor?" Dax questioned, pulling her focus. She nodded, watching him. "Let me help you with this one. I might have an idea."

Henley searched his eyes, nodding after a few seconds. Clearly, Dax needed something to focus on, which gave him a way to help her.

"Of course. Thank you." She leaned up and kissed his cheek.

"Perfect. I'll put Dax down to take care of it, and he'll update us in a few days. That leaves the Society, which you don't have to decide for a week, giving us time before we need to stress. Was there anything else on your mind, Baby Shaw?" Fletcher asked. He pierced her with a smug smile as he waited for her to argue his point.

Henley gaped at him, her mouth opening and closing like a fish. "Well... I... Um..."

"I believe the correct answer is, 'No, Fletcher. You're a God among men. Thank you for helping me see the error of my ways.'"

Henley sputtered, her cheeks turning red, and she followed it with a hearty laugh. She shook her head no, conceding.

"Great. Then I suggest we find something to eat and chillax. We can do all the girlie shit you pretend to hate but secretly love, like painting your toes and doing one of those mask things with cucumbers."

"Cucumbers?" Henley asked, a giggle erupting. Fletcher narrowed his eyes at her, but they had no menace behind them.

"I have some spa products a client gave me once," Dax offered, frowning in thought.

"What's wrong?" Henley asked when she noticed. He shook his head, the look leaving him as he stared at her.

"Nothing. I was just thinking. Can I wash your hair?" he asked.

"Sure. I'd like that."

"I'll grab some food. Reed, do you want to join me?"

I debated if I was ready to be away from Henley yet. The need to protect her and make sure she was safe even from her own emotions was overwhelming. Watching her with Dax I knew she'd be okay, reminding myself it was the purpose of this type of relationship. Plus, it seemed like Dax needed some time alone with her, and I could give him that.

"Yeah. Let me take care of Lady Sterling first, and then I'll be ready."

Fletcher nodded as I stood and ensured my cat had fresh water and food in her bowl. I quickly cleaned out the litter box and grabbed a treat for Lady. It looked like she'd done well without us for a day, and I wanted to reward her for not tearing up any shit.

She eagerly ate the treat, licking her lips even after it was gone, begging me for more. Patting her on the head again, I scratched behind her ears as I smiled, happy I had her. My mom continued to prove how right she'd been. Opening myself up to people, having a job I enjoyed, and having something depend on me, had rooted me back in life instead of the grief.

It still hurt to think of my mom missing my life, and it was hard to imagine doing some of the big things without her. But the pain no longer over-whelmed me, and that was something to be grateful for.

I met Fletcher outside and climbed into the Jeep. It was quiet as we drove, neither needing to speak or perhaps we were both in our heads. I, for one, was tired of conversing with people after the long weekend.

Fletcher parked at a diner and turned off the engine but didn't get out. I glanced at him out of the corner of my eye, figuring he had something to say and would when he was ready.

"We have to keep her from the Society," he said after a few minutes passed.

"If Henley wants to do something, she'll do it. I don't want her to join, but we have to let her decide for herself."

His jaw ticked, not liking my answer. Probably because he knew it was true.

"That doesn't mean she has to make it alone," I added. "If we continue to show her we're going to be there for her, no matter what, I think she'll say no."

"And if she doesn't?" he asked, turning to me.

"Then I'm sure you have some crazy possessive ideas we can do."

It was silent for half a second before Fletcher laughed, the sound coming out like a honk, surprising him.

"Tell me I'm wrong?" I lifted my eyebrows, knowing I wasn't. Fletcher had cool vibes on the outside, but I could sense the need to control and possess her underneath it all, mainly because I felt the same way most of the time when it came to Henley.

"Fine. You're not wrong. It's just not something I want Henley to know about yet."

"You think she doesn't?" I scoffed, truly amazed if he thought that.

"What? She does?" he asked, his face stricken.

Snorting, I climbed out of the Jeep. "Oh, she knows and loves you. You don't have to hide any parts from her. She'll accept it."

Fletcher looked off into the distance, a little confused before nodding and following me into the diner. We ordered enough food for a whole hockey team, the staff's eyes going wide when we listed everything. While we waited, I decided to discuss the other topic we still needed to deal with.

"You need to add Dax's brother to the list. I have a feeling he's going to try to cause a problem for him. Not to mention Gareth is still out there. The police are on it, but there hasn't been a sighting since that day. I think the constant having to look over his shoulder is starting to get to him."

Fletcher sighed but nodded, pulling his phone out. "You got anything going on we need to worry about?" he asked, lifting his eyebrow in question. It felt more like an attack than a general query.

"And if I did?" I challenged, crossing my arms.

"We'd be there to help. Sorry if that came out

wrong. I just like to be prepared for what attacks we might have to face."

I sighed, letting his comment go. We were all under a lot of stress, and I'd rather him take it out on me than Henley.

"No. My mother died over the summer, so I'm still dealing with that. I want to spread her ashes one weekend, but so far, we haven't had the time. There are no exes, siblings, or scumbag parents to worry about. I have a few hockey enemies, but they typically stay on the ice. I don't let people in, which might be a good thing for once."

"Sorry to hear about your mother. Were you close?"

I nodded, swallowing. I couldn't talk about her this openly around people, not after thinking about her earlier. It was still too fresh.

"I know this might sound empty, but... I know what it's like to lose someone you care about. So, if you ever need to chat or hit things, just let me know."

Letting out a breath, I met Fletcher's eyes, noticing the sincerity there. He had lost someone he cared about. I recognized the sadness in his eyes. It wasn't an empty platitude. After a few seconds, I gave a single nod, letting him know I'd heard him.

The rest of the time, we discussed the team and what players had done well during the game. It was easy to focus on that instead of all the other things. When we returned to the house, both Dax and Henley seemed a little more relaxed, and I got a twinge of envy for the time they'd spent together.

As the night went on and I painted her toenails as she laughed at some ridiculous movie, I knew she needed me just as much as I needed her, and that was all that mattered.

It wasn't until I was lying in my bed that I remembered I never asked Fletcher if there was anyone or anything in his past we needed to worry about.

# CHAPTER 28

## *Henley*

AS MUCH AS I didn't want to admit it, Fletcher had been right about taking the night off. Nothing else would've been solved, and worrying about it was only borrowing trouble. I woke up with a fire in me, ready to tackle this day and anything that came my way.

Pulling up to the building Scarlet was staying in, I sent a text to let her know I was there. After five minutes passed, I sighed, realizing I'd have to go inside. Scarlet was notoriously late for any and everything other than hockey.

Locking my car, I headed up the stairs to the room she was staying in. Knocking, I jumped back when a loud moan echoed from behind the door. Okay, so maybe she wasn't still asleep. Smiling, an idea popped into my head, and I started to smack and bang against the door as I yelled obnoxious things.

"Your dildo delivery is here! Congrats, you've won a lifetime supply of hemorrhoid cream! Act now to get this amazing offer on a gallon of lube. It can all be yours for $19.99 a month."

The door finally opened, a giggle escaping me as

Scar narrowed her eyes at me. She had a sheet covering her body.

"I don't know what's funnier. The fact you think that embarrasses me or that I'm sad it's not true. I could use a gallon of lube right now."

"And here I thought we had a good thing going!" I joked as I shook my head in mock outrage before I smiled at my friend. "I thought you wanted to get breakfast?"

"I do. Just give me a minute to put on some clothes. I'll meet you downstairs."

"If you're not down in five, I'm leaving you!" I shouted as I walked away, chuckling to myself while wondering who she had in there. I knew Keaton, Monty, and Cody had all been interested. Huh. Maybe she'd gotten her harem after all?

Five minutes later, Scarlet zoomed out of the building, practically skipping to the SUV. She grinned wide as she opened the door and got in.

"Hello, lover."

"I'm not sure that applies anymore." Wiggling my eyes at her as she happily sighed, putting her feet on the dash. I knocked them off, giving her a look.

"After the game on Friday, a bunch of us went out for drinks. The tension between me and a few of the guys had been off the charts all week, but I'd wanted to focus on the team, so I hadn't given in. Plus, it was fun to play with them and see how far I could push the limit."

"I hope you're not breaking any hearts, Scar."

"I can't help it, Hen. I'm a lovable person. But... I think you've finally shown me a solution I could get behind."

"Oh?" I asked, pulling into a parking spot in front of the coffee shop.

"Monogamy never felt right. Whenever I tried it, it was like I was wearing skates two sizes too small. It was uncomfortable, and someone always got hurt. So instead, I thought I'd just be a serial dater and bed hop. But even that isn't enough sometimes. I get tired of going through the same dance, not having real intimacy, or being scared someone would catch feelings."

I turned off the car and faced my friend. It felt important, like she was sharing something more than just a hookup. Scarlet grabbed my hands, squeezing them.

"When I saw you with your three guys and how happy you were, it made me believe I could find something like that, too. I know I joked about it, but it felt like the answer to what I'd always felt, and I was too scared to admit it."

"So, I take it you've found a few guys who don't mind sharing?" I asked.

She nodded, a tear escaping down her cheek. "Yeah. I think I have. Oh, Hen. It's more than I ever thought possible. But also, how do you walk? And do you have any tips?"

Chuckling, I hugged my friend, rubbing my hand

on her back. "Come on. I need coffee before we start to talk about dicknometry."

"Ooh, now there's a subject I could get behind, or would it be in front of? You know what, I'm good with all of them," she declared as she climbed out of the car.

I couldn't help but laugh every second I was around Scar. She was good medicine.

Ordering coffee and a breakfast bagel, I grabbed a table off to the corner that had two cozy chairs next to it. Scarlet joined me a second later, and I stared at her, waiting for her to spill who the mystery men in her life were.

She managed to take the longest time to situate herself, fixing her necklace and tying her shoes before she finally looked up with a coy smile.

"Oh, were you waiting on me?" she asked, placing a hand on her chest as she batted her eyelashes.

"You're the worst." I rolled my eyes, taking a drink of coffee. I was going to need it to deal with her nonsense this early.

Scarlet chuckled as she took a sip. "Well, I'm guessing you could guess who."

"Fine. I'm desperate to know, so I'll play your games. Keaton?" I asked.

She nodded, a soft smile on her lips. "Oh my God, Hen. He's the absolute sweetest. And the things he can do with his tongue. Girl!" She fanned her face, and I noticed the slight blush. Scar might be onto something. She'd never blushed about any of her other lovers.

"He asked me if you were going to eat him alive," I admitted.

"Ha! Probably. Especially if it was just him. But since it's not, I can embrace the softer and sweet things he does without wanting to run away in hives."

Our food was delivered, interrupting her spiel for a second. We took a moment to eat while the server returned to the counter. I peered around, noticing only a few other patrons sitting as most people got their order to-go. After I took another drink of my coffee, I eyed her, curious to know more.

"I'm going to say Monty next."

"Yep." She nodded, taking a bite. "Now, I knew the sex between us would be off the charts. He's the type of hockey guy I usually gravitate toward, the ones I can climb like a tree." She fanned her face, and I chuckled as I kept eating. "I wasn't sure if he'd go for the arrangement I wanted, but he was the first to suggest it. He's a voyeur and likes to share, so win-win for me!"

I finished my bagel and pushed the plate away, folding my legs under me as I leaned against the armrest with my coffee. "I wonder if playing on a team for so long helps that? The guys are used to working with someone?"

"Who the fuck knows?" She giggled, crossing her legs. "I think it's the air in Utah, honestly. All the fresh mountain air makes people happier and hornier."

"Is there one more?" I asked.

"Yep. I'm sure you can guess who."

"Cody?"

"He's so much fun. I've never laughed so much in my entire life."

"I'm happy for you, Scar. You deserve all the happiness... and sex."

"Yeah, I do!" She laughed as she danced in her seat. "Now, spill. What was it like to meet Carly, and how will she nail Dakota's balls to the wall?"

I sighed, knowing she'd ask. "It wasn't at all like I thought it would be. She lives on a private estate in the woods. There was a dress code to follow for every meal, and even had outfits for all of us. The clothes were nice, but it was strange how she knew our sizes. Right?"

Scar's eyes went wide. "A dress code? Sizes? Okay, I think you've broken my brain."

"That's just the beginning of it, too." I sat forward, eager now that I had someone's attention who knew our world. "There was a pool party with a lot of other hockey players, some business owners, and politicians. It was a very odd group to mingle together. She introduced me to the whole party, making me feel like a specimen to be auctioned off."

"I'm just having a weird visual of old people in swimsuits. You've definitely broken my brain now."

Snorting, I smiled, taking a breath. "Then, after the party was a formal dinner. The guys were all in suits, and I wore a ball gown. It was gorgeous. After everyone ate, all these performers came in."

"Performers? Like a band?"

"No, more like a Cirque du Soleil show. It was fascinating to watch, and it was nice to pretend I belonged in that world for a little bit, but eventually, this Cinderella's shoes were too small."

"I have no words. That's a lot for one day."

"It was, wasn't it? I kept questioning myself if I was being too paranoid. She was nothing but nice and provided everything I could possibly need, going out of her way to host a party full of people she thought I'd like to meet with. But I dunno. It felt like it was too much. I kept waiting for someone to jump out and scream, 'Fake!' which made it hard to truly enjoy it."

"That sucks, Hen. I know how much you were looking forward to seeing her."

"She was lovely, really, and I feel bad for thinking she had a hidden agenda." I dropped my eyes because, in the end, Carly had one.

Scarlet reached out and clasped my hand. "Don't ever feel bad for listening to your gut. It's what makes you so great. So, I'm guessing you still don't have a solution for donkey balls?"

"Donkey balls?" I spat.

"Dakota, donkey balls. It's all the same." She grinned, lifting a lot of my worry.

"Dax is going to look into something. When we

landed, I found out that Carol's trying to contest the court order that terminated her rights."

"That bitch! Sorry, I know she's your mother, but damn, that's cold."

"No apologies needed. Carol *is* a bitch. With that and the team, I didn't have it in me to deal with Dakota. Fletcher and Reed are helping with the team, so I only have to focus on Reese for the moment."

"Another point for a harem. Seriously, there haven't been any negatives yet."

Laughing, I told Scar my story about doing laundry and cursing the number of socks.

"But you ended up being fucked up against the washer? I'm trying to see the negative here, Hen?"

My face blushed, and I shrugged. She had a point.

"So, how do you deal with the whole group thing? Do they get weirded out if someone's balls are in their face?"

Coughing, I looked around, noticing an older lady had looked up from her book at Scarlet's question. Another girl closer to our age snorted as she scrolled on her phone. She looked familiar, and I figured I'd seen her around town before. When my cheeks returned to normal, I focused back on Scar.

"Ah hem, well, I just had my first one, and it wasn't that type of group scene. One person went, and then the other two were together. It was my first, you know," I whispered, suddenly embarrassed.

"You popped your DP cherry! High five, girl! How

was it? It's nice, right? I remember my first time." She sighed wistfully after smacking my palm.

"Do any of your guys like one another?" I asked, curious.

She scrunched up her nose as she thought. "I'm not sure yet. I could see it as a possibility. Yours?"

"No. I tried to get Reed and Dax to kiss, and they looked at me like I had three heads. So, it's not something my guys are into." I chuckled, finishing my coffee when I noticed the time. "I need to get back to campus. There's a meeting, and I need to review the game film before practice later."

"Ah, the life of a coach. You're great at it, Hen. It suits you."

"Thanks, Scar. It feels right."

The two of us cleaned up our area and headed out. The older woman who'd been reading put her book down, grabbing my attention as we passed. I tensed, worried she would tell us we were sluts and going to Hell.

"It's so nice to see women embracing their sex life. I wish I'd cared less when I was younger. Now, I have to read about it vicariously in books." She lifted the one she was reading, and I noticed the scantily clad man and woman on it. "To be young," she sighed.

"Hell yeah! I'll get some for you, ma'am." Scar lifted her hand, getting a high-five from the woman. We giggled the rest of the way out of the shop.

"Never thought I'd hear you telling a grandmother

you'd get some for her. Oh man, you're good for the soul, Scar. Never change. I'm going to miss you when you're gone."

I placed the car in reverse as I backed up, jumping when Scar slapped her forehead, and I slammed on the brakes.

"Shit, I forgot to tell you why I wanted to get breakfast."

"Holy crap! Don't do that. I thought I hit something."

She cringed, and I registered what she said.

"If it wasn't about your new sex life, what was it?"

"I'm not leaving. Dmitry offered me a position to hold skills workshops. He liked how much the kids worked last week and wanted to keep it. So, you're stuck with me, lover!" She threw her arms around me in a tight squeeze.

"Seriously? That's so awesome. I'm so happy to have more time with you." I hugged her back just as tight.

Confidence that I could do this on my own returned to me each time I regained my footing. A car honked, breaking our hugfest, and I realized I was halfway out of the parking spot. Whoops. Waving the person an apology, I finished backing out and headed back to campus, excitement bubbling in me.

# CHAPTER 29

## *Henley*

THE NEXT FEW days flew by as I focused on Reese and hockey. I hadn't heard anything from Carol yet, but I knew it was only a matter of time. Both my lawyer and the caseworker were confident she had nothing to contest, listing the same reasons I had to Reese that day.

It made it even more obvious my mother was up to something. She didn't want Reese back, but something else. The problem with Carol was it could be anything.

The team played better than ever, making me excited for the week's upcoming game. As much as I hated that Fletcher had stepped away from his post on the junior team, I loved having him and Reed with me. The three of us complimented one another in our areas of skills. Not to mention how nice the view was. On the days I got to spend time with Dax, too, I felt like I'd won the lottery.

Blowing my whistle, I motioned for everyone to gather around. The team hustled, their hair slick with sweat as they removed their helmets. It had been a long practice, and they'd all worked hard on the drills.

"Good practice, you guys. I can tell your dedication

is paying off. You're finally playing like a team. Tomorrow's practice will be shorter after conditioning, so everyone has time to participate in the Lux charity drive. This is a perfect opportunity to practice networking and giving back to the community. One of my favorite parts of being a professional athlete is the good I can do with my platform. So, I hope you all will take it seriously."

I paused as I searched their faces, hoping they were all listening. Satisfied, I continued.

"This Friday is the family and alumni game. I know many of your parents will be attending, which adds pressure. Keep your focus on the game, and celebrate once we kick some Penguin's butt. Everyone will be looking to see if last week was a fluke. So, was it?" I asked.

"No!" a few kids shouted, slapping their sticks against the ice.

"I agree. We're a good team, and now we can prove that. Hit the showers. I'll see you tomorrow."

The team dispersed, excited chatter filling the space. It was a nice sound compared to the first week's grumblings.

Reed and Fletcher had already collected all the gear, so I took a few seconds to stretch out my legs as I skated around the rink, running through the practice. It had become my routine by this point to replay it and then leave it on the ice.

Feeling confident about our plays, I skated off,

taking the guards that Fletcher handed me. Susie, Cody, and Tyler headed toward us as we neared the locker room.

"Hey! How did your ice time go?" Susie asked when she saw us.

When she'd returned earlier in the week, she'd shared that Dmitry had offered her a position for the season. Cody and Tyler were sharing the head position since Ty still wanted to be part-time so he could work with his dad at some security firm.

"It went well. This game should go a lot differently this week. How's your team looking? Any new recruits?"

"There are a few interested, but they won't be here until next week," Cody answered.

"You going to the charity drive tomorrow?" Susie asked.

"Yep. You?"

"Of course. We can chat more there. Maybe we can do a girls' night with Scar after?" she asked, glancing at the two guys next to me.

"Yes!" I nodded, my eyes wide. "That would be great. Let's do it."

"Perfect. I'll talk to you then." She waved as she followed the others onto the ice.

Fletcher wrapped an arm around me, pulling me closer. "I'm happy you have some girlfriends here, Baby Shaw. Though I think our spa night will be tough to beat."

"Oh, most definitely," I agreed, peering up at him. "Reed gives a great pedicure."

Reed grunted next to me, having heard my words. Grabbing his hand, I swung our arms as we made our way, loving our relationship.

The three of us quickly changed, heading out of the building together. It was getting dark already, and I regretted parking on the side of the building, but it was the closest to the side exit, so it felt worth it at the end of the day.

Two guys appeared wearing black, full-face masks, jumping out from behind a van and grabbing Reed and Fletcher by their arms. In that moment, I realized how dumb I'd been. We were completely cut off. A scream left me as the guys were shoved down to the ground, my body freezing on the spot.

"Stop!" My eyes pinged between two of the guys I loved, worry and fear filling me.

"Run, Hen!" Reed shouted as a knee pressed down on him. He and Fletcher bucked against the men, but the ambush had surprised us. I could hear their grunts and sounds of pain as fear clawed up my body.

I debated for another second if I should do something or follow Reed's instructions and run. Ultimately, I decided to turn tail and get help. I'd only get hurt if I tried to attack the men, and then we'd all be screwed.

I only made it two feet before I ran into a chest, smacking my face, and jolting back. Meaty hands reached out to grip me, squeezing my biceps and pulling me back to his body.

"Let me go," I shouted, attempting to fight as best I could. His grip crushed my arm, and I cried out in pain, a whimper leaving me.

"Shut the fuck up," the man hissed.

"Wh-a-a-t do you want?" I hated how my voice trembled.

"This is the last warning I'm giving Dax. I'll start breaking bones if he doesn't deliver what I asked for. Though you, I might save for a different type of breaking."

The mention of Dax had me straightening my spine. This had to be the jackass that broke his ribs.

"You might as well do it now then, because Dax isn't going to give you shit, asshole!" I spat.

"Looks like this one has some spunk. Don't worry; I'll break that out of you quick."

"Good luck doing that from prison."

"And here I thought only blondes were dumb." He rolled his eyes like he was bored with me. My whole body shook as the adrenaline rushed through me.

"What's that supposed to mean?" I asked. I was trying to stall him, hoping someone would leave or see them on the security cameras.

"I have friends in high places, sweetie. You can't touch me."

Narrowing my eyes, I felt the fire return as I stared this man down. He was used to his size intimidating others, but I could see the desperation. He was an addict and needed his fix. Once I calmed down, I remembered my training and stomped down on his instep, kneeing him in the head when it fell forward. His arms let go of me, and I didn't hesitate as I ran, screaming at the top of my lungs.

"Help! Help! Fire!" I hit the cars as I passed, setting off any alarms, hoping they would alert someone. I screamed 'fire' a couple more times, remembering a study that people were more willing to respond to it over 'help.' I didn't look back as I ran, worried he'd be hot on my tail and I'd stumble.

I made it around the corner just as Dax and a security guard exited the building. Dax saw me and took off for me. I didn't stop; rushing toward him as I pointed to the side.

"Call the cops."

The security guard pulled out his walkie-talkie and taser as he continued around the side. My body shook as I fell into Dax's arms. The tears I'd been holding back ran down my face now that I was safe.

"Hen, what's wrong? What happened? Where are the guys?"

"Gareth," I croaked, my voice hoarse from screaming.

"I got her, Dax. Go," another voice said.

I whimpered, not wanting to let go now that I had someone I trusted. The touch on my arm was gentle, familiar. Opening my eyes, I spotted the kind doctor.

I couldn't remember his name, but I knew he was safe.

"Let Milo look at you, Petal."

Nodding, I stepped away. Dax's eyes were haunted as he scanned me.

"Go help the others," I whispered, my eyes pleading. Milo placed a jacket over my arms and moved me toward the front of the building.

It took Dax a few seconds before he could turn and dash around the corner. I moved in a daze, my mind shutting off now. Milo checked me over from head to toe. Even though I didn't believe I had any injuries. I couldn't remember all Gareth had done; I just remembered he held my arms.

"Are you hurt anywhere?" Milo asked.

"I… I… I… don't think so. He just grabbed me." Milo nodded, lifting my arm and looking it over. While he was doing that, a police car pulled in, followed by an ambulance. The police continued around the building as the ambulance stopped.

The noise and lights drew a crowd as students gathered, trying to figure out what had happened. Milo helped me to the ambulance, telling the EMT what he knew. They flashed a light in my eyes and had me open my mouth. Eventually, they placed a blanket over my shoulders once they'd examined me thoroughly.

I stared out into the night, my body and mind numb. I was so tired of being beaten down. Every time

I thought I was thriving, something popped up and reminded me I wasn't allowed to. When would I get to be happy without fear of the consequences? When would it be my turn?

My questions were stopped as a body slammed into me, thin arms going around my neck. The numbness wore off as I held Reese.

"What happened? Are you okay?" they asked.

"I'm okay," I said, hoping if I repeated it enough, I'd believe it.

When I didn't say anything else, Reese asked Milo. He didn't have much info, so they returned to me quickly.

"Where are the guys, Hen?"

"I don't know. They were being held down. Dax went to help, but no one has returned. Do you think that means they're dead?"

As I voiced the question, the sobs erupted, my body shaking more as I let out all my fear. Reese hugged me, rocking with me as they tried to soothe me. I berated myself for being weak, for falling apart in the parking lot with so many people watching, and for making my younger sibling have to comfort me. But no matter how harsh I was to myself, I couldn't stop the tears.

Hands gripped my cheeks, hands that were rough from work and much larger than my siblings. That knowledge had me looking up, blinking tears out of my eyes. Reed stood in front of me, his mouth moving, but I couldn't understand what he was saying.

The realization he was standing in front of me finally penetrated the fog around me, letting sound and reality return.

"Henley, I'm here. I'm okay. Henley, come back to me. To us. We're all okay, baby. We just need you."

"You're okay?" I asked, lifting my hand.

Reed nodded, his body relaxing at my spoken words. He pulled my head to his chest, holding me to him. "I've never been so scared in my life, Hen. Thank you for listening to me. Thank you for running."

"I didn't want to," I admitted into his chest. "I didn't want to leave you."

"I know. But I'm glad you did. I'm okay. I promise." Reed drew back, his thumbs wiping my tears away as he stared at me.

"Give her to me," Fletcher barked, making me jump. I peered over Reed's shoulder, spotting him there.

"Calm down. You'll scare her more."

"I'll calm down once I know she's okay," he argued.

I patted Reed's hand, getting his attention and breaking the stare-off with Fletcher. "Let me go. I'm okay."

He sighed and kissed me, holding me to his chest for a second. When he stepped back, I watched as he wrapped an arm around Reese. Their face was ashen, but when they met my eyes, they nodded, smiling at me. Reed nodded that he had them, so I stood up and stepped into Fletcher's arms.

His body shook as he held me. The shock wore off, so I made soothing sounds, letting him know I was okay, that we were all okay. Once he calmed, I looked for Dax, needing to know he was safe, too. Plus, I had a feeling he'd blame himself, and I didn't want him to do that.

"Where's Dax?" I asked. Reed and Fletcher were both being looked over by the EMT, but it didn't appear either of them had any injuries outside of a few scratches from being face down on the pavement.

"He's over there with Officer Delaney," Reese said, nodding. Squeezing their hand, I walked over. Dax wouldn't look at me as I approached, and I knew my hunch was correct.

Not questioning it, I stepped into his space, wrapping my arms around him. His body was taut, but I kept holding on, needing him to know I was there.

"I love you, Dax. This wasn't your fault."

He dropped his head, his arms embracing me as he held me. When he was able to meet my eyes, he searched them. I held his gaze, knowing he needed to know with certainty that I meant what I said.

He sighed and kissed my lips, holding me to him for a long time. It was soft but reassuring, and I stored the feelings I gathered from it in my heart, knowing I'd need them.

Once we'd all been looked over and released by the EMT and Milo, we gave our statements to the police officer. Apparently, after I kneed Gareth and ran screaming, he'd run after me until I met up with Dax and the security guard. Then he'd backtracked, took his guys, and ran off in the other direction. By the time the security officer arrived, they were disappearing around the corner.

"I heard you screaming, Petal, and I knew something wasn't right. I've never been so scared before," Dax admitted. It brought tears to my eyes, but there wasn't anything I could do. It had been scary.

The police officer thanked us and offered to have a patrol car sit outside our house and monitor the hockey rink. Dmitry told him it wouldn't be necessary as the school would hire a private firm. It had shocked me since I hadn't noticed him arriving, but it made me feel better knowing there would be someone here to protect the kids.

After a lot of hugs from Reese, I coaxed them to return to the dorm with Braden and Briana, and promised to text before I went to bed.

There were a lot of other people watching, but I was done for the day. Climbing into my car, I handed the keys to Dax, too tired to drive.

That night, we managed to all cram into Fletcher's king bed, no one wanting to sleep alone. It took me a long time to fall asleep, despite the exhaustion. I couldn't quit replaying the scene over and over in my head and imagine how it could've been so much worse. It would take a while to stop feeling Gareth's hands on me.

I was beginning to believe the only option I had was to join the Society in order to keep everyone I loved safe.

# CHAPTER 30

## *Henley*

A LOUD BANG had me jumping, a startled scream escaping as I turned around, looking for the danger. When I spotted a metal sign on the ground, I realized someone had just knocked it over. Placing my hand over my heart, I took some deep breaths, attempting to calm myself.

I'd been like this all day—jumpy and scared of my own shadow—and I hated it.

It wasn't who I was.

Spotting Reed, I watched his muscles flex as he lifted a few cases of water onto the table. Weirdly, it calmed me. In a way, it made sense; his muscles were hypnotic. He turned and caught me staring, his stoic face softening as he watched me. He lifted his brow, and I knew he was asking if I was okay.

Nodding, I returned to the table I was sorting, happy to get lost in a task for a bit. Dmitry had wanted to cancel the charity drive after the events of last night, but I wouldn't let him. If people treated me like a glass doll, then I would break.

What I needed was to keep going so I could remind myself how strong I was. The routine and predictable nature soothed the sense of security that had been stolen, allowing me to find my footing again.

"Do you have any more name tags? I recruited a few more people to help," Reese asked as they came around the table.

"Yeah. One sec." I placed the last t-shirt on the pile and turned to face my sibling. Reese watched me with careful eyes, probably assessing my mental state. Smiling at them, I grabbed a package of name tags from under the table and handed them off.

"How's it going so far? Looks like we have a good turnout."

Reese nodded. "Yeah. There are a lot of parents here. I guess most people's families come in for the whole weekend. We've collected a lot of good stuff so far."

The charity drive was to gather gently used or new sporting equipment to give to communities where the sports programs were underfunded or nonexistent, allowing kids who might not normally have access a chance to find a sport they loved.

"There does seem to be a lot of people." I surveyed the crowd, some anxiety returning at the realization Gareth could be hiding among them. My eyes flitted over one of the security guards, and I calmed, remembering we weren't unprepared this time.

A woman approached with an envelope in her hand. She had a sense of familiarity, but I couldn't recall why. Pasting on a smile, I faced her as she approached.

"Hi. Are you signing up to participate in the parents' events, or would you like to buy some merch?"

She gave a crooked smile, and I suddenly remembered where I knew her from.

"You were at the coffee shop." My acknowledgment made her smile broader.

"Ah, so you do remember me." She glanced at Reese, who was still standing next to me with the package of name tags. "Perfect. You're here too."

The hairs on my neck rose, and I knew this wasn't a parent or someone here for the charity drive. This woman had a purpose, and I'd bet money that it included Reese.

Shifting so I stood in front of my sibling, I kept my smile as I waited. When she just kept staring, I caved, hoping I was wrong. "Did you need something?"

She sighed like I was inconveniencing her. "Some days, I really hate my job," she mumbled before sliding the envelope across the table toward me. "I'm sorry to do this because you seem like a nice person, and that's rare in my job. But at the end of the day, you're not my client."

I refused to take the envelope, leaving it there. I crossed my arms as I dropped the smile.

"And who is your client?" I asked, the sound practically a growl, and I wondered if I'd picked it up from one of the guys.

"Carol Henshaw."

My blood froze at the name, my breath getting lodged in my throat. Reese shifted behind me, their elbow knocking into my side, and I remembered to breathe. Slowly letting it out, I narrowed my eyes.

"And just what are you doing for Carol?"

"I'm a PI. She hired me to find dirt on you."

A shocked laugh escaped me. Of all the things I'd thought she would say, that wasn't one of them.

"Dirt on me?" I scoffed. "Sorry to disappoint you, then. I don't live a fascinating life." And while that was historically true, I knew the last few months had been different. But I still wouldn't call them scandalous.

She gave me that crooked smile like she thought I was cute or dumb. I didn't know which I preferred.

"You sure about that?" she questioned.

"I don't have time to do anything worthy of blackmailing. I'm sure that's what my mother intends to do. She made a big stink about refilling for custody, and now this. She's grasping at straws."

She lifted her hands, stepping away. "I just find the information. It's not up to me what my clients do with it."

"So why are you giving it to me, then?" I asked, confused.

"As I said, you're a nice person. I've been watching you over the past month, and I don't think you deserve what she's planning. In good conscience, I couldn't give her the ammo without warning you to wear a bulletproof vest first."

"You could just not give her the ammo," Reese said.

The woman glanced back at Reese, shrugging. "I could, but then I wouldn't have a business, and a girl's gotta eat."

"Wait!" I shouted, an idea forming in my head. She smiled, and I wondered if that had been her intention all along. "What would it take for you to work for me instead?"

She grimaced, and I wondered if I'd said the wrong thing. "Sorry, this isn't TV. You can't just pay me double to make it all go away. I signed a contract, so I'm obligated to report back to my client any of my findings."

My shoulders slumped, and my eyes dropped as I bit my lip, racing through all the possible solutions I could think of.

"What about if we hired you to find dirt on her?" Reese asked, surprising me. A shadow fell over me, and I looked up, finding Fletcher had joined us. He searched my eyes as he tried to figure out what was happening.

The PI stepped back to where they'd been, smiling at Reese's question.

"Now, that is something I can do. They didn't opt for the exclusive package, meaning once my job for them is done, they become fair game." She smirked, and I found myself liking her despite the fact she'd been snooping on me.

"What's going on?" Fletcher asked, clearly sensing something was afoot.

"Carol hired... Sorry, what's your name?" I asked, realizing I hadn't got it.

"Veronica. Veronica Mars."

"Seriously?" I asked, my mouth gaping open. She laughed, making me like her more than I wanted to.

"It would be cool if it were, wouldn't it? I'm Macy McPherson, owner of M&M Investigations."

She held out her hand, and I shook it, a little dazed by this woman. I turned back to Fletcher, my eyes wide as I tried to regain my footing. He smirked as he waited for me to compose myself.

"Right, so... Macy was hired by Carol to investigate me. She's just delivered the information she's gathered and was giving me a heads up on what Carol has planned."

"Why does it sound like you use quotations around her name when you speak about her?" Macy asked curiously. It felt like I was the question to a puzzle she couldn't entirely solve, and if she could figure me out, then she'd understand something better. I didn't like it.

"And Reese asked if we could hire you to investigate Carol..." Fletcher finished. "What's your daily fee?" he asked, all businesslike now that he knew. I wanted to be pissed he stepped in, but I wasn't. This was one thing I'd be happy to hand over and let someone help me with.

"I can send you my packages if you're interested," Macy replied, looking Fletcher up and down. It wasn't necessarily sexual, but I didn't like it. I narrowed my eyes as I stared.

"We'll do the best one you have with the exclusive feature so she can't use you ever again," he said before I could respond. They continued talking as I watched them go back and forth; I'd become a spectator to my own conversation.

"Done. My card's in the envelope. I look forward to hearing from you. This offer only lasts for twenty-four hours, so don't dally!" Macy gave a finger wave before spinning on her heel and walking away this time. It made it even more obvious the first time had been a ploy.

"Thanks, Fletch. I got a little overwhelmed by it all."

"Anytime, Baby Shaw. I meant what I said about not being in this alone. You and Reese are ours now."

He wrapped his arm around me, pulling me to his side. I glanced at Reese, finding them blushing. Reaching out, I took their hand, wanting them to be included in this moment. It had been a long time for either of us since we'd felt like we belonged.

Reese cleared their throat after a few seconds. "I

guess I better get these name tags to my new recruits. The hockey gear isn't going to sort itself."

I stepped away from Fletcher to hug Reese. "I love you, and no one will take you from me," I whispered. Reese nodded into my embrace, squeezing me back. "Now, go do something, or I'll get the coach after you," I teased.

"I hear they're a real toughie," they said, smiling.

"You hear that, Fletch? I'm a toughie." I chuckled as he stared down at me. Reese waved as they left, leaving us alone for a second.

"You doing okay?" he asked, his hand coming up to cup my cheek. I closed my eyes, letting myself soak in his comfort for a few seconds.

"I'm... managing. I think that's all I can handle today."

He nodded, his eyes sweeping back and forth. The gold in his eyes shimmered in the evening light, and I wanted to stay there where it was safe.

"Do you want me to open the envelope? Or do you want to stay in the dark?" he asked.

Sighing, I dropped my head to his chest as I thought about it. I knew I should be prepared and look at it, but the part of me that had already dealt with enough shit for the past twenty-four hours didn't know if I could peek into another dark corner and not run away screaming straight after.

"I can look and just tell you without you having to

see it. Would that be better? Half in, but not completely?"

I debated and realized that it might be about all I could handle today. Nodding, I stepped back, picked up the envelope, and handed it to him. He didn't hesitate to open it, pulling out a couple of photos. I watched his face, attempting to gauge how bad it was.

Fletcher flipped to the second one, but his face told me nothing, remaining more stoic than Reed. That fact alone was causing me to freak out.

"It's bad, isn't it? I didn't think I had anything to hide, but now you're making me question myself." I shook my hands in front of me as the anxiety crept up my neck. After he glanced at the last one, he placed them all back into the envelope, putting a business card in his pocket.

"They aren't bad, but I can see how they might look to a judge."

"Okay. What are they of?"

He cleared his throat, his eyes scanning the surrounding area. "The first two are pictures of us all out at the pub. There's beer and dancing with Dax and me. Neither of which is very incriminating. It could be spun that you're out late drinking and are promiscuous since it's with two different guys."

I rolled my eyes, not concerned about those two things. They could be spun however they wanted, but I was over twenty-one and a consenting adult. Neither of those things were illegal or kept me from performing my duties as a guardian. Especially since Reese was in school and not waiting up for me at home.

"What's the last one?" I asked, knowing it had to be worse.

Fletcher pulled his shirt away from his neck as red spread up it. "Ah, well, hmm. Apparently, we didn't shut the curtains the first night you were with Reed and me."

I stood there, my mouth open, trying to picture what he was saying. But that would mean... No... not again. The violation of my privacy hit me full force, and I swayed. If another photo of me was leaked, I would be unable to show my face. It didn't matter that I was safe and committed to both of them. The narrative about me being unwholesome was already there, thanks to Dakota. This would be the cherry on a screw-Henley-over sundae.

"Well, fuck."

"It's not as bad as you're probably thinking. It just could—"

"Make me look like someone with a sex problem," I interrupted him.

"Yeah." He swallowed. "It sucks, Hen, and isn't fair. How do you want to get ahead of it?"

"You think I could?"

"Possibly. You have the advantage of knowing about it this time."

I tapped my finger against my lip, debating my options. "I don't know where to start."

"I'll talk to Dax and see what he was planning. Perhaps we can take down two enemies with one story."

Nodding, I licked my lips, liking his idea. "Yeah. Let's hope. I'm tired of being executed for my choices. And if you want any more sexy times in the house, you need to install self-closing curtains or something."

Fletcher chuckled, the sound deep and dark as it rumbled through my body. He pulled me close to him, kissing the top of my head. "Will do, Baby Shaw, will do."

# CHAPTER 31

## Dax

MY PHONE VIBRATED for the thousandth time, and I hit the reject button again. I'd been staring at the computer screen, attempting to devise a solution to the Dakota problem, but my mind was stuck on last night.

Hearing Henley scream would haunt my nightmares, as would finding her running for her life. The look of terror on her face wasn't something I'd easily forget. Scrubbing my hands against my face, I tipped my head back to stare at the ceiling and prayed for some type of divine intervention to give me the perfect solution to all my problems.

The vibration began on the table, so I righted myself to answer it, knowing it wouldn't stop until I did.

"What?" I growled.

"Dax Memphis Cassel! I know you're not talking to your mother with that tone of voice."

My face flamed, and my fists clenched as I realized my mistake. Taking in a deep breath, I let it out slowly.

"Mother. I'm sorry; I thought you were someone else."

She tutted, the sound loud through the tiny speaker. "I know exactly who you thought I was, and I'm calling to tell you I'm over sitting on the sidelines with this feud with your brother. It's been years, Dax. I know what he did wasn't right. I don't blame you for being angry at him. But I don't want my family to be torn apart. I miss you, Son." The fire in her voice disappeared the longer she spoke, pulling at my heart-strings.

"I miss you too, Mom. It's just not that simple to forgive him. He *betrayed* me."

"I know, Dax. I get it. Really, I do. I slapped him and put him on grandfather duty for an entire year. So, don't think he didn't go unpunished."

"He's a grown man, Ma. You're not the one who's supposed to be punishing him."

"I'm his mother until the day I die, so if he does something dumb, then I'll make sure he knows it."

"Did he have to change his diapers and bathe him?" I asked, suddenly feeling a little better at the thought of Derek in his thousand-dollar suit giving our grandfather a sponge bath.

"You bet your cute butt he did!" She chuckled proudly.

"Ma! You can't say my butt is cute. I'm a grown man."

"You're 29, Dax. I can say your butt is cute. Do I need to remind you I'm your mother?"

"No, Ma." I chuckled. "I know you are."

"You sure about that? Because a boy is supposed to call his mother and see her, especially when important things happen." I could picture her crossing her arms, lifting her eyebrow in a challenge. I'd been ducking her calls for months, and she was letting me know it.

"Sorry. You're right. Things have just been busy with school starting."

"Humph. That's not what I heard."

Cursing under my breath, I rubbed my temple, regretting answering the phone. This was so not the conversation I wanted to have right now.

"Oh. What have you heard?" I hedged. I could practically hear the smile over the phone as she spoke.

"That you have a girlfriend."

Exhaling, I counted to ten, so I wouldn't explode on my mother. "It's still new." As soon as the words left my mouth, I regretted it. As much as I didn't want my mother, or my family for that matter, in my business, it didn't feel right minimizing what Henley and I had together.

"Is that why she's dating three of you?" she asked hesitantly.

"No. She's dating three of us because she wants to, and we want her to be happy. We're all on board with the idea. And I lied before. It might be new, but it's…" I paused, searching for the right word. "It's real. Henley gets me and accepts me for who I am, even with all the things from my past."

"Well, that's… I'm glad, Dax. You deserve someone

who sees how special you are." Her love for me was evident, and I relaxed, happy she'd accepted my situation. "And if you're happy with this... arrangement... then I'll find a way to understand it. As much as I love Jennifer, I never thought she was the right woman for you. So, when can I meet her?"

"Ah, um, I'm not sure. Things are pretty busy with the school. She's the hockey coach, so yeah, lots of games and practices." I slapped my forehead at how ridiculous I sounded.

"A coach. That's exciting. When are the games?" she asked. The question sounded innocent, but I knew my mother was fishing for something, and I needed to tread very carefully.

"They play on Friday evenings. They have one tomorrow night."

"So that means she's free on Saturdays? Perfect. You can both come to the wedding then."

And there it was. Pressing my lips together, I tugged at the strands of my hair. I'd walked right into her trap.

"It's not a great time, Mom. There are some issues going on that Henley needs to focus on."

"Nonsense. You can spare a day. It will be good for you to come home and see your family. Some of your cousins you haven't seen in years will be here. Ainsley just married that big-shot sports reporter, and they're going to make it."

Dropping my hands, I replayed what she said in

my head as I tried to recall who she was talking about. Maybe this could be the break I needed. I'd get my mom off my back, have Henley to shield me from all the pity looks, and introduce her to a hotshot reporter that could make Dakota go away.

"Mom, you're a freaking genius!" I shouted, standing up and making the chair screech as it slid across the floor.

"Language! But thank you, Son. I do think I'm rather intelligent. Not that your father would agree," she grumbled. "You forget about the cookies in the oven once because you're tired from an energetic toddler and a colicky newborn, and he won't ever let you forget it."

Coughing, I tried to hide my chuckle, having heard my father comment on mom setting a timer more times than I could count.

"What time is the wedding?" I asked, anxious to get things rolling now that I'd found a solution.

"Pictures are at 4 pm, the wedding is at 5 pm, and the reception will follow. It's black-tie, of course, so make sure to bring something appropriate. Or I could have your tux dry cleaned for you if needed."

"Yes, on the tux for me. I don't have the need for one here. I'll make sure Henley has something appropriate."

"I'm so excited to see you, Dax. I'm glad you're finally coming home. It's been too long."

After finalizing some more details about the

upcoming nuptials, I hung up the phone and smiled, knowing I had a solution for Henley. Now, I just had to convince her to come to a wedding with me.

For the first time in a year, I didn't get nauseated thinking about the wedding. In fact, if I thought back to when I bumped into Jenny at the party, I hadn't felt a thing. I'd been surprised and then irritated that my brother was there, but there wasn't any pining on my part.

Blinking, I smiled at the significance of that. At one time, I thought Jenny was it for me, and a life without her would be meaningless. So I'd settled for a life of hookups, knowing it would be all I was capable of.

Henley changed that. She showed me my life could be more than I believed.

"What's up?" Reed asked as he stepped into the kitchen and downed a bottle of water.

"My mom called. She manipulated me into attending my brother's wedding this weekend."

"Shit, dude. That sucks. You can't get out of it?" he asked, scrunching his nose.

"No." I sighed. "But I think it could be the answer to our Dakota problem."

"What about Dakota?" Henley asked. My head turned to find her behind me. Her eyes were still sad, and she'd lost some of the natural shine she usually had. I motioned for her to come to me, wanting to hold her and soothe away the aches I'd caused.

Her feet patted against the tile floor as she neared,

her leggings and oversized t-shirt doing things for me. She climbed into my lap, and I wrapped my arms around her, placing my head on her shoulder. Kissing her neck, I breathed her unique Henley smell.

"Would you be my date for my brother's wedding?" I asked instead of answering.

Her head tilted in my direction, her eyes searching. "You decided to go?"

I nodded. "Yeah. My mom called and manipulated me into saying yes. Derek told her about you, and she wants to meet you."

She swallowed, her eyes big. "Does she know, you know?"

"Yeah, Petal. She knows." I smiled, her presence already making me feel better.

"Oh. Um." Her fingers came up to her lips as she debated.

"If you don't want to, I understand. But I think there's a way to take care of Dakota once and for all."

"How?"

"My family runs in a lot of upper-class circles. They know a lot of people, and my cousin apparently just married a reporter."

"A reporter? For where?"

"Oh, just ESPN."

Her eyes went wide as she gulped. "Okay, yeah, that could be interesting. But I'll go even if we don't take care of Dakota. I'll be there for you."

I kissed her nose as emotions that felt too big surged through me. I wanted to say them, but I knew I wasn't ready. So for now, I'd just have to tell her with my kisses.

"Thank you, Petal. It means a lot. I'm not as anxious as I was before about going, but having you there will be even better. It's black-tie, so you'll need a dress. Do you have anything or have time to get something?"

"Hmm, I can make it work. I'm supposed to hang out with the girls tonight, so maybe we can hit a few stores before they close."

"How was your day?" I asked, genuinely wanting to know.

Her eyes fell as she played with my hands in front of her. "It was okay. I had a few jumpy moments. Then a PI gave me a folder with some pictures in it."

"What?" Reed and I said at the same time, making her jump.

"Sorry, Petal." I glanced at Reed, and he sat, curious to know what it was, but realized he needed to be softer.

"Um, my mom hired her to dig up dirt. I'm guessing Carol plans to blackmail me or something. There wasn't much to find because, hello, I'm boring. She had a few pictures of me and you guys dancing at the pub, and then there's one of me, Fletcher, and Reed in a compromising position."

"Say that again, Petal?" I asked. The thought of someone violating her privacy again had my blood boiling.

"Yeah, so the curtains didn't get shut the first time the three of us were together after you were injured."

"Fuck," Reed hissed, running his hands through his hair. "I'm so sorry, Hen."

"It's okay. The three of us didn't think."

"Shit. So she's probably planning to release it to the public, and what? Show you're a healthy twenty-something with an active sex life?"

"Yeah, well, I could play that off maybe if there wasn't already a video of me masturbating for public view."

Despite her distress, her words had my dick waking up and taking notice until I remembered everyone could see it. Then my possessive instincts kicked in, and I wanted to hide Henley from the rest of the world. No one but the three of us got to see her like that. This photo needed to stay buried. I didn't want to see her go through that scandal again.

"What are we doing?" Reed asked.

"Fletcher hired her to dig up stuff on Carol so we can try to fight it from the front. If not, I might have to cave and give her what she wants, so she doesn't threaten to take Reese away."

"What do you think it is?"

"Usually, I'd say money. But she has her new sugar daddy. So, I don't know what she could be after."

The uncertainty was too big, and I knew it would eat Henley alive. I'd need to get with Fletcher and find out what this PI knew and how we planned to protect our girl.

# CHAPTER 32

## *Henley*

I SORTED THROUGH THE DRESSES, the hanger sliding against the metal as I pushed it aside. The fabric was smooth against my fingers, but I didn't see the dress. I might've been standing in a boutique with two of my best friends, but my mind was a million miles away.

Outside of Carol and the shit with Dakota, I had a ticking time bomb on a decision to make. One that had significant consequences attached to it. And I had no clue if they were worth it.

"Hen! You gotta try this one," Scar shouted across the store, breaking me from my stare down with a mannequin.

Sucking in a breath, I blinked as I turned to see what she was shouting about. Susie touched my arm, and I jumped until I realized it was her.

"Sorry. I'm a bit out of it," I admitted, crossing my arms over my chest.

"Why don't you leave the dress picking out to Scar? You know she gets great enjoyment out of dressing her friends. Let her find the perfect thing."

Susie's touch was gentle as she directed me to the dressing room.

"Yay! You're here. Try these on." Scar shoved me into a dressing room, and I laughed, unable to sulk too much in her presence.

I looked at the dresses, scanning them over before picking the one I liked the best. It was mostly black lace with a black slip underlay. It hit just below my knees and had capped sleeves with only a slight dip in the front. I absolutely loved how it was tasteful and sexy.

Stepping into it, I pushed my arms through the sleeves and zipped it up as far as I could reach. I sucked in a breath as I took myself in. It fit perfectly, and I loved the way it moved. Opening my door, I peeked out, spotting my two friends.

"Can I get a hand?"

"Yes! Finally, it's my moment," Scar cheered as she stood, holding a hand to her chest. "It would be my honor to unjam your clam."

"I don't even want to know where you come up with this stuff." I laughed, turning so she could zip me.

"Urban dictionary. She spends way too much time on there," Susie disclosed, not caring when Scar narrowed her eyes at her.

"Anyway," Scar said, turning back to me. "I knew this dress would be perfect. Do you love it?" she asked, bouncing on her toes.

I twirled in the mirror, a smile gracing my face as I looked at my silhouette. "Yeah. I do. It's perfect. Thank you."

"Eek! Okay, there's this perfect pair of shoes to go with it too."

Scar and Susie spent the next half hour helping me pick out shoes, the perfect clutch, and jewelry. By the time we left the store, some of the weight of the past few days had lifted, and I felt better. I pulled them into a three-person hug, the clothing bags hitting them on the back. But I didn't care. I'd needed this more than I knew.

"Thank you. I'm so glad you're here. I didn't realize how much I missed girlfriends until you both crashed into my life again."

"Aww, we love you too, Hen," Scar said as she squeezed us back and forth.

"Anytime, Hen. You're our girl. Always."

Letting them go, we walked over to the car and deposited our bags before walking down the sidewalk to a bistro we wanted to try.

"Oh, Suze…" Scar started, tilting her head toward our quieter friend. Scar had a mischievous smile on her face.

"Yeah?" Susie asked, glancing over. She immediately froze when she spotted the look Scar was sporting.

"Um, what am I missing?" I asked, looking between the two.

Scar rubbed her hands together, her grin growing wider as she shuffled back and forth on her feet. Susie's eyes widened as she waited for Scarlet to share.

"Oh, just a tall, broad, and gruff man leaving her room this morning."

Susie's cheeks reddened, but she clamped her lips tight, shaking her head. My brain spun as I tried to put the clues together since neither was saying who.

"Wait... Maks?" I asked, my jaw dropping.

Scarlet nodded, her eyes sparkling as she watched Susie. "Yep. And if I'm not mistaken, he was doing the stride of pride."

Giggling, I wrapped my arm around Susie. "I'm happy for you, Suze. It's been a while since you liked someone."

She sighed, her shoulders dropping. "Yeah. It's still new, so I didn't want to say anything. Especially after how my last relationship ended."

Grimacing, I nodded, completely understanding how it felt when starting a new one.

"I'm just proud of you, girl. I heard you through the wall, and damn. It got me all hot and bothered." Scar fanned herself. She could never let either of us off the hook for something. Susie groaned, tossing her head back and rubbing her temples.

"Really, Scar? You couldn't let me live in the bubble where I pretended we didn't share a paper-thin wall?"

"What's the fun in that?" Scarlet blew her a kiss, hooking her arm back in hers to keep walking.

"Besides, it's nothing to be embarrassed about. I'm sure you've heard me this week. I'm not going to censor myself just because you might hear. Fuck that."

"Oh, I know." Susie giggled, the color in her cheeks lessening the more we walked.

"If anything, I want to know what you were doing to make him sound like that. It was the most I've ever heard from Maks."

Susie groaned, her face flaming again as we stepped into the restaurant. I glanced back, spotting the security guy that was escorting us. The guys had insisted he accompany us if they couldn't join us. He'd been staying hidden so well, I'd almost forgotten he was there. He nodded as I stepped into the restaurant, and I released some of the fear I'd been carrying that Gareth might try to jump me when I was alone.

Looking around the bistro, I enjoyed the cute decor and homey atmosphere. An electric fireplace crackled in the center, bringing the whole look together. Following the girls to a table, I checked my surroundings and noticed everyone around me. I'd been more hypervigilant since last night, and I didn't think it would go away anytime soon. At least not until Gareth was captured.

Placing the napkin in my lap, I picked up the menu and surveyed the options. My mind was beginning to overload again, so I picked the first thing I recognized and placed the menu down.

"Yum. It all looks so good," Scar mumbled, rocking in her seat. I appreciated her enthusiasm and effortless way of being. I knew it wasn't easy to be so carefree, despite what other people thought. Scarlet had her own demons to battle, just like everyone else.

"I can't decide. What are you getting, Hen?" Susie asked, pulling me from my thoughts.

"The barbecue chicken mac."

"Ooh, could I try a bite? I'm stuck on that and the chicken and bacon panini."

"For sure."

The waiter approached us a second later, stopping in her tracks when she spotted us. "Holy shit. You're Henley Henshaw, and you're Susie McNeil and Scarlet Stephens!"

The young girl bounced as she looked between the three of us. It had been so long since someone recognized me and responded this way; I was slightly stunned.

"Hey, it's nice to meet you," Susie said, pulling me out of my shock. "You a hockey fan?"

The girl nodded, her hair swinging with the movement. "The biggest. I play for the rec team. I'm not the greatest, but it's fun. I've watched all of your games, Henley. And when I heard you would be the coach here, I hoped I'd get to meet you one day. Like, wow. You're real." Her hands shook as she stared at me.

"How about we get a picture, and if you have

anything you want to be signed, we can do that?" I asked, hoping to settle her some.

"Really? Oh, man. That would be epic. Like I have no words."

Scar and Susie chuckled as they watched the girl gush over me.

"We do love our Hen. She's the best," Scar said, giving me a wink.

After we had taken a picture with me and then with the three of us, our waiter, Heather, took our order, promising to have it out quickly.

"Ah, that never gets old," Scar sighed, bracing her head on her hands. "You should invite her to the game tomorrow. Let her see you in action."

"Yeah, that's a good idea."

"So, how are you doing this week? I know the stuff from last night had to be scary," Susie asked after our waters were dropped off.

I pulled the wrapper off and played with the straw, searching for the right words.

"This week has been a lot. I thought I was dealing with it well, and then last night happened, and I feel like I'm on the brink of crying at all times. I almost peed my pants earlier today when someone dropped something near me. I need to get out of my head with the game tomorrow. I'm just not sure how."

Susie reached across and squeezed my hand. "We're here to listen if you need to talk about it. But if you want the distraction or something else, we can do that too."

I bit my lip as I debated what I wanted and what I needed. I had a feeling they were two entirely different things. Blowing out a breath, I assessed my two friends. They were watching me with careful eyes, making me wonder how delicate I must look, which made my decision for me.

"I hate feeling this way. Like I'm scared of my own shadow. I'm not sure how to make that feeling go away."

"Maybe because you're not supposed to. Something scary happened to you, and you need to recognize the effect it will have. If you run from it or push it away, it will only catch up to you," Scarlet said. Her face was serious, her brows drawn down as she studied me. A haunted look crossed her face, and I knew she spoke from experience.

"I can still feel his hands on me," I admitted with a shaky voice; my eyes fell to the table in shame. "Part of me wants to rage about the fact this man touched me and held me against my will. Another wants to curl into a ball and hide away, so nothing like that can ever happen to me again."

"Unfortunately, it takes a while for that sensation to go away," Susie said, drawing my attention. It was then I knew that they had experienced something similar before. It might not be the exact same, as they likely didn't have one of their boyfriend's drug-addicted macho men after them. But it shed light on the realization that this was way too common of an occurrence for women.

This wasn't something I wished to share with anyone. Nor would I assume that three strong and successful women such as ourselves would have this shared trauma. The fact that we all accepted it as part of being a woman? Nope. Fuck that.

Maybe it was that knowledge that incensed me, that burned away the shame and fear and replaced it with a bone-deep strength I didn't know I possessed. Taking a deep breath, I lifted my head and met my friends' eyes. I didn't find pity or shame but pride as I looked at Susie and Scar.

"There's our girl," Scar whispered, reaching to squeeze my hand.

"Thanks for knowing what I needed better than I did."

"That's what friends are for," Susie answered.

Our food arrived then, stopping our serious conversation as we discussed the game the next day and who we thought was ready. I knew I'd still need to face the things that had occurred last night, but I felt more secure in myself, which made a world of difference.

After a few more pictures and signatures, I invited Heather to the game, letting her know I'd leave a few tickets for her at the box office. Her squeal of joy made me realize all the shit I'd been through this week was worth it if it meant I got to make a difference in even one person's life.

Now, I just had to make a difference in my own life, and the picture of what that looked like became clearer by the minute.

# CHAPTER 33

## Henley

I DRIFTED in and out of sleep, finding myself in that place between waking and restlessness where dreams felt real. My mind had decided to take a holiday, or more aptly, a sexcation—tired of dealing with all the shit in my day to day.

Not that I could blame myself. The current dream was much preferable to reality, anyway. Sighing, I focused on the pleasure dream I was receiving and what a lucky bitch she was.

Legs spread wide, I threaded my fingers through the long locks of my lover as he feasted on me beneath the sheets. His tongue licked up my center, hot and firm, as it flicked my clit, releasing a moan.

"I wish I wasn't dreaming. This would be the best way to wake up," I moaned as my back arched up.

"You're not dreaming, Petal." Dax's hands flexed on my thighs as he pulled me closer to his mouth; the feel of his calloused hands on my sensitive skin made me whimper. "Open your eyes and watch me lick you clean. You're the best type of breakfast, Petal."

I could feel his stubble against my skin as he rubbed his face back and forth. His nose brushed against my sensitive bud, shooting tingles through me. My pussy throbbed with need as my wetness dripped onto my thighs.

I wanted to believe him that this was actually happening. But I was too scared it was only a dream, and if I opened my eyes, it would all end.

Pulling his face closer to where I wanted him, I felt his fingers flex against me as he hummed in appreciation. I rode his face, spreading my arousal all over him. I'd never felt this desperate before, needing something to tip me over the edge.

"Open your eyes, Petal. Look at me feasting between your legs."

I shook my head, keeping my rhythm as I rocked against him. His head drew back, and I whimpered as the pleasure stopped.

"Open your eyes."

The command in his voice was clear, and I snapped them open without another thought. Dax's face came into focus, his chin shiny from my arousal. His hair was a mess from my hands threading through it, giving him that effortless sexy bedhead look. His fingers twitched on my legs as I took him in and accepted that I truly was awake.

"Good morning, Petal." Dax smirked at me for a second before he dove back between my legs to enjoy his breakfast.

My back arched as his tongue speared me, and I reached out to grip the sheets, coming into contact with a hard body on one side instead. Turning my head, I met crystal blue eyes full of heat; the pupils blown wide. Reed stared intently at me, and I wondered how long he'd been awake. His eyes dropped to where Dax was feasting on me, and he licked his lips.

I glanced down as well, taking in the tank top that had been pushed up to my breasts and my sleep shorts, nowhere to be seen. The hand that had landed on Reed moved on its own, feeling the dips and curves of his muscles. Moaning, I forced my eyes open to turn back to Reed. The sheet that still covered him was tented, his hard cock enjoying the early morning wake-up call.

"Touch yourself," I moaned, my voice husky with need. My legs shook as Dax licked and sucked my clit, his hands holding me firm to his face. Reed's eyes flicked back to me at the request. "Please. I want to watch," I begged.

Reed swallowed, and I knew a throat had never looked as sexy as it did at right that second. My hand stayed on his abs, my fingers trailing through the small patch of hair. His hand pushed the sheet down, allowing his dick to spring free from the confines. Licking my lips, I held my breath as I watched his hand wrap around his thick cock.

It was a battle as Dax pleasured me, my eyes wanting to roll back and the need to watch Reed stroke himself. His hand moved slowly at first, going from tip to base in a firm grip, his thumb rolling over the tip and spreading the bead of pre-cum.

"Yes. That's hot," I whispered.

My fingers ached to reach him, but I couldn't at this angle. His free hand reached out and rolled my nipple, and everything became too much as I crashed over the ledge. My legs trembled as I came, my insides clamping down on air as they sought something to squeeze. I cried out, my back arching and my fingers clawing at whatever they could find. Dax didn't let up, continuing to lick and suck me until the last waves of my orgasm stopped.

Dax pulled back, and my eyes blinked open as I caught my breath. His face was covered, his tongue licking his lips to savor every last drop of my release as he pulled my taste into his mouth. Glancing back over at Reed, his hand had stopped moving, squeezing at the base of his dick.

"More. I need more," I said once my voice had returned. Dax glanced at Reed and then back at me as he thought things through.

"Reed, sit in the middle of the bed. Petal, between his legs with your head on his thigh." The direction was clear, and neither Reed nor I hesitated, moving into the positions Dax wanted us. Reed's cock twitched as it rested against my shoulder, and it was only the curiosity of what Dax was up to that kept me from wrapping my lips around it. Reed pulled my hair over his leg; one hand massaged my scalp, and the other palmed my breast.

I looked up at him from beneath my eyelashes, finding his crystal blue eyes pinned to me. They swirled with emotion, the blue darker as he watched me.

"You're so fucking beautiful, Petal. Your skin is flushed from your orgasm, and your nipples are pebbled and ready to be sucked. I look at you and want to devour every inch of you. It's so hard to know where to start."

Facing Dax, I sucked in a breath as I watched him stroke his cock, his lip between his teeth as his eyes trailed over me, leaving a fire trail in their wake. His powerful thighs flexed as he moved forward, stopping his ministrations to touch me.

"I could spend hours between your legs, bringing you to one orgasm after another, watching you writhe in pleasure as I wring you dry."

I whimpered at his words, my pussy throbbing for him. "I need you."

"I know, Petal, and you can have me. All of me."

His hands traveled down my legs, reverently touching my skin as his fingertips brushed over me. When he reached my thighs, he bent my legs at the knees and pressed them back, practically folding me in half. I sucked in a breath at the stretch of my muscles, knowing I'd feel this later.

"Reed, take her legs and hold them for me." Reed

did as instructed, banding an arm around my legs, the other in my hair. "Suck his dick, Petal. Reach your tongue out and lick his tip."

Tilting my head slightly, I did exactly as he said and licked around the tip, dragging that bead of pre-cum into my mouth. Reed's body tensed beneath me, his muscles flexing as I reached out and stroked him with my hand. His eyes were laser-focused on me, watching my tongue as it jutted out to swirl around his head. Moving closer, I brought him further into my mouth, sucking him as far as possible. The corner of my mouth stung as it stretched to accommodate his size.

Reed's hand in my hair tugged at the roots as he helped to move me back and forth. I wasn't sure how this would go with Reed and Dax without Fletcher, but Dax had fallen into the leadership role effortlessly. It was nice to trust him to get us where we wanted and not have to think about anything else but the pleasure we were giving one another.

"Fuck," Dax hissed. "I don't know why it's so hot to watch you blow another man. But it is. It's the best type of porn."

Whimpering, I attempted to shake my butt to remind Dax to get to it. My desperation from earlier hadn't quelled, and I needed to be filled. Pulling back slightly, Reed's dick made a popping sound as I let him go to focus on Dax.

"Fuck me, Blondie, or I'll jump on Reed and make you watch instead."

Dax smirked, his eyes heating at my words. "Yes, Coach," he purred, bringing his dick closer to my entrance. I watched as he lined himself up, rubbing his tip over my folds and coating himself. I knew he was dragging it out, making me wait for my sass. His eyes met mine, the corner of his mouth twitching seconds before he slammed into me.

The fullness was everything I needed, and I moaned as I twitched around him, adjusting to his size. His length was hard and warm, giving me exactly what I wanted.

"Suck, Petal. I won't move until you do."

Somehow we'd entered into a game of sexual checkers, daring the other one to make a move. Reed's hand flexed in my hair, tugging slightly on the strands and reminding me he was there. Turning back to him, I flicked my tongue, licking around him before closing my lips. As soon as I sucked him down, Dax moved, pulling out and slamming back in.

His hands gripped my ass, lifting me to angle himself better. The two of them held me where they wanted me as they moved in unison. My pussy stretched around Dax, my walls clenching with need as he pushed into me. With the way he held me, he could drive his dick deep, filling me completely full. When Reed reached around and rubbed my clit, I knew it wouldn't take long to fall apart in their arms.

"Come for us, Hen," Reed commanded, his voice rough and gravely; letting me know they were the first words he'd said today. That knowledge sent me flying, and I tumbled over the edge.

I screamed my release around Reed's cock; the sound muffled as I came. My body trembled and convulsed as pleasure racked through me, the feel of both of them too much to handle. Reed followed not long after, groaning as he came down my throat. His salty cum hit the back, exploding over my tongue as I swallowed every drop.

His free hand caressed the side of my face as I blinked up at him. The hand in my hair soothed away the places he'd pulled, massaging my scalp tenderly. My eyes closed at his touch, cherishing this moment with him.

"You're so warm and tight, Petal. Every time I'm inside you, I never want to leave. You grip my cock so well, squeezing me until I have no choice but to unleash."

Dax's thrusts were frenzied, his words coming out in pants as he pistoned into me. His movements became sloppy as he rushed to get in one more thrust before he came. With a stuttered shout, his muscles flexed against me as he held my hips up high in his hands. I watched as his abs twitched, his head thrown back, with his hair falling around his shoulders. His lips parted in a silent scream as he made shallow thrusts, riding out his orgasm.

When he stopped, his eyes met mine, the emerald green orbs shining bright back at me. I knew Dax didn't believe he could love anyone, too scared to get hurt again, but I saw it written all over his face. I'd give him time to realize it and love double for us both until then.

"I love you," I said. He smiled softly at me, and I knew it was important I kept reminding him how I felt.

"Ah, man! Not fair. Flag on the play!" Fletcher shouted as he walked into the room, alerting us all to his arrival. The three of us chuckled as he frowned, taking us in. His eyes roamed over my naked and well-spent body, heating me up again.

"Wrong sport," Reed said, chuckling.

"Yeah, well. It sounded better than an illegal check," Fletcher huffed, his hands on his hips. His eyes met mine, his smile returning, and I knew he wasn't actually upset.

"Where were you?" I asked, sitting up.

"I had to go pick up my family from the airport."

"Shit. Are they here?" I asked, looking around desperately for something to cover myself. Reed and Dax froze as they waited for him to respond.

"No." He chuckled, and I realized he said it to get back at us for the sexy times. "They're staying at the B&B. They'll be at the game later and want to go out afterward for dinner."

My body relaxed at his words, the threat of his

family finding us naked gone. "Oh, good. I didn't want to see your mom again as your girlfriend with another man's cum in me."

Fletcher's eyes heated, and before I could blink, he scooped me up off the bed and marched toward the shower. "My turn," he growled, waking up the rest of my body.

Fletcher spent the next thirty minutes reminding me how good he felt as he fucked me up against the counter and the shower wall. After my third orgasm, I waved the white flag, my legs shaking so badly I could barely stand.

With a satisfied grin, he washed my hair after leaving a hickey on my breast to remind me who'd made me boneless.

It was the best way to start a day in the history of starting days. Hands down. Or tied, if that was your thing.

# CHAPTER 34

## *Henley*

AFTER MY FRIDAY breakfast with Reese, I'd been stuck in meetings all morning to discuss the team's progress with the Board of Trustees. While not everyone on the board was team Henley, it looked like I'd made progress with a few. It helped that Dmitry had supported the three of us and the direction we were taking the team. It also eased my anxiety about where he stood, confirming he was on our side and not aligned with Carly. I still hadn't had time to talk with him about everything that had occurred last weekend, but I felt reassured he trusted us to do what we needed.

"The charity drive yesterday was successful. We're still crunching the numbers and sorting all the inventory, but it looks to be our best yet," Tammy, the head of the charity drive, reported.

"Humph, that's surprising since some of our wealthiest families are no longer part of our school," Mr. Jacobson tutted. The man was in his fifties, with graying hair and the most prominent nose I'd ever seen. He'd been opposed to everything I'd done so far as the coach and wasn't afraid to voice his opinion.

Mr. Jacobson *was not* on team Henley.

"Enough, Bernard," Mrs. Monroe-Smith said, rolling her eyes clearly over his tirades.

From what I could gather, Mrs. Monroe-Smith was one of the founding families of the school and town. She'd recently joined the Board of Trustees this summer. She looked like a sweet grandmother, but I was learning she didn't put up with bullshit.

I instantly liked her. She *was* team Henley.

"Thank you, Tammy. The last thing on our agenda is a reminder that team photos will be taken next week. I hope to see most of you at tonight's game. Go get 'em, Coach," Dmitry said, closing the meeting. He nodded to me before he stood, walking over to talk to someone.

Gathering our stuff, I was ready to get out of this room and onto the ice. I'd much rather spend hours in my skates than sit in a conference room listening to people debate the best way to spend the budget. At least these meetings were only once a month. I doubt I'd make it if they were weekly. If the boredom didn't take me, it would be the deadly stares Mr. Jacobson sent my way.

The guys climbed to their feet just as eager to escape these four walls. Before I could take two steps, Mrs. Monroe-Smith intercepted me, placing her hand on my arm.

"Hello, Henley dear. I was wondering if I could speak with you for a moment."

Despite my desire to leave, I couldn't deny this woman her request, especially when she was one of the few on my side.

"Of course, Mrs. Monroe-Smith."

"Call me Aggie, dear. All my friends do." She smiled, giving me that warm chocolate feeling inside, like I'd just drank a mug of hot cocoa.

"Alright, Aggie. How can I help?"

"I know you're busy, but I was hoping I could run a proposal by you. Perhaps you could do brunch at my house sometime?"

"Oh, um, yes, that would be lovely. I'll be out of town this weekend, but maybe the next?" I asked, curious as to what she'd want.

"Perfect. I'd also love to meet Reese, and your men are welcome to join us. My adoptive granddaughter is eager to meet you both as well. I believe you know one of her boyfriends, Tyler Matthews?"

I blinked as the information processed through my head. "Sawyer is your adoptive granddaughter?" I asked when I put the pieces together.

"That's the one. I'll check with her that next weekend works. She and Henry are away at competitions some weekends, and I can't always keep track." She smiled with fondness, proud of their achievements. "My husband Charlie's a huge hockey fan. So, I'm not going to tell him who's visiting so I can watch him go all fanboy." She giggled, the sound so refreshing I felt it liven up the room. I loved that even in her sixties, she still played jokes on her husband.

"Then I'll definitely bring Reed and Fletcher. Do you have my number?"

After putting my contact information into her phone, I felt mine vibrate as she sent a message with her address. Pulling it out, I opened my phone and found two messages from unknown numbers. Entering Aggie's name, I said my goodbyes and opened the other as I headed out into the hall to find the guys. The rascals had escaped, but I knew they wouldn't go far.

555-8746

Hey, Marshmallow. I've got something for you. Want to grab lunch?

It took me a few seconds to work out who it was. Shaking my head, I chuckled as I realized. Again, I wasn't sure if I liked her or found her incredibly annoying. The jury was still out. Changing her name in my phone, I grinned as I typed in a response.

HENLEY

I'm beginning to think you're obsessed with that show.

MACY (VMARS WANNABE)

It's comedic gold, and you know it.

You didn't answer my question.

HENLEY

Sorry, too busy changing your name in my phone. I have an hour. Can you come to campus?

MACY (VMARS WANNABE)

As long as you buy me food, I'll meet you wherever.

HENLEY

Deal. See you in a few. I'll wait outside the cafeteria.

MACY (VMARS WANNABE)

Later, Marshmallow.

Tucking my phone back into my bag, I spotted the guys talking to one of the security guards further down the hall. When I drew nearer, I realized who it was.

"Asa Walsh," I called out.

The tall blond turned his head at my voice, a smile spreading across his handsome face. He took two steps, picked me up, and hugged me tight. I chuckled at his antics, slapping his arm to put me down. From behind him, I watched as Reed and Fletcher's faces changed, their smiles morphing into deadly stares at his arms wrapped around me. Thankfully, Asa set me down, stepping back to look at me.

"Henley Henshaw! Girl, I can't believe it's really you. I heard you were here but hadn't had a chance to make it over yet. How long has it been?" he asked.

Reed and Fletcher moved closer to me, making me

laugh. It didn't go unnoticed by Asa, either. His eyes sparkled, and I wondered if he'd known and had wanted to ruffle their feathers.

I blew out a breath, trying to remember how long it had been since we last saw one another. We'd both played on the Olympic teams and had gotten close during the training and games.

"I wanna say four years? You were on the team at my second Olympics, right?" I asked.

He nodded, agreeing. He crossed his big arms over his chest as he looked at me and the two men practically glued to my hips.

"You're right. Wow! So much has changed since then. How are you liking being the coach?" he asked.

"Ha. That answer changes on which day you ask me. But overall, I love it. It's been great getting to do it with these two." I elbowed my two guard dogs, smiling at them. "What about you? What are you up to these days?"

He motioned with his hands down his body, pointing out the Alpha Security Solutions logo on the black polo he wore. "It's a long story, but my biological father opened a security firm here, so I took a break from hockey. Reed took my job, actually." He laughed, glancing at the blue-eyed man on my right whose eyes had narrowed. Reed didn't like that if Asa hadn't stepped down, I could've been working with him instead.

"My girlfriend still works at Lux, though, so I decided to help Samson while Fin and Milo are here."

"Milo, as in Dr. Milo?" I asked, lifting my brow.

"The very one. He's part of my family. Have you joined the harem club?" he teased, glancing between the two guys.

I chuckled, wondering if there really was something about the mountain air here that made everyone want to be in unconventional relationships. Perhaps it was the fact it was readily accepted or that at a school that catered to elite athletes, it wasn't uncommon to find a group of people who wanted to belong to something bigger than themselves. We'd all worked so hard for so long, to the peril of most of our relationships, putting everything that wasn't our sport on the back burner.

Then one day, you wake up and realize that while you were busy pursuing your dream, believing it would be the key to your happiness, everyone else was out living their lives, leaving you empty and alone.

Gold medals were nice, but they weren't great at cuddling or even giving a shoulder to cry on.

"It seems I have. These two, plus Dax Cassel. They make me happy." I looked at the two next to me, love radiating from my eyes. They softened, realizing Asa wasn't a threat. I turned back to my old friend. "I haven't met Fin yet. We should all get together for dinner sometime."

"Yes, absolutely. That would be great. We have a

house outside of town where we all live. You guys should come over." He looked between the three of us, lifting his finger to Reed and Fletcher. "Henley's like a big sister to me, so don't think I won't punch you in the junk if you hurt her."

"I know a good thing when I find it," Fletcher said, wrapping his arm around me. "And dinner sounds like a good idea. Maybe next week?"

"Sounds like a plan. I hate to dash, but I need to meet someone in a few minutes. It was so good to see you, Asa." I gave him another quick hug before racing out of the admin building with the guys following.

"Who are you meeting?" Fletcher asked as we marched toward the dining hall.

"Macy. She said she had something for me. I want to be surprised that she already found dirt, but I'm not. You can't throw a rock without hitting something sketchy with my mother."

Reed grimaced, his face taut as he walked next to me. I reached over and took his hand, rubbing my thumb across it. He looked over at me, his face softening as he met my eyes.

"What did Aggie want?" Fletcher asked as we stepped through the first set of doors. Macy stood within, leaning against a column. She waved as we neared.

"Aggie invited us over to her house for brunch. Wow, my social calendar is getting full." Chuckling, I motioned for Macy to get in line with us. The four of us grabbed food and headed to a table off to the side.

"I need to eat here more often. This food's way better than my microwave."

"The benefits of an elite academy," I said. "They go all out to ensure everyone is in tip-top shape."

She shrugged, taking a bite of her meal. Her eyes practically rolled to the back of her head. Taking a deep breath, I sat my fork down, wanting to know what she'd found.

"Not that I don't enjoy watching you eat... but what did you want to talk about?"

"Spoilsport," she huffed. Macy reached around and pulled out a large envelope from her bag, much like the one she'd handed me yesterday.

"Did you buy these in bulk?" I asked as I picked it up.

"I'm a bargain shopper."

She went back to her food as I opened the envelope. My heart raced as I pulled out the papers and photos. There was a lot more than what she'd had on me yesterday. It confirmed that no matter what my mother believed, I was the better fit to be Reese's legal guardian.

With shaky hands, I flipped over the first photo, not surprised by what I found. My mother and her latest sugar daddy. There were pictures of clothing, hotels, and jewelry receipts, adding to around one hundred grand. It shocked me she found someone to spend that amount of money on her and how quickly she'd done it.

Not surprisingly, there was an email to a reporter from my mother about doing an exclusive with her daughters as they took the male hockey world by storm. While I'd suspected she'd been up to something, it disgusted me she'd gone to such lengths to exploit us.

When I finished looking, I'd hand it off to Reed who then passed it to Fletcher in a weird assembly line. The three of us sat quietly while reviewing the evidence Macy had collected as she ate.

"How did you do all of this in one night?" I asked when I was halfway through.

"I felt I'd need it when she came to me. Plus, your boyfriend promised me a bonus if I did it quickly. So, Voila. Money and food are my big motivators. No shame in my game," Macy said, doing a happy dance in her seat. She was now eating a piece of cake like she'd never had any before. I didn't know if that was true or if she just really enjoyed food like she said.

Flipping through a few of the last pages, I froze when I came to the second to last document. My hand trembled as I read it, then rereading it to ensure I hadn't hallucinated it. My eyes jumped up to Macy's. She was already watching me with a coy smile.

"Is this real?" I asked, swallowing around the lump in my throat. My heart felt like it would jump out of my chest.

"Yep. I had to dig real deep to find that gem." She leaned back, crossing her arms.

"What is it, Baby Shaw?"

"It says that Reese…" I stopped, licking my dry lips as I took a deep breath. Looking between Fletcher and Reed, I shared the piece of information that would change everything. "It says that Carol isn't Reese's biological mother."

Their mouths dropped, mirroring how I felt on the inside. If Carol wasn't Reese's mother, then who was? And how had Carol raised her? And why?

"How is this possible? I remember my mom being pregnant. Did she… Did she steal a baby?" I asked in quiet horror.

"Nothing quite that sinister. From what I could gather in the hospital records, your mom miscarried late term."

I blinked, not grasping what Macy was telling me. "Then how?" My nose scrunched, knowing I was missing something.

"Your father," she said, and my eyes shuttered. I hadn't thought about my dad in so long that hearing her bring him up shook me. Macy cleared her throat and continued. "It looks like he had an affair. Reese is *your* biological sibling."

The fear I'd lose them lifted a little, not that I'd let who our parents were change our relationship. Reese was my sibling. Simple as that. But I didn't want to have to give Reese to someone else. It would break me.

"And Reese's mother?" I asked, my voice cracking.

"Matilda Rivers died during childbirth. I'm guessing with your mom losing a baby a few months prior; it was easy for your dad to convince her to raise Reese as her own."

Licking my lips, I tried to make sense of everything. "How do I not remember any of this? I would've been around eight or nine."

"Memory isn't linear, Hen," Reed murmured, his voice soft and low. His hand covered mine, his thumb sweeping back and forth across my palm.

Shutting my eyes, I took a deep breath and nodded, a memory resurfacing.

*My dad picked me up from hockey camp, telling me he had a surprise for me. I walked into the house, worried I'd find Mommy sad on the couch like she'd been before I left. My mom rocked a small bundle in her arms, a smile on her face. I ran over, staring at the baby. Reese had reached their hand out, grasping my finger, and I fell in love. Promising to protect them forever and be the best big sister.*

"I... I... sorta remember now. She'd been so sad before I left for camp. I remember feeling happy I got to leave the house and play hockey for a month, so I wouldn't have to be around it. When I returned, Reese was there, and I was so excited to be a big sister. Things were good again. At least until... until my dad was killed in a car wreck. After that, she changed. I was starting high school, so I focused on hockey, knowing it was my escape. It wasn't until a few years ago that I learned how bad things had gotten. I should've never left Reese in that house."

"You were just a kid, Hen. You can't blame yourself for wanting to pursue your dream. When you found out, you did something about it. Focus on that," Fletcher encouraged.

Wiping my eyes, I sucked in a breath before facing Macy. "If she isn't Reese's biological mother, why is she fighting for custody now? She'd been so relieved when I stepped in."

Macy shrugged. "I just find the information. I don't make assumptions. If you look at the last sheet, it might shed some light, though."

Glancing down at the lone paper on the table, I picked it up to look closer. The information didn't make sense. "I don't get it. Who is this?"

"That would be your new stepdad."

"But he's broke... Why would Carol marry him?"

Her eyes twinkled, shoving the last bite of her dessert into her mouth. "The con-artist got conned."

A giggle traveled up my throat, surprising me. Out of everything I'd learned over this lunch, that had to be the funniest. Carol thought she'd married a rich guy, setting herself up for life. But instead, he'd played her just as well. And now they were desperate and hoping to get a huge payday from me.

"Wow, I don't even know what to say."

"Thank you, works," she teased. "Also, I think you need to change my name to fairy godmother in your phone."

"Why's that?" I asked, my brow raised in question. Macy constantly surprised me, making her interesting and frustrating all in one.

"Her payment bounced, meaning I'm no longer under contract."

"How much?" Fletcher demanded before I could process what her statement even meant.

"I knew I liked you," she teased, smiling big. "Reimburse me the cost of the film, and I'll call it good."

"Done." Fletcher pulled out his phone and typed something into it. A second later, Macy's chirped, and she glanced down, smiling.

"Thanks for lunch, guys. Good luck with everything. I'm rooting for y'all." She stood, picking up her trash. My mind still whirled from the last few seconds. "And next time I see you, Henley, I hope it's for fun. You're a cool chick. Hit me up if you ever need a friend. Laters."

She waved as she strutted out of the cafeteria, drawing attention from all the kids. Macy McPherson was a force to be reckoned with. I glanced between Reed and Fletcher, a laugh bubbling out of us as we processed the past thirty minutes.

"Did anyone else find her slightly terrifying?" Reed asked.

"Oh yeah. I'm glad she's on my side." I nodded, wiping the tears from my eyes.

As much as I tried, I couldn't shake the impending doom sitting on my chest. How was I going to tell Reese?

It was the smoking gun I needed to get Carol off our backs, but I wasn't sure what it would do to Reese. This changed everything... and I wasn't sure if it was for the better or worse.

# CHAPTER 35

## *Henley*

MY EYES SCANNED the ice as the players skated by, the game in full play. Purple and black blurred in front of me, the players indistinguishable. The buzzer sounded for the end of the second period, waking me from my trance.

"You okay, Hen?" Reese asked, their eyebrows lifted in concern. We skated through the door in the boards to head to the locker room.

"Yeah, sorry. Just a lot on my mind." I gave a brittle smile and pushed away the thoughts consuming me. Get it together, girl.

"Alright, Blizzards! How are you feeling out there?" I asked, clapping my hands to get their attention. Everyone sat around the locker room in various stages of disarray as they drank water or a sports drink.

"Good. We're kicking as... butt!" Jack shouted, stuttering on the last word. His teammates chuckled as his cheeks heated.

"You guys are playing great. We're up by four points, so going into this last period, we need to play tight and not let them get any shots. Watch your blocking and don't give the refs any reason to call a penalty. Take a moment to catch your breath and get back out there. We have a game to win."

The kids cheered, smiles forming on most of their faces. It was a stark difference from a month ago.

Reed and Fletcher watched me as I took a drink, giving myself a few seconds to calm my mind.

"We got you, Baby Shaw," Fletcher whispered, effectively reminding me of his promise.

Nodding, I patted his arm and headed back out to the ice. The rest of the conversation from lunch replayed in my mind as I skated. I couldn't keep this from Reese. I had to tell them.

Feeling confident in my decision, I looked up and spotted that the team had joined me on the ice during my self-reflection. I scanned the crowd gathered, taking in all the happy families. Sadness threatened to overtake me as I looked on in envy. I'd never had that. After my dad died, there had been no one at my games.

My eyes landed on Dax, who sat with Fletcher's family a few rows behind the team bench. He smiled when he noticed me, lifting some of my sadness. Frankie, Fletcher's sister and my college roommate, waved when she spotted where Dax had been staring. Waving back, I laughed at her exuberance. Frankie hadn't changed one bit.

Sera and Sean were a few rows over with Briana, along with Susie, Scar, and their various partners. I even spotted Rhonda and Rowen sitting with some other familiar faces. Each face I landed on smiled and waved, offering their support and encouragement.

I might've been alone, with no family in sight, but I'd made my own. And Reese had that now. We didn't need Carol because we had each other and the people we'd gathered around us, celebrating our wins and grieving our losses with us.

Reed skated over, lifting an eyebrow. "You good?" I nodded and smiled because I got it now. I knew how to tell Reese.

"Yeah. I am."

His body relaxed as he scanned me. "See you after." He gave me one last look before heading toward the booth. My heart settled, and my brain no longer buzzed with a million thoughts as I climbed onto the team bench. The crowd grew louder as the players met in the center of the ice, their sticks slapping against the surface.

Once the whistle blew, the game resumed. The players skated up and down the ice, no longer a blur as I watched them, focusing solely on the plays. The period flew by as our team managed to keep them from scoring. I held my breath as Reese passed to Braden and the clock counted down. An enforcer rushed toward him, and I sucked in a breath, worried we'd have a repeat of the last game.

Somehow, in the congestion of players, Braden pushed the puck over to Jack and out of the way of the opposing team. Lifting his stick high, Jack sent the puck flying through the air as the timer blared.

The whole stadium held its breath, watching the black disc as it neared the goalie. They reached out, their thick glove closing as the puck approached, but it wasn't enough. The red light flashed on top of the goal as the puck landed behind the line.

Jumping over the wall, our team descended onto the ice as gloves, sticks, and helmets were thrown down. Cheers and screams echoed around the space with everyone's celebrations. I hugged Reese, rocking back and forth with happiness. This game brought us to a winning record of 2-1, proving the team had what it took to succeed. It might be only one game, but it showed us we could do this.

"You played so well!" I shouted, attempting to jump on my skates. Reese grinned so wide that their dimples were on show. "I have some news to tell you about Carol. Macy came through and… well, we won't have to worry about her any more if that's what you want."

Reese assessed me; some of their happiness faded, and I wanted to punch myself for stealing it from this moment. But the fear clawing at my throat that something terrible would happen before I had the chance to explain had made me blurt it out.

"Okay. Whatever it is, I trust you." My pulse slowed, and I pulled them in for another hug, kissing their temple. "We can talk more at dinner." They

nodded, and we skated off together, shouts of congratulations following us.

Back in the locker room, I gave a brief speech on
how well everyone did and to enjoy the weekend with
their families. It was the first one I'd managed to give,
but the words were few as I eagerly wanted to celebrate with my loved ones, too.

Fletcher, Reed, and I returned to our locker room
and showered in record time so we could meet up with
his family for dinner. I felt both nervous and excited
about it. Fletcher wanted to share our relationship
with his family and not keep it a secret. His pride in us
warmed my heart, so I pushed aside the fear that they
would hate me.

Reese waited in the lobby, waving goodbye to the
B&B twins when we neared. Fletcher wrapped an arm
around Reese's shoulder as he steered us toward a
large group. Dax spotted me and broke away, coming
to stand with us. Fletcher wanted to tell them about
the four of us right off the bat so no one had to pretend
they weren't with me. I appreciated his thoughtful-
ness, even if it scared me.

"Hey, fam!" Fletcher shouted, grabbing their
attention. "This is Reese, Henley's sibling." He placed
his hands on their shoulders like a proud parent. If I
hadn't already loved the man, seeing him show off
my sibling with pride would've sent me over the
edge.

"It's so nice to meet you, Reese. I'm Harriett, but

you should call me Mama Cromwell." Fletcher's mom hugged Reese, accepting them as their own.

"Hey, Hen!" Frankie said, bouncing over to me. Even with a kid on her hip, it seemed she had a boundless amount of energy. "I see my brother took my advice and made you his girl," she teased.

Fletcher wrapped an arm around my shoulder, his eyes sparkling as he stared at me. "I did. And because she has such a big heart, I knew I couldn't keep her to myself. So, Hen's our girl." He broke his eyes away to nod to the other two men beside me. Frankie blinked for a second, and I worried I'd lost her friendship before she grinned and chuckled.

"Well, damn. Why hadn't I ever thought of that?" she asked. A man I assumed was her husband kissed her temple as he took the baby off her hip.

"Because your heart is the size of a pea, and if you had more than one man, you'd run away screaming that you needed your space. I only locked you down because I was persistent and knocked you up." Frankie's mouth dropped open for a second, followed by another laugh and shoulder shrug.

"He's not wrong. I am a bit of a commitment-phobe. I can't even commit to a brand of laundry detergent."

"Oh god, I'm getting flashbacks of us fighting over whose turn it was to pick dinner."

"Still a thing," her husband said, reaching out a hand. "I'm Anthony. It's nice to meet you, Henley."

"You too." I shook his hand and turned to his mother. Surprisingly, she wore a smile, no hint of judgment on her face. She stepped closer, her arms open.

"It's so good to see you again, Henley. I'm so happy that you and Fletcher are together, whatever that looks like." She hugged me, her arms reassuring and firm, and I relaxed. "He's been so much happier since you came here. I worried he'd never get past—"

"Mom, we should head to the restaurant so we don't lose our reservation," Fletcher cut in, his voice firm.

She tutted at him, nodding, and patted my arm. "Yes, of course. And don't forget; I brought everyone some banana bread." Her smile returned, directing the large group out the doors.

A shout followed by a screech of my name greeted us as we exited. My body locked up, worried Gareth had returned to take us out. I quickly swiveled my head back and forth, looking for the danger. My eyes landed on my mother, and a different sense of dread encompassed me. It wasn't Gareth, but we were far from free of danger.

Reese glanced at me, biting their lip as Carol rushed toward us, waving her arms.

"My darlings, there you are. I've been waiting forever to see you. They wouldn't let me into the game."

That news shocked me, and I wondered which of

my guys had thought to do that ahead of time. Whoever it was, they were getting a blow job when we got home.

"This isn't the time, Carol," I said, hoping to brush her off until we weren't surrounded by others.

She reared back like I'd slapped her. "It's *family* weekend, Henley. I know you like to pretend I'm not your mother and that you girls don't need me, but I still have rights, and I want to be here to support you both."

The amount of bullshit in her speech sent me over the edge. But I'd caught her carefully placed words. *She said I like to pretend, not that we both like to pretend she wasn't our mother.* I guess even Carol couldn't lie to my face about this.

Taking a deep breath, I glanced at Reese, hoping I was doing the right thing because it looked like we were doing this right here, right now. Reese stood with their arms wrapped around their middle, probably in an attempt to protect themselves from Carol's hurtful words. It gave me the strength to push forward.

Eyes narrowed on the woman who birthed me, I placed my hands on my hips, going into full warrior mode. "That's funny, *Mom*. Last time I checked, you'd signed your rights away to *me*. So, no. You don't have any rights, nor are you *our* family. So don't pretend that's why you're here."

Her face morphed to rage, and it turned almost purple; her eyes narrowed to slits, her lips in a sneer.

"You think you're so high and mighty. Just wait until I'm done with you. You won't be able to get a job anywhere without taking off your clothes."

The words hurt, but I brushed them off, knowing she couldn't truly hurt me. I wouldn't let her.

"I think you'll find that you don't, in fact, have anything. Next time you decide to marry a rich man to make all your problems go away, you might want to verify he's, in fact, *rich*." Her eyes shifted slightly, my words registering, and I spotted the first sign of fear. "This is your last warning to leave Reese and me alone."

"I'm not going anywhere until I get what I want," she seethed, stepping closer and not backing down. I hated that Fletcher's family was witnessing this, but I was done playing her game. It was time to take Carol off the board.

"Suit yourself, but don't say I didn't warn you." Sucking in a breath, I let out the truth. "I know you're not Reese's biological mother, so your claim to rights has no value."

Her face fell at my words, and her whole body deflated. I heard Reese gasp behind me, but I kept my focus on the woman who'd raised us both so I didn't falter.

"You're out of moves, Carol. It's time you packed your bags and never set foot anywhere near either of *us* again."

I took a deep breath, my hands shaking as I stared

down at my mother. Warm hands settled on my shoulders, massaging some tension away and reminding me I could do this. I wasn't alone.

"Because I have a heart, I'll give you one final choice. I'll help you get a divorce and your own place, in exchange for you never contacting me or Reese again. You'll also sign an NDA prohibiting you from ever speaking anything about either of us to the press. Or you can go down in flames with him after the FCC finds out what he's been doing. Stealing from his investors to pay for his lavish lifestyle will not go over well."

Carol didn't hesitate, proving she had some sense of self-preservation.

"I'll take your offer and sign whatever."

My shoulders dropped, the air I'd been holding leaving me in a rush. I'd done it. I'd won against Carol.

"Where are you staying? The lawyer will send over the documents and a cashier's check once they're signed," Fletcher said, stepping up when all the words escaped me.

Despite feeling relieved Carol would no longer be a problem, an overwhelming sadness appeared. My mother had chosen money over us. A hand squeezed mine, and I peered over, my eyes meeting Reese's.

As a united front, we watched the woman who'd raised us give her information to Fletcher and leave without another thought. Turning to my sibling, I squeezed their shoulders, hoping to offer comfort.

"I'm sorry you had to find out like that. I didn't know how to tell you. I'm sure that wasn't easy to watch."

"Are you kidding? It was brilliant. You were magnificent, Hen."

"But..." I stuttered, confused.

"Honestly, I feel more relief than anything. I never felt a true bond with Mom... Carol. I just assumed it was because of not knowing who I was for so long, and then when I did, not feeling accepted for it. This makes so much more sense. I'm just sad I never got to know my real mom."

"Oh, kiddo." Pulling them into my arms, I squeezed them tight. "I can help you find her family if you want. I just learned about your mom today, but if you're curious, we can look them up."

"Maybe someday, but for now, I'm good with the family I have. With the people you've brought into my life who accept me."

My eyes watered, the weight of everything lifting as I stared at my sibling.

"You're still my sister, though, right?" Reese asked, biting their lip.

"Always. Even if we didn't share DNA, I'd always be your sister. I'll tell you what I know later. Let's head to dinner since we've already given everyone here a show."

Reese's smile covered their whole face, those

dimples returning. Linking our arms together, we walked to catch up with our group.

"By the way, thank you for sacrificing your savings for me. I know that's where you're taking it from to pay her."

"I'd do anything for you, Reese. I'd pay whatever cost if it meant you were protected from someone like her. You're going somewhere, kiddo, and I support you in that. And now, we don't have to look over our shoulders, waiting for her to drop in."

"You're the best, Hen. I know I wouldn't be where I am without you."

Giving them another squeeze, we joined the rest of our crew as we split into vehicles for the drive to the restaurant. Thankfully, the remainder of the evening was filled with laughter as we got to know Fletcher's family better.

# CHAPTER 36

## Dax

I LOADED the last bag into the car, in no particular hurry to head to my family's home. While I no longer dreaded being around them, I didn't specifically like their company. Spending the day with them wasn't on my list of favorite things to do.

"We ready?" Henley asked, stepping out with Reed.

Both of the guys had wanted to tag-a-long for moral support, but in the end, Fletcher had opted to stay back so that Reese wasn't alone in case Carol had a change of heart. With his family in town as well, he wanted to spend time with them before they headed back home.

At least, that was his reasoning.

Fletcher had been acting strange since his family arrived, but I couldn't determine why. He'd been on board to tell them, not hesitating to be honest about who we were to Henley. So, I didn't know what it was about their presence that had rattled him. He'd given in so easily to staying behind that it seemed more like an excuse than the real reason.

Henley had been dealing with so much of her own stuff that I didn't think she'd noticed his odd behavior.

And with the stress of my brother's wedding, dealing with Dakota, and her decision about joining the Society looming, it wasn't something I wanted to bring up yet if it wasn't critical. The first thing I planned to do on our return Sunday evening was to corner him and make him talk. He said we didn't have secrets in our group, so it was time he shared whatever was bothering him.

Huh, it looked like I could do this communication thing after all.

"Yep. Last chance to back out before we enter a level of Hell no one knew existed."

Henley rolled her eyes, walking closer to me. Her arms wrapped around my waist, her head tilted to peer up at me.

"Wherever you go, I go. And if it's Hell, then we'll get through it together."

My eyes roamed over her face, taking in all her features. I knew I didn't deserve her, but I wouldn't let her go anymore. Bending down, I kissed her softly, her lips smooth and plump.

"Okay, Petal. You got a deal." She beamed up at me, her smile taking my breath away.

The next few hours zoomed by as we got onto our plane and landed in Las Vegas. The desert heat hit me as we exited the airport. I hadn't missed this dry heat at all.

"Did you see those slot machines?" Henley asked Reed, her eyes wide with excitement.

"Yeah. They have them practically everywhere," he answered, smiling down at her.

Despite living close to Las Vegas most of my life, Henley's excitement at every new thing made it fun again. I got to see everything again for the first time.

"How far is your family's house?" she asked as we settled into the rental.

"Depends on traffic, but it could take an hour to two. I can make it take longer if we take the scenic route," I teased.

"As much as I'm sure I'd enjoy that, we should get there so we're not late. Plus, they might need our help or something."

"You're cute, Petal. They have people for that."

"Oh." Her eyes became owlish at the implication. Reed chuckled in the back at her expression. She was just too cute sometimes.

"I'm not sure what we'll encounter when we get there. They see me as the black sheep, the bad spot on the family name, so my reception might not be the greatest." I grimaced, dreading my father's response.

"Just tell me who to punch," Reed grunted, flexing his knuckles.

"And I'll kick them for good measure or give them a really good stare down," Henley added, scowling in my direction. She looked like a chihuahua.

Their jokes did the trick, and I laughed, knowing whatever happened, I wasn't in it alone.

TURNING DOWN THE DRIVEWAY, MY HEART RACED, AND MY stomach jumped up into my throat. I stared at the expansive brick two-story house that resembled more of a museum than a family home. The shrubs and flowers out front were impeccable, groomed to perfection by the staff of gardeners my mother hired. A catering van blocked the drive, several people dressed in white shirts and black pants scurrying in and out of it as they carried trays and dishes.

"Whoa. You said your family was connected, but I hadn't expected this for some reason."

I grimaced, knowing I'd purposefully downplayed my family's influence and wealth. Coming to a stop on the side of the house, I cleared my throat before I faced them.

"Yeah, sorry. I'm so used to people knowing or using me to get something that I omitted some details."

"We understand. Families are complicated. The only thing I want from you is—"

"Your dick," Reed interjected, shocking both Henley and me.

"Reed!" she shouted, laughing as she turned and smacked him. He shrugged and chuckled, dodging her attack.

"Damn straight, Punchy. It's just that good." I

puffed up my chest.

"Oh, my God. I give up. You're both impossible." Despite her frustration, Henley had a bright smile on her face. Cupping her cheek, I leaned close and rested my forehead against hers.

"Thank you, Petal. You're the first person to see me for me and tell me I was worthy." I kissed her nose, jumping out of the vehicle, worried I'd say those three little words that kept getting tripped up on my tongue.

"Should we take in our bags or wait?"

"Grab them now. We won't want to come back out once we get to our rooms. It's going to be a madhouse."

The three of us walked toward the front door, our luggage in tow, and those nervous butterflies returned. Would my mom be embarrassed another guy was with us and tell me my life choices still weren't good enough for the family name? The white door opened as we neared, stopping my thoughts as my mother stepped out to embrace me.

"Oh, Dax. You're here."

Desirae Cassel stood at five-four, but that didn't stop her from pulling me down and inspecting every inch of me. She tutted at my hair length, cupping my face in her delicate hands as she stared into my eyes. Her matching green ones looked back, searching for something.

"You look happy, Son."

"I am, Mom. Henley, this is my mother, Desirae."

She smiled as she stepped back, letting me go, and faced my guests.

"It's so nice to meet you, Henley." She pulled my girlfriend into her arms like it was the easiest thing in the world, welcoming her to our home.

"It's nice to meet you as well, Mrs. Cassel," Henley said, smiling warmly at my mother.

"Mom, this is one of my roommates, Reed. He's also dating Henley."

I had to give it to my mother. Despite her words the other day on the phone, I wasn't certain how she would respond face-to-face, worried it had been a ploy to get me here. But as the wonderful woman she was, she turned to Reed and warmly welcomed him before she stepped back to look at the three of us. I needed to quit lumping her in with the others and call her more.

"Please, call me Desirae. Thank you for coming with Dax. I know this day will be hard for him, so I'm glad he has your support. I, um," she stuttered, the action so unlike my mother. "I know relationships are more evolved nowadays than when I was young, so while I might not understand your situation, I'm just glad that Dax has someone who makes him happy."

"Thanks, Mom." I kissed her temple, the anxiety I'd been carrying dropping off my shoulders at the acceptance. It wouldn't be this easy with anyone else, but she was the only one I cared about.

"Come in, and I'll show you to your room. Sorry, there's only one bed. I wasn't expecting three people."

"It's alright, Mom. We'll make it work."

The three of us followed her into the house, my childhood memories resurfacing as I passed rooms and photos. Not every moment here had been bad, but there weren't many good memories either. Thankfully, we avoided running into Derek or Jenny as Mom led us to a guest room.

"People will be arriving shortly. Your tux is in the closet, dear. I just need you down for pictures by 4 pm. Until then, you can avoid the chaos."

She kissed my cheek, giving me another pat, and walked over to give Henley and Reed a squeeze. I knew this couldn't be easy for her, so I was happy she tried. The door shut, closing the three of us in the room, allowing me to take a breath.

"Your mom is lovely, Dax," Henley said, walking closer.

"She is. Just remember that when you meet my father. Derek takes after him."

Reed grimaced, setting his luggage on a dresser and hanging his garment bag that held his suit. I'd been surprised when he had something appropriate to wear since I only usually saw him in sweats and hockey gear.

The three of us piled on the bed and sent pictures to Fletcher, rubbing in what he was missing. He, of course, sent back an image of his middle finger. Henley messaged Reese, checking in with them, and then we spent the next hour watching mindless television.

"I guess I should get ready," Henley moaned, lifting herself from the bed. She'd been lying in Reed's lap with her legs in mine. I loved how she always gave us equal attention whenever she could. "I'm excited about my dress."

"I can't wait to see you in it and then take you out of it," I teased. My voice turned husky, and I debated whether there was enough time to dirty my girl up before we had to face the masses.

"Nope. I know that look, and I won't cause you to be late. Once we make it through this, then you can ravage me as much as you want and we can even call Fletcher, so he's not left out."

I glanced at Reed, his eyes as hungry as mine at the idea.

"Sold. Go get dressed, Petal. We have a wedding to crash."

Henley rolled her eyes but jumped off the bed and entered the bathroom. Reed and I watched as she curled her hair, fixing it into a fancy updo. Our attention never strayed as she applied her makeup, and we took in every inch of her. She turned, spotting our eyes glued to her.

"Have you been watching me the whole time?" she asked, her cheeks reddening.

"Yep. You're the best entertainment."

"Hmm. Well, I'm going to close the door, so my dress will be a surprise. You better get yours on too."

"I'm not wearing a dress, Petal." I smirked, loving getting a rise out of her.

Henley rolled her eyes, waving her hand at me. "You know what I mean. See you in a few minutes."

Begrudgingly, Reed and I climbed off the bed and changed into our wedding clothes. I hated wearing the tux, feeling like an overgrown penguin. I couldn't move as freely as I could in gym clothes.

"Who decided ties were formal?" Reed huffed, pulling his away from his collar. He wore a charcoal gray suit with a black shirt and tie.

"Probably the same person who invented high heels," Henley said. "Though you look hot in that suit."

She fanned herself, not noticing how Reed and I had frozen. Her dress hugged her body, showcasing all her best features. The black lace gave enough of a peek without being indecent, making me want to know what was under it. Combined with her hair and makeup, she was stunning.

"Fuck, Hen. You look gorgeous. You're going to make the bride mad."

"Why?" she asked, not understanding.

I nodded, agreeing with his statement. "Yep. Everyone is going to be looking at you instead of her."

"Oh." I didn't think it was possible to watch her blush so much, but I discovered I liked it.

"Shall we?" I asked, offering her my arm.

Her phone rang as we stepped out into the hall, so Henley paused to answer it.

"Hello? Oh, hey, Keaton. Uh-huh, yeah. Um, okay, well, I'm not in Utah. I'm with Dax at his brother's wedding. Yeah, it's not that far. Shoot, Reese is back in Utah. Hmm, Fletcher might be able to bring them. What time? Yeah, that should work. Is this your number? Okay, I'll text you once I confirm with them. Uh-huh. Talk to you soon."

"What did Keaton want?" I asked, my voice tense. I knew it was ridiculous to get jealous that my friend had called her, considering I'd been the one to introduce them, but being at my brother's wedding to my ex-girlfriend had me feeling a little more fragile than usual.

"He wanted to see if we could fly to LA tomorrow to do that campaign. The photographer he wanted had a last-minute cancellation, so he's trying to get us in. I just need to check with Fletcher. Go on ahead to the photos. I'll be right behind you."

I hesitated, not wanting to leave her by herself, even if Reed would be with her. In reality, I didn't want to face my family alone. I glanced at my watch, noting the time, and knew I'd have to or endure more of my father's wrath.

"Don't take too long."

I kissed her cheek and continued down the stairs. I passed a few staff members but no one I knew on my way out to the backyard. Exiting through the glass doors, I spotted my brother and his bride as they posed for pictures.

I stopped, my feet not wanting to move as I waited for the misery and loneliness to hit me. This was supposed to be *my* day.

But the longer I watched them, the more I noticed how little I felt those two emotions. Letting out a deep breath, I took the last few steps to where my mother and father stood.

"Dax, just in time," my mother cooed, brushing off invisible lint as she appraised me. "Dashing as always."

My father eyed me but kept his mouth shut. I nodded in greeting, too scared I'd say something to upset him otherwise. His jaw clenched as he stared; my mother narrowed her eyes at him after an uncomfortable amount of time had passed.

"Glad you could make it, Dax. I thought your mother mentioned a new girlfriend. Or was that a lie as well?"

Right off the bat with the barbs there, huh, Dad?

"She had to take a phone call. She'll be out in a moment."

"Hmm. With one of her *other* boyfriends?" he said, his words cutting.

"Henry!" my mother admonished, glaring at him. "Dax is home for the first time in years and has brought someone he cares about. For the sake of the day and my heart, please be respectful. I won't have you making him or his guests feel uncomfortable."

My mouth gaped as I stared at my mother, speechless. While my mother had always been fierce, I'd never had her stand up for me so spectacularly.

"Fine. I'll behave—holy shit, is that Reed Cole?" my father asked, his turn to have his mouth hang open. My mother slapped his arm at his use of foul language.

The last few seconds had given me emotional whiplash, a laugh erupting at the situation. I'd been so worried about being here, but it was apparently all for naught. I kept laughing, drawing Jenny and Derek's attention, but I couldn't stop. Whenever I looked at my father's face, I would chuckle again.

Reed and Henley joined me, casting me questioning looks at my behavior. I attempted to stop, dragging Henley into my side.

"Henley, this is my father, Henry Cassel, former governor of Nevada."

Her eyes widened for a fraction of a second before she held her hand out to shake his. "It's a pleasure to meet you, sir."

"Henley Henshaw? As in, a two-time Olympic gold medalist?" he asked, looking from me to her.

"Um, yes, that's me. Are you a hockey fan?"

He nodded, his eyes moving to Reed. "I've been a huge fan of yours since your college days. It's an honor to meet you." He extended his hand to Reed, and the big man glanced at me before looking back at my father.

"Your son is a great man," Reed said, not taking my

father's hand. I was shocked he'd said anything at all, and for him to say that had me puffing out my chest.

"You know Derek?" my dad asked because, of course, he would associate greatness with his protégé and not the screwup.

"No." Reed narrowed his eyes. "Derek's a dick. Dax has a higher caliber character than Derek ever will."

Everyone froze, staring at the man who dared to speak so highly of me. My mom appeared proud, her eyes a bit misty. My dad's jaw had fallen back open, his eyes narrowing the longer he stood there. Henley beamed at me, squeezing me around the waist. I didn't know if Derek and Jenny had heard him, but based on Derek's pissed-off expression, he'd gotten the gist.

"Well, hmm," my father said, at a loss for words.

"It's time for the full family," the photographer said, calling us over. I bent down to kiss Henley, squeezing Reed's shoulder.

"Dude, I'd totally kiss you too right now, but I'm worried you'd fall for me, and my dick only gets happy for Hen, so just know I love the hell out of you, man. I've never had a friend as honest and supportive as you. So, thanks."

Reed only nodded, having used his words toward my father. I posed for a hundred pictures with my brother and ex-girlfriend, not even having to fake my smile. This might be the best wedding I'd ever attended.

# CHAPTER 37

## Henley

AFTER THE PICTURES WERE TAKEN, Dax was ushered off to greet some of his family members and entertain them. Reed and I stood together, marveling at the comings and goings of the staff and guests. The wedding started promptly on time, and we were seated on the groom's side. Dax was pushed into standing up with his brother, despite his obvious feelings about Derek and the wedding in general.

"Is it me, or is this the most boring wedding ever?" Reed whispered, leaning close. He draped his arm over my shoulders, his thumb caressing my bicep.

I nodded. "Yeah, I'm usually at full blubber at this point. It's like they don't even like each other. I don't understand how someone as nice as Jenny is, who dated Dax for years, would choose to marry Derek instead. Is being a governor *that* impressive?"

Reed shrugged, his eyes sweeping across the people gathered. There were about fifty people in attendance, all of whom seemed to be more important than the last. I leaned into him, his minty smell relaxing among all the overpowering colognes. I sighed in relief, glad he was here. Dax needed us both.

"You may kiss the bride," the officiant said, almost as enthused as the couple kissing.

The crowd stood, clapping their hands as they were announced as Mr. And Mrs. Derek Cassel. Everyone's eyes were on the happy couple as they walked down the aisle, but I only had eyes for Dax. His blond hair sat on his shoulders, a slight wave in it. His emerald green eyes stayed focused on me, filled with a hunger I'd never get tired of.

He made no effort to watch the proceedings, causing a few people to turn and look at Reed and me. When he reached our aisle, he held his hand out and waited for me to take his. Once our fingers were interlocked, Dax pulled me into the aisle with him. His free hand cupped my jaw, his eyes boring into mine.

"Standing up there, I realized I've been an idiot, Petal. I'm obnoxiously, hands down, no take-backs, in love with you. You're never getting rid of me now. I hope you're prepared to deal with my dirty socks and my complete and utter addiction to your pussy."

Tears streamed down my face, and I hiccup laughed at his words. I didn't care if people were staring. The only person I had eyes for was standing right before me.

"I love you too, Dax, dirty socks and all."

The most brilliant smile spread across his perfect

lips a second before he pulled me closer, slamming our mouths together as both of his hands captured my face. Dax kissed me, stealing all the air from my lungs. It was adoration and possession wrapped in one hungry lip lock. My feet tingled, goosebumps rose all over my body, and I wasn't sure if I'd be able to stand if he wasn't holding me.

His kiss slowed, the world returning to me in slow seconds. Our breaths mingled together as we panted for air. Dax's forehead rested on mine, his pupils blown as he gazed at me full of love.

"I wish we could leave this farce right this second. I have so many plans about how to make you cum all over my face again."

I sucked in a breath, very much wanting what he promised, and wondered if there was a way to make it happen. Hands slid over my shoulders from behind as a body warmed my skin. Hot breath skated over my neck, and I shuddered.

"I'm completely on board with where this is going, but may I suggest we make contact with your cousin's husband so we can take care of a gnat first?" Reed suggested, his voice husky. My eyelashes fluttered against my cheeks, and I gasped. His words were important, but I found it difficult to remember why.

"Dakota. Right. Jackass removal," Dax said, blinking as he regained his composure. "Let's get through this. Reed has just properly motivated me."

Dax kissed me quickly, his smile returning. His eyes sparkled with joy, and I giggled, enjoying seeing him so carefree.

The chairs around us were now empty; the rest of the guests had already vacated the area. We walked together with me in the middle of my very sexy boyfriend sandwich. A few people watched us, but most of them focused on their conversations, too busy impressing one another to care about us.

Dax pulled us over to a table where a petite brunette sat in the lap of a very recognizable man—Saint Bishop.

"You didn't say she was married to Saint Bishop," I murmured out of the side of my mouth, slightly screeching.

"I didn't know who he was. My mom said some ESPN reporter."

"*Some* reporter. Geez. That's like saying Muhammed Ali was just *some* boxer."

Dax stopped, his eyes widening as he looked from me to the man. He hadn't noticed us yet, too absorbed with the woman on his lap. He swallowed, nodding that he understood.

"Hey, Ainsley. I hear congratulations are in order," Dax said as we approached the table.

The couple looked up from their love bubble. Ainsley smiled when she spotted Dax, jumping up to come around the table.

"Daxy! How are you? It's so good to see you. It's been so long." She gave him a hug, her joy clear on her face. I instantly liked her.

"I'm good, and it has been a long time. I couldn't believe my little cousin was married when Mom told me." He pulled back, holding her arms as he spoke, a genuine smile on his face.

She returned his grin, stepping back as her eyes moved to her betrothed. "Marriage is the best. You think you'll ever do it? Oh, shit. I forgot." She covered her mouth, her eyes wide. Saint stood, pulling her back to him, his hand on her waist in a protective gesture. It was cute to see the big man so besotted. He was always so serious on the air.

Dax laughed, shaking it off. His arm moved to my shoulders, pulling me into his side and kissing my cheek.

"It's all good. I don't know about marriage, but I'm where I'm meant to be." He peered down at me as he said it, and my insides melted.

"I'm happy for you, Daxy. I never agreed with what your brother and Jenny did. So, I'm glad you found someone. I wish you all the happiness in the world." Her shoulders relaxed, settling back into her husband.

"Thank you, Ainsley."

"Oh, this is my husband, Saint. Babe, this is my favorite cousin. We used to get into so much trouble together. He was the only one who would play with me because I was younger than the rest. It got boring once he went away to school."

Saint's eyes sparkled as he listened to his wife reminisce. "It's a pleasure to meet you, Dax."

"Likewise. And this is my girlfriend, Henley, and her other boyfriend, Reed."

"Henley Henshaw and Reed Cole. I was shocked to see you both here. This isn't your usual crowd," Saint said, lifting an eyebrow in question.

It seemed he was already on the hunt for a story. I stiffened, not sure what he was fishing for. Maybe this was a terrible idea.

"Two boyfriends?" Ainsley asked, her eyes big.

"Three, actually. Fletcher couldn't make it."

"Fletcher Cromwell?" Saint asked, his eyes widening as well.

"Yup." I didn't falter; firm in my choice and belief in our relationship. The guys hadn't hidden me, so I wouldn't either. Besides, it only gave people something to talk about if I acted ashamed.

"You know them?" Ainsley asked, a crease forming between her eyes.

"They're hockey players," Saint explained, staring at Ainsley with heart eyes. He placed a kiss on her forehead before glancing up at us. "There was something about you in the news, wasn't there? I've been off for the past month. We just got back from our honeymoon a few days ago. I'm still catching up on everything I missed."

"Which time? The one where my jerk of an ex-boyfriend released a private video and got me placed on leave for the hockey season? Or the time he stole my phone and faked an engagement, only to come on air and say how desperate I was afterward? Oh, and it was during my first game as a coach for Lux's senior hockey team, where his accomplice locked me in a room, so I missed the last period," I spewed, unable to hold it back.

Saint's eyes grew so big I was afraid I'd broken him. Ainsley gasped, covering her mouth. "That is terrible! I can't believe someone would do that. How did he get away with it?"

"Because he's Dakota-fucking-Hughes, and he believes he's untouchable." And protected by a club that would cover up anything for their gain. A shudder rolled through me at the thought.

"Oh, Henley. I'm so sorry. That's horrible. I can't believe he's allowed to make whatever claims he wants without repercussions. It's just..." Ainsley stopped, her lip quivering as her eyes watered. She waved a hand in front of her face. "Sorry, I'm really emotional at the moment. Your story is bringing up a lot of feelings I thought I'd dealt with. Saint and I met because of an initiation prank gone wrong. He saved me from the side of the road in a downpour." She looked up at her husband, the love clear as day in her eyes. She moved in front of him, his arms wrapping around her. "I hate bullies. Is there anything you can do?"

I shrugged. "My PR team believes I should let it go. That any statement I make will look like I'm covering something up, giving his story more credence even though I have video of his accomplice stealing my phone, proving it wasn't in my possession at the time of the tweet."

"What do you want to do?" she asked, understanding in her voice. I hadn't expected to meet someone here I'd like, but Ainsley was proving to be a firecracker wrapped in a tiny package.

"That's a bit of a loaded question. I'm the legal guardian for my sibling, so what I might *want* to do, I have to consider for their sake." I took a second to think about what she asked. "If there was no recourse for my actions, then I'd make him suffer as much as I have at his words and actions. He's violated my privacy twice and made me doubt myself. He took away hockey, the one thing I could always count on, and when I moved on and started to flourish again, he returned and shoved me back to the ground."

Saying all that, I realized how true it was. Dakota was a narcissistic bully who couldn't stand that I'd moved on and had succeeded without him.

"Oh, Saint, can you do anything?" Ainsley asked, tilting her head upside down.

He stared at her, a conversation passing between

them. He licked his lips, lifting his head to meet my eyes. "I'm not sure what I can do, but if there's something you think I could help with, I'd be glad to do it. The divide between women's and men's sports is already too great. I don't like when male players use their platform to keep it that way. If I can be an advocate for you, please let me know."

"Thanks, I'll keep that in mind."

The conversation went to safer topics after that before the happy couple left us to dance. Reed and Dax watched me closely, their brows drawn down.

"I thought you wanted his help, Petal? That felt like you left it open instead of jumping on it."

I licked my lips, nodding. "I'm not saying I won't use his help at some point, but as I was relaying everything, I knew I needed to be the one to take down Dakota. He won't respect me or my choice any other way. If I use another man to convey my message, he'll see it as shots fired. He'll come back at me, and Reese might be collateral damage this time. Knowing what I know now, I can't let anything jeopardize my guardianship of them. It wouldn't be fair."

"You're sexy when you go all mama bear for Reese, Hen." Reed kissed me, pressing his lips to mine.

I could feel the heat in his eyes burning a path along my body. Only the announcement of food being served kept me from racing back to the room. The three of us ate in relative silence; all the words had been spoken as we bided our time. We survived through the speeches and suffered through the cutting of the cake. When the mandatory dances began, Reed peered around at the crowd.

"How much longer do we need to stay, Dax?"

The man in question lifted his arm, checking the time on his watch. "I say we've put in enough face time. Let's escape before I'm roped into catching the garter." He did a full-body shudder, and I knew he was completely over Jenny. The three of us escaped to our room without being trapped by any other family members.

Both men watched me, their gazes tracking every step I took. Remembering my promise, I placed my phone on the dresser and video called Fletcher. He answered immediately.

"Hey, baby. How's the wedding?" he asked, his face coming into focus.

"Are you alone?" I asked, not wanting to scar my sibling or his family.

"Yeah. Are you?" he asked, squinting at the screen. Only a tiny amount of light filtered into the room from the window, highlighting my face, but nothing else.

"No. I'm not alone. Dax, lock the door."

Fletcher's eyes grew at my command, his throat bobbing as he swallowed. "You're serious?"

Nodding, I winked before I spun around, facing Dax and Reed. I took my heels off and placed them to the side. Turning in front of Reed, I lifted my hair so he could unzip me. Fletcher cursed as he moved closer to the camera.

The dress pooled at my feet as it slid off. I picked up the phone and climbed on the bed, setting it on the nightstand. Laying back, I slid off my bra. Both guys in the room were still dressed, their eyes glued to my movements. I watched them as my breasts came into view, their reactions spurring me on.

Tossing it to the side, I hooked a finger at them. "You going to fulfill your promises?"

They moved instantly, their clothes being discarded as they neared the bed. I peeked over at Fletcher; his bare chest was on display as he made himself comfortable. His hand rubbed his length over his boxers, and I licked my lips as I watched.

The bed pressed down on both sides, my view becoming filled with naked flesh. Reaching out my hands, I trailed my fingers down both sets of abs, feeling all the muscles and how they flexed under my touch. Dax moved first, dropping down between my legs and ripping off the last scrap of clothing I wore. When the air hit my sensitive flesh, I gasped.

He stared at my center, licking his lips. Trailing his nose up my inner thigh, I tossed my head back from the soft touch. Reed captured my mouth with his, kissing me so passionately that my toes curled. Soon, I was lost in the pleasure the two of them were giving me.

Dax took his time, trailing his fingers through my

folds, using my slickness to glide along my pussy and clit. When his tongue flicked against my bud, my legs shook, a gasp opening my mouth further for Reed. My hand took Reed's cock, stroking him from root to tip. His eyes shuttered, and this time he took a breath in.

Peeking back at the camera, I found Fletcher had his cock out, his hand stroking his thick length as he watched. Reed licked my nipple, sucking it into his mouth, and my back arched. Dax had pulled me onto his face, devouring me more with his devil tongue. Pleasure coursed through me, and I didn't know if I could make it much longer.

My heart raced as my muscles tensed, my skin sensitive and full of goosebumps. My orgasm crested, taking me by surprise. Reed moaned around my breast, my hand gripping him tightly. Turning my head, I took him into my mouth, swirling my tongue around him. Dax thrust his fingers into my drenched pussy, holding true to his promise to adore me down there. The man had a passion for oral sex, and I'd happily oblige to his ministrations anytime.

After another orgasm, Dax flipped me on my stomach and lifted my ass to him. Reed stayed before me, and I took him back into my mouth as Dax pushed his dick into my soaking-wet entrance. With each thrust, I was pushed forward on Reed's cock, which slid further down my throat. His hands threaded through my hair, guiding me, my hands braced on his thighs. I was helpless to their touch as they rendered me speechless.

Dax roared, his hot cum flooding me as he jerked inside me. I moaned around Reed, and he pulled out of my mouth the second Dax stilled. In a daze, I let Reed pull me down onto him, my legs wrapped around his waist as he gripped my hips and pushed up into me.

"Fuck, Hen. Every time I'm in this tight pussy, I think it can't get better than this. And every time you prove me wrong."

He kissed me hard, his tongue taking control as I felt him lose control, his fingers digging into my flesh; I knew I'd have marks. Reed came, his body twitching from the force, and I laid panting in his arms, my body sated.

"Eyes on me, baby," Fletcher barked from the phone.

I'd forgotten he was there in my orgasm fog. I met his eyes; the intensity making me suck in a breath. Fletcher bit his lip, his head falling back as he came all over his hand, his cum shooting out in spurts. My pussy quivered as I watched, and Reed cursed as I flexed against him.

"Holy fuck, that was hot," I whispered.

Fletcher winked and stood, showing me his cum filled chest. I found it intoxicating to know even miles apart, I had that effect on him. The camera came closer to his face a few seconds later.

"Love you, Baby Shaw. I'll see you tomorrow."

"Love you too, Fletch. See you tomorrow."

"Night, fellas," he said before the phone disconnected.

Sighing, I got cleaned up and ready for bed in a daze, crashing between Reed and Dax, knowing what decision I had to make in the morning.

# CHAPTER 38

## *Fletcher*

MY PHONE RANG AGAIN, and I ignored it and sent it to voicemail like I had all the others. The notification ticked up to 102 a second later, making it another message I wouldn't listen to. Turning my phone over, I tried to put it out of my mind. I only kept it on because I didn't want to miss anything from Henley or Reese.

Focusing back on my family, I smiled as my sister made silly faces at her youngest, Hailey. I'd spent most of the weekend with them, so I wouldn't be alone in the house. I'd never minded before, but it felt so empty without the other three now. Plus, it hadn't been a hardship tagging along with my family. I missed being around the loudness and chaos they seemed to exude so effortlessly.

Looking at my nieces, I realized how much I'd missed out on. They were growing up so fast. Hayden zoomed into the room, jumping into my lap when she neared.

"Hey, Uncle Fletch." She smiled up at me, a few teeth missing.

"Hay-Hay," I sang, tickling her. She giggled,

squirming on my lap until she jumped down and ran off.

Anthony sat down in the chair next to me, a soft smile on his face as he watched his girls. He turned, assessing me with his knowing eyes. I'd known Anthony since pee-wee league, and I couldn't think of a better man for my sister. He'd been smitten with her since he was fourteen and patiently waited until she returned from college to wear her down.

"You good?" he asked, sipping his coffee.

"Yeah. I am."

He nodded, not needing any other explanation. "We miss you back home."

I sighed, rubbing my beard. My mother had already made the same claim, pleading for me to come for Christmas this year. It had been a few years since I'd been back there.

"Yeah. I miss home too. It's just... hard to be back there. It's not the same without..." I cleared my throat, emotion rising in my throat.

"I get that, Fletch. We all grieved Emila's loss. She was a light that shone brightly, and without her, it's a little dimmer."

My right fist clenched as I stared at the carpet. I knew I was being unfair. Of course, he would grieve for her, along with my family and everyone from our hometown. She'd been the best part of that place.

But she'd been my best friend, and when everything went down in the end, I was the one by her side when she died.

"It's not the same," I gritted out, my heart racing. My jaw tightened, my molars grinding into one another. I shut my eyes tight, needing to rid myself of the images that had flooded me. *Her frail body, all the monitors, the hope and fear in her eyes. The plea to help her.*

When I calmed, I opened my eyes; the light flooded back in, and I took a deep breath, pushing it all away. Anthony kept watching me, an apologetic look on his face.

"I didn't mean to push your buttons, Fletch. I just wanted you to know we miss you. With your new lady love, I thought maybe you might be ready to return."

He paused, taking a sip of his coffee as he watched me. My hands gripped the arms of the chair as I waited for him to ask.

"Does she know about Emila? About who that made you become? About what you lost?"

I shook my head once, the move stilted and tense. A pit in my stomach opened as bile threatened to move up my throat. *Who I'd become. What I'd lost.* What a fucking joke.

"No. I try to forget myself." When I lifted my hand, I was shocked when it shook as I ran it through my hair. I couldn't be *that* person. Not anymore.

"Hmm," he hummed, taking another sip. "Is that who you've been avoiding, then? The board?"

Nodding, I focused on breathing, needing to calm the fuck down so I didn't lose it in front of my family. It wasn't Anthony's fault, but I hated him at this moment for bringing all this up. I'd worked hard to forget it, to shove that part of my life to the back of my mind and never think about it.

And until last weekend, I'd been successful in doing that. Being around *that* crowd again, seeing some of the same faces that belonged in my worst memories, I couldn't ignore it as easily. It didn't help that my phone had been blowing up ever since; their insistence on me fulfilling my duty was a constant reminder of a life I wanted no part of.

But I'd known deep down they'd descend on me like bloodhounds when I used some of my wealth and influence to help Henley. I didn't regret it, feeling like it was the first time it had ever been useful and not the collar around my neck it really was. But now that I'd poked my head out of the sand, they weren't letting up. They wanted their pound of flesh.

Almost on cue, my phone vibrated against the seat cushion. I flipped it over, spotting the familiar number, and sent it to voicemail yet again.

"I won't tell you what to do, Fletcher, but avoiding them never makes them disappear."

I jumped, forgetting Anthony was sitting next to me. My nostrils flared for a second before I calmed myself. He wasn't the enemy.

"I never wanted this. I don't know how to explain

it to her... to them," I whispered. The agony in my voice shocked even me.

"I didn't get to spend much time with Henley or the other guys, but from what I saw, you four are a unit. If you tell them the whole story, *the real one,* they'll understand and see what you did as the greatest act of kindness anyone could ever give."

I scrubbed my hands over my face. I didn't want to admit he was probably right. The fear consumed me at times, making me hide instead of doing the one thing I'd been preaching from the beginning—communicating.

"I love her, and I'm worried she'll leave if she knows. I don't want to lose her. Honestly, I don't think I could go through heartbreak again."

"Do you really love her, though, if you're unwilling to give her all of you? You're not trusting that she loves you and sees the best in you, despite all of your flaws. And despite your *almost* perfection, you Cromwells aren't as perfect as you believe."

"Shut your mouth, babe! I'm perfect," my sister shouted, confirming that she could hear our entire conversation. She stood, carrying Hailey on her hip as she walked closer, sitting in her husband's lap and holding Hailey to her chest. Anthony stared at her like she was the sun, kissing her nose.

"You're absolutely right, sweetheart."

My sister preened as I gagged, her face turning to me, her eyes narrowed.

"Listen here, Brother dear; I'm going to give you one piece of advice. If you can't be honest with Henley, you don't deserve her. Don't be a jerk like her ex and underestimate her."

It was the slap to the face I needed. If my sister had clumped me together with that asshole, then I needed to change. Taking a deep breath, I let it out as I nodded in understanding.

"You're right. I'm so used to how most people respond when they find out, that I assumed she would too. But Henley sees me for who I am, so I need to trust her with all of it—even the hard parts."

"And my job is done," Frankie said, snuggling deeper into Anthony's arms.

The display had my heart aching, missing my girl. Turning my phone over, I sent her a quick message, needing her to know I was thinking of her.

FLETCHER

Hey baby, is it clingy to say I miss you already? You've been gone for 24hrs, and I miss you like a part of my soul is gone.

HENLEY

Not clingy at all. I miss you too. It's not the same without you here. I'm glad I'll see you soon.

FLETCHER

Same, baby.

Listen, there's something I want to talk to you about. Something from my past. I've been scared to talk about it. Most people don't respond well to the info.

HENLEY

Whatever it is, I'll listen. It won't change how I feel about you.

As long as it's not that you kick puppies. I couldn't deal with that.

FLETCHER

It's not kicking puppies.

HENLEY

Reed wants to know if it's that you sniff underwear? He's confident he caught you once.

FLETCHER

Not that either. And tell Reed it was his own reflection he caught.

HENLEY

*laughing face*

Dax said that you're secretly a billionaire and own a whole house full of tiny china dolls.

FLETCHER

Dax is an idiot, and dolls creep me out.

HENLEY

He said it takes one to know one.

FLETCHER

Is he looking in the mirror with
Reed too?

HENLEY

*dead*

Thanks for the laugh, Fletch. I guess I
should get out of bed and face Dax's
parents. We have to suffer through
breakfast before we leave. We can
talk more tonight.

FLETCHER

Good luck, and thank you. I'm picking
up Reese in an hour. See you soon,
baby. I love you.

HENLEY

I love you!

I stared at the messages for a few minutes as relief
and love coursed through me. I'd been an idiot.
Frankie and Anthony were both right. I was making a
bigger deal out of this than I needed. The rest of my
visit was carefree and light, and I promised my mom
I'd talk with everyone about visiting at Christmas.

"Ok, Ma. I promise."

"Even Reese. That cutie needs some Cromwell
cheer."

The image of all of us sitting around my family
home in matching PJs flashed through my mind. It
didn't cause me dread or anxiety, but happiness and
excitement. Things would be different because I was
different, and I had a family who loved me. I believed

we could use some Cromwell cheer. No one did Christmas as well as my mother.

"You're not wrong there. I'm not sure what Dax's plans are, but I think Henley and Reed would be all for that."

She patted my cheek, a warm smile on her face. "It's going to be okay."

Her words held a double meaning, and I nodded, worried my voice would croak if I spoke right then. Swallowing, I licked my lips.

"Love ya, Ma. Let me know when you're all back home."

"Will do, Son. Now, go be the incredible man I know you are."

She kissed my cheek and stepped back, letting me leave the suite they'd all gathered in. Waving over my shoulder, I shut the door and jogged down the stairs. I said goodbye to Rowan at the front desk but didn't stop to chat, eager to see my girl.

I threw some clothes into a bag, unsure if I needed anything. Henley said we'd be back tonight, but I knew things could come up, so it was better to be prepared so I wasn't stuck wearing the same outfit two days in a row.

I patted Lady Sterling and ensured she had fresh water before jumping into my Jeep and heading toward campus. Reese waited outside with her two friends, waving goodbye to them when I pulled up.

Reese smiled as they opened the door, climbing into the passenger side.

"Hey, Fletch."

"How was your night?" I asked as I pulled out of the parking lot and drove toward the private airfield. Keaton hadn't been able to get us on a flight this last minute, so he'd sent a jet to us, stating we could all fly back on it after the shoot.

"Uneventful. Hung out with the twins and watched some movies."

"You doing okay after everything on Friday? I know that had to be a shock."

Reese shrugged. "It was and wasn't. I never felt close to Carol, so discovering she wasn't my biological mother didn't change that. I'm just glad she's out of my life."

"You're part of my family now, kiddo. My mom invited everyone to the house for Christmas."

"Really?" Reese's eyes lit up. "I've never had a big family Christmas. Are we going?"

"I still need to talk to Henley, but yeah, I think she could be persuaded."

"Sweet. I was dreading staying in the dorms. I was going to see if I could convince Henley to let me go stay with the twins. But I didn't want her to be alone; this is even better."

"I'm glad you like my family so much."

"They're the kind of family you see on TV."

I smiled, warmth spreading through me. The airport came into view, and I turned into it, feeling more invigorated and ready to share my past with the people I loved. The guys had become my friends and brothers, and I knew the four of us could get through anything. We'd shown that dealing with all the shit thrown at Henley. We could figure out how this fit into our lives as well.

I parked the Jeep, and Reese and I hopped out, grabbing our small bags. I spotted two planes on the tarmac and headed toward the first one with the SnowPoke logo.

Four black SUVs zoomed toward us, making me jump back. Pulling Reese behind me, I stood my ground as they slowed, blocking us from all angles. When the person stepped out from the closest one, I knew my time ignoring them was up. Fucking hell.

"It's okay, Reese. I'll handle this."

Their hands gripped my shirt, their body pressed into mine. Henley was never going to forgive me for this.

# CHAPTER 39

## *Henley*

BREAKFAST at the Cassel's consisted of a full buffet with more food than I could ever eat this early in the morning. Thankfully, neither Henry nor the newlyweds were present, making it an enjoyable feast with Dax's mom.

"I'm so glad you could come and visit us, Henley. It's been lovely getting to meet you. I hope you'll return and bring your other boyfriend as well?"

I had to give it to Desirea; she swallowed down the fact her son was in a polyamorous relationship better than I expected.

"That would be lovely. I'll have to check when we have some free time. We're about to enter our busy season with two games a week, plus National and Olympic trials coming up," I said, hoping it didn't sound like I was brushing her off.

"Yes, of course. We'll figure something out." She hugged me, stepping back to give Reed, then Dax one. After he said goodbye, the three of us filed out of the house and climbed into our rental. Dax sat there quietly for a few seconds, needing to process everything.

"You good?" I asked, reaching my hand out to rub his thigh.

"Yeah. This is the first time I've been home that hasn't ended with me fighting with my dad or brother in years. Thank you both for coming with me. I needed to close this chapter of my life more than I realized."

"No problem, man. We're here for you," Reed said, reaching between the middle of the car and squeezing his shoulder.

Dax blew out a breath, nodding as he winked at me, backing out of the drive. "I must say, I'm excited about Henley being the center of attention next. It's not my forte."

"Hmm, that's funny since you have a bit of an exhibitionist streak in you," I teased. "The first time we were together, you had me pressed up against a glass window with a club dancing below us."

Reed growled, surprising me. "You let other people see her?"

"Fuck, no. It was tinted on the other side. No one could see in. It just gave the illusion. Which she knew." Dax's eyes narrowed at me, a giggle escaping me at his look.

"Oh. Well, that's kind of hot, then. Where was this club?" Reed asked, shocking me further.

"Reed Cole! Not you too."

He sat back as he rubbed his jaw in thought. "What? I like to watch, and the thought of you naked and pressed to a glass with people below who can't see is thrilling and exclusive." He shrugged like he hadn't just blown my mind.

"Well, okay then." I laughed, turning back around.

"It's in the city. We can go one weekend. I know the bouncer there. Speaking of, how are we going to get back at Fletch?" Dax lifted his eyes to Reed's in the rearview mirror.

"What for?" I asked, turning to stare at the side of his face.

"He tried to embarrass us in front of you. It's only natural that we join forces for payback. It's bro code, Petal."

"Bro code." I chuckled, shaking my head. Secretly, I liked that they were bonded and close. It made our relationship feel more valuable. It wasn't just sex holding us together, but a group of people loving each other, even if it was in different ways.

We'd been driving for a while when Reed bolted forward, pointing off in the distance. "Can you pull off there?"

Dax nodded, doing as directed. I peered back at Reed, trying to read his emotions. Did he need to pee or something?

The car stopped a few seconds later, and I took in our surroundings. A greenhouse stood directly in front of us, flowers bursting everywhere. It was surrounded by a small house and a pond with a man-made waterfall built into the side of the hill. Turning the other direction, I encountered the mountains and desert. This place seemed out of place, but there was no denying it was beautiful.

"What is this?" I asked, stepping out of the car.

"It's just someone's home. I spotted it on the way here, and something about it called to me. I think I need to spread some of my mom's ashes here," Reed said.

Grabbing his hand, I squeezed. "It's a beautiful spot. Should we ask the owners?"

"I'll take care of it," Dax said, striding forward. I wrapped my arms around Reed, holding him as we leaned against the car and waited for Dax. We watched as he knocked on the door, an older woman answering it. She glanced out at us as he spoke, giving him a soft nod and patting his hand, then she stepped back into her house and shut the door.

Dax jogged back over to us, a smile on his face. "She said she'd be honored. This is her oasis in the desert, a place for weary souls."

Reed exhaled and nodded as he worked his jaw back and forth. "Will you both come with me?"

"Of course." I didn't have to think about it. If Reed needed us, then we'd be there. Dax nodded, taking my hand. Reed stepped out of my arms and grabbed something from the back seat. Shutting the door, he held out his hand, and I took it as he led us over to the pond. The waterfall fell into the water, the sound soothing as it rippled across the water.

"She filters the water from the greenhouse through the pond. It's all self-sufficient," Dax said.

"It's amazing. I never thought something like this could survive in this weather."

"Beautiful, strong things find a way to survive, no matter where they're planted," Reed whispered.

He dropped my hand to open the container he had. It was small, and his hand shook as he stared at the water. I wrapped my arms around his waist to give him some of my strength at this moment. Dax moved to his other side, placing his hand on his shoulder. Reed closed his eyes, his body relaxing under our touch.

"Mom, I hope you enjoy this place. It reminded me of you." He took a deep breath, closing his eyes as he stared at the sky. "Thank you for loving me and pushing me to keep trying, even after you were gone. I've... I've done that, and it's more than I could've ever hoped for." He swallowed, tears streaming down his face. "I miss you, but I see and feel you everywhere. I hope you're proud of the choices I'm making. I love you, Mom."

I wiped the tears from my face as Reed turned over the small container. The ashes flew through the air, some landing in the water and others carried by the wind into the greenhouse.

"That was beautiful, Reed. I know she'd love this place."

He nodded, kissing my forehead, his lips lingering on my skin. With a sigh, he stepped back, and we returned to the car. The rest of the drive was quiet, but as we stepped into the airport, Reed stopped, drawing our attention.

"Thank you. That meant a lot to me to have you both there."

Smiling, I locked our fingers together, and the three of us walked through the airport to catch our flight. Something magical was growing between all of us, and I knew my decision was the right one. When we landed in LA, I'd call Carly and let her know.

THE CAR KEATON HAD SENT PULLED UP TO THE BUILDING, and excitement built in me. I missed Fletcher and Reese and couldn't wait to hug them both. My leg bounced as the driver slowed, Reed's hand falling to my leg.

"You're like a kid on Christmas morning," he teased. He seemed lighter since spreading some of his mom's ashes, and I made a mental note to make sure he did it some more. He'd told me how she wanted to be spread in different places.

"Oh no, I'm way worse on Christmas." I laughed, leaning over to kiss his cheek. Shaking his head, he climbed out with me, Dax meeting us around the back with our bags.

Walking into the building, my eyes tried to take in everything. It was all marble and shiny chrome. Instantly, I worried I'd leave footprints or something on the immaculate surfaces. I glanced back to ensure I wasn't earning another laugh from the guys. I stuck out my tongue to hide my blush.

The elevator was quiet as we rose, that nervous energy returning as I bounced on my heels. The guys talked together, but I was too amped up to pay attention. The elevator opened, and I bolted out, searching for Fletcher and Reese. When I didn't find them, I sagged.

"Looks like we beat them here," Dax said. "Come on, let's go chat with Keaton." He pointed in the direction his friend was going over something with a woman on a screen.

"Actually, I need to make a phone call first. I'll be right there."

Dax searched my eyes, eventually nodding and letting me go. I walked over to a large window, my hands shaking slightly as I pulled out my phone. I didn't have any new messages from Fletcher or Reese, so I pulled up my contacts and selected Carly's.

The phone rang a few times before she answered. "Hello, Henley. I'm glad you're calling. Have you come to a decision?"

My heart raced, and my palms sweated, my vision

blurred as I fought the panic. Pressing my forehead against the cool glass, I grounded myself and remembered my earlier conviction. I could do this. It was what I needed to do for myself. For us.

"Hey, Carly, and yes, I have."

My voice was strong, and I tilted my head up, pushing my shoulders back. I wouldn't buckle under the pressure. Just like with a deadlift, it would be challenging to lift the weight up on my own and deal with the complications in my life.

But I trusted in my muscles and the work I'd put in. The burn, that stretch of muscle as I lifted, would be worth it in the end. I'd stand on my own, the weight on my own shoulders, knowing I'd conquered it.

And my men, Reese, and my friends would all be there spotting me like the incredible people they were.

"Wonderful. I'll have the steps to remove Dakota started and let you know when I'll need you here."

"You misunderstand, Carly. I appreciate your generous offer to join the club and all the perks that come with it, but I will have to decline."

It was quiet on the line for a second, and I wasn't sure if she had heard me or not.

"I see. Is there anything I could do to change your mind?" she asked.

"No. I want to do this on my own."

"Even with everything you know, you'll still walk away? You won't be protected from Dakota after this."

"I don't need to be. He'll hang himself at some

point. I'm tired of having to prove I'm worthy, of having to belong to the right club in order to be taken seriously. If I want to make a difference, I need to do that on my own. Use my own platform and not one that was curated for me."

"I think you're making a mistake, Henley. The Society could do so much for you."

"Maybe. But it's not the life I want. I'm confident in my decision. Again, I appreciate the offer and everything you provided last weekend, but I'm saying no. I hope we can still respect and support one another."

"The frivolity of youth." Her voice hardened, and I debated changing my mind for a split second as fear enveloped me. "If you're not with us, Henley, you're against us. Best of luck. It's a tough world out there."

The phone clicked, and I stood motionless as I stared down at the device. Swallowing, I squeezed it until the fear dissipated from my body.

I didn't need the Society to succeed, but something told me they might've needed me. And in rejecting them, I'd potentially made a powerful enemy.

But it didn't change my decision. They were no different from Dakota. In fact, they'd let him run unchecked, making my life hell. The Society and Dakota were both bullies, and I was sick of being pushed around.

The best way to fight a bully was to beat them at their own game, and I had an idea of how to do that now.

Walking into the main room, I smiled, feeling better and solid in my decision. This campaign would be the starting point of a new life for Reese and me. My phone pinged, and I pulled it out, hoping it was them. Instead, it was a message from my lawyer. My brows furrowed as I read it, not understanding it.

HOWARD PENNINGTON

What do you want us to do with the cashier's check? It was sent back with the signed papers.

HENLEY

I don't understand. Macy confirmed she cashed it a few seconds after the courier left.

HOWARD PENNINGTON

*pic attached*

I stared in disbelief at the picture. Sure enough, the check with the amount I pulled from my savings stared back at me. My heart sped up, and I quickly opened my message to Macy.

HENLEY

Hey, quick question. You're certain Carol cashed the check and left?

MACY MY FGM

Yeppers. She was on a plane an hour later.

HENLEY

That doesn't make sense. The lawyer has the one I sent.

Looking up, I spotted Reed and Dax. One glance at me, and they headed toward me, concern etched on their faces.

"What's wrong?"

"I don't know. I just have this weird feeling." I flapped my hands under my armpits like a chicken as I walked in a circle. "I told the Society no, then immediately I got a message that Carol didn't cash my check, but one for half a million dollars. But Macy says she signed everything and left on a plane. I just need Reese and Fletcher here. I'm freaking out." My voice had risen to a volume only dogs could hear by the end.

"I'm sure there's a plausible explanation. Let's not jump to conclusions just yet," Dax said, placing his hands on my shoulders. The fact Dax was calm startled me. Nodding, I took a deep breath and allowed him to pull me into his arms. His hand rubbed up and down my back, soothing me.

"Oh shit," Keaton said, drawing our attention.

"What?" I asked, my heart jumping back into my throat. His face paled as he read whatever was on his phone. When his eyes met mine, my legs gave out, tears falling before I even knew what he said. I just knew it was something terrible. I told the Society to fuck off, and now they were punishing me.

Why did I think I could do this on my own?

"Where are Fletcher and Reese?" Reed asked, his voice demanding.

"They never got onto the plane."

"What?" I screamed.

Keaton glanced up, his eyes worried. "The pilot says they were headed to the stairs when four SUVs pulled up and took them both to another waiting plane. He assumed they were meant to go, so he went home."

"Where is my sibling? Where's Fletcher? What plane was it?" I shrieked, no longer pretending to be calm.

Keaton swallowed, glancing down at his phone. "He said it had an HTC logo on it."

"Why would they get on a Hat Trick Co. plane?" Dax asked, frowning.

"Did you say Hat Trick?" someone I didn't know asked. Keaton nodded, motioning for them to continue. "There was something on the news about HTC a few seconds ago. Their missing CEO had been spotted returning to the building. News is there's a huge deal about to be made, and they all have to be present to vote."

I heard what he was saying, but they didn't

compute. What did the CEO of Hat Trick have to do with my missing loved ones?

Reed stalked over to the TV and flicked through the channels until he found a news one. The color drained from me as I watched, dizziness washing over me. What the ever-living-fuck?

# CHAPTER 40

## The Society

THE CALL DISCONNECTED, and I threw the device against the wall, a shrill scream leaving me. Crouching down, I tugged at my hair, my breath leaving me in short pants as I fought for control.

"Madame Arbitrator?" my new personal assistant asked, stepping into my office. I waved him off, not wanting a witness to my ire. He cleared his throat, not leaving as I'd asked. If he didn't start following directions, he wouldn't make the cut to full member.

He was already on thin ice for being an idiot, and quite honestly, the last type of member we needed. But the old men clung to ways of the past, too scared to acknowledge the world had changed. Henley was meant to be my A-bomb, wiping out the old cronies and paving the way for the next generation of the Society.

"What?" I barked, turning my head slightly, sending daggers with my eyes. I'd had my fill of insolent people today.

"The West members have arrived, Arbitrator. I've directed them to the formal meeting room."

My nails dug into my palms, and I stood, collecting myself. Smoothing down my hair, I walked over to my desk and gathered the tablet I needed.

"Thank you, Kurt. I'll be out in a second," I said, dismissing him. His lip twitched, a sneer disappearing before it fully formed. It looked like I needed to deal with two pieces of trash tonight.

Pulling out my mirror, I smoothed on my red lipstick, checking my hair and the rest of my features. It was such a shame I had to dress this way to gain the respect of the members. Before my post here, I'd only worn heels and a skirt when I'd been forced to, which wasn't very often. Back then, no one forced me to do anything.

Unfortunately, the same sentiment couldn't be said today. I'd thought taking this position would earn me the respect of my fellow male athletes, but instead, it had made me a sex symbol for them to drool over. And the Society did nothing to discourage their behavior, spouting tradition and elegance.

They could take their fucking elegance and shove it up their assholes.

Snapping the mirror closed, I leaned against the desk and took a second to breathe. It would do those men some good to wait on me. Taking stock of my emotions, I knew the real reason I was angry at Henley. I envied her. When she'd been given a choice to join this club, she walked away.

I hadn't had the same luxury.

And now I was owned by the Society, their perfect little puppet to show off, making all the old and rich members more likely to continue with their investments. I'd been given a title, but Arbitrator might as well be synonymous with pet.

I'd thought I could make a difference, gain respect, and use that to make fundamental changes. Instead, I was forced to control and manage a group of insufferable man-toddlers who only saw me as the pussy who wouldn't let them do all the shit they wanted—like Dakota-fucking-Hughes. God, I'd wanted to punish him so badly.

Henley had been my one chance to bring a real force into the fold. To bring about change these men couldn't brush off. I'd researched everything about her, crafting the perfect seduction, and trusted Carly to seal the deal like she had so many other times.

But I hadn't expected the three men she'd brought with her. They were a complication I hadn't prepared for.

Sighing, I rubbed my temple, knowing I had to let that asshole off his leash.

While Henley had been given a choice, only one was acceptable. As much as I respected the girl, she was now an enemy.

And the Society dealt with enemies only one way—total annihilation.

**The story will conclude with Breakaway. You can preorder it here.**

# Letter from the Author

Oh hey there! How are you doing? Do you want to throw things at me? Curse my name?

Yeah, I know. This one didn't end as gently, but I promise it's not as bad as it seems. Fletcher has a secret and it will be revealed in the next book.

Henley and the guys grew so close in this one, proving that they were the family they wanted to be. Now they'll have to put that bond to the test for what's to come in book 3.

One of the things I love about this book is the bond that Henley and Reese have. I knew it was a risk to add a NB character, but it was one I believed was important for representation.

Overall, I hope you enjoyed this second book and are dying for the last one. It should be out in June if all things go well.

And hey, if you need something new to read in the meantime, you can check out my backlist and upcoming releases.

This book wouldn't have been possible without a few people. So, I'd like to take a moment to thank the ladies who keep me sane through this process.

Emma, I'm not sure how much more I can gush, but thank you for being the first one to fall in love with my characters and supporting me with each new project I think of. I'm sure one day you won't receive any more of the "so listen, I've been thinking..." messages. Maybe. Probably.

Megan and Heather, thank you for being my first feedback and helping me find teasers, plot holes, and making sure things sound right. Your thirst traps do a soul good. Don't ever stop sending them.

Lindsay and Kayla, thank you for always saying yes and finding time to dive into my words. I appreciate the feedback as I finalize the draft and polish it up. You're the fresh eyes I need after reading it for the millionth time. So thank you.

To all my ARC readers, thank you for spreading the word and getting my book in front of people. You make this job so fun, and I love every mention, like, video, and edit you create.

And to the person reading this far, thank you for giving a new series a chance. I hope you found something you loved between the pages.

# Also By

For the most up to date look at my releases. Check out all my books here: https://authorkrisbutler.com/my-books

## LUX BRUMALIS

Penalty Box

Dead Lift

Breakaway

## THE COUNCIL SERIES

(completed series)

Damaged Dreams

Shattered Secrets

Fractured Futures

Bosh Bells & Epic Fails

The Council Boxset

# THE ORDER DUET (COUNCIL SPINOFF)

Stiletto Sins

Lipstick Lies

# DRESSED TO KILL SHARED WORLD (STANDALONE)

Raven

# F*CK STEAL KILL

F*ck Steal Kill

# DARK CONFESSIONS

Dangerous Truths

Dangerous Lies

Dangerous Vows

Reckless (Cami's Novella)

Relentless (Nat's Novella)

Dangerous Love

# TATTOOED HEARTS DUET

Riddled Deceit (Part 1)

Smudged Lines (Part 2)

Open Road (Road trip Novella)

Tattooed Hearts Completed Duet

# MUSIC CITY DIARIES

Beautiful Agony

Beautiful Envy

# VACATION ROMCOM

Vibing

# SINNERS FAIRYTALES

(standalone)

Pride

# About the Author

Kris Butler writes under a pen name to have some separation from her everyday life. Writing has become her second love, providing a safe place to normalize mental health through her characters. Kris enjoys writing emotional books with flawed characters, sassy heroines, and all the book boyfriends she loves to drool over. You can find her at home most nights reading with her husband and furbaby, trying to maintain her nerdy sock collection, or playing tabletop games with her friends. Kris loves to talk with readers about her books, even if it's just them yelling at her for that cliffhanger. If you enjoyed her book, please consider leaving a review. You can find her in her reader group or on social media.

Join my newsletter
Join my fan group
Check out my website

www.ingramcontent.com/pod-product-compliance
Lightning Source LLC
Chambersburg PA
CBHW061209190726
48288CB00001B/112